ALSO BY ALAN B. GAZZANIGA

Seeds For All Seasons

The Seeds We Sow

SEEDS OF DOUBT

Alan B. Gazzaniga

Arrowhead Classics Publishing Company

First Edition May, 2006

ISBN 1-886571-21-X
EAN 978-1-886571-21-1

Tim Graves (*Seeds for All Seasons*) was a sperm donor while doing his surgical training. Without his knowledge his sperm was used for reproduction purposes rather than research. In collaboration with *Globe* reporter Meg Logan Tim learned that he had three offspring, two of whom had died from an apparently genetically acquired cerebral aneurysm for which Tim himself had been treated when he was in high school. The third child he found unexpectedly when he was called to the emergency room to treat Joey Santori, Red Sox pitcher and "son" of mobster Tony "Lefty" Santori. Joey, too, suffered from a cerebral aneurysm but Tim was able to save his life.

Tony's right hand man and muscle, Paulie Strata, stumbled upon the biological connection between Tim Graves and Joey Santori. In order to keep the relationship a secret from his boss and his boss' enemies, he murdered the infertility doctor and plotted to kill Tim and Meg. This became unnecessary when the neurosurgeon and his girlfriend were killed in an auto accident. Later this was determined to be a hoax (*The Seeds We Sow*) and Tim returned to his old life and prepared to marry Meg Logan. Paulie Strata was arrested and entered the witness protection program so he could testify against his old boss.

In *Seeds of Doubt* Tim experienced up close and personal the complex nature of litigation that doctors must face when, as he is trying to resume his old life he must endure a malpractice lawsuit carried over from a surgery he performed before he "died." While Tim is depressed over the suit, Meg is fighting mad.

One

Jerry Cleary sat in a booth in the gloomy hotel lounge and stared at his second glass of wine. It was not unusual for Betsy to keep him waiting, but something in the tone of her voice when they had arranged to meet this afternoon made him wonder. The room key was burning a hole in his pocket. He knew he should be spending this time preparing for his case tomorrow and, in fact, he had all his papers stuffed in his briefcase, but an afternoon with Betsy was not to be denied.

Jerry is a successful personal injury attorney (Jerry Cleary For Personal inJerry). His practice was growing so rapidly that in the past year he'd added ten more associates just to keep up with the flood of new claims coming through the doors. His underlings handled all the mundane, bread and butter cases, and he saved all the high profile cases for himself.

Glancing at the television over the bar, Jerry saw that President Reagan was signing a bill in the Rose Garden that would extend the budget to Boston's Big Dig, while Tip O'Neill looked on. *Nice,* Jerry thought, *more construction means more injuries, meaning more business coming my way.* As his eyes scanned the room he saw that Betsy was standing in the doorway. He raised an arm to get her attention and half stood as she approached the booth.

"What the hell kept you?"

"I'm fine, and how are you?" the pretty young woman snapped back at Jerry's rude greeting."

"I'm sorry. Just being a pain in the ass lawyer as usual. But where have you been?"

She sipped from the glass of wine the attentive waitress had placed in front of her as soon as she sat down. Betsy Gallucci was not intimidated by overbearing attorneys. She was an out-standing young court reporter who had learned quickly that when dealing with attorneys, the best defense was an offense.

Somewhat mollified, Betsy relaxed into the soft leather of the booth. She was a very attractive woman in her mid twenties with raven hair and riveting blue eyes. Her lips were full, she had olive skin, and the body of a goddess. Although she was blessed with a good genetic combination—an Irish mother and an Italian father— she knew that looks alone wouldn't get her where she wanted to be. After stenography school, she had started her own court reporting business and, along with her three associates, was considered the best in the business. Jerry had met her several years earlier when he was deposing a defense expert in a medical malpractice case. As far as he was concerned, it was love (or maybe lust) at first sight.

"I was taking a statement from a mafia informant. You better believe there was security around this guy," she said, as though continuing a story she had already started. "By the way," she went on, "this room stinks of cigarette smoke. You know how I hate that."

"Take it easy. This is the non-smoking section and I don't smell anything," Jerry replied.

"I bet. Anyway this guy is trying to nail his boss, Tony Santori. Have you heard of him?"

"Heard of him? Is the Pope Catholic? Hey, I grew up South of Roxbury, of course I've heard of him. What an asshole. You know, people still don't seem to understand that you can make money and still use the strong arm techniques *legally*, like I do."

"Well, just maybe he didn't have the same opportunities you had!"

"If you call busting your ass going to night school and hold-ing down two jobs part of my 'opportunities', then you're right.

I never had anything handed to me. I didn't go to Harvard, BU or any place fancy. Just Suffolk Law School, and I'm one of their most successful graduates."

"Says who? Jerry Cleary." She signaled the waitress for another glass of wine. "How does a lawyer define success? Money?" she teased.

Jerry was now definitely encouraged. If he were careful, he would have a very successful afternoon. On rare occasions Betsy could shut off her charm and turn a cold shoulder. But that's what he liked about her. He liked the challenge and he liked the rewards even more.

"Of course. It's all about winning and losing, and I don't lose."

"Yeah. I read in the paper yesterday about that poor doctor who committed suicide last week. You sued him, took all of his assets, then, the straw that broke the camel's back, according to *The Herald*, you garnished his earnings. Is that what you call 'winning'?"

"My, my aren't we the angry one today? That *poor* doctor, as you describe him, was underinsured and the settlement was more than fair."

"Four million dollars for a stroke after gallbladder surgery?" she looked at Jerry skeptically.

"That's what the jury decided. My client's in diapers, is unable to care for himself. He requires around the clock nursing. Besides, the doctor took it personally when the real issue was his incompetence. Maybe by taking his life he saved another victim down the line. Hey, somebody has to clean up the messes," he chuckled and took another sip of wine.

Betsy shook her head in disgust. She snapped back, "I was at that doctor's deposition. You were mean and nasty to him. He was a nice guy, and the stroke, according to your own expert's admission, could have happened whether or not there was bleeding during the operation. That expert witness, by the way, was a real prize. Where did you find him? In the old soldier's home?"

Jerry didn't like this exchange, but he knew he would have to work through it. "He was a retired surgeon from one of the big hospitals in West Los Angeles. He was quite a good surgeon in his day. You can't hold his testimony against me."

"Couldn't you find a doctor in Boston or anywhere in Massachusetts? Or did the 'practicing surgeons' she made quotation marks with her fingers, "feel there was no case?" Betsy didn't hide the fact that she was quite familiar with the way the system works.

"Nobody would help, so I had to go out of state. Can I help it if doctors don't like to testify against each other. Besides, I just present the facts. It's the jury who actually decides."

"Yeah, the jury decided after you destroyed the doctor on the witness stand."

"So he didn't have good counsel. That's not my problem. Hey, can we talk about something else now?" Jerry felt his promising afternoon slowly slipping away.

"I wonder, when you get through suing all the doctors, will there be anybody left who will want to take care of you?" Betsy wasn't ready to drop the subject just yet.

"Listen, there are plenty of good doctors out there, you just have to know who they are. And you, of all people, should know that doctors are only obstacles to get at the insurance company. If it weren't for lawyers churning the system all the money would be held by the insurance companies. We are just moving that money around." Jerry was waxing eloquent, having used this rationale more than once.

"So where are you going for medical treatment?" she asked.
"The doctors in Sweden."

"Of course not. I go to the doctors at St. Mary's Hospital. I'm on the Board of Directors. Most of the doctors there have me on contingency for two thousand a year. So's I can't sue them, conflict of interest," he laughed.

Jerry Cleary was a commanding presence in the courtroom. At just over six feet tall, with broad shoulders and a straight back, he had piercing gray eyes that were intensified by their contrast with his coal black hair. In college he was a formidable debater who was able to argue any side of an issue, and he often attributed his eloquence to his Irish heritage. At the moment, however, he needed more than eloquence to appease Betsy.

"You have got to be kidding me," Betsy said shaking her head.
"Look, it's my business to do the best for my client. It's a

numerator/denominator problem. I work on the numerator. If the doctor has a bad outcome we sue. The doctor looks at it differently. He or she says I did one hundred of these and 99 went fine but one didn't. I have a good record, why am I being sued? It sullies my reputation unfairly to be so severely judged by one bad outcome."

"Let me get this straight. A patient has a bad outcome and you sue. The doctor has a good record but you destroy his reputation because he screws up *once*. Is that how it works?" Betsy was outraged.

"The doctor will do alright. It's only money. They shouldn't take it personally. Enough of this, okay?" Jerry was not accustomed to being put on the defensive. Things were going from bad to worse. He glanced at his watch.

Betsy was ready to change the subject. "Let's talk about us. We've been 'seeing" each other for more than nine months. The last time we were together you complained that my...what's the word, oh yeah, *pheromones* had changed."

"Hey, that wasn't a complaint. It was an observation. I thought you might have changed your shower soap or something. You know."

She had thought at the time that it was an odd statement coming from a man who over the last few months had been slipping in the personal hygiene department. He had taken on the sour odor of someone who does not wash on a regular basis, so unlike the fastidious Jerry Cleary she had met several years ago.

"I haven't changed anything, and by the way, sometimes you smell like you just left the gym after a workout." Betsy was sorry she said that, but at times Jerry could be so infuriating, she just had to strike back.

"Why don't we drop this subject, too?" Jerry finished the last of his wine and mentally counted to ten. He looked over at Betsy who remained silent, with her arms folded stiffly against her chest. Jerry broke the silence in softer tones with, "Who was the mafia guy you met today?"

Betsy looked up and sighed. "You know that's confidential."

"Come on. It's in the newspaper that some little twerp named Strata was under protective custody."

"I know you're a big time attorney and all, but that 'little twerp,' as you call him, has killed about ten people. So I would be careful how you characterize him."

"Ah, that mafia crap is bullshit and you know it. Did you know he was the one who tried to kill the doctor I'm suing right now? A neurosurgeon named Graves. If I knew what was going on between them it could help my case."

Betsy was silent a moment then said, "I don't know. I can't say too much, but the informant was adamant that the relationship between him and Dr. Graves was strictly personal. It had nothing to do with his criminal activities. His lawyer said he wouldn't answer any questions about it. In fact, he said the doctor saved his life." Betsy became animated as the conversation shifted to a subject she could control.

"It must have been real 'personal' if he was going to kill the doc. Where did you do the depo?"

"In the Federal building. Where else? You know the feds don't trust the BPD. They want to put the Santoris out of business permanently."

"Hells bells! It was the BPD that arrested your guy for murder! The Feds are the ones that blew that investigation. So where are they hiding him? You can tell me *that* can't you?" Jerry pleaded.

"They have him stashed in a safe place. They don't tell me where they keep him," she said sarcastically. Then she brightened and said, "But I did hear one of the guards who brought him say they were headed back to the Island."

"Island? Must be one of the Harbor Islands. I've heard they used Lord's Island before. Anything else?"

"Since this is already in the newspaper, he did cop to bumping off this fertility doctor and his secretary in Vermont. He said there was a link between that killing and your Dr. Graves."

Jerry stared unbelievingly at Betsy, "You mean he admitted to murder? Was his lawyer present?"

"Oh yeah. The lawyer went along with it because Strata said the hit on the doctor was ordered by Lefty Santori. You know, another nail in Lefty's coffin." Betsy yawned as if to say this was nothing unusual in her daily life.

"Why in the world would a mafia chief order a hit on a neuro-surgeon and a fertility doctor? It doesn't make any sense." Jerry was getting excited now. If he could prove that the doctor he was suing was involved in some kind of underworld activity then he would score big.

Betsy jumped in, "Whoa! Slow down. Who said Paulie Strata was telling the truth? During a break I overheard one of the federal attorneys mention that they had two informants and the other one says Paulie acted on his own."

"Did the attorney mention the name of the other informant?" Jerry asked hopefully.

"No, he didn't, but he did say he was a relative of Lefty Santori."

Suddenly Betsy reached across the table and took his hand in both of hers. "I think it's over between us, Jerry. It was fun, but we're going nowhere with this relationship. You're on your second wife and I don't want to be involved anymore." She smiled at him. "Besides, you'll be looking for a new plaything in another four or five years." She stood up and started to walk away.

Jerry reached for her arm as she passed him. Betsy looked at his hand clutching her arm a little too forcibly and Jerry immediately released it. "Is it something I'm not doing? You know. In bed?"

"Look who's taking it personally now? There might be a heart in your chest after all," Betsy raised one eyebrow before adding, " but I'm not going to stick around to find out. Good-bye, Jerry. And don't get too close to those mafia guys. It could be bad for your health." She relished having the last word and vowed to herself as she walked through the lobby that never again would she leave her self-respect at the door of a cheap hotel room.

After a few moments of stunned silence, Jerry signaled for the check, paid the tab and left the bar.

PLEASE DEPOSIT ROOM KEYS HERE

With a shrug he tossed the key into the box and walked through the lobby and out into the street. He still had hours of work to do.

Two

Jerry was sitting in his office mulling over the events from the day before. It was bad enough he couldn't get laid, but he also hadn't gotten enough information from Betsy about Tim Graves. He would miss Betsy, though he knew he would find a replacement before too long. For now, however, he was more interested in capitalizing on what little information he had. Dr. Graves was somehow mixed up with a mafia figure and had nearly lost his life. Actually, he had lost his life once before, but that was fake. Jerry was on a roll when Graves was "dead" because there was no defendant to fight back, but when the doctor had returned from the dead it forced Jerry to rethink his case. Now he had a live defendant to contend with and there were additional unanswered questions about his activities. So far, the case was moving along fairly well, and he was meeting with his client in several minutes to go over her testimony prior to an upcoming deposition by the defense.

Jerry didn't spend a lot of time thinking about his next move, he would leave the Graves/Strata issue up to the experts. He was too busy and didn't mind paying a little extra for the help of someone who knew more than he did about things other than the law. He flipped open his telephone book and dialed a number. The phone on the other end rang twice before it was answered by a gruff voice saying, "Collins Investigation Service. Who's callin'?"

"Eddie, it's Jerry Cleary. When are you going to get a secretary who knows how to answer the phone? It's better for business," Jerry chuckled.

"Hey Jerry. What's up? I can't afford a secretary, not like you big shot lawyers."

"Now Eddie, that's no way to talk to a potential customer, is it? How're the wife and kids?"

"They're fine, but it's tough paying college tuition on a retired detective's salary."

"Hey I thought that award we got from the city for your wrongful termination was going to help. Is that all gone?" Jerry was surprised.

"Long gone. But I'm doing okay with this little business I've started. What can I do you for?" Eddie didn't like wasting time with idle chatter.

"Same ol' Eddie. I think I have some work for you. Remember that doctor who faked his death to avoid a mafia hit?"

"Of course. It was all over the newspapers."

"This is confidential, but yesterday Paulie Strata gave a statement to US Attorneys that he killed a fertility doctor in Vermont—a doctor who had been on the staff at University Hospital with Graves, the doctor I'm suing now. Both of the docs were on Strata's hit list. I want to know what went on between Graves and the mafia guys. They have Strata hidden away on one of the Harbor Islands. On Lord's, I think."

"There're eighteen islands out there. But why didn't that guinea punk tell why he was out to get them?"

"He said Tony ordered the hit and he didn't know why. He said it was personal business, not mob connected. He wouldn't give any more information."

"Does any of this have to do with that phony transplant mess that left one of our guys out to dry? I keep in touch with the precinct and there's still a lot of bitterness about all that." Eddie had been dismissed early from the police department for drinking on duty. But it was determined by the courts that it was an unjustified termination. He was reinstated to a desk job in order to finish his last year and get full retirement. Although he had his enemies when he was on the Force, for the most part he had been very popular and had worked closely with Patrick Kennedy during a fourteen-year stint in homicide. The latter was the detective that investigated the heart transplant irregularities that led to Teddy Murtaugh, a fellow officer, missing his chance for a new heart. Teddy was so devasted that he died shortly afterward.

"I don't know, but the papers have been uncovering connections between the genetics lab, the med school and the mafia. Some graduate student was feeding information to help the mob buy organs." Jerry knew it was more complicated than that, but he didn't want to waste time on details. "This is privileged, Eddie, but I've discovered during the prelims with this suit against Graves that he was suspended because of the way he performed in the operating room. It seems his son had recently died of the same thing. The pressure must have got to him."

"Yeah, I read that in the paper too. The last part I mean. The kid died from a busted blood vessel in his brain. What's that got to do with Paulie Strata?"

"I'm not sure. But my hunch is that a murder and an attempted murder of two doctors from the same hospital must be tied together somehow. See what you can find out." Jerry hung up and swiveled around in his chair. He looked out of his corner window at the Boston Commons. The trees were still bare and he could see all the way across to the courthouse. His office was in a renovated building that formerly was a hotel on the corner of Boylston and Arlington. He had bought the entire third floor and painted his name in gold script on each of the 30 windows facing the street below. "Jerry Cleary" was written along the top arc of a circle and he had the logo "For Personal in-Jerry" written along the bottom arc. Corny, but it brought in the clients.

His intercom sounded as his secretary announced that Mrs. Bradford had arrived and was on her way in.

Jerry greeted her warmly and led her to a chair across from his desk. He had forgotten how attractive the thirty-two year-old widow was. She was dressed in a gray wool suit over a pink blouse. Her brown hair was in a pageboy style, making her look even younger.

"Can I get you something?"

"I'm fine. But I'm worried about this deposition next week. What am I supposed to say?"

Jerry walked over to the chair next to her and sat down. He resisted the impulse to put his hand on her shapely knee. "Well, that's why I wanted to meet with you today. The short answer to your question is this: tell the truth. You have brought an action against a doctor and the hospital. They are going to fight tooth and nail to win it. You are the one who is claiming that the surgery on your deceased husband was done incompetently and that incompetence led to his death. They want to know why you think they are responsible for killing your husband and how you came to that conclusion." Jerry smiled at his own brevity.

"But I don't know how it was done. All I know is that he was alive when he went into the operating room and he was dead when he came out. I realize he had a serious condition, but I never thought he would die. He was young and healthy, people like that don't just die. Dr. Graves was upset when he came out from the surgery. He looked almost out of control." Julie Bradford was very steady and couldn't have been more sincere. Jerry was quite pleased with her poise. She was going to make a great witness.

"There, you have just told me how you feel and what you think. That's all you have to do at the deposition and you'll do very well. However, there will be many more questions and I won't necessarily be able to coach you on the answers. But I can almost guarantee what the defense lawyers will ask you. You ready?"

"Yes."

"These are not in any particular order," Jerry had the questions memorized and he rattled them off as easily as breathing, " How did his death affect you financially? What are you doing now? Did you have to sell your house? Did he leave you with any life insurance? How are your children doing? What happened to his business? What was your income before he died versus now? What did Dr. Graves tell you before the surgery about the risks of the operation?" he stopped to let the litany sink in, then added, " Do you get the idea, Mrs. Bradford?"

"Yes. You and I went over the financial stuff during our first meeting. It was devastating. John didn't have life insurance. Since we last talked six months ago I had to sell John's shares in his business to his two partners. They were very nice, but had to borrow money to buy me out. Wouldn't you know after I sold his shares, the business really took off as John had always dreamed it would?" She let out a long sigh and shook her head. She continued, "Remember? It was a software company that finally developed a program John had been working on for years. Something for positioning satellites. I only got a hundred thousand dollars for his shares and today they are worth over thirty million."

Jerry had practiced for years never to show emotion or let out an unexpected response to statements by others. He was a master at the poker face. Julie's last statement put his discipline to the test as he rose out of his chair and walked to the window, hiding his face from his client. He was overjoyed.

He gazed out the window, blinking several times to clear his eyesight. It seemed for a second that he was looking at two Boston Commons. Or had he teared up over the thought of a large award or perhaps a substantial settlement without going to trial? Finally his vision cleared in more ways than one. With his back still turned to his client he said, "Well, now that does pose possibilities that I did not consider. Perhaps we are asking for too little? Anyway that will work itself out as we approach trial." His conversation with Betsy Galucci and the efforts of Eddie Collins might just pay off big time. He turned and looked at Julie Bradford.

"But, let's get on with your deposition. What's essential to a successful outcome here is to show the jury that Dr. Graves acted callously and did not inform your husband, or you for that matter, about the risks and alternatives to surgery." Jerry moved closer to her, making sure he could see her response. That was all that mattered in front of a jury.

"Well, that will be very simple to prove. I never spoke to Dr. Graves about the risks. I did speak briefly to a student doctor who talked about death and possible brain damage. But he didn't seem to know what was going on. But Dr. Graves never mentioned alternative treatments. John told me that Dr. Graves said it was surgery or death from a ruptured....aner...rysm. I believe that's the word."

Jerry breathed slowly now as he geared up for the next question. "What did he say the risks were? I mean, what were his chances with surgery?"

"I don't know. All I remember is that John told me as they wheeled him into surgery that Dr. Graves said it would be a piece of cake. That he'd be home in five days."

"Piece of cake?"

"Yeah, that the operation would be easy and not to worry. Why is that so important?"

"Well, if Dr. Graves quoted a low risk to this risky surgery and did not offer a safer alternative, then he acted recklessly, thereby exposing himself to punitive damages. Now I will have to amend the complaint against him to include punitive damages and will let his lawyer know this afternoon. I also have an expert that says your husband was not a surgical candidate and that he should have had the aneurysm clotted with a catheter."

"Wait, just what are you saying? Are you saying John didn't need the surgery and something else could have been done?" Julie was becoming angry. "Who's your expert neurosurgeon? I want to talk to him, right now."

"Well, he's both a neurosurgeon and fancies himself a neurologist as well. And I know how this information might upset you, Mrs. Bradford. But my general experience is that it's not a good idea to speak with other witnesses in the case before your deposition. If it came out during your depo that you had conversations with others you would have to reveal his name. Now, I keep such things confidential because I don't want to tip off the other side." Jerry had been sitting next to Julie and stood up and walked behind his desk. He remained standing, forever practicing his courtroom technique. "You said Dr. Graves was very upset when he talked to you after John's death. Did you know that he had a son with the same condition?"

"Not then I didn't. I read something about it in the papers later on."

"Did you know that Dr. Graves had been suspended for his actions surrounding your husband's care?" Jerry was pressing hard and his questions were asked in a very direct manner. He wanted to gauge his client's response.

Julie looked startled and hurt. "You mean he did something bad and then tried to hide it from me?"

"Well, what did he say when he came out to the lobby?" Jerry wanted to establish her response to this question in her mind so that if it differed from the doctor's recollection then he could make a big deal about it in court.

Julie thought for a while and then said, "I remember exactly, because he was so upset. He said that the ane...urysm had burst when he was working near it and that the bleeding was so bad he couldn't stop it."

"That's all he said?"

"No. He said he was sorry he couldn't have done better." There were tears welling in the corner of her eyes when she finished. Jerry could barely contain himself over this performance.

He knew the circumstances were quite different from the way Graves had portrayed the surgery to his patient's wife. While in law school he made it a point to eat lunch or dinner in the nearby hospital cafeteria to learn how things go. He overheard nurses and doctors talk about complications and how they were covered up. This was a classic case.

Having finished his eloquent direct questioning of Julie, Jerry came around from behind his desk. He approached his client and tenderly put his hand on her shoulder while she dabbed her eyes with a handkerchief.

"You have my deepest sympathy Mrs. Bradford. Perhaps that's enough for today."

With reddened eyes Julie gave an apologetic smile to Jerry and said, "Thank you. I have to be going anyway. I'm meeting my fiance` for lunch at Lock Obers."

Jerry was taken aback and pulled his hand off her shoulder "I didn't know you were so involved with someone."

"Oh yes. Actually it's John's old partner. In fact, he was the one who made the breakthrough in the computer program. John was proud of that because, Seth, that's my fiance`, was a student of his at MIT. Actually Seth and I are about the same age and we have become very close."

Jerry was getting sick to his stomach. "I don't mean to be personal here, but what do you mean by 'close.' "

"If you are asking if we are intimate then the answer is 'yes'," Jerry noted the swift change in his client's apparently innocent demeanor. " I'm sure that question will be asked at my deposition since we are claiming loss of consortium. But by the time of the trial we'll have been married. So having sex with my husband won't be an issue. Will it?"

"Married? To your dead husband's former partner who undoubtedly will be, or *is*, worth millions of dollars. That's not going to gain much sympathy from the jury." For the first time in a long time beads of sweat broke out on Jerry's forehead. It would be difficult to make a case on damages at trial. In fact, her husband's death was actually going to make her a rich woman. Things weren't looking so good anymore.

Julie smiled knowingly and said, " I suppose we could postpone the marriage. Actually we were planning to book a time at the Protestant church in Wellesley. June perhaps. You think we should hold off for now?" she asked gazing at the stunned attorney.

Jerry smiled in return, "I think that would be wise. We expect to go to trial in less than two months, so it shouldn't be much of a delay."

"I suppose not. But really, I don't need this lawsuit any-more. Maybe I'll just drop it."

Jerry flinched. He felt himself getting angry at the "griev-ing" widow. He spoke slowly and calmly, "I have spent a lot of time and money on this case. It would be unfair to me to stop it now."

Julie Bradford paused for a moment before conceding, "I guess you're right. Maybe we could alter our arrangement."

She added in a more businesslike tone, "You stand to collect a third of the judgment after expenses. Unmarried, I'm worth more to you than married. So let's say I remain the grieving widow until after the trial and your fees get adjusted to twenty percent of the award. You eat any expenses, of course. That still should provide you with a tidy sum. Just redo our contract and send it to my lawyer." Julie stood and started to leave with a wave of her hand. Her eyes were quite dry now.

Jerry realized that Julie Bradford was a smart business-woman who was going to do well in court. *How is it that a street-smart lawyer like me gets outfoxed by an uppity, suburban WASP?*

Three

Eddie Collins leaned back, put his feet on the desk, and closed his eyes. He needed to organize his approach to Jerry Cleary's request for information on Tim Graves. Eddie had always been a respected homicide detective who was an excellent investigator, and he never started an investigation without first creating a thorough outline of the case in his head. He likened it to anthropology. You start with the skeleton and build out. His first plan of action would be to find out as much as he could about the players. Graves, the fertility doctor, and Paulie Strata. Since he already had a lot on Paulie Strata, it was Graves who represented the real mystery. Eddie remembered reading the newspaper accounts of his faked homicide and then his attempted murder by Strata, but he knew the papers only presented one side of the story. Newspapers presented the facts superficially and inaccurately. Eddie knew the muscles and skin of this skeleton had yet to appear.

Ready for action, Eddie swung his feet to the ground and reached for the phone. He first called the Massachusetts board of medicine to get a brief timeline of Dr. Graves' education and employment. Tim Graves attended USC, graduated from Harvard Medical School in 1960, and then went into training at University Hospital. He had been on the staff there since 1968 and currently holds an active license. Eddie thought he would start looking at USC, but since it was only seven in the morning in Los Angeles he decided to wait. In the meantime, he would see what he could get from his favorite associate and Southie buddy at the Boston Police Department, Patrick Kennedy, Chief of Homicide.

After several rings and several transfers, Eddie finally reached him. When all the greetings were over, Eddie asked, "Do you have anything you can tell me about this Dr. Graves? He was supposedly killed by the mafia?"

"What have you read in the papers?" Patrick asked, immediately on guard.

"Not much. Hey, maybe we should talk about it over lunch? My treat," Eddie said, knowing that his friend would feel more comfortable discussing the matter outside the department. Patrick accepted the invitation and they agreed to meet at the Rainbow Cafe near the station at 12:30.

After Eddie hung up, he decided it was still too early to call Los Angeles. He hated wasting time, so he closed his office and headed for the public library. They had a great collection of the Boston daily newspapers dating back three years; he might find something useful there.

Once inside the library, he made a beeline for the section set aside for newspaper cataloguing and storage. The older editions had been bound into large books and the more recent editions were still in their newspaper format with all the junk advertisements removed. If only they could do that to every newspaper, he thought.

Since there had been nothing recent about the case in the news, he started six months prior to when the transplant scandal was exposed. He read Chief Rastellini's statements about the conspiracy to redirect organs and the department's sadness over the missed heart transplant of one of their officers. After working with Chief Rastellini for many years, Eddie knew that whatever he said was on the level.

He had always respected the Chief, but he gained new admiration for him after his suspension ordeal. While working in the department, Eddie lost his temper with an assailant they were questioning and broke the guy's nose. Several people in the department held a grudge against Eddie for being so tight with the Chief and trumped up accusations against him. They claimed he had been drinking on duty when he hit the suspect, calling for an internal affairs investigation of his "harmful problem." Later, Eddie was forced to undergo an unannounced blood test, which showed that he was legally drunk, but the results given by the hospital had been read from the wrong sample. At least that was what was said. Eddie thought it was a plant by someone in the department. It didn't matter—Eddie was suspended and later terminated.

The Chief had supported him during the internal affairs investigation that led to Eddie's suspension and he maintained his support by giving Eddie a desk job after winning a court ordered reinstatement. The Chief had always believed in Eddie's competence as a detective and he never succumbed to the self-serving opinions of others trying to convince him otherwise. For that, Eddie trusted every word Chief Rastellini had to say.

Reading through the articles about the transplant scandal, Eddie was surprised to discover that Luther Kennedy's lab was mixed up in the mess. Apparently, one of Kennedy's lab assistants had used data to steer organs to the mob. Luther Kennedy was Patrick's older brother and Eddie had known him while growing up in Southie. Eddie remembered the days when he, Luther, and Patrick would hide in Patrick's attic to drink Cokes and look at Playboy magazines. Further in the article Eddie found a quote by Dr. Graves that mentioned Luther Kennedy as a classmate of his in medical school who had helped out Graves when he was on the run. *This story is getting more and more interesting.*

He continued reading until he had learned all about Tim Graves' son dying from a ruptured cerebral aneurysm, the death (or was it murder?) of the infertility doctor, and the supposed death of Tim Graves and Meg Logan (which he already knew about from his work on the force). He also read about the amazing story of Joey Santori being successfully treated by Dr. Graves for a ruptured cerebral aneurysm. *This thing reads like a dime store novel.*

Eddie glanced at his watch. It was a little after twelve and he had been looking through articles for nearly two hours! He only had twenty minutes to get to the Rainbow Café for his meeting with Patrick. Eddie quickly shut his notebook and headed out. He had gathered some interesting information, but he knew the real story was still not there.

Eddie entered the very full Rainbow Café, thankful that he had called ahead to reserve a booth in the back. The maitre' de was his old friend Shamus O'Connor. Shamus had been a troubled kid from Southie. Eddie had straightened him out years ago after Shamus was busted for selling pot. Shamus felt he still owed a debt of gratitude to Eddie, but Eddie never believed in calling in markers on old friends from the neighborhood. It would be like putting the arm on your own family.

"Let me bring you a drink, Eddie," Shamus said, after showing him to his table.

"No thanks, Shamus. I'll just have water."

A moment later Eddie watched Pat Kennedy come into the restaurant. Shamus immediately brought him over to the booth.

"I'll have some coffee." Pat said as he was sitting down. He then picked up the menu and shrugged.

"Bring us two specials, Shamus. Thanks." Eddie said. Shamus nodded, retrieved the menus, and went straight to the kitchen to place their orders.

"Good to see you, Eddie." Pat looked around the restaurant and added, "I don't get in here very often, policeman's salary. Is this one of the perks of having a private practice?"

"Nothing but the best for the guys on the Force. Besides, I'm on an expense account and my employer can afford it. How's it going?" Eddie asked.

"Great. Things are quiet and that's the way I like it. Someone whacked a small time punk from Southie, a leftover from Sean Connor. I'm pretty sure we know who did it." Pat unfolded his napkin and placed it on his lap as he spoke, "Now, enough about me. What's going on with you?"

"Things at home are great. The kids are out of the house, but still on the dole…for another couple of years, at least. Joan went back to nursing, and between her and my business, we seem to be doing fine. Nothing like being on the Force, but it's interesting enough," Eddie smiled.

"What do you see?" Pat asked. He was interested in Eddie's private practice. His retirement was coming up in several years and he thought he might team up with Eddie.

"Infidelity, divorce, investigating for lawyers who are trying to win cases. I get a lot of deadbeat dads. You know, finding them and squeezing them…and let me tell you, it's fun when you find them. I see just about everything, and I couldn't be any busier." Eddie was trying to put the best spin on it to keep his old partner on the hook. "The best part, though, is that it's mostly cash up front. Interested?"

"Yeah. Sure. Sounds like you'll need a partner in a few years. But what's the story now? Why the lunch today?" Pat asked.

Shamus set down two bowls of clam chowder, compliments of the house. Eddie crumbled some crackers into his soup and said, "I won't beat around the bush. My client is Jerry Cleary…the personal injury attorney?" Eddie waited to see if Pat recognized the name. Pat nodded that he did, and Eddie continued, "Anyway, it's about a lawsuit he has against Dr. Tim Graves, the guy I believe you and the Chief rescued from that piece of shit Paulie Strata. My sources tell me that Strata copped to the murder of a fertility doc in Vermont. That doctor was an associate of Graves. I'm interested in the connection between Graves and the mafia punk. Why would a mafia guy want the doc dead? I just wanna know what gives?"

"The Chief and Graves are old buddies. Before I forget, I ran into the Chief on my way out and told him I was having lunch with you. He sends his regards. Anyway, they go way back to the time they served in the Navy together. The doc saved his daughter's life. So, asking me questions about the doc sorta puts me in a bind, do you see?" Patrick ate his soup while Eddie contemplated an answer.

"Hey, I'm with you there," Eddie said. "The Chief looked out for me when IA cooked up that phony charge. I would be in a bad way if it weren't for him. Stepping on his toes or offending his loyalties is the last thing I want to do. But I also owe Cleary a lot. He was the one that found out my blood test had been 'screwed up'." Eddie threw up his hands to put air quotes around his last statement. " So, what can you tell me?" Eddie continued with his soup, but kept eye contact.

Pat picked up his napkin and wiped his mouth. After looking around the room again he said, "We had Paulie Strata on tape talking to a shooter about doing the doc. That's when the doc and the Chief hatched the fake death idea to get the doc off the hook and go after Strata. It was always strange why a Lefty Santori henchman would do the doc when only a month earlier the doc had saved Lefty's son. Believe me, I couldn't figure it out and I still can't. But the Chief knows why and he isn't talking. You'll have no luck getting anything out of him…it's all hush hush. Danny wouldn't even let us investigate that Strata creep, turned it over to the Feds with some conditions attached." Shamus arrived with shrimp linguini, steaming focaccia bread, and two large spoons. He set the food down and rushed to another table as more lunchtime customers arrived.

"I read an article about the Chief helping out the doc, but there's something missing. Anything I can get…any scrap… would be a big deal to me." Eddie said, spooning up his linguini with a piece of bread.

Pat put down his spoon and chewed thoughtfully. He was caught between his loyalty to Danny and his long time Southie buddy. He didn't have the answer to Eddie's question, but he knew his brother Luther did. When he interviewed Luther after the transplant scandal broke Luther told him about his graduate student lab assistant who had relayed information to Paulie Strata. Luther also tipped him off as to the reincarnation and location of Tim Graves. Pat decided that since most of this information, with a few key exceptions, was already public knowledge. He wouldn't be betraying anyone's trust by telling Eddie about it.

Pat told Eddie the story of how Meg Logan and Tim Graves met his brother Luther. He gave him all the details about the interactions between Strata, Luther, and Graves. He finished by saying, "Luther probably could tell you as much as I can…maybe more. It still isn't the whole story, but Luther might shed more light on it."

Eddie smiled. In less than three hours he had learned a lot and was well on his way to giving Jerry what he wanted. But Eddie didn't want to solve this mystery too quickly. He needed to pad the bill. He also didn't want to let Pat know how much he had given him. Eddie wondered if he could play on Pat's guilty conscience. "Well that's not much to work with, but I suppose it's a start," he said with a frown.

Pat didn't bite. "Sorry. That's all I have," he said. Pat knew the game, and he knew he had given Eddie a lot of information. He wasn't about to give him anymore. He also knew that getting information out of Luther would be like getting gold out of Fort Knox. Pat felt a twinge of guilt about shunting Eddie over to Luther, but Eddie and Luther had known each other for a long time and Luther could handle it.

"Luther still at the school?" Eddie asked. "I haven't talked to him for a couple of years. Remember when we used to hide in your attic and look at Playboy magazines. Luther used to go nuts over those pictures."

"He's at the same place he's been for the last twenty years. He's a big shot now, but still unmarried with a string of girl-friends. Actually, I'm thankful for that. For a while there I thought he was a fag. Of course, Ma had everything figured out…she knew what we were doing up there."

"How's Edna doing? Still living in the same house on 5th street?" Eddie asked.

"Yup, still living in the same house she and Pa, God rest his soul, bought forty-five years ago. Ma's actually doin' great. Retired ten years now, the high school just isn't the same without her." They were both grinning at the shared memories of their high school years as Shamus approached the booth.

"How was lunch? We have a wonderful tiramisu for dessert," he smiled.

"Lunch was great." Eddie shot a questioning glance at Pat. Pat shook his head and patted his belly. "Okay. I guess we're through. I'll take the bill," Eddie said.

"Hey Eddie it's on me," Shamus said.

"Forget it. I'm on an expense account." He gave Shamus his credit card and looked at Pat. Taking up where they left off, he asked, "Do you think Luther would talk to me?"

"Can't say. Luther does have a soft spot for you. You did get him out of a lot of scrapes when we were growing up. But, you know, he isn't my skinny kid brother anymore. He's a big time professor who takes his work seriously, and I just can't see him doing anything that smells the least bit unethical. Not even for me. So, I guess it's Luther's call."

"I'll call him when I get back to the office," Eddie said.

Shamus returned with the credit card, and Eddie left a big tip courtesy of Jerry Cleary.

Four

Luther was cordial on the phone. He agreed to meet Eddie at his office the next morning, but he could only give him half an hour. Eddie left his office on Massachusetts Avenue and caught the green line from Huntington. He got off at Longwood and hoofed it over to the school. He found Luther's building with twenty minutes to kill. Instead of waiting around inside he walked out to a corner coffee shop to buy a *Globe* and a cup. Sitting at a stool near the window, Eddie's thoughts turned from the paper in his hand to the papers he had read in the library yesterday. His trip to the library and his meeting with Pat Kennedy had proven to be very productive. He definitely knew more about Tim Graves and the situation with Paulie Strata, and it was clear how their paths must have crossed when Joey Santori was brought to the emergency room after his collapse on the mound during a Red Sox game. But if the doc operates on Joey and saves his life, then why does Paulie try to have him killed a month later? It still didn't make sense to Eddie why the doc, who was hailed as a hero for saving Joey Santori's life, would then be Lefty Santori's number one target. An infertility doctor too was in the sights of Lefty. Was Paulie acting alone, he asked himself.

Was it more than just coincidence that the doc's kid died of the same disease Joey had? That the doc's kid, like his dad, was once a great a left handed pitcher? He would have to track down

39

some experts on brain aneurysms.

Eddie glanced at his watch and saw that he had five minutes to get to Luther's office. He headed back down the street and entered the research building. He climbed up to the second floor where he found Luther's office. He pushed the door open and stepped into a small waiting area where a middle-aged secretary was sitting shuffling papers. She looked up and raised her eyebrows.

"Eddie Collins. I have a ten o'clock with Luther," Eddie said.

The secretary smiled and offered him a seat while she buzzed Luther. Within seconds the door flew open and Luther bounced out to shake Eddie's hand. "Hey Eddie! Come in. Come in," Luther said, leading him into his office.

As Eddie looked around, it reminded him of his old office at the precinct: gunmetal desk and chairs with metal filing cabinets in the corner near Luther's chair. One window looked out on the school's common, and there was just enough room for three or four people to sit. Eddie took a seat, but continued to size up the situation. He focused on the filing cabinets and saw that the rectangle identification card on the top drawer read: **DNA STUDY**. Now that would be an interesting drawer to peruse, he thought.

Eddie's musings were interrupted by Luther. "Same old Eddie. Doesn't miss a trick. You were always the one who could size up a situation and make it work for you. I haven't talked to you since you started your new practice. How's that going?" Luther looked over at the filing cabinet after Eddie stopped staring at it.

Eddie had always liked Luther, and his old friend was way too smart for any bullshitting. "Everything is going well. But I think you know why I'm here. I'll be up front, Luther. I talked to your brother yesterday and he recommended I talk to you. If I know Pat, he must have mentioned our conversation to you."

"Go on," Luther smiled.

"Well, I'm working for Jerry Cleary. That fact is supposed to be confidential, by the way, but we are old friends." Eddie was trying to get chummy with Luther, hoping he would open up.

Eddie continued, "Cleary has legal proceedings against Tim Graves. I know Graves was an old friend and classmate of yours, but I'm neutral here. You may think it disloyal to talk about him, but sometimes what you say can help steer the lawyer away from something potentially damaging."

"I can answer questions as long as they don't violate any confidentialities," Luther said. His tone suggested to Eddie that the old neighborhood stuff wouldn't apply here.

"I understand." Eddie was a little disappointed in losing his advantage, but he didn't let it show. He went on, "Pat told me you used DNA from Graves and Meg Logan for your database. So the confidentiality, at least for that, no longer exists. Right?"

"Yes, we did draw blood from them about two years ago because I wanted to expand my data base. As a matter of fact—and this has been in the newspaper—we used that information to confirm that Meg Logan was *not* the person killed in that crash staged to protect them from Paulie Strata."

"Did they ask you to draw the blood or were they doing it just as a favor to you?" Eddie asked. He eyed Luther carefully, trying to read his body language as he answered the question. He knew that the noted geneticist did not tell lies very well and was not known for his political astuteness.

Luther slumped back in his swivel chair and laced his hands behind his head. He rocked himself from right to left while staring at the ceiling. Finally, he said slowly, "Let me see, how did they happen to come to me? You know I don't remember. I think they dropped in one day and it came up in our conversation." Luther leaned forward onto his desk and cradled his face in his hands.

That's lie number one, Eddie thought. "So it just happened? No other reason? They weren't worried about possible birth defects if they had children together. Something like that?"

"Could have been…but it was two years ago, Eddie. I just don't remember," he said, looking down at the counter rather than into Eddie's scrutinizing gray eyes.

I'm not going to get anything here. He's lying like a kid who just threw a baseball through the neighbor's window.

Shifting gears Eddie asked, "Was Dr.Graves involved with the transplant scandal and that lab tech of yours? The papers said the tech tipped off Strata about the doc being alive, nearly got the doc killed. There has to be a tie in somewhere." Eddie figured it wouldn't hurt to keep pressing Luther.

"If there is a connection then I'm unaware of it. Peter, our *former* lab tech, did whatever he did here entirely on his own." Luther paused and added, "Now, I do admit that he worked closely with Strata. I guess he was also living with a nurse who spotted Tim one night in Cambridge. She told Peter. He told Paulie. I don't know. Peter said it was all done in innocence…he just wanted to inform Paulie's boss that Joey's surgeon was still alive. Like it was good news or something. I have a feeling he told the truth."

This story was becoming more bizarre as far as Eddie was concerned. Knowing that Paulie might have been acting alone still didn't explain why he wanted Graves dead. One thing was clear, though, Eddie wasn't going to learn anything from Luther. The old neighborhood friendships ceased to matter for Luther somewhere along the way.

"Well, I'm sorry to take up your time," Eddie said. "It seems like I may never find out what went on. I don't know…maybe that's for the best. Give my love to your mother when you see her," Eddie said as he stood up to shake Luther's hand. Even if he couldn't get much out of Luther this time, he still wanted to part on good terms—just in case something else came up.

"Eddie, it was good seeing you," Luther said. He smiled sincerely, but shrugged his shoulders as if to apologize. Luther knew he hadn't been much help to Eddie, but he also knew that Eddie understood the bind he was in. Luther pointed to a door next to the one Eddie has used from the waiting area and said, "Take that door, it goes directly to the hallway."

As Eddie left, he checked out the lock on the door. He saw it was a simple contraption that would be easy to break into. He shook the thought out of his head and continued down the hall. Eddie was disappointed he didn't find out more from Luther, but he felt sure that Luther was hiding something. No need to worry about padding the hours. This was going to be harder than expected.

Five

Jerry Cleary pleaded, begged, threatened, and intimidated defense lawyers to agree to take depositions in his office. He considered it essential to his success, though he didn't tell them that. He sold the idea as a winner for both sides: the defense attorneys could bill their travel time to their clients and he didn't waste his expensive time on contingency cases. Little did they know that Jerry used the opportunity to subtly manipulate the case. He conducted his depositions in a large, enclosed conference room with no windows. The walls were painted a soft orange color for its calming effect. In the center of the room was a long, rectangular oak table with 16 matching chairs. The deposed victim always sat in the center opposite a wall on which hung three evenly spaced paintings. If the individual being deposed was one of his clients or experts then he used upbeat pictures, like seascapes or young girls running in a field of flowers. If the deposed was on the other side, however, he chose from a collection of pictures that depicted despair and turmoil. The starving child in Biafra was his favorite, but he had many to choose from.

Jerry was as controlling as a shark in a fish tank. Determining the venue of his depositions also meant he could choose his own court recorder. He wanted to show Betsy Gallucci there were no hard feelings by enlisting her services for Julie Bradford's deposition. And perhaps she could be persuaded to give him some more "personal" attention…

It was early afternoon and Julie Bradford was waiting in Jerry's office. Jerry excused himself and went to check out the conference room where they would hold the deposition. Inside he found Betsy plugging in cords and placing paper in her recorder.

When he walked in the room she looked up with a tight smile. Possibly a good sign?

"Glad you could make it. I hope you're glad to see me." Jerry said. He looked around to make sure they were alone and then whispered, "I've missed you. Oh how I have missed you."

"Well I'm glad to hear that. I've missed seeing you Jerry." Betsy said, deliberately not whispering. "Don't think this has been easy for me. But we can talk about that later. Who are you crucifying today? Must be on your side since the pictures are easy to look at." Betsy was familiar with all of Jerry's tricks.

"Caught me. Yes, it's my client Julie Bradford. She's bringing the action against Dr. Graves."

Jerry sat down in one of the chairs. The deposition would start in fifteen minutes, giving him some time to pump Betsy for information. "Still hanging around the mafia types. Any news?" he asked.

"Sure, Jerry, I've got a lot of news, and it's mostly confidential. I did overhear one of the guards talking about how they just got back from the harbor. Looks like they have Strata stashed in an old, abandoned lighthouse on some island. Quite a fortress from what I can gather. They don't want to lose this stoolie."

"I guess not. When do they bring him in?" Jerry stood, getting ready to leave.

"Early in the morning to avoid crowds. Six AM. Around there. They keep him sequestered in the Federal Building until ten, then he spills his guts and I am the lucky one to record it," she made it sound like it was no big deal. "Oh, by the way, and this may already be in the papers, but that other stoolie the feds are holding was Lefty Santori's nephew, Lenny DeGrazie. He is the son of Lefty's only sister. She's the one who had a heart transplant last year…stole the heart from the cop. Apparently Lefty and Lenny have kissed and made up."

"The mafia going soft?" Jerry asked.

"Maybe. But, from what I gather they both have a common enemy in Paulie Strata. They can't wait to see him dead." Betsy squeezed lotion on to her hands and rubbed them together. She was ready.

"Interesting. I'll be a minute," Jerry walked out of his conference room and told his secretary to have the parties assemble for the deposition. He would talk to Eddie Collins later about what he had learned.

As he walked back into his office he smiled at Julie Bradford and asked, "Ready?"

"I'm a little nervous," she sighed "but let's get it over."

Julie was dressed in a plain, gray cotton dress with a black sweater. Her hair was clean, but not styled. She wore black shoes with no stockings and no make-up except for a colorless lip-gloss. *Perfect*, Jerry thought.

"Don't worry. I'll have an attorney on either side of you with me sitting at the end of the table. These attorneys assisting you are young, but very smart. They have studied your case inside and out, so you need not fret about the questions too much. Just remember what I told you: if your attorney objects to a question then that means you should think carefully about how to answer it. They can't speak for you, but they can help keep your answers consistent and open to interpretation by me in court later on. Understand?"

"I think so, but I would feel better if you are at my side," she said.

"Well, I want the defense to think that I am so confident in your testimony that I am willing to let one of my junior associates handle it. Also, it will allow me to leave if necessary. The defense is doing the same thing, you see? Mr. Stokes is having a junior associate take your deposition. Now, she's quite fair and will not hassle you...too much," Jerry added. There isn't an attorney alive that wouldn't go for the jugular vein if it were exposed.

Meanwhile, the attorneys were gathering like locusts in the conference room: counselors for the hospital and the anesthesiologist, Julie's personal attorney, the attorney for Graves, and an attorney representing the medical group, who was also named in the suit. In total, there were seven attorneys present. Personal business cards were soon sliding across the large conference table as some attorneys were meeting each other for the first time. It looked like a miniature shuffle board game was underway when Jerry entered the room. Now there were eight lawyers working on somebody else's dime or, in the case of Jerry, somebody else's future dime. Jerry shook everyone's hand and offered up some refreshments. He was clearly in charge, and he could be a gentleman when necessary.

"Shall we get started?" He smiled and sat down in a chair at the end of the table nearest to the door.

Betsy Gallucci asked Julie to raise her right hand and swear to tell the truth, the whole truth, and nothing but the truth.

The attorney for Tim Graves began, "Hello Mrs. Bradford, I am Lisa Harding. I represent the firm of Stokes, Bradley, Murphy and Goldfarb. Have you ever had your deposition taken before?"

"No, I haven't," Julie answered.

"That's okay. Let me just explain that I would like you to answer the questions I ask, but I ask that you let me complete my question before you answer. These are not trick questions. If you do not know the answer then just say so. Do you understand?"

"Yes."

"I will try to make this as painless as possible, but I must warn you that some questions will be personal. If you feel uncomfortable answering any of them you may consult with your attorneys. They cannot answer the questions for you, however, and I expect all responses to come from you and you alone." Lisa went on with the usual disclaimers and homilies about the process, emphasizing that the deposition was just like giving courtroom testimony. After several objections by Julie's flanking attorneys, Lisa was ready to begin.

"You have sworn that the testimony you are about to give is the truth and the whole truth. Were you the wife of John Terry Bradford of 13 Aspen Road, Wellesley, Mass?"

"Yes," Julie said.

"How long had you been married before Mr. Bradford succumbed to his medical problem?" Lisa was looking down at her notes as she asked her question.

"Ten years."

"Was it a happy marriage?"

"Objection," the attorney on Julie's right blurted out. "Question lacks foundation and calls for a conclusion."

Lisa was prepared for this and said, "You have claimed loss of consortium in your complaint and that's a fair question. I am not going to rephrase."

The plaintiff attorney sighed and said to his client, "You may answer if you can."

"John and I were happily married. We had...have...two girls, Kimberly and Karen. We tried to spend as much time together as we could—going on weekend trips, that sort of thing. John was very busy starting his own company after he left MIT, but somehow he managed to spend time with the girls and give me attention as well. We had a very happy household...we never argued and the two girls are quite normal. I mean they aren't seeing a psychiatrist if that's what you really want to know. " Julie was over her initial fright and began to dig in her heels.

"If John was so busy then how often did you have sex together?" Lisa asked, ignoring Julie's last comment.

"Objection, lacks foundation," one of Julie's attorneys said as he scribbled something on his legal pad. He added, "But you may answer the question as best you can." Julie's attorney felt like he was earning his salary until he glanced over at Jerry who gave him the slightest, almost imperceptible, headshake. Julie could answer these questions without qualifying remarks from her attorney.

"John and I were very much in love. From the first day of our marriage to nearly the very end we enjoyed each other.... sexually... as much as we could. If you want a number...as much as four times a week." A couple of the male attorneys raised their eyebrows just slightly. They'd be happy with four times a week.

Very small tears appeared in the corner of Julie's eyes. She reached into her handbag for a tissue and then dabbed both her eyes and nose. *Wonderful*, Lisa thought. *Straight out of Hollywood.* She should have insisted on videotaping this deposition— this performance could win the academy award. Lisa thought about pinning down her sexual habits more precisely, but decided to let it go for now. After questioning Julie's current financial situation and future financial needs, Lisa finally got to the area that would pertain more to the impending trial.

Jerry could sense which questions were coming next, and excused himself from the room. He wanted to speak to Eddie Collins, but, more importantly, he didn't want to be around if Julie started "misrepresenting" herself. If it turned out in future discovery she was lying, Jerry could always claim that he wasn't present when the fraud was underway.

Lisa was watching Jerry leave as she continued, "In your complaint you stated that Dr. Graves did not inform you or your husband about the risks of surgery and possibly safer, alternative ways to treat your husband's condition. Do you still contend that?"

Julie did not want to appear like the angry consumer who thought all doctors were in it for the money. Bitterness, she thought, might be used against her. "First, I want to say that Dr. Graves was a very nice man...he was a very compassionate doctor. As to your question, the answer is yes. My husband spoke with Dr. Graves when they first met and then again on the night before surgery. I was not involved in either of those two discussions. I met him after the surgery, and he was clearly upset."

Lisa chose to ignore the last part of Julie's answer for the time being. "So what was discussed between your husband and Dr. Graves?" she asked.

One of Cleary's lawyers immediately interjected, "I object to that question. Lacks foundation. Any answer would be speculation and hearsay. She was not present at the meeting."

Lisa agreed with the young attorney, who seemed to be following things quite nicely. She said, "Fair enough. Did your husband say anything about the meeting with Dr. Graves when you arrived later?"

"Yes he did. He said that Dr. Graves had told him the surgery would be a piece of cake. Dr. Graves told my husband he would be home in five days. My husband also said that the doctor seemed busy and had spent only a few minutes with him."

"Is that it?", Lisa asked.

"Yes." Julie sighed and wiped new tears from the corner of her eyes.

"Now, you said you met Dr. Graves for the first time after the surgery?"

"Well no. I said I met him after the surgery, but that wasn't the first time. I saw him just before surgery when John was being wheeled into the operating room. Dr. Graves introduced himself and said he would be out to see me after the surgery. There was no discussion at all about the surgery. He seemed very nice and considerate."

Ignoring the clarification of her earlier answer, Lisa asked, "What did he say after the surgery, when you *met* him?"

"Well, he was very upset. He said the aneurysm was a lot worse than expected and that it ruptured during the procedure. He seemed very agitated. He was sighing repeatedly, running his hand through his hair and shaking his head. He kept saying that he did the best he could."

"Did he tell you anything more about the details of the surgery?" Lisa asked.

"No, only that there was a lot of bleeding. He didn't say he was sorry for John or anything. He only talked about the aneurysm and how difficult it was…like something he'd never seen before." Julie took a drink of water.

Lisa was careful not to press her witness too hard. She knew Julie Bradford was a savvy woman who was playing at the grieving housewife. Despite her young age of thirty-two years, Lisa was an experienced attorney. She was attractive, pert and well groomed. Her deposition questions were well thought out beforehand. However, there was no way to shake Julie's testimony without running the risk of making her look like a victim of an aggressive attorney.

"One further question and then I will turn the questioning over to the other attorneys here. Did Dr. Graves at any time tell you or your husband about ways to treat cerebral aneurysms other than surgery."

No he did not. In fact he said the only accepted treatment was surgery."

"Thank you. I have no further questions." She turned and looked at the hospital attorney.

He was a plumpish older man with balding hair. He had been through this over and over again and had only one question. "Did the nurses or anybody review with you the possible problems with the type of surgery your husband was about to have?"

"Yes. A very nice nurse and a 'student doctor' went over the risks. They said Dr. Graves was too busy to come back and speak to me." Her voice had just a touch of sarcasm.

"Thank you. I have no further questions."

The attorney for the anesthesiologist asked a similar question and was satisfied that the answer did not implicate his client with the informed consent issue. The attorney for the medical group had no questions.

Looks like the hospital is off the hook…at least for this part of the suit, Lisa mused.

Julie stood up and excused herself. The attorneys began stuffing yellow legal pads into their briefcases while Lisa tried to look casual and positive. Underneath, however, she worried that if her firm was going to prevail in this case it was going to be an uphill fight. The hospital, medical group, and the anesthesiologist were clearly minor players who were not about to help her in some kind of united battle against Jerry Cleary.

Jerry rationalized his decision to leave his client during her deposition. He felt assured that she didn't need his help, and his inevitable interruptions would have been an unnecessary distraction. He also had other business to conduct on her behalf, like calling Eddie Collins. Really, though, Jerry didn't want to be around for Julie's testimony because he wasn't sure about the truthfulness of her testimony. Ever since she wangled him on his fees he was wary of her. When his secretary got Eddie on the phone she put him through.

"Hey Eddie, it's Jerry. Any news?"

Eddie appreciated cutting to the chase, "I have been all over this case, and this guy Graves is a hard one to read. I had to hire an investigator in Los Angeles to do some digging around. It appears Graves was quite the athlete in high school. But he also had a ruptured brain aneurysm and was operated at the children's hospital there."

"So?"

"Well, don't you think it's odd that father and son had the same brain problems?" Eddie was disappointed in Jerry's lack of enthusiasm, "I checked with a neurologist at the MGH and she says cerebral aneurysms are pretty common, one in a thousand births. But here's something odd—no one before him had it. His mother and dad are in their late 70's and neither of them had this problem. Anyway, he got over his brain surgery in high school and went on to be a great pitcher...and I mean *great*... at USC."

Jerry was getting impatient. He couldn't make any meaningful connections, "Can you get to the point? I'm in the middle of a deposition here."

"Hold your horses, Jerry, for chrissakes. I told you this is not a quick study," Eddie paused to let Jerry calm down and continued, "Graves has two brothers. One is a big shot lawyer with a large firm in LA and the other is an aeronautical engineer...graduated from Cal tech. They don't have any medical problems either *and*, here's the real kicker, they don't resemble this Graves guy in any way. They are both short and neither of them is athletic."

Jerry sat silent for a moment trying to process everything Eddie was saying. Dr. Graves has any genetic condition, but none of his immediately family has it? Could it be that he was adopted and therefore totally unaware of his condition? Did he pass it on to his own child unknowingly? If so, that would be a source of serious guilt, even though it really wasn't his fault. Jerry still couldn't figure out how all this tied in with Paulie Strata, or is there a connection at all? When he finally spoke, it was the calm, interested, and in control Jerry who said, "That's a lot of information, but I'm not sure what it means, if anything."

"I understand. But, and I am only guessing here, what if the fertility doctor…who, by the way, was world renowned…as if it couldn't get any more interesting…what if he used sperm from a medical student or from a surgical resident on Maria Santori. I mean, Joey Santori is a left-handed pitcher, just like the doc, who then pops up with an aneurysm, again just like the doc, *and then*, by chance, the doc is the one who saves his life…," Eddie ran out of breath.

"You might be onto something. But isn't that a slightly crazy scenario, and what proof do you have? I can't go walking into court with wild theories. How do you know Maria Santori had artificial insemination?"

"I don't know. But remember when Graves was allegedly killed? Afterwards, Maria Santori was immediately admitted to the spook house. Maybe she was shocked by the death of her son's real father? Look, this is just my theory today. Maybe it will change next week, but I'm working on the proof angle, don't worry. " Eddie didn't want to compromise Jerry by revealing his plot to break into Luther Kennedy's lab for a peek at his DNA files.

"Okay, keep working. But listen to this. I learned today from a very reliable source that a second Santori informant was let go by the feds. Apparently they couldn't use him as a witness because of the crooked FBI guy. You remember that?"

"Yeah, he was using Sean Connors as an informant, but he was using wire tap conversations which were illegal. I never heard who it was, but I have an idea." Functfionally Boston was a small a town and Eddie kept up with all the rumors spread around the Force.

"Well, I'll tell you who it was. It was Lenny DeGrazie, the son of the lady who received that heart meant for the cop. She's Lefty Santori's sister," Jerry couldn't help gloating, pleased with his own ability to dig up information.

"Just as I thought. Whatever happened to loyalty amongst the guineas? I guess the Santoris wanted to get rid of Lenny because he disrespected them, and he had a big mouth. He tried to put the arm on a Sox guy, pissed off Lefty. So where does that leave us?" Eddie was going around in circles.

"I don't know, but my informant tells me that Lenny and his uncles have kissed and made up. I'm sure they have a common enemy in Strata, since the papers connected him to the car bomb that killed his dad." Jerry kept up with the seedy side of Boston's underworld, having been exposed to it while growing up South of Roxbury.

Jerry went on, "Also they bring Strata in by boat when they are grilling him. The Fed Building. He's on one of the Harbor Islands. One with a lighthouse, most likely Lord's Island."

"Interesting." Eddie knew all about Lord's Island and that the Feds had used it before to stash protected witnesses.

Jerry gave Eddie the go-ahead to continue his investigation. He hung up the phone and massaged his eyes with a balled fist. His head hurt and he had a full afternoon of work ahead of him. He usually avoided drugs, preferring to tough things out, but today he'd take any help he could get. Jerry buzzed his secretary and asked her to bring him two *Advils* and a glass of water. When she entered his office with the *Advils* and a sympathetic look, Jerry spotted one of the attorneys who had sat in on Julie's deposition in the waiting room. Jerry waved him in as he swigged down the pills and water. Jerry's secretary flashed him a flirtatious smile as they passed each other in the doorway.

Jason Damon had been the attorney in charge of keeping Julie out of trouble. He was a little less than six feet tall with an athletic build and handsome, chiseled features. He had been a hockey player while in college at Northeastern and later graduated from Tufts law school at the young age of 26. Jerry liked him the first day he met him and had brought him into his practice five years ago. Although Jerry preferred doing his cases on his own, he had succumbed to the demands of a growing practice and his need for more help. He didn't take partners but paid his employees good salaries with incentives and most stayed as long as they could before seeking greener pastures. Being from South Boston, Jerry would tell Jason, had nothing to do with his attraction to the young attorney. But Jason knew better. His boss was a homeboy who believed the Irish had better stick together. For that reason, Jason was the only attorney in the office who had unfettered access to the boss.

"Well, don't just stand there. How did she do?" Jerry asked.

"I didn't need to be there. She knew the answers to all the questions and played it perfectly. She will be a hard witness to shake up in court. I know Ms. Harding was impressed, even if she did a good job of hiding it. With a few exceptions, I didn't need to slow things down at all." Jason never minced his words, a trait Jerry appreciated.

Jerry rubbed his forehead. His headache was receding, and Jason's summary of the deposition made it feel that much better. "I am putting this case on the front burner to accommodate the client. I'd like you to work with me…get up to speed with everything. We've got the doctor's depo two weeks from now and some nurses later this week. You do the nurses and I'll do the doc, but I want you there when I do his."

Jason smiled. It was a real compliment to have such an important role in a big case and he was going to learn a lot. "Consider it done, and thanks." Jason walked out, shutting the door behind him.

Jerry spun around in his chair and gazed out at the Commons. Things were happening quickly—he had to keep his eye on the ball. He knew this was going to be a tough case to win because it was always hard taking down a well-known and popular neurosurgeon like Tim Graves. He needed every bit of ammunition he could get. If Tim Graves was involved with the Santoris he would need proof and he would need to be careful how he used it. If Graves had donated sperm for money, knowing he had an inherited condition that could be fatal, then that wouldn't look good. Jerry had to be careful how he got his proof and he had to be sure, whatever he does, that nothing backfires.

Six

Tim slammed his locker shut and swore under his breath. He had just completed a successful surgery for a frontal lobe tumor, but he couldn't feel happy about it. He was troubled by what Luther Kennedy told him about his visit with Eddie Collins last week. So, he thought, Jerry Cleary hired a private investigator to snoop around. To top it off, Tim had a meeting at four o'clock with an attorney who was representing him in the Bradford law-suit. He had never been sued before or, for that matter, given a deposition. He practiced in a high-risk specialty and could have been a legal expert, but he shied away from doing it because he was too busy being a doctor. Some of his less busy colleagues got involved in legal stuff because they liked the limelight and thrill of the trials, or they liked the extra money. Tim wasn't interested in either of those things.

The lawyer assigned to meet with him was a junior associate of a large firm that did only defense work for doctors. Stokes, Bradley, Murphy, and Goldfarb was about as ethnically balanced as a circus high wire performer. Stokes was the senior man and was a black lawyer who had stuck by the doctors from the very beginning of his practice. The other partners, depending on the level of remuneration, had been on both sides of the fence during their legal careers. For that reason Tim requested Stokes as his attorney of record and the insurance company agreed.

He pulled on his white coat over his scrubs and headed to the recovery room to see his patient. After things appeared stable, he headed to his office where Lisa Harding was waiting for him. Tim noticed immediately that she was young and attractive. He introduced himself to her in the waiting room and led her into his office. He asked his secretary to hold all calls and messages.

"No offense, but you look young enough to be my daughter," Tim joked as he sat down behind his desk and motioned for her to take a seat.

Lisa smiled, "I get that all the time. I've been with the firm seven years and made junior partner recently. I'll be working with Mr. Stokes on your case. You'll meet with him as we go along, but I'm the one doing all the preliminary work. It's a better use of time and resources."

"Sounds good. What do we need to do?" Tim tried to be positive.

"To begin, I have some questions to complete the interrogatories." She saw the puzzled look on his face and explained. "Plaintiff counsel gets to ask questions about you after he serves the complaint and before he meets you at deposition. He wants to know if you were on any drugs before the surgery, if you had taken any alcohol, your general state of mind, etc... I have filled most of this out using your curriculum vitae."

"I suppose they are going to say because of my personal problems that I should not have done the surgery. Is that it?" Tim already knew the answer to that question. He didn't want to make Ms. Harding uncomfortable, though. She was only trying to help. "No, I don't use drugs and I didn't drink before the surgery."

"Okay. Well, Mr. Cleary is very thorough when he prepares a case, so we must be able to answer all of his questions—including questions about your state of mind."

"Why is my state of mind any of his business?" Tim shouted, and immediately regretted it. He was upset that he couldn't control his emotions more. "I guess I'll have to avoid those kinds of outbursts..."

"It's best if you do," Lisa said without a smile. "I realize this is hard for you, but you need to depersonalize things and take a more analytical approach. The attorney for the other side can query you any way he wants and you have to answer his questions, whatever they are…unless, of course, they invade attorney client privilege. Unfortunately, for these kinds of proceedings, client privilege is a gray area because not only are you a defendant but you are also one of the leading experts on brain aneurysms. You should keep that in mind."

"I think I understand. But I was not under any emotional duress during the surgery. My son died nine months before Mr. Bradford's surgery and I'd already resolved the issues between my ex-wife and me."

"Okay. Now, I don't need to know everything, but tell me what you can about your 'untimely demise'. How did you get involved with someone like Paulie Strata?"

"I knew that would come up," Tim let out a big sigh. "I haven't told you yet, but I learned from a friend of mine that Jerry Cleary hired an ex-cop to investigate my relationship to Strata."

"What!" Lisa was shocked. "How come you didn't notify us about that? Mr. Stokes would put a stop to that right away. Unless, that is, it has something to do with Mr. Bradford's care." Her last statement was actually a question.

"My relationship to Paulie Strata has nothing at all to do with the Bradford case. I didn't tell you about the investigation because the ex-cop happens to be an old friend of the person who told me about it. I promised not to reveal my friend's source, and I can't reveal anything about the reasons for my death and disappearance."

"That may be so, but you can expect questions about it during your deposition. I can't make you tell me anything about it, but it would help for me to know so we can avoid any surprises. For example, he may ask, simply, why did you disappear? Do you always duck out when you are in tight situations? What is the relationship between your practice and organized crime? I hope you understand what I mean, Dr.Graves."

Tim thought about it. He didn't see how his problems with Strata would have any bearing on Mr. Bradford's case. He wasn't about to tell his attorney the details of his past sperm donation and biological relationship to Joey Santori. He had promised Maria Santori he would never reveal those secrets and he wasn't going to start now, even to his own attorney.

"Well, I simply can't tell you anything about my disappearance. That stuff happened well after my experience with Mr. Bradford. It is strictly personal and has nothing to do with me as a physician. Mr. Cleary can dig into it all he likes, but he won't find anything to use against me...at least as far as the Bradford case is concerned," Tim said.

Lisa wasn't pleased with his answer. She was, after all, a defense lawyer who knew most of the tricks of the trade. She knew what the other side could do to discredit her client. "That's fine. But if, during the course of this litigation, you need to reveal anything then it will be only between Mr. Stokes, myself, and you. I just want to make that clear."

"So noted."

"Now, let's get down to the case at hand. There are questions about the informed consent. Last week I deposed Julie Bradford, who is bringing this action against you. She is a very cool customer under questioning. She'll make a good witness in the courtroom," Lisa said.

"Well, what did she say?" Tim was suspicious.

"That she had never met you before surgery, that she wasn't told anything about the risks of surgery or alternate ways to treat brain aneurysms." Lisa looked at the legal pad propped on her lap and looked up again.

Tim thought for a moment. What he was being told didn't square with his way of practicing medicine. Early in his practice he had been through the painful process of delivering bad news to a family he had never met before surgery. He swore he would never do that again. He always made it a point to talk to a spouse, offspring, parent or concerned friend before performing surgery, no matter how difficult or easy the procedure. The only time he didn't adhere to that rule was in the case of emergency surgery.

"What Mrs. Bradford says is simply impossible. In fact, I remember she was in the room with me when I talked to Mr.

Bradford the night before surgery. I might have mentioned that in the pre-op note I wrote," Tim said.

Lisa reached down and pulled out a bound copy of the patient's hospital record from her briefcase. She thumbed through it and scanned the progress notes. After several minutes Tim said, "Let me look. I can find it faster."

"Here it is," Lisa said, smiling at Tim's impatience. She pointed to a progress note dated before the surgery and asked, "Is this it?"

Tim looked at the note Lisa was pointing to and said, "Yes. Patient seen and risks, complications, and other treatments explained to patient. He agrees to surgery."

"It doesn't say she was present at that meeting. And I couldn't find it in the nurse's notes or anywhere else in the chart," Lisa said.

Tim reached for the bound chart, but Lisa withdrew it.

"Can't I look at it?" Tim asked.

"I would prefer that you didn't review the chart before your deposition. If you do then Mr. Cleary can ask you questions about it with the intention of catching an inconsistency in your statements. So, it's best if you don't see it."

Tim was beginning to realize exactly what he was confronting here. He concluded that the less he knew the better, though it made him nervous. "What kind of a system do you have? How can I defend myself without knowing the facts?" he asked.

"The facts you know today are the ones he can find out about. The more you review about this case the more potential questions he can ask. The more questions he can ask means more opportunity you have to screw up." Lisa gave Tim her no nonsense look. She could see he still wasn't quite getting it and added, "Let me give you an example of what I am talking about. If you were to review the record now, at deposition he could ask you what Mr. Bradford's blood pressure was shortly after you got into trouble in the operating room. If you answered, let's say, 90 and it was recorded as 70, then he could ask you to look at the record. When you see it was something different than you answered, he would ask you why you didn't know the correct number. Implying that you weren't aware of how serious the situation was."

Tim was starting to like Lisa's direct approach. It made sense to him now: this case isn't like a medical school oral exam. This is about trying to catch him in a lie. Mr. Cleary's job was to discredit him and any answer he gave during a deposition would have to be the same in court. Tim didn't want to have to backtrack on something he said during the deposition. "This is your playing field and I suppose I have to go along with your rules…or else get smashed by Mr. Cleary."

"You're getting the idea," Lisa said.

"Then I should say I haven't reviewed the record and don't recall the exact number."

"You could. But the point is this: don't guess or try to show what a great memory you have for facts. This is a common mistake physicians make in their testimony. You simply cannot guess or speculate. If he wants to pursue it further then you can ask to see the record. Now, if you were an expert witness then, of course, you would need to know as much about the hospital record as possible."

"So I'm an expert who is kept in the dark. I don't understand," Tim said.

"You are an expert on the neurosurgical treatment of aneurysms, but as far as this case is concerned we have an expert witness. You are not the expert for this case. Understand?" Lisa was going to have to be patient here. Things that were intuitive to her legal mind might not be to someone else. Doctors thought the same thing about lawyers when they tried to explain medical facts. It was like explaining the secret of a golf swing to a beginner.

"Ok. Who is the expert for me?" Tim asked.

"We'll get to that later." Lisa did not like getting out of step. She had an organized approach to client interviews and was careful to control the agenda. She continued, "Mrs. Bradford also testified that you didn't talk to her or her husband about safer alternative treatments. I'm afraid Mr. Cleary has made a big issue of this and has expanded the complaint to include punitive damages."

Noting the perplexed look on Tim's face she went on, "These are damages outside of the medical case. They are meant to hit you personally because your insurance doesn't cover them. Most lawyers threaten punitive damages hoping it might scare you into settling the case. But with Mr. Cleary, one never knows his intentions."

Tim moaned. "I feel like I'm being hit from all sides here. It doesn't even sound like *you* believe me. I tell you, I talked to both of them in his room the night before surgery and went over everything…including alternative methods of treatment. Those methods, by the way, can be just as hazardous as surgery. They are a long way from equaling surgical results and would never be used for an aneurysm like Mr. Bradford's."

Lisa looked at him and could tell from his demeanor that he was telling the truth. In court, however, it didn't matter what she thought. Without more documentation, it was what the jury believed that counted. The case boiled down to whom was more believable—a successful neurosurgeon with everything to lose or a grieving widow with everything to gain. She had been tough on Tim, but only because she wanted to see how he responded to hard questions. He had responded well and she decided to lighten up.

"Let's go over the operative report and then we'll be done," Lisa said, softening her tone a bit. "Educate me exactly on what the problem was and why the surgery ended up the way it did."

As Tim was getting ready to address her question the phone buzzed. He picked it up and listened for a bit. "Tell Meg I am in a conference now and will be home in an hour or so and just leave my messages on your desk. He thanked his secretary, who was leaving for the day, and turned back to Lisa.

"Where were we? Oh yeah. Let me give you a quick sketch about cerebral aneurysms and what we were confronted with in Mr. Bradford's case." Tim proceeded to go over the history and treatment of brain aneurysms, relating in detail the circumstances of the surgery. It was painful for him to relive that horrible day, and just talking about it conjured up difficult emotions. When the aneurysm burst in front of his eyes and he was unable to stop the bleeding, frustration led to a rare moment of decompensation in the operating room. The feeling one would have after hitting a world series winning home run only to be tagged out because you forgot to touch first base.

When Tim had finished, Lisa could tell that just recounting the events were painful for him. "I understand how difficult this must be for you. But you should know how bad your story appears on the surface. Here you have a bleeding artery which you are unable to control, and you simply sit down and let the resident take over."

Tim slumped down in his chair, defeated. He saw that Lisa was not impressed with his story. If he couldn't convince his own lawyer then how would be able to defend himself in front of twelve lay people who don't know the first thing about the difficulties he encountered? Again, it seemed as if Lisa was on the plaintiff's side. I'm the only one who can educate the jurors, he thought, so I guess I need to do more. He took out a sheet of blank paper from his drawer and drew a diagram of the left brain with the middle cerebral artery coursing over it. He sketched in an aneurysm, roughly the size of the one Mr. Bradford had, and then showed the drawing to Lisa.

"A cerebral aneurysm is like a balloon with a very short stem. I have to place a clip across the stem and clamp it down. That's when trouble can occur if the clip is not applied correctly. The stem, which connects the artery to the aneurysm, is usually only about a millimeter or two. In this case it was broader than that. This is called the neck of the aneurysm, and if it tears there is no way to stop the bleeding without clipping the artery. I saw that I couldn't stop the bleeding without clipping the artery, so I simply gave up."

"We have an incident report here that says you sat down and told the resident to take over," Lisa said softly, indicating that she was beginning to understand the problem and frustration.

Tim sighed. Maybe he had become unglued because of his experience with his own son. He regretted his behavior perhaps more than he regretted not being able to clip the aneurysm. He wished he could go back there and do it all over again, but thinking about past mistakes now was just a waste of time.

"The resident was the chief resident and he had worked with me for nearly four years. He was very skilled and, in many ways, better technically than I am. He did clip the middle cerebral artery and stopped the bleeding, but the brain infarcted." He saw that the word infarcted puzzled Lisa. "Infarcted means brain tissue died. With the swelling and blood loss there was just no hope. We pronounced him dead in the operating room," Tim said.

"I don't think the opposition needs to hear your opinion of the resident's technical skills. For obvious reasons, that's an example of attorney client privilege and will go no further than this room. Confessions and mea culpas are good for the soul, but they have no place in these proceedings," Lisa explained.

"Okay, I understand."

"I'm still a little uncertain about why the bleeding could not be controlled. Isn't that what surgeons are supposed to do?" Lisa asked the one question Tim knew he needed to address. It was going to be hard, but he needed to make people understand the complexity of working on the brain.

"I'll give you the long answer to that question...with a little background. This hospital, years ago, was distinguished for its pioneering neurosurgical expertise. One morning the chief surgeon was removing an accoustical neuroma—that's a tumor of the hearing nerve—under local anesthesia. The patient was awake, but he had a cloth draped over his face. So while he's operating, this surgeon encounters severe bleeding he knows he can't stop. He puts down his forceps, walks around to the front of the patient, lifts the sterile sheet, and tells him that it will soon be over."

Lisa shuddered, "Sounds gruesome."

"It is gruesome...but the point is this: bleeding during a neurosurgical procedure on the brain is unlike bleeding anywhere else in the body. You can't simply free up vessels and clamp them. We work in a very confined space with hardly any room to move around. We essentially have one shot at our objective or else it's often a bad outcome."

Lisa remained silent. She liked Tim's answers after he got over the emotional aspect of the case and stuck to the facts. He came across as compassionate, but not obsequious. "I guess brain surgery isn't a walk in the park," Lisa smiled. Telling a joke meant her interview was over. "Well, I think that should do it for today. You should know that Mr. Cleary has not named any experts yet, but I hear he has someone who will testify that this aneurysm should have been treated with a catheter."

"That's bogus! Those techniques are still in their developmental stages and this aneurysm was way too big for that. It had a fat neck as I said making it impossible to clot completely. Who's their expert? " Tim asked, trying to control his anger.

Lisa raised her hands as if in surrender and said, "Remember, I'm just the messenger here. Save your venom for Mr. Cleary."

She placed the medical records in her briefcase, and snapped the locks. "If you want to know who the expert is then we would need to make a motion to dismiss and force him to respond, which would consequently force him to reveal the name of his expert. But Mr. Stokes doesn't like playing games like that. We will soon know what Mr. Cleary is up to. He pushed the trial up to next month. Says his client is anxious to get it over with."

"Who is my expert then? You mentioned an expert for our side but we haven't discussed it."

Lisa smiled. "Oh. Right. During your 'disappearance' we were forced to find someone and we did. It was easy, actually. Dr. Davis at NYU. He is very much in your favor."

Tim was relieved to hear that someone would stand up for him, especially someone of Dr. Davis' stature. Tim had only met him once or twice at meetings where they both sat on panels. He was a well-known and well-respected neurosurgeon in New York. "That brightens things up a bit. So far I've been accused of lying, incompetence, callous behavior, fraud, malfeasance, and, to top it off, my attorney doesn't quite believe all my answers. Finally I have someone as respected as Dr. Davis in my corner."

"I am on your side, Dr. Graves, please believe me. But however tough I may have seemed to you, Mr. Cleary is going to be ten times worse." She stood up and offered her hand to Tim.

"Your deposition has been calendared for next Tuesday at Mr. Cleary's office. Your secretary cleared your schedule. I will meet you there at one thirty." Lisa and Tim walked to the outer office and said goodbye.

Talking with Lisa made Tim doubt whether he even had a chance to win this lawsuit. He went over to his secretary's desk and picked up four messages. One was from the recovery room saying his patient was stable, another from a patient he needed to call back, a third from Bill in audiovisual saying he would try again later, and finally a message from a vendor who also said he would try again later.

Tim called his patient and then called the pharmacy to order a medication for him. He went to the locker room to change out of his scrubs. On his way out of the hospital he swung by the recovery room to find everything stable and then drove home.

Later on, when he entered the front door of his condominium Meg was there with a big kiss and a hug but sensed immediately that something was wrong. "Bad day?" She stood back and tried to gauge his mood.

"My medical day was fine, but my legal day was awful. I met with the attorney from Stokes' firm and it was definitely not fun." Tim threw his overcoat onto a hall rack. "Let's have a glass of wine. I'm not sure I want to replay my meeting with the lawyer just yet. It's too depressing."

Meg tried to be cheerful for him and said, "One glass of wine, coming up. Go sit in your favorite chair and we'll talk about something else."

SEVEN

A week had passed since Eddie spoke with Jerry about his latest discoveries. During that time, Eddie had snooped around some more and found out that Lenny DeGrazie was living with his mother in her old house in Somerville. Lenny had rented the small house in the backyard to a college student and moved into the main house so he could keep a closer eye on his mother. He needed to make sure she took her medicines, which amounted to about twenty pills per day. Lenny had taken over his father's brick laying business after he died and it fell to him to keep things going. To his surprise, he liked his new role so much that he was making the business grow. There were days when his crews were so busy that he himself would have to fill in as a hod carrier or bricklayer. Mainly, however, his role was to schmooze customers and keep his long term, skilled employees happy. His exposure to the feds had cured him of any ambitions to follow in his uncle's footsteps. The demand for brickwork was going to be around for a long time, and he was going to play it straight and safe.

Eddie would worry about Lenny in due course. First, he had to learn if there was any reason to pursue his investigation of Tim Graves. The idea of breaking and entering Luther's lab was difficult to rationalize, but, after stewing over it, he grew to accept it. After all, he wasn't going to steal anything…he was only going to look around. Besides, it's not like this would be the first time he collected evidence without permission or a subpoena.

Eddie planned his break-in for Saturday night. The doors to the science building were locked at 5:00 on the weekend, so Eddie entered one of the lower floor classrooms at 4:30 and waited in the shadows of a filing cabinet. He heard the guard make his final check of the building and then lock the outer doors. Now that the easy part was over, Eddie left the classroom and quietly climbed to the second floor towards Luther's lab.

He stopped suddenly and listened after hearing a door some-where in the building bang shut. It seemed like hours before he continued climbing the stairs, but it was only a few minutes. When he reached the main door of Luther's lab he jiggled the door-knob. Locked. He proceeded to the back door he had used several days earlier. It was a keyed lock from the outside and a snap doorknob lock on the inside. He pulled out his collection of pass-keys from his pocket and, after several tries, opened the door. Eddie breathed a sigh of relief—a jimmied lock would have aroused too much suspicion.

The office was pitch black and Eddie clicked on his pocket flashlight. He tiptoed over to the file cabinet he remembered see-ing earlier and opened the top drawer, which wasn't locked. *No need for tight security here*, he thought, as he began to go through the files. They were labeled with such things as reagents, main-tenance records of lab equipment, reprints of Luther's articles. Finally, at the back of the drawer, Eddie saw a folder labeled "Initial DNA Study". He opened it and found a computer print-out with a list of names entered into the DNA database.

Suddenly, the door to the main lab rattled and Eddie heard someone shuffling down the hall toward the backdoor. After he heard keys jingling outside the door, he knew who it was. *Christ*, he thought, *I left the door unlocked. What an idiot! If I'm caught then I can kiss my investigator's license and my pension goodbye.* Eddie felt beads of sweat forming on his brow. He quietly pushed the file cabinet door shut and slid himself into the space under Luther's desk, which thankfully had a modesty board. He heard the doorknob turn and then the door opened. The guard stepped into the office and cursed the careless people in the lab who had left the door unlocked. He flashed his light around the small office and, satisfied that it was empty, snapped the lock shut and left. It was a full minute before Eddie took a breath.

He crawled out from under the desk only after hearing the guard's footsteps in the stairwell. Eddie needed to work quickly if he was to get out before the guard made another round. He opened the file cabinet and retrieved the computer print out from the "Initial DNA Study" folder. He skimmed through the names beginning with G but didn't see "Graves." There was an "anonymous" listed between "Grange" and "Gross" with the word "attic" written under the results column. He tried looking for "Santori" and again found that in the place where "Santori" would fit the word "anonymous" was written instead. The results for that anonymous listing were again noted as "attic." He found Meg Logan's name and no other anonymous names. He returned the printout to the file and put the file back in the cabinet. Satisfied that things in the drawer were as they were when he opened it, he slid it closed and took a quick look around the office. He hadn't left anything behind, and only breathed a sigh of relief when he exited the building undetected.

As Eddie drove home he mulled over what he had learned. He was pretty sure the two anonymous names stood for "Graves" and "Santori," and he figured that "attic" must mean that those files were hidden in Luther's attic. The attic had been their hide-out while growing up in Southie and now Luther was probably using it as a storage area...or hiding place... for laboratory results. It was still only a theory, and until he looked at those results Eddie had nothing but conjecture.

Breaking in and entering a low security medical school office was one thing, but breaking into the house of his old friend's mother was another. The next day Eddie decided that looking in the attic would be reserved as a final, desperate measure. Instead, he would see what Lenny had to say. Eddie knew Lenny from the days when he was a cop chasing down small time crooks in Somerville. Lenny was a guy always on the edge—not enough to be brought in for questioning, but just enough to capture Eddie's attention. Eddie figured he could use what he knew about Paulie's whereabouts as leverage for extracting information from Lenny. Lenny would be happy to pass along any tips about Paulie Strata to his uncles.

When Eddie called Lenny's office his secretary told him that Lenny was out building an add-on to a high school in Lowell. It was a long drive to Lowell, but Eddie reasoned that it might be worth the trip. And what did he care anyway? Jerry Cleary was paying for it.

It was almost lunchtime and the students from the high school were milling around in the recreation area. Eddie spotted construction going on behind the cafeteria and walked over to check it out. As he approached he saw Lenny engaged in an animated conversation with one of his bricklayers. He appeared to be explaining something when Lenny caught sight of Eddie and nodded to let the ex-cop know he had recognized him.

As Eddie approached him Lenny reached out and offered his hand. Eddie was surprised by the gesture and accepted it.

"How's it goin' Eddie? My secretary called to say you might be coming out here. I understand you got your own gig now?" Lenny walked over to a low retaining wall and sat down. He pulled out a cigarette and offered one to Eddie, who declined. He went on, "As you can see, I'm busy. Business has never been better and it's all legit. If I knew it could be this easy then I would have started doin' it sooner," he laughed. "What can I do for you? I know you didn't drive all the way out her to ask about my health."

"You're right about that," Eddie said with a chuckle. "What ever happened to the Lenny I used to know? The one with a chip on his shoulder, always looking for trouble?" he asked.

"I'm sure you know about the troubles with my uncles. That's over. In fact, they steered me some work. I'm out of the stoolie business. That shit's enough to give anyone religion. If they want your ass the Feds will get you no matter how long it takes. Fact is this: the longer it takes the worse it is cause you never know when the other shoe is gonna drop. On the other hand, it isn't hard to figure what you dickheads at the BPD are up to and then take precautions," Lenny laughed and slapped Eddie on the back a little too hard. The work and outdoor life had made Lenny fit and of course he was strong as an ox.

"You may be kidding, Lenny, but there is some truth there. We don't have the resources like the Feds. I'm here for my client—he wants to learn about some things that you might be able to shed light on. I figure you are out of it now, maybe can talk a little," Eddie said.

Lenny stiffened. Whenever a cop or, for that matter, a private cop wants information it can only turn out bad. "If I remember you correctly, you are a no bullshit kinda cop. Straight to the point. So why change now? Give it to me straight," Lenny said.

"Okay. What can you tell me about the relationship between Paulie Strata and the doctor he was hired to kill?" Eddie asked.

Lenny whistled low and shook his head. "You don't want much! If I could get my hands on that little asshole Strata I would take his head off. That little piece of shit killed my old man. I know it was meant for me, probly deserved it the way I treated my uncles, but that's all over with, now Paulie has gotta get dead. That doctor Paulie killed up in Vermont was part of a plan, but I don't know the details. I was with him when he did it, only along for the ride—I had no idea what he was up to. I was only followin' orders by going with him, you know, to see if he needed muscle. About that other doc, now, I got my own ideas."

"That other doc is the one I'm really interested in. What can you tell me about him?" Eddie asked.

"That depends. What do you got for me?" Lenny wasn't offering any freebies here.

"I got a line on Paulie Strata. But you gotta go first."

"Okay, here it is. After Joey's surgery, Paulie and me took Joey's ma to the hospital one day. I was waitin' in the car when all a sudden Paulie comes out with that killer look in his eye." Lenny stopped and took a long drag on his cigarette before flicking it to the ground. Exhaling through his nose he thought for a minute, making sure to find the exact words for what happened next. "Then Paulie gets in the car, hits the steering wheel with his fist, and says 'the doc's gotta go'."

"That's it? He said 'the doc's gotta go'? Nothing more?" Eddie was disappointed.

"No, that ain't all. Then he says…and I didn't tell this to the Feds…'fucking infertility doc's gotta go too'. As if he was thinking out loud and I wasn't there. After that, he never spoke another word about it." Lenny stood up and stretched his massive arms over his head. "Paulie scared the shit out of me then. But now I would kick the living shit out of him," he said while yawning.

"What do you make of all that?" Eddie asked, knowing full well that he had his own ideas what it meant.

"Dunno. There's some kinda connection between your doc and that fertility doc, but I don't know what it could be. I don't really care either. All I know is on that day, when Maria got back in the car, she was the most peaceful and happiest I'd ever seen her."

"Nothing more? That's it?" Eddie was happy with what he got from Lenny, but it didn't hurt to squeeze more out of him, if there was any more to tell. It was no good letting Lenny think he was satisfied. In Eddie's mind, Lenny's story tied everything together, but he still lacked proof.

"That's it. Wha'dya got for me?" Lenny asked.

"Here it is…and it's the best I can give you…Paulie is spilling his guts to the Feds. They have him locked down on some island in the harbor. When he testifies they bring him to the wharf at harbor patrol headquarters. This happens usually at around six in the morning. There's heavy security waiting for him at patrol headquarters and then he gets escorted to the Fed Building"

"For chrissakes there's a shitload of islands out there. What island?" Lenny asked before Eddie had even finished speaking. Lenny detected some resistance and added, "Come on, Eddie. You promised."

"Take it easy." Eddie stood and stretched too. "He's on Lord's Island. I confirmed that with the cop on harbor duty. But you never heard it from me. Now, I gotta head back." The two men shook hands, and Eddie left. He had advanced his investigation, but proof still rested in the attic of Edna Kennedy's house.

Eddie spent the weekend driving his wife crazy. He moped around the house in his pajamas, barely mumbled a full sentence, and watched every sporting event on TV. He couldn't come to grips with what he knew he had to do—he had to break into Edna Kennedy's house. He ruminated over how he could justify breaking into the house of an old friend and also kicked himself for promising Jerry that he would deliver the goods. He couldn't go back on his word to Jerry, but he also couldn't stomach the idea of violating his friend's trust. Eddie figured he had no choice— he had to see what was in Edna Kennedy's attic. *Maybe I can get a little extra out of it*, Eddie thought. Things were getting tight at home and a little bonus for the extra risk—not to mention the blow to his conscience—would at least make his decision easier to swallow.

When Eddie picked up the phone on Monday morning he heard Jerry Cleary's voice on the other end say, "Eddie, it's Jerry." Jerry exaggerated the vowels in each name to let Eddie know he was not happy. "Long time no hear, pal. You're getting your bills in on time, but what have I got to show for it?" Jerry asked.

"I can understand your frustration Jerry, but I'm just about done. Things are a bit dicey right now. I know where I can find corroborating evidence to back up my theory about Graves, but it's ...ahhh...how should I say it? It's a delicate situation. Let's just say you wouldn't want know where it is or how I plan to get it."

"And what theory are we talking about again?" Jerry asked.

"We went over it. Member? My theory about Graves being adopted and donating his sperm...about passing along a gene to a certain baseball player who is related to a certain mob boss."

"Yeah, I remember that crazy theory all right. But how sure about it are you?" Jerry was getting interested.

"How does 99.9 percent sure sound to you?"

"Wow." Jerry was suddenly more interested. "I won't ask

how you're so damned sure. I know you well enough to take it to the bank. When do we get the other point one percent?" Jerry had the feeling that this was going to cost him some hard cash.

"Well, we should discuss that. Like I said, I can get it, but there are certain risks I'll be takin'. The hourly rates you're paying right now won't cover it. In round figures, Jerry, I need five thousand payable upon delivery. I'm not trying to gyp you either. It's just that sticking my neck out is worth more than one hundred dollars an hour."

Jerry mulled over what Eddie had just said. The money was chicken feed compared to a settlement in the millions, but he didn't want to sound too eager. He could maybe get Eddie to come down a thousand if only for the satisfaction of being able to bargain down an ex-cop.

"Four thousand and you gotta deal," Jerry said.

"Shit. You shyster," Eddie laughed. "Okay, it's a deal. But I am still chargin' my regular rates...the four thousand is surplus. Agreed?" Eddie held his breath. He didn't think Jerry would even go that high. He must really want the information, he thought.

"Okay, you son of a bitch, but this better be worth it. I know you won't have it by tomorrow, so the question is when?"

"Who says I won't have it by tomorrow? I'm planning to...um...obtain the documents today."

"Great. Call me on my back line tomorrow morning. You've got the number," Jerry said, and hung up.

Jerry swiveled his chair around and stared out the window. Things were shaping up. He had a great witness with a great story, a so-so expert in Los Angeles, and a defendant with a suspicious personal life. Jerry knew he had to be careful about using his information wisely—he already knew what it was like to have a rock solid case turn to mush because an expert witness went sideways on him or because his client bombed out on the witness stand. In this case, his expert witness seemed more likely to screw things up than anything else. The real question Jerry needed to face was whether he had enough facts to destroy Graves or whether he needed to go dirty and use this other data he was gathering. It remained to be seen. Jerry glanced at his yellow legal pad and began jotting more questions for Tim Graves. He liked using the algorithm approach in which he wrote down questions and then wrote down possible answers to those questions and then thought of more questions based on the possible answers. It was a long process because every question had more than one answer, but Jerry would rather spend a long time sketching out all the possibilities than get trapped by not knowing which direction to go when he was deposing a witness. Defense attorneys could smell such a weakness right away.

Eight

On his way to the office early Monday morning Eddie took a little detour. He cruised by Edna Kennedy's house before turning down the alley behind it. He found a parking space two houses away from Edna's and decided to park there when he returned in the afternoon. He felt certain that one of his entry keys would work on the lock to the back door of Edna's house. He just had to be certain that she wasn't home. Even though she was retired, it was quite possible that Edna would be gone for most of the day. She was very active in the church and neighborhood social groups and she often tutored students at Southie. Remembering why she might not be home gave Eddie a slight pang of guilt, but he quickly recovered. Driving out of the alley, he decided that he would call Edna before he left the office, just to make sure she was out.

Eddie called Edna's number at 11:30 and no one answered. She was probably out on a lunch date, which would give him at least an hour. It would take him twenty minutes to drive to her house in South Boston and another 10 minutes for parking and entering the house. He immediately hopped in the car and sped off. He found his parking spot free, so he eased the car in the space and cut the engine. The house appeared empty from the back. He couldn't detect any activity at all. Acting as though nothing were unusual, Eddie nonchalantly walked through the backyard and closed the gate. He quickly covered the ground between the gate and the backdoor, being careful not to look around or appear suspicious. Within a minute he had found a key that fit the lock and he entered the door that led into the kitchen. Sweeping through the kitchen he noticed that the morning dishes were already washed and the place was spotless. Nothing changes, he thought. He moved down the hall leading from the kitchen towards the staircase and tiptoed up to the second floor. Once on the second floor, his cop instincts took over and he searched every room for signs of occupancy. No one was in the house.

Eddie remembered from his childhood that access to the attic was through a shallow closet that only contained a pull down ladder. He spotted the closet and opened it. He pulled down the ladder, which came out on hinges, and rested it neatly on the floor. After testing it for traction and sturdiness, Eddie climbed up several rungs, reached up over his head, and pushed aside an access panel. He climbed the remaining rungs until his head, shoulders, and upper torso were in the attic. He glanced at his watch. It was twelve fifteen. He pushed himself up onto the attic floor, keeping his head low to avoid the studs of the gabled roof. He left the ladder in place and moved the access panel out of the way.

The dusty attic had obviously been untouched for many years, though there was an old throw rug in the center of the confined space along with a rocking chair. Someone must have used this space at some time to read or meditate, Eddie thought. There was a single light hanging from a cord over the chair, which, to Eddie's surprise, still worked. Looking around the room he noted that the space was much smaller than he remembered. When he was a teenager hiding out up here with Luther and Patrick the place seemed like a palace. Now, it just looked cluttered. There were boxes along one wall and an old steamer chest along another. Several pieces of old furniture filled one corner, and things looked as though they hadn't been moved for several years. Everything was covered with dust except one cardboard box sitting on top of a table. Eddie made a beeline for the box but was disappointed to find it empty.

Since there was so much junk in the attic and so little time, Eddie needed to make his search a methodical and efficient one. He divided the space into quadrants and started searching in the one containing the most boxes. He found only old photographs, newspapers, and personal letters. He turned to the second quadrant where an old, beat up looking dresser stood. He opened the first drawer to find medals and citations that Luther's dad had received in World War II. Luther's dad had never mentioned the war to anyone and here he was a clear-cut hero. It was typical of him to hide something like that, Eddie thought. A pang of guilt hit him again...he was violating the closest confidences of friends by poking into their private lives. He almost decided to quit, but figured he might as well see it through... after all, he had come this far.

The third quadrant in Eddie's grid of the attic was filled with old chairs and books, which he quickly searched to no avail. The last quadrant left to explore contained only a bedside table with a single drawer. Eddie went over and pulled on the drawer, but it wouldn't open. When he looked along the side of the table he could see that someone had nailed the drawer shut. He shook the table and heard nothing. It didn't sound like anything was in the drawer and the table didn't feel any heavier than it should. Somebody must have nailed the drawer shut years ago so it wouldn't be used. Annoyed with himself for this futile errand, Eddie shook the table again and then turned it over. He was surprised to find, taped to the bottom of the drawer, a manila envelope. Both the envelope and the tape looked clean, as though someone had placed it there fairly recently. Eddie felt a surge of excitement as he peeled the envelope off and tore open the seal. Jackpot! His excitement quickly turned to panic, however, when he heard a door slam and someone yell from downstairs, "Ma! Are you home?"

Eddie froze. He remembered Pat telling him about being on duty this weekend...which meant today would be his day off. *Shit.* Eddie cursed himself for being such a bonehead. First leaving the door unlocked in Luther's office and now this. This was the kind of sloppy work he used to berate his fellow officers for doing. He stuffed the envelope into his coat pocket and tiptoed over to the attic opening to listen. Edna Kennedy's house was not an acoustic marvel and the slightest noise made in any room could be heard throughout the house. He heard rustling in the kitchen and what sounded like the refrigerator door opening and closing. It sounded like Patrick was helping himself to a free lunch while his mom was out. *If Pat comes up the stairs then I'm finished.* The ladder was down and there was no way he could reach down to pull it up again. Eddie heard some more movement in the kitchen and then heard Patrick walking down the hallway to the stairs. He climbed on the first step before shouting up the stairwell, "Ma are you there?"

Eddie heard Patrick climb another step. *It's all over.* There was no sense trying to hide in the attic since the ladder told the story. Suddenly the phone rang and Eddie heard Patrick moving to get it.

"Hi Ma," Patrick said. There was a pause and Eddie listened intently. After a few seconds he heard Patrick say, "Okay. I'll put the cake in the fridge. See you tonight…and remember it's a surprise. Kevin doesn't know anything."

Kevin was Patrick's older son. Eddie figured that they were planning a family get together for his birthday. Moments later the front door was pulled shut and Eddie breathed a sigh of relief. He realized that he hadn't charged Jerry enough for what he just went through. As he climbed down the ladder Eddie felt as though he just won the Super Bowl. Not only did he dodge a big bullet, he also got what he came for.

Later that evening, in the quiet of his home, Eddie looked more carefully at the contents of the envelope. His working hypothesis was true after all, and now he had the proof. Piecing together Lenny's words and the information in his hand, Eddie felt sure he knew the answer to the question Jerry had asked him just three weeks ago—Why did Paulie want to kill Tim Graves? Eddie replayed the scenario in his head: Paulie takes Maria to see Graves after Joey Santori's surgery. He overhears their conversation in which she admits to having been inseminated with

Graves' sperm. This enrages Paulie who is loyal to his boss and will go to any lengths to protect him. If news of Maria's duplicity were to get out, the damage to Tony's image as a crime boss would be immeasurable. He decides to act by killing the fertility doctor and destroying any evidence that points to Maria's medical history with him. Then he tries to kill Tim Graves, but fails.

Eddie felt uncomfortable with his new findings. This was his job and he did it well, but at what price? Jeopardizing his friendships, breaking the law, exposing himself to lawsuits and the loss of his license? Not to mention exposing the artificial insemination of Maria Santori, which she obviously had hidden from everybody, including her husband. What would he tell Jerry in the morning?

Eddie awoke the next day after a fitful sleep. He showered, shaved, and dressed. The whole affair was hanging on him like a football helmet lined with lead. It was 8:30 when he sat down for a cup of coffee and the morning paper. He had tried to be upbeat when he came home last night, but he couldn't even talk to his wife, who suspected he was under more strain than usual. Joan Collins was a sympathetic woman and a devoted wife who deeply loved her husband. Even though his bouts of depression and anxiety were sometimes exhausting for her, she had always been there for him.

"Eddie this is the worst I've seen you," she said as she placed a cup of coffee in front of him.

Eddie tried a smile, but it didn't work. He stirred sugar into his coffee before answering, "I've been working for Jerry Cleary and now I'm in a bind. I have information that could help him in a case. Trouble is I got the info' by bending some rules, if anyone found out about it that could be the end of my investigating business."

Joan was impressed. "Wow. That's more than you usually tell me when I ask what's bothering you. What gives?" She removed two slices of toast from the toaster and started to butter them. "You almost never let me in on what you're doing. Why now?" She turned and stared at him, not entirely pleased.

"I know I was a pain in the ass when I was on the Force. I was young and carried the weight of my work on my back. Now that I'm on my own, it's a little scary. There's no monthly paycheck unless I produce results, and it's gotten me to do things I wouldn't ordinarily do. I guess I'm just feeling really guilty right now. Irish Catholic guilt and this is my confession time." Eddie was able to respond to his introspection with a real smile.

Joan softened and said, "You've always been a great provider. But I'm working now. I think we could manage living on your pension and my salary. The house is nearly paid for. Only one more kid in college….by the way, remind me to talk to you about that." Joan slid into the chair opposite her husband and took a sip of coffee.

"Talk to me about it now. I need to make a decision today about Jerry."

"Well," Joan tilted her head back and forth as though her gesture might take the sting out of what was coming, "Rob's last tuition bill is due. You know he works and saves and tries to help, but it isn't enough. I'm worried that his job outside of school is taking away from his studies. I have seven thousand put aside, but I need another three thousand… plus minor expenses. I know it isn't always about money, but if you could scare up four or five thousand it would get us over the top."

Eddie closed his eyes. The big payoff from Jerry was gone in a flash. Why did money always have to rule his life? "Okay, I'll see what I can do. When do you need it?"

"The bill came yesterday and it's due in three weeks." She sat stirring her coffee and looking Eddie in the eye.

"Okay, I'll get it," he said. "I gotta go." Eddie stood and came around to kiss Joan goodbye. "Love you," he whispered.

On the way to the office Eddie decided he would give Jerry the best information he had, but hold back on the documents he had purloined from Edna Kennedy's attic.

It didn't take Eddie long to find Jerry who seemed rushed. Eddie said into the phone, "I have obtained documents that fulfill the scenario we talked about yesterday."

"When do I get to see them?"

"You don't want to see them. You have to trust me on this.

Tim Graves in all probability is the father of Joey Santori and I would be very careful how you use that info."

Jerry was in too much of a hurry to go into the details of what Eddie had revealed but he had heard enough to use during Graves' deposition. "Okay, Eddie. Thanks for the advice. But the mafia doesn't scare me. Let's talk tomorrow." Jerry hung up.

Nine

Tim hated everything about this day. It was Tuesday, his big case day, and it was also the day of his deposition. Driving to Jerry Cleary's office after lunch was the hardest thing he had done in a while. He was about to face the one thing he had dreaded since medical school: a lawsuit. He was about to be grilled by some smartass lawyer who could be as smooth as silk or as rough as sandpaper depending on the situation. Tim feared lawyers primarily because he could never quite understand what made them tick. He knew his brother very well, of course, but he could never understand what attracted him to the law. Legal studies were boring and involved no science or physiological mechanisms. In fact, as far as Tim was concerned, it was the anti-science. The jury and adversarial system had started in the twelfth century and hadn't advanced since. Were these the musings of an educated man or the grumbles of someone about to be toasted by a clever attorney? As far as Tim was concerned it didn't matter. Mr. Bradford was dead. He'd tried his best and everything after that—like this whole process—was about money, pure and simple. This wasn't about advancing the future care of patients with cerebral aneurysms. It was about greenbacks.

After searching for several minutes, Tim finally found a parking garage about two blocks from the office where he was to meet Lisa Harding. His initial impression of the young attorney was favorable, and he actually looked forward to seeing her again. He dodged cars as he crossed streets to get to Cleary's office. Once inside, he took the elevator to the third floor and found Lisa Harding sitting in the waiting room by herself. After they greeted each other, Lisa told Tim that her boss, Edwin Stokes, would arrive shortly. Just as she finished speaking, the door to the office opened and a tall, trim, black man with a legal brief-case in his hand entered the room. Mr. Stokes appeared to be in his late fifties with graying hair. He wore clear-rimmed glasses and had a very engaging smile. Tim liked him immediately.

Edwin Stokes was born in Boston in 1930 and grew up south of Roxbury, where Italians and Irish lived together in neighbor-hoods containing some black families. Edwin's ancestors origi-nally immigrated to Boston from Canada in the late 1880's, and they were able to buy land, own homes, and go to the public or private schools of their day. Massachusetts is the only state in the union that never had slaves. Mr. Edwin Stokes senior owned a successful chain of grocery stores while his mother had her own accounting business. The family lived modestly and within their means, and Edwin never felt deprived as a child in any way. He did, however, suffer from asthma, which frequently left him look-ing out the window of his house to watch the neighborhood kids—mostly white—play in the street while he sat inside struggling just to breathe. It was during this period of his life when he realized that to succeed in a predominantly white society meant he would have to integrate himself.

Edwin was exposed to literature and history at a very young age. His parents read to him all the time and they often read stories about slaves who had escaped bondage to live free, pros-perous lives. He grew to love books and could almost always be seen reading the black authors such as Tubman, Douglas, and Carver. Yet, he knew that to integrate himself he would need to read the white authors as well. So, he would plow through Dickens, Shakespeare, Longfellow, and Lincoln. Being so close to such a historical area of America, Edwin also became inter-ested in the history of Boston and read the writings of Edwin

White and John Adams. It was really the writings of Adams that got him interested in the law, and he pursued his interest all the way through law school. After graduating near the top of his class at Boston Latin and then attending Harvard, he was accepted at Harvard Law School. It was a significant achievement for him because affirmative action was not in effect when he was applying. He entered the ivy-covered halls of that white, elitist school on his own two feet.

As an undergraduate at Harvard, Edwin was one of two or three black people attending the school. He suffered the taunts and crude jokes from some of the white students, and from the black kids running in the street of Cambridge, where he was called an Uncle Tom. But, by and large he was accepted simply because of his broad knowledge in literature and American history, both black and white. Since his asthma prevented him from participating in sports, Edwin spent his free time pursuing public speaking in the debating society. He became a formidable opponent not only because he was an articulate black man, which seemed to intimidate the white students, but because he was able to recall facts from history to support his positions. Black or white, Edwin stood out as one of Harvard's best students.

Edwin passed the Massachusetts bar when he was twenty-five years old. It was after the era of Jackie Robinson and during the beginning of the civil rights movement. On an emotional level he could accept the reasons for such a movement, but he had trouble with it from an intellectual viewpoint. After all, hadn't he accomplished everything in his life entirely on his own in spite of his color? He took on the white establishment on his own by learning what they knew and more—it was education that provided the key to success and it was the individual's responsibility to engage in his own learning process. It was also as an individual defiant of prejudices and expectations that he would practice law. Instead of being a token black in a firm of white lawyers, he opted, instead, to open his own practice.

He went back to the neighborhoods in Roxbury and South Boston in order to build up clientele. It was only after he had defended a doctor against allegations of malpractice and won

that he decided to be a defense lawyer with a specialty of representing physicians. In those days it was easy to defend doctors
because juries were very favorable to the medical profession and
had a measure of respect for physicians. It used to be hard for
plaintiff lawyers to win malpractice cases. Consequently, Edwin
did very well, enabling him to build a large practice and take on
associates. Over the years, however, improved technology and
greater expectations imposed upon the medical profession made
it more and more difficult for Edwin to win cases. Juries were
more sophisticated and would not bend in favor of a doctor as
frequently as before. To make matter worse, doctors with good
reputations were taking the stand against their colleagues in in-
creasing numbers.

Aggressive plaintiff attorneys were becoming more hopeful
that their cases would win in front of a jury and so they took up
more malpractice suits than ever before. As the cases became
more and more marginal, so did the experts. Many who testified
against doctors would say outrageous things about what consti-
tuted standards of patient care, and by the early 80's the plaintiff
attorneys were on a roll. So much so that the legislature tried to
reign in the plaintiff attorneys with tort reform. Results were still
pending. At fifty-eight Edwin Stokes had seen it all and was about
as shrewd a lawyer as there was in Boston. He was always positive in his approach, but laced it with a little skepticism to keep
his clients on the side of reality.

"Good afternoon, Dr. Graves," Edwin said without an intro-
duction, " I don't believe we've met before. I know you've met
with Lisa, and she has been keeping me up to speed. I wanted to
be here for your deposition since I consider it as important as the
trial itself."

"Nice to finally meet you. You have a great reputation among
physicians and I'm sorry to meet you under these circumstances,"
Tim said.

Edwin was familiar with doctors and their egos. Whenever
they were presented with legal action they immediately felt like
their reputation was smeared. Whether the claims were thrown
out in court or not, doctors always felt that the accusation itself

was just as good as being convicted of a felony. Edwin also respected the naivety of doctors because it spoke to their good nature as people who just wanted to help others. He explained, "I want you to understand that this is a civil proceeding but it won't be civil. Mr. Cleary is out to get as much money as he can from you and your insurance company. You have not committed a crime, but you are being challenged because you stand in the way of the money. It's important for you to realize that you have an excellent and justified reputation. But as far as Jerry is concerned, you're the scum of the earth."

"Sounds like you and he are friends? I mean, you called Mr. Cleary by his first name," Tim questioned.

"We are friends. I grew up next door to him and knew his older brother Sean quite well. He got me out of more scrapes than I can name…saved my butt many times. Sean became a career sergeant in the Marine Corps and was killed in Vietnam. I loved him like a brother. You could say he was the brother I never had. But, that's as far as it goes with the Clearys. They're Irish, and if you don't understand the Irish then you will never win a case in this city. They are clannish, tough, give you the shirt off their back, and won't back down from a good fight. The other things they are, let's say are not pertinent right now."

"Seems a little ironic that you would have such great respect for a group that fought school integration. How do you feel about Louise Day Hicks?" Tim was fascinated with Edwin Stokes. He had never dealt with black people in high school and he only knew a few during his undergraduate years at USC. They seemed to be on the fringe and he always felt like he was holding back, and visa versa, when interacting with them. But he felt comfortable with Edwin Stokes. There didn't seem to be any inhibitions clouding the conversation.

"We could carry on with this, but it's time to start the deposition and we need to go over some things," Lisa interjected as politely as she could.

"Right you are," Edwin said. He knocked on the glass window where the receptionist was sitting and pointed to a door leading to the inner offices. She nodded and Edwin headed through the door to the conference room assigned for opposing counsel to meet with their clients.

They settled around a small table in a room adjacent to the main conference room. Lisa spoke first. "One of the main issues in this case seems to be that of informed consent, or the lack thereof. I deposed Mrs. Bradford last week and she claims to have not spoken to Dr. Graves at any time prior to surgery. She claims not to have been told about treatments other than surgery. The other issue here is that of the surgery itself…the unexpected clipping of the middle cerebral artery. Finally, we have to deal with the circumstances surrounding Dr. Graves' disappearance for a year."

Edwin sat silently and thought about what Lisa had said. He watched Tim's reaction as well, noting that the doctor looked completely at a loss. Tim didn't know what to think. The issue of the informed consent was a complete lie and the surgery had a bad outcome. Finally, Edwin spoke, "Tim, I want you to remember everything about the circumstances of the surgery and answer the questions succinctly. Do not guess, elaborate, offer explanations, speculate, approximate, prevaricate, or delineate. Understand?"

"Yes," Tim said.

"The only information Mr. Cleary can get from you is what you give him. That information can be twisted, squeezed, and manipulated…I think you know what I'm talking about."

"Yes, but how do I know when I'm crossing the line or I am being asked a loaded question?" Tim asked.

"Fair enough," Edwin said, "If I think the question is a lead in to some other question that will compromise you then I would interrupt and say something like 'lacks foundation, hypothetical, privileged'…anything to slow things down and get you thinking that this is an important question. Let me give you an example. How long is your index finger?"

Tim chuckled, "Actually, it's funny you should ask. I measured it once and it was about 8 or 9 centimeters. I had to know how long it was when I took a physical examination class and we were learning how to estimate depths of cavities." Tim seemed proud of his answer. It wasn't long winded, he had explained why he knew the answer, and he gave an approximate answer.

Mr. Stokes sat staring at him and then said, "I asked you how long your index finger is and you just gave me a history of your life. I didn't ask you how you knew how long it is or why you knew, you volunteered that. You don't even know for sure how long it is."

Chagrined, Tim bowed his head and said, "You're right. I don't know exactly how long it is."

There was a sudden knock on the door and Mr. Cleary's secretary poked her head in to say they were waiting for them in the conference room. Tim's heart leapt in his chest—the moment he had been dreading had finally arrived. He followed Edwin into the main conference room with Lisa trailing behind. Jerry, who was sitting in his usual position at the end of the table, stood and shook hands with Edwin and Tim. He waved a hello to Lisa and sat down.

"There's water in front of you, Dr. Graves. If you need anything else just speak up," Jerry said.

Tim nodded as he sat down in the middle of the table facing three pictures on the opposite wall. For this ordeal Jerry had chosen pictures of Dunkirk, Bill Buckner booting a grounder in the world series, and the blackened, defeated faces of GI's in Vietnam. *What a downer*, Tim thought.

"Allow me to introduce you to Betsy Gallucci. She is the reporter for this deposition," Jerry said.

Tim nodded at her and then raised his right hand as she administered the oath to swear in his testimony.

During the formalities leading up to questions about the case, Jerry was pleased to find out that this was Tim's first deposition. He spent time explaining why they were there and how Tim should wait until Jerry finishes his question before answering. When Jerry finished running through the protocol he said, "We're here because my client, Julie Bradford, has brought action against you. She is claiming that you did not inform her or her husband about the dangers of surgery for a middle cerebral artery aneurysm nor did you inform her of the possibility that other methods could be used. Also, the surgery was performed in an incompetent manner and ultimately led to Mr. Bradford's demise. Do you want to respond to that?"

Edwin jumped in, "The question is overbroad, lacks foundation, assumes fact not in evidence and I ask my client not to answer it. It's not even a question"

Jerry nodded and said, "Okay. When did you first meet Mrs. Bradford?"

"I first met her when she and her husband came to my office for consultation."

Tim could add more to his answer, but decided to play it his lawyer's way.

"What was the date of that visit?"

"I would have to look at my office records," Tim answered.

Without missing a beat, Jerry slid the records across the table to him. Tim nervously looked at his record and found the date and read it to Betsy.

"Thank you," Jerry said, "Now, does your office record indicate that Mrs. Bradford was in the office with him on that date?"

Tim fumbled through the chart and kicked himself for not documenting that she had been with her husband. Maybe his secretary would remember. Tim made a mental note to ask her.

"No," Tim said, and then added, "But she was there." He felt Edwin Stokes hit his leg under the table. He got the message.

"So you say. But the records do not reflect that do they?"

"No."

"Where were you when you saw her again?"

"Assumes facts not in evidence," Stokes interrupted, "assumes he saw her again." The other defense lawyers for the hospital and anesthesiologist agreed.

Jerry sighed, "I see this is going to be a deposition managed by esteemed counsel. Other than in your office, did you ever see Mrs. Bradford prior to surgery?"

"I saw her in the hospital the evening before surgery" Tim said.

"Is that documented in your office records?"

"I don't know." Jerry slid over Tim's office records. He briefly reviewed its contents. "I don't see any reference to it here."

"How about the hospital records?" Jerry had a soft patient tone to his voice indicating he knew the answer to that question.

"I haven't reviewed the medical records," Tim looked at Lisa when he said that but she stared straight ahead. He was on his own.

"Okay. Fair enough. Here is the medical record." He pushed it over to Tim who spent about five minutes reviewing it knowing what the answer would be but hoping to spot some entry by a nurse.

Finally Tim said, "I don't see any reference to it here." This time he didn't fall into the trap of adding any more information.

Jerry half expected some long diatribe about how he had seen her in the room and how the nurses were supposed to document those visits but didn't. Most doctors would have found someone else to blame in a similar situation, but Tim was remarkably concise. For his first deposition he was doing well and seemed composed. Jerry would have to do something about that.

"At that alleged meeting with Mr. and Mrs. Bradford, did you discuss alternative ways to treat cerebral aneurysms?"

Jerry's smugness was starting to piss Tim off. *Alleged my ass,* he thought. So this is the game: call me a liar, make me mad, and then wait for me to say things that will damage my case. I'm not going to fall for that!

"Yes," Tim answered.

Jerry blinked. He was hoping for an answer to build upon, at least something more than a simple 'yes.' He noted that Tim hadn't even flinched at the word "alleged."

"What exactly did you say to Mr. Bradford?" Jerry asked, deliberately ignoring the fact that Tim also talked to Julie Bradford.

Edwin Stokes couldn't hold back. "I object to that question. That's privileged information between the doctor and patient. Mr. Bradford is dead and I urge my client not to answer that question," he said.

Jerry frowned. It was an odd thing for the opposing counselor to say. Of course patient/client privilege is honored even when someone is in the grave, but obviously Julie Bradford had waived that privilege with her lawsuit. She was the sole executor of her husband's estate.

"My client has waived privilege and your client must answer the question or I will seek the court's help," Jerry said.

"I would like a moment to discuss this with my client," Edwin said. Everyone stood and stretched while Tim, Lisa, and Edwin went into the adjoining conference room.

When they were all seated Edwin turned to Tim and said, "I wanted to take a break here and go over this part with you. Are you absolutely sure Julie Bradford was in the room when you discussed the surgery with her husband? She swears that she wasn't there, and if she is believable to a jury then it's going to make you look bad."

Tim eyed his attorney. Lisa had doubted his story and now Edwin Stokes was doubting it. They both were acting as though he had given them a standard answer that all doctors rehearse when asked about their patients. Had he been wrong about Julie Bradford? Was she really not in the room with him? *No*, Tim thought, *I will not let them intimidate me*. He said, "I understand you are trying to do what's best for me, but I sense a certain lack of trust. When I say something then it's the truth. I have an excellent memory for such events. I can even tell you exactly what she was wearing. I didn't expect my own attorneys to doubt my word."

"Take it easy," Edwin said, "I know this is unpleasant. We are just telling you that your answers need to be accurate and precise. This may come back to bite you. The fact that she was or was not there is not important. What's important is your answer." Edwin seemed miffed to be challenged by his own client.

Tim was not going to give in on this point. "Shall we return? I have a lot to do when I get back to the hospital." He was tempted to add a dose of sarcasm about how he had more important things to do but decided to hold it back.

After the conference room settled down Edwin said, "We are back on the record. Pending proof that Mrs. Bradford is the executor of Mr. Bradford's estate, I have instructed my client to answer the question. Could the court reporter read it back?"

Betsy read the question back. Tim quickly responded, "Mr. and Mrs. Bradford were in the room together. She was sitting in a chair to the left of her husband. She wore a blue blouse with a dark purple or black skirt. Her hair was cut in a pageboy style and she had on a beret that matched her skirt. I remember noting to myself that she must be left-handed because she wore her watch on her right hand." Jerry shifted in his seat. Tim knew the detail of his recollection would make him uncomfortable. He continued, "I told both of them that there were options other than surgery. Since he had a large aneurysm he couldn't be assured a reasonable chance of success with alternative treatments. The only proven technique was surgery."

Jerry was surprised by the sincerity and detail of his answer. He began to wonder whether or not his client had been entirely candid about her story. Well, he thought, there's nothing I can do about it now. He decided to move on and spent the next hour going over the details of the surgery and Tim's response to it.

Jerry seemed to be winding down his interrogation. He had stopped looking at Tim and had started straightening the papers into neat piles in front of him. But Jerry was only trying to project a casual attitude in order to set up his final question, which he knew would bring Edwin Stokes to a boil. "One last question, Dr.Graves, have you ever had your license suspended or your hospital privileges suspended?"

"I object to that question," Edwin said, "It's overbroad and lacks foundation. But my client may answer if he wishes."

Edwin's interruption had alerted Tim to be careful with this answer. The briefer the better. "No, I've never had my license suspended. I can't answer the second part of your question because I don't know what you mean by hospital privileges?"

"Did the medical staff at University ever suspend your surgical privileges?" Jerry asked, as if he knew the answer.

This time both the hospital attorney and Edwin objected. They both quoted statutes that prevented discovery of medical staff suspensions. The hospital attorney also added that if the suspensions were for more than thirty days then they were reported to the medical board and became public record.

"I recommend that my client does not answer that question," Edwin said.

Oblivious to Edwin's objection, Jerry asked, "Dr. Graves are you going to answer the question?"

"On advice of Mr. Stokes, I will not respond to that question."

"Edwin this is inappropriate. I don't want to go before the judge and force him to answer," Jerry threatened. He was using a favorite ploy by plaintiff attorneys to scare their adversary.

Edwin hunched forward and looked down at the floor between his legs before saying, "Shall we move on? He has nothing further to say on this subject." He was getting tired of Jerry's games.

Jerry sat in silence until Edwin raised his head. They exchanged dirty looks.

"When there was trouble during the surgical procedure, did you or did you not sit down and let the chief resident take over?" Jerry's question was laced with sarcasm as he glared at Edwin.

Tim stared at Jerry. *This asshole has no clue what it's like.* Tim gave the only answer he could give, "I sat down when I knew there was no hope of clipping the aneurysm and stopping the bleeding. The resident wanted to try so I let him. He managed to stop the bleeding, but he did so by clipping the middle cerebral artery."

"We have been at this for over two hours now and I think my client needs a break," Edwin said as he stood and motioned for Tim to follow him. Tim and Edwin headed for the men's room down the hall. Lisa stretched and rubbed her neck.

"Now that was better. Your answers were concise and believable." Edwin said to Tim as they stood over the urinals.

"These questions have not been particularly tough, but my answers are the truth. Sorry I got cranky during the last break. Do you think I'm telling the truth?"

"I'm afraid the idea that 'the truth shall set you free' does not always apply to the courtroom. It's more like the one who *appears* to be telling the truth shall be set free. As I said before, your story is believable, but so is hers. It will be up to the jury. I think Mr. Cleary has not really opened up the big guns yet. It's four o'clock and he saved the best for last. Unfortunately you have kept your interactions with the mafia thugs to yourself so I may be of little help in guiding you."

"I assure you that has nothing to do with this lawsuit."

"That's not the point. He's trying to discredit you and, frankly, that whole business looks questionable, to say the least. Remember when a lawyer says 'by the way' it's not something he just thought of. It usually means he is about to ask a question he already knows the answer to."

"I figured as much. That suspension question caught me off guard, but your objection helped me be alert. Thanks."

"Just doing my job."

"How did he know about my suspension? That's supposed to be confidential."

"Yes, it seems odd. Maybe he really didn't know about it and was just fishing around. But I have to admit he sounded as though he knew the answer. I suppose he could find out from other people at the hospital. People can come forward and volunteer information about what goes on and it's all legal." Edwin frowned as he wiped his hands with a paper towel and tossed it in the trash. He mustered up a smile and said, "Time to get back."

Jerry resumed his questioning. His demeanor was more hostile than it had been earlier.

"Doctor, do cerebral aneurysms run in families?" he asked.

Tim stiffened. He was getting tired and had to stifle the hostility he felt toward Mr. Cleary. "That's pretty basic medical school stuff. Yes they can."

There was a new aggressiveness in Jerry's voice as he read from a small, torn piece of paper. "By the way, were you a sperm donor when you were a medical student or resident at University Hospital?"

"I object to the question," Edwin nearly shouted, "lacks foundation and is overbroad."

Jerry knew Edwin was pissed off. The other lawyers joined Edwin's objection.

Jerry sighed. "Okay. Doctor, was it common practice for medical students to donate sperm when you were in training?"

"I don't know what you mean by common, but yes there were some people who donated?"

"Were you one of those people?"

Edwin had no idea where these questions were going but he had a feeling they were related to the Strata problem. He just looked at Tim with raised eyebrows.

"Yes. I donated," Tim answered, defeated.

"It's late," Jerry said. "I'm going to stop here with the understanding that I reserve the right to recall the doctor for further questions." With that Jerry stood up and gave Edwin his most winning smile. *Gotcha!* Jerry glanced over at Betsy who gave him a withering look. *Uh oh.* He'd pissed Betsy off, too. *Oh well, all in a day's work.*

Tim, Edwin and Lisa left together. As they stood at the elevator and out of earshot, Edwin said, "He has something up his sleeve and we don't know what it is. But I have a feeling you do." Edwin looked pointedly at Tim. Lisa also waited, hoping Tim would open up and help them understand what the plaintiff's attorney was planning.

"You're going to have to trust me. This has nothing to do with the suit and I doubt he knows more. It's nothing but a fishing expedition."

Edwin decided to drop the subject.

All three of them left the building and headed up the street. The workday was over and the sidewalks were crowded with people rushing to catch the MTA. Others were hurrying down to the Combat Zone to be entertained by the x-rated bars and porno shops. Tim remembered his days as a medical student when he would let off steam down in the Combat Zone. He would go to the Peppermint Lounge with Chubby Checkers, have a beer and maybe dance the twist. Now, twenty-seven years later, he was standing on a familiar street corner dodging pedestrians and listening to his lawyers discuss a major lawsuit that could not only destroy him professionally but financially as well.

Edwin maneuvered himself to avoid all the oncoming human traffic and turned to Tim. "You asked me about Louise Day Hicks.

She was...is a great lady. At least she stood up for what she believed in and didn't roll over because someone challenged her. The NAACP tried to muscle her around, but she stood firm. She did what she had to do to protect her neighborhood from idiotic court orders. And you know she never left her neighborhood. She still lives in South Boston on Columbus Avenue." Edwin paused a moment and gave a look of honest reflection before adding, "It's too bad about the busing issue because now there's all that white guilt going around. This city has become a haven for liberals. We've gone from John Adams to Ted Kennedy. Need I say more. But really, white people aren't all bad. Why, some of my best clients are white," Edwin smiled. "Good day Dr. Graves. We'll be in touch." Edwin shook Tim's hand and Lisa gave a small wave as they joined the throng of people crossing the street.

What the hell was that all about? Tim asked himself. He was dejected as he headed back down the street to his car. He had stereotyped Edwin Stokes as a disenfranchised black attorney who would love sticking it to the white Irish lawyer. He had never imagined him to be a conservative. A conservative, black lawyer has to be as rare as a Red Sox World Series pennant. Tim immediately remembered the Bill Buckner picture from Cleary's office and felt even more depressed. "This is stupid", he mumbled. He was like a kid needing a pat on the head. He wanted to hear from Lisa and Edwin that he'd done well in the deposition, but instead he got a speech about Louise Day Hicks. He drove back to the hospital and saw patients for the rest of the day feeling as though he had the weight of the world on his shoulders.

Ten

After Tim's deposition, Jerry had a meeting with some junior associates to review the status of his firm's pending cases. He knew the meeting would take another three or four hours so he called his wife to let her know he wouldn't be home for dinner. He added that he might even have to sleep in the office overnight. After a prolonged pause she gave him a bored "okay." She had plenty to do with the kids anyway. Jerry was used to his wife's guilt trips and quickly shook it off. He went back into his conference room where Betsy was checking over the spelling of her transcription. She looked up as Jerry entered the room and watched as he closed the door behind him.

Always the optimist, Jerry asked, "Well, what do you think?"

"I think you are a clever lawyer. I want you on my side if I ever need it. But, you are a first class weasel. What's with the personal stuff about Dr. Graves and sperm donation? Where are you going with that?"

"I meant what do you think about you and me getting it on later tonight," Jerry said, almost pleading.

"When pig's fly. I have to get started on this deposition. You're not the only one who has to work late, you know." Betsy saw Jerry flinch a little before adding, "Hey, I'm not saying never, but now's not the time."

"Well, at least that's better than the other day when you left me high and dry."

"Very funny, but I suggest you pay attention to your work, hot shot, because I was there for your client's deposition and, if you ask me, she's not believable at all. Married ten years and does it four times a week? Give me a break!"

"People tend to exaggerate about their sexual escapades. It's just like in high school when guys would say they've laid every girl in the school."

"In your case I would believe it."

"I'm glad you recognize my virility."

"No kidding now. You have another problem with this woman. She said she never met with the doctor before surgery, but Dr. Graves was very convincing. I'd believe him over her any day." Betsy closed her notebook and medical dictionary as though punctuating her opinion. She unplugged and folded up her stenograph, grabbed her purse, the recorder and books, and started to leave.

"What's the hurry? I don't have another meeting for an hour. How about going to Lock Obers' for a glass of wine?" Jerry looked hopeful.

"You never quit, do you?" she demanded. Then she softened her tone and added, " Jerry, I really do have to go. But I can leave you with something to chew on, though I'm sure you'll see it in the papers tomorrow. It's about Strata, your mystery man. The Grand Jury meets in two weeks. That means if I were the Santoris, I woulda heada backa to Sicily." Betsy's father was second generation from the old country and had picked up the habit of placing vowels at the end of words from his parents. She loved to imitate his Italianized English when she wasn't being serious.

"Well thanka you," Jerry mimicked back. "Who's the lead attorney? I want to talk to him."

"Where have you been? George Krosnowski. He came back to run the organized crime task force after he was cleared of any wrong doing in that FBI fiasco. He's good. Maybe not as good as you are, but actually, you two have something in common."

"What's that?"

"You both have egos bigger than the Hancock Building."

"Thanks," Jerry chuckled. He pecked Betsy on the cheek before she could make a clean escape out of the room.

Jerry was happy that Krosnowski was the lead attorney. He had worked with him on some cases with the V.A. Hospital, back when he had been off the mob stuff for a while. He was a tough guy who, in a short time, found out how to get around this town. Jerry hoped that Krosnowski had learned something new about Strata and be willing to share it.

Jerry awoke the next morning to the sounds of the city. Cars were belching their gas and honking their horns in the streets below. Occasionally someone shouted out an expletive. Even though it was St. Patrick's day it sounded like people were coming to work. The sun was shining through the corner window when esteemed counsel rubbed his eyes and looked at the clock on the wall. For a moment there seemed to be two clocks, but as he rubbed his eyes one clock disappeared. *Damn. What a night.* He had worked until one a.m. guiding his associates through cases in preparation for arbitration or trial. Even though he missed out on scoring with Betsy, he was glad to have gotten so much work done. The clock told him he had forty-five minutes until the office started buzzing again. He would have to change his crumpled shirt and smelly socks. Luckily he had his own shower and fresh wardrobe in his office. He sniffed his armpits and decided he could skip the shower and get away with just brushing his teeth, washing his face and putting on a clean set of clothes.

After freshening up a bit, Jerry decided to grab a cup of coffee. On his way to elevator he ran into his secretary arriving for work. "Long night?" she asked.

"Yeah but we got a lot done. I'm going out for a coffee and a roll. Do you want anything?"

"No. Thanks for asking."

"I'm going to need to talk to Eddie Collins when I get back. Also George Krosnowski
at the U.S. Attorney's office."

Jerry stepped into the elevator and pressed the button for the first floor. Around the corner from his office was a hole in the wall coffee and donut shop. He grabbed a *Bulletin* from the newspaper rack and thumbed through the sports page. When he finished reading all the basketball box scores he looked at the front page to find a picture of George Krosnowski and an article entitled *GRAND JURY TO HEAR MOBSTER TESTIMONY. Wow, Krosnowski sure gets his name around.* Jerry read the article and found out that Strata was his witness, something everyone else in Boston probably knew already. Just as Betsy had said, he read that the Grand Jury was to meet in two weeks. He needed to get to Strata before that. He waved at the young girl behind the counter and headed back to his building.

As soon as he entered his outer office he told his secretary to get Collins on the phone first then Krosnowski.

By the time he settled down at his desk Eddie was on the line.

"Eddie, anything, tell me? I was in a bit of a hurry yesterday."

"Anything such as what?" Eddie asked carefully.

"Cut the bullshit. I read in the papers this morning that Strata is appearing before the Grand Jury in two weeks. So what gives? Is he through with his testimony or what?"

"You should know better than me. All I know is they bring him in from Lord's Island every Wednesday morning like clockwork. Six a.m. sharp. Plenty of security, they take him to the Federal building. I know for a fact it's Lord's 'cause the cop on duty at the harbor told me."

"Ok. When do I hear more about what you talked about yesterday?" Jerry wanted more details, but he wasn't sure how much.

"We still got that deal? Four thousand?"

"Of course. When have I ever let you down? You can come by and pick up a check today if you want. I'll make it out for that plus your expenses, which I see you have invoiced."

"Deal. I have in my possession factual documents that show that Joey Santori's DNA and Tim Graves' DNA are so close that the probability of their not being related is one in two billion."

"Shit. That would be the combined population of China and India," Jerry said.

"And then some. So you gotta figure that it's extremely...no, make that *totally* unlikely that those two have the same DNA by chance."

"I doubt the doc laid mama Santori but she could have been artificially inseminated with the doc's sperm. He admitted in his depo that he donated sperm when he was a resident at University. That also would explain the mob hit on the fertility doc," Jerry said.

"Bingo. But so what if Graves donated his sperm? There's no law against it, and I'm sure he didn't know who was gettin' his sperm," Eddie said.

Jerry was not about to go into any more detail. It was a matter of whether or not he wanted to use this information at trial. But he still needed to know more and the only one who could help him was Paulie Strata. "You're right. Thanks for your help. I'll take it from here."

"I know you're a big deal lawyer, but those families in the North End don't give a shit about any of that. I spent a good deal of time trying to nail those assholes and they are cagey and tough. Almost got 'em once. Would have too if it wasn't for that mess you bailed me out of."

"Goodbye Eddie." Jerry hung up without waiting for a reply. He sat staring at the ceiling while he put the pieces together. He wasn't going to worry about some guinea goombas. He had to verify this story before he walked into court. He buzzed his secretary and told her to get Krosnowski on the line.

When he was buzzed back in five minutes he pushed the blinking light on his phone and picked up. "Hello. Jerry Cleary speaking."

"Jerry, George Krosnowski here. How are you?"

"Good, George. How are you?"

"Not too bad. Don't tell me you have another malpractice case against the V.A.? I'm beginning to think you've got someone on the inside feeding you cases," he laughed a little, though he was half serious.

"You know me better than that. It's not another V.A. case. I understand from reliable sources you have a certain mob punk by the name of Strata you're about to parade before a federal Grand Jury."

"That's no secret, it's in the papers today," George said.

"I've read the article. I'm calling because I would like to talk with Paulie Strata about his involvement with a doctor he tried to bump off. I'm up against a trial date so I just need to verify a few facts."

"So you don't want much. Look, he's already pleaded to the murder of the doc in Vermont. That's the deal. He pleads and gets five years. In return we have enough stuff from his testimony to put the Santoris away for good." Krosnowski was on guard. He wouldn't risk blowing his case to help some greedy plaintiff attorney, even if he and Jerry did have a history. "How badly do you need to talk to him?"

"Bad enough that I will get a subpoena if necessary. You know, a subpoena could delay your Grand Jury hearings.... "

Kroskowski snorted in exasperation as Jerry continued.

"It's just between the two of us. No tape recorders or court reporters. I just want to verify some things I uncovered in preparation for trial."

"Are you talking about the neurosurgeon he planned to hit?" George perked up a little. He already knew that Paulie would never talk about his relationship with the doctor he claims saved his life.

"The very one."

"He already said he wouldn't talk about it. It was part of his plea bargain. Besides it has nothing to do with the mob. He said he acted alone and whatever beef he had with the doc is long over." George knew this wasn't going to put off Cleary, but it was worth a try.

"I want to talk to him man to man. Just let me know if you can arrange it or not?" Jerry was running out of patience.

"Back off! I'm not a defense attorney you're trying to intimidate. We bring him over to our offices here on Courtway every Wednesday. We would have him today but it's St. Patrick's Day." Krosnowski had spent enough St. Patrick's days in Philadelphia to know that few people go to work when you give them an excuse to drink all day. "We're bringing him over on Thursday morning. Be in my office at nine sharp. I can give him to you for an hour."

"Great! So you think he'll talk to me?"

"Hey this isn't Lubyanka. If he doesn't want to talk to you he doesn't have to." George laughed. He didn't care what Cleary did. Paulie would be a tough nut to crack. "By the way, your name came up during one of our sessions with him."

"It did? What'd he say??"

"He said there were two cops on the Santori payroll, they framed a Detective Eddie Collins who was about to lay the hammer on Tony and Gianni. Sweet huh? Only thing was you bailed his ass out but it still worked. He was assigned to desk duty and they never heard from him again."

"I always suspected an inside frame job on that case."

"Keep it under your hat. Paulie doesn't know who the dirty cops are but I hope to find out when the Santoris are bargaining for their lives. Ok?"

"You seem confident about having the mob under control, but I'd be careful. You never know with that bunch. People have tried to nail them without success."

"Thanks for the advice. See you in the morning, nine sharp." George hung up.

Jerry sat for a while at his desk and looked out into his office waiting room. There were no clients and his afternoon was clear. It was St. Patrick's Day and somehow it had come without him noticing it. He remembered when he was a kid and counting the days until March 17th. He and his brothers would get the day off from school and fool around on their bikes in their neighborhood south of Roxbury. They would sneak a beer or two from the local pubs and arrive home giggling. Their mother always suspected what they'd been up to and she would send them to bed without dinner. It's not so unusual for an Irishman to welcome a day that promotes excessive drinking, but unlike the stereotype, Jerry was not much of a drinker. He had the occasional glass of wine and that was about it. He didn't even like beer anymore. Reminding himself about the rest of the population who did like beer and lots of it, Jerry decided not to drive home late and run the risk of being hit by a drunk driver. He would go home early today, after he finished his paperwork.

Later, when he walked into his house in Wellesley he was greeted by his three daughters who shouted "Daddy's home! Daddy's home!" They had been lying on the living room floor watching a Disney movie for the hundredth time when Jerry opened the front door. Jerry lived in an expensive brick two story, 8000 square foot home that overlooked the Wellesley campus and Lake Waban. He had gotten the 2.5 acre property years ago in payment for fees incurred when he defended a white-collar real estate broker. That was back in his defense attorney days and he was proud that he pleaded the poor sucker down to probation and community service. He was even more proud that he could place his family in such nice surroundings. He had the house built along with a tennis court, pool, and structured garden. He was oddly moved when he walked through the front door and saw his young girls jumping up and down trying to kiss him. His oldest daughter Diane reached up and kissed him. She shouted, "Phew you stink dad. You have B.O."

Jerry lifted his arms and sniffed his armpits just as his wife walked into the front hallway. "Girls", she said, "go back to your movie. Dinner's ready in half an hour."

They went storming back into the living room pushing and shoving each other. Jerry and Deidre had three daughters aged two years apart from eleven to seven. He adored them and didn't see them enough. But what was he to do?

"Hello Jerry, happy St. Pat's Day," she said in a flat voice. There was no kissing or body contact. "You had a busy night, huh? Do you want to shower before dinner?" She was standing two feet away. "I agree with Diane. You need it "

Jerry shrugged. Deidre Cleary was tall and attractive with a commanding presence. She had shoulder length black hair that was perfectly brushed. Her eyes were a chocolate brown and with her prominent cheekbones and upturned nose she appeared cold and intimidating at first glance. Jerry knew better, though. Deidre had grown up in Maine and her maiden name was Craven. The Craven's were a powerful family with lumber and hardware holdings making up only a part of their fortune. At first, Deidre's father was opposed to their marriage, saying, "Why do you want to marry a mick from Boston?" The cold stare Deidre leveled at him was enough to assure that the slur was never again uttered in her presence.

Jerry had met Deidre when she was a social worker for the welfare department in Boston. Being a graduate of Simmons College, she could at least keep up with Jerry, unlike his first bimbo wife who was still demanding alimony. Deidre, like many people from Maine, was not what she appeared to be. She was kind, compassionate, and thoughtful, but it just took a while to get to know her.

"I smell that bad? I didn't notice. I did skip a shower this morning, but I thought I was okay."

"You skipped for the past two days, remember? And that was after playing tennis on Sunday." Deidre abruptly turned and walked back into the kitchen.

Jerry knew he had some major fence mending to do. He glanced into the living room and saw his three daughters lying prone in front of the television. They had their heads cradled in their hands and their legs bent up in the air as they watched the movie. Suddenly Diane laughed, rolled over and punched her sister playfully. Jerry shook his head. He might as well be on another planet for all he meant to them. Deflated over Deidre's reception and the short attention span of his children, he climbed the stairs, threw his clothes in the hamper and took a shower.

The next morning Jerry took another shower and left home early. His attempts to communicate with Deidre over the course of the evening had been met with cold indifference, and he resolved to pay more attention to his family. She would come around. She always did. Hell, he didn't have any vices. He kept himself fit. He didn't smoke or drink. *Well, three out of four wasn't bad.* He thought of Besty Gallucci.

In an effort to commit to going home that night he decided to take the MBTA into South Station and cab it to Krosnowski's office. He parked his car in the Wellesley Square MBTA parking lot and got a cup of coffee from the local cafe. He grabbed a *Bulletin,* bought a ticket and sat reading the newspaper and sipping coffee until the commuter car arrived.

It was 8:30 a.m. when he entered the Federal Building on Courtway. He checked out the building directory to confirm that Krosnowski's office was on the fourth floor and then headed over to a coffee kiosk in the lobby. There was a small line waiting to get to the 'designer coffee' from the kiosk because most of the early arriving employees could only afford the cafeteria's watered down brew. He hurried over, not paying attention to the other people in the lobby, and settled into line.

Within moments he heard a familiar voice behind him. "What are you doing here Jerry?"

He turned and stared into the gorgeous face of Betsy Gallucci. Her looks overwhelmed him momentarily, but he recovered. He immediately noticed her form-fitting denim jeans and black high heels. She was also wearing a denim vest bordered with red lace over her white tee shirt. She looked sexy in the trashy sort of way that Jerry liked.

"Fancy meeting you here. Doing your snitch's depo today, I assume?" he asked, while tapping his fingers on make-believe keys.

"Shh," she frowned as she looked around. "If it gets out I talked to you I'm done."

"Relax. You didn't say anything to me that wasn't already in here," he whispered as he waved the folded *Bulletin* in her face.

"I know. It just looks bad. Sometimes you act like such an ass."

Jerry raised his eyebrows and straightened his already straight shoulders. "I like it when you talk dirty," he said.

He was next in line to order coffee. He turned to Betsy and asked what she wanted. "My treat," he said, winking at her.

"Forget it. I can get my own. And don't follow me. We can't be seen together." Betsy was again whispering.

"You mean never?" Jerry was still fishing. Last night's resolve to improve things at home seemed a distant memory.

"Give it a rest. This is business."

Jerry paid for his coffee and waved back at her as he headed for the elevators and Paulie Strata.

A bored secretary ushered him into a small interrogation room promptly at nine o'clock. The windowless room was just big enough to hold a gunmetal table and three uncomfortable looking straight back chairs. Jerry immediately noticed the warning sign on the wall that read: *ROOM NOT MONITORED. RECORDING DEVICES NOT ALLOWED.* He hoped they wouldn't search his briefcase.

Jerry placed his empty coffee cup on the table and sat down. When he opened his briefcase he shoved aside his hand held recorder and took out a legal pad. He quickly closed his briefcase and started jotting down questions on a yellow legal pad when the door opened. A stocky young man with a dark crew cut came to the door. *Right out of central casting*, Jerry thought.

"Mr. Cleary, I'm Agent Girardi. Please stand up." He closed the door and walked over to Jerry. "Raise your arms." He frisked Jerry with measured and almost robotic motions. "Please take off your coat, tie, and shirt."

"Hey, I'm not armed," Jerry complained.

"Not with a weapon, but maybe with a recording device." He waited for Jerry to comply with his orders.

As Jerry stood bare-chested he felt vulnerable and a little embarrassed. The agent ran a probe over him looking for an electronic signal. "You can get dressed. Are you attempting to record this conversation?" Jerry shook his head. "Please open your briefcase."

"Now wait a minute. I have rights."

"Krosnowski's orders," the agent deadpanned. "You don't have to cooperate if you don't want to, but the meeting is over if you don't." He stood waiting impatiently while Jerry put on his shirt.

"So much for the second amendment," Jerry mumbled and opened his briefcase. The agent searched it and held up the small tape recorder. "That's for dictation only," Jerry stammered. He finished tying his tie.

The agent jerked his head towards the sign on the wall and said, "You can pick it up when you leave." The way the agent was carrying on, Jerry felt like he had been busted for cocaine possession.

"I'll bring the witness in. You have fifty minutes." He hit the eject button on the recorder and handed the tape over to Jerry. He walked out with the recorder, shaking his head.

Moments later, the door opened and Paulie Strata walked in. Jerry was shocked at the short stature of the mafia thug. He was husky with thick shoulders, but he couldn't have been taller than 5'6".

After eyeing Jerry, Paulie looked back at another agent standing outside the room. He shrugged his shoulders as if to say "no big deal".

Paulie appeared neat and well groomed. He was dressed in a black silk shirt with an open collar and a pack of Parodi cigars in the left breast pocket. He wore coarse cotton brown pants without cuffs and dark penny loafers. His black hair was combed straight back exposing a narrow forehead. Despite the New England winter, his skin was still dark and swarthy. He had the characteristically high Sicilian cheekbones below dark, expressionless eyes hooded with lids chronically at half-mast. Those eyes were leveled at Jerry.

"How was the boat ride?" Jerry asked.

Paulie pulled out a chair and sat down. "I don't get seasick if that's what you mean. What's this about Cleary? How'd you know I was stuck on that island?"

"You weren't hard to find. I have good investigators."

"Cut the bullshit. You want to know something, ask me straight out. No sucking up."

Jerry stared at Paulie and was struck by how such a short man could immediately take over the room. There was no question who was taking charge of this conversation. He had encountered similar types of criminals when he worked for the DA's office, but at least being with the DA gave him some leverage. Here he couldn't threaten to subpoena or incarcerate. It was best to cut to the chase and not blast him with questions. Still it was hard for Jerry to imagine how this pipsqueak could be responsible for at least ten murders.

"Okay," Jerry began, "I'm in litigation...er, I am suing Dr. Graves for malpractice." Jerry decided to keep the words simple. No lawyerspeak. He continued, "Of course your involvement in his disappearance and attempted murder have been in the newspaper. I just need to know why he was your target."

"It's none of your business. Next question." Paulie's face did not show emotion, but his eyes told the story. Jerry now knew why people feared him. If looks could kill... He shuddered inwardly as if someone had run an ice cube down his spine.

"Okay. I can see why you don't want to answer that question." Paulie shifted in his chair and took the pack of cigars from his shirt pocket and shook it. He lipped out a cigar and lit a match with his thumbnail. After lighting his cigar, he shook the match and tossed it into Jerry's coffee cup. Jerry ignored Paulie's show of contempt and instead glanced at the **No Smoking** sign. Paulie took a deep pull on the cigar and then blew out the gray smoke in Jerry's direction.

Shit, Jerry thought, *what the hell am I doing here? This guy isn't going to give me squat.* He decided to try a different approach.

"Let me tell you what I think." He didn't wait for Paulie's acknowledgment as he proceeded to tell the story of how he came to bring legal action against Dr. Graves, how his faked death and reappearance had affected the lawsuit, and why the story about Paulie Strata wanting to kill him became important. All of this, Jerry explained, led to his own investigation of the matter in which he had uncovered information biologically linking Joey Santori to Dr. Graves. Jerry was walking around the room as he reeled out the facts while Paulie kept staring straight ahead, puffing on his cigar.

"Nice story," Paulie said when Jerry finished. He still hadn't made eye contact. "You married?"

"Yes."

"Kids?"

Even though Paulie spoke in a steady, almost bored voice, his body language was very threatening. Jerry didn't like it.

"Yes."

"How many?"

"Okay, hold on. I'm supposed to be asking the questions." Jerry sat down opposite Paulie in an effort to establish eye contact.

"You're saying that Joey Santori ain't the son of Tony Santori. If that story got around you can't even imagine how it would piss off Lefty. Piss off his brother Gianni even worse. Now Lefty... would kill you. Gianni would kill your kids. Slowly. Maybe make you watch. Capice."

"You guineas are animals! I thought you just stuck to business and left other families alone?"

"Families are civilians. True. But you're tryin' to destroy innocent people with your bullshit lawsuit. Doc Graves saved my life and he's off limits." Jerry thought Paulie was through because he paused to take a pull on his cigar and blow more smoke in his face. "You guineas, huh? What about you sick micks. Always too much. Too kind, too loyal, too stubborn, too bigoted, too mean, too much booze, can't keep it in your pants, always on the take. Never just right. You're just a crook with a license usin' the courts to rip people off."

Jerry sputtered and reddened, "First you threaten my family, then you denigrate...no, let's not mince words here...then you shit on my race and profession." Jerry had let Paulie get under his skin. He struggled to calm himself and went into his automatic lawyer mode as a way to regain whatever control he had lost. He smiled and said, "This interview is over."

He placed his legal pad into his briefcase and closed it. He glanced at Paulie, but Paulie wasn't moving. He was smiling and looking straight at him.

"You'd think that someone who says he loves his family would be more careful."

"What are you talking about? More threats?" Jerry stood up and straightened his tie.

"No, I mean you gotta be more careful about who you sleep

with. How long you been doing Betsy Gallucci? I see her every week. She don't look all that happy to me. You got a problem with Cleary junior?" Paulie asked.

Jerry's practiced courtroom composure quickly faded. His face turned red again and he blustered, "Listen you two bit picce of guinea shit. You're outta line."

Paulie stood and barely looked down at Jerry. "That's why I could never work with micks. They never think beyond their dicks. I know all about you. Betsy Galluci's dad is a barber, knows everyone in the North End. He and Tony, that's Mr. Santori to you, went to Eastie together. He cuts Tony's hair. Been doing it for years."

Jerry felt gut shot. All of his attempts to keep his affair with Betsy a secret were a waste of time. If some goombah on an island knew then lots of others must know too. Paulie turned toward the door and said, "I'm going away for a nickel and I can proudly say I never cheated on my wife. Good luck on your lawsuit counselor. You're going to need it."

Jerry watched Paulie disappear through the door and Agent Girardi come in to return the tape recorder he had confiscated. "Worthwhile interview?" he snickered and then disappeared again.

Krosnowski poked his head through the door. "All done?" he asked noting the empty chair. "He wrinkled his nose. I told Paulie not to smoke those stinking cigars in here!"

"I don't smell anything but dago sweat."

"Are you sure of that? He seemed pretty cool when he came out, but you look like you've been through the ringer."

Jerry passed Krosnowski on his way out of the interrogation room. He looked back and said, "I won't be calling him as a witness. He can't help me. Thanks for giving me the opportunity without a lot of hassle. He's going to be a good witness for you, I can tell. I just don't how you can deal with these punks."

"It's a living….and remember, you owe me one."

Jerry waved at him and said, "You got it." On his way to the elevator Jerry spotted Betsy through the glass partition of an enclosed office. She was sitting at her recorder poised to take more of Paulie's testimony. She glanced up at Jerry, but he quickly turned away and pushed the elevator button.

What a day! Jerry knew he had the story right, but he would never call that obnoxious, little rat Strata to the stand. He could only hope that the defense doesn't call him for some godforsaken reason. When he stepped out of the building he was hit with a cold blast of air. The bright, sunny day of earlier had turned as glum as his mood. He hailed a cab and headed back to his office.

Eleven

Lenny wasted no time calling his mom after his meeting with Eddie Collins at the Lowell job. He had some info that his uncles would love to hear and he wanted to deliver it personally and on his home turf. He was no longer the worthless nephew and he wanted to take this opportunity to show off. "Tell those brothers of yours I have some important news for them and we should have dinner," he told his mother. She said she would make some linguini if he would bring home some mussels and crusty bread. Lenny stopped at his favorite fish store in the North End and bought enough mussels to last for several meals. When he got home he cleaned and brushed them, throwing away the spoiled ones.

When Tony and Gianni heard what was on the menu for dinner they had eagerly accepted the invitation. They arrived at seven o'clock, coolly shaking Lenny's hand and hugging their sister. They all stood in the kitchen while Celeste made the final preparations for the meal. She tossed some linguine pasta into a pot of boiling, salted water and gave the red sauce simmering next to it a quick stir. The kitchen was warm and filled with the aromas that only Italian cooking can give.

"You look as good as new, Leste," Tony said, using her childhood nickname. "You can't even tell you have a black man's heart."

It was Tony who had arranged a heart donor for his sister when, less than a year ago, she was dying of congestive heart failure. The donor was a young, black motorcyclist who had been killed on the way home to his son's birthday party.

"Yeah, you look great Celeste. When do we eat?" Gianni added. Gianni was shorter and stockier than Tony and his personality matched his stature. He usually had very little to say. He lacked Tony's good looks with his round face and wide prominent nose. Tony, by contrast, was tall and sported a narrow, classic Roman nose—he seemed to have inherited the best traits from his Italian father and American mother.

"Lenny, pour some Chianti for my favorite brothers and then let's sit at the table here in the kitchen. The linguine isa nearly done and the mussels are cooking. I mada the besta sauce," she said as she kissed her two fingers together and threw up her hands. While Celeste fussed over the stove the men seated themselves at the table and made small talk. Soon Celeste was serving the food and old memories dotted the conversation. Celeste crossed herself every time Vito, her murdered husband, was mentioned. He had died in a car bomb meant for someone else, days after her heart transplant, and the news nearly halted her recovery.

Celeste had pistachio and dried fruit cannoli for dessert. Once coffee was served Lenny shooed his mother out of the kitchen promising her he would clean up. She knew this meant time for her to leave and let the men talk about stuff she didn't want to hear. When she could be heard climbing the stairs to her bedroom, Lenny said, "I talked to Eddie Collins today. You know he still has a hard on for Paulie, that little prick. Anyway, he says the feds have Paulie stashed on an Island in the harbor."

Tony perked up. He had been skeptical about meeting with Lenny to discuss his "hot tip," but what he just heard sounded promising. "Is that the same Eddie Collins who was a cop chasing Paulie a coupla years ago?" he asked.

"The very same. He's retired now and has his own investigating business. I hear he's doin' well," Lenny said.

"We nearly nailed his ass but some smart lawyer got him off.

Never bothered Paulie again tho. Maybe that was a mistake," he said slapping his hand on the table.

Even Gianni perked up, "What island? There's a shitload of them out there."

"I have a map here. It's called Lord's Island. You see it way out. Has a lighthouse and all. He's guarded around the clock, comes to town every Wednesday to rat you guys out."

"Just like you were gonna do with us," Gianni whispered. "But you didn't know anything so it was okay," he smirked.

"It wasn't okay. You guys botched the job and killed my pop," Lenny said clenching his fists. Paulie had been sent by the Santori brothers to kill Lenny, but ended up killing Lenny's dad Vito instead.

"Okay, cool down.   Vito was Paulie's mistake, but what's done is done. It's water under the bridge now, so let's move on," Tony said. "Look, I been fishing out at that island. Someone could get to Paulie if they were real good. Tell me, Lenny, why would Eddie Collins give you this stuff?"

Lenny unclenched his fists and tried to relax. "Eddie's working for this lawyer, Jerry Cleary, who wants to find out why Paulie wanted Joey's surgeon dead. He's suing the doc for malpractice," he said.

"So tell me what you gave him." Tony was getting impatient. He didn't care about lawsuits.

"I told him Paulie killed this baby doctor in Vermont. That Paulie was pissed about something to do with Joey's doc and this other doc. That's all I know. Paulie is a psycho. He had his reasons."

"I don't wanna know his reasons." Tony said. The only thing Tony wanted was a dead Paulie Strata. "Thanks Len for the heads up, and thanks for dinner. Gianni and me will take it from here. Best you don't sit here no more. We'll find our way out."

Gianni, without raising his folded arms off the table, waved his right hand to acknowledge Lenny's goodbye as his giant nephew brushed past him and left the room. Gianni turned to his brother and shrugged, waiting for Tony to speak.

"Paulie goes to the Grand Jury we go to jail, simple as that.

We got no choice here. This is going to take an expert." Gianni nodded but didn't say anything. "I'm moving on this tomorrow. You agree?" Gianni nodded again. They left without saying anything to Lenny who was sitting in the living room watching TV.

The next morning Tony made a call from a payphone to Silvio Testa, his cousin in New Jersey. Ten minutes after Tony gave him the payphone number he got a call back. "Can't be too careful," Silvio said. "What's up?" he asked. Silvio agreed to a face-to-face meeting and would go half way. He and Tony would meet in a strip mall outside of Hartford sometime in the early afternoon.

Silvio Testa was the head of a New Jersey mob that, for many years, had been successful dealing with stock scams, prostitution, and other forms of illegal business that prayed on human weaknesses, such as gambling. Silvio didn't like the rough stuff that other mobs got involved with, but he was not opposed to using muscle when necessary. For Silvio, Paulie Strata fit the category of everyone's problem because he was a loose cannon—you never knew who he was gonna hit next.

It was a Tuesday afternoon and the lunch crowd at the Chicken 'n Burgers restaurant had mostly disappeared. Tony and Silvio settled into the last booth and ordered hamburgers and coffee before getting down to business.

"Did you bring the stuff?" Silvio asked, his double chin jiggling as he spoke.

"Yeah. Maps, money, a picture and some notes about where he's being stashed. This is a rush job 'cause they're gettin' ready to have him testify to the Grand Jury. They'll probably be movin' him soon."

"How much you bring?" Silvio asked as he spooned sugar into his coffee.

"What you told me. Twenty-five and five."

"Slip me the five under the table." Tony did as he asked and Silvio said, "Now here's the deal. No guarantees. We all want Paulie dead. It's important, it's gonna take someone good. I can't say if this guy will take the job or not. If he does, even if something goes wrong, he keeps the twenty-five…because of the risk. Capice?"

Tony didn't have many options. Money, especially 25,000 dollars, wasn't going to do him any good in jail. That's provided he had any money left after he paid off his lawyers.

"Capice. It needs to be done like yesterday."

Tony reached into the breast pocket of his coat and brought out an oversized thick brown envelope. "The money's in hundreds, like you asked." He started to hand it to Silvio who immediately held up his hands.

"No, I ain't touching the envelope. Set it on the table and take down this address. You got a pen?" Tony pulled out a Sharpie and waited for Silvio to give him the address. "No, no," Silvio said. "Print with your right hand. You never know whose gonna find this envelope. Ready? New England and New York Private Mail, Bethany Road, Box 783, Albany, New York. Tony found it slow and tedious to write with his non-dominant hand, but he finally completed the address and it was legible. Silvo said, "Now look out the window. See that sign that says New England and New York Private Mail. When we're done here, you go over there, give them the envelope and pay the postage. That's all you have to do."

Silvio Testa knew who the envelope was going to, he just didn't know how it would get there. He didn't want to know. His only role was to approve sending the envelope and collect ten thousand for his effort—five when the contract was drawn up and five if and when there was a completed contract.

Tony put the envelope back in his pocket and moments later their lunch arrived. Silvio plowed through his hamburger as if he hadn't had a breakfast of eggs, sausage, toast and jam only hours earlier. Tony only nibbled at his hamburger, eating just half. While Silvio was finishing up a slab of apple pie and ice cream, Tony paid the waitress and went over to the private mail store to post the envelope. He hoped it would work. By eight o'clock that evening he was back at home in Nahant with his future in the hands of a hired killer.

Twelve

Dominick Milano walked into the Post Office in Utica, New York and waved at the man working behind the counter.

"Thanks for the call, Pete," he said as he walked to his post box.

"No problem."

Dom fished out his keys and opened his box to find a thick manila envelope. The address on the envelope had been written with a childish scrawl.

"How's my account here?" Dom asked the postal worker who had been watching him pick up his mail for the last ten years.

Pete looked in a logbook and said, "You're paid up until June. Including the forwarding costs of that package."

"Thanks, I won't be needin' the box after that."

Dom had told Silvio when they last met that he would do one more job and then call it quits. He was grateful to his uncle for looking after him and his mom so well over the years, but he had made good on all his debts and it was time to start his own family while he was still safe and financially able.

Dom knew he had a lot to thank his Uncle Silvio for. He remembered the day, twenty years ago, when his dad had been shot to death during a robbery of the family grocery store and how Uncle Silvio avenged his father's death by catching the Puerto Rican low life who'd gunned him down. After that Dom entered the Marine Corps where he was a sniper with the expeditionary forces. He won a silver star for heroism when he saved his battalion from an ambush. When Dom returned from his service in Vietnam, it was Uncle Silvio who put up the money for him to buy his apple farm in New York. Dom had agreed to help his uncle "deal" with people who threatened his business in exchange for the down payment on a farm. Despite the violent nature of the work his uncle was asking him to perform, Dom didn't mind the idea of eliminating threats to his family. In fact, he took pride in his role as a protector. "I only have one condition," he told his uncle, "I'll take care of snitches or other made members in your organization who are giving you trouble, but I won't touch civilians." In the seventeen years since being enlisted by Uncle Silvio, Dom had eliminated eight targets for his uncle while also making his apple business a success, selling his produce under the Milano name to grocery store chains throughout New York and New Jersey.

But the envelope he now carried out of the post office would be the last one he'd ever see and he felt lighter for it. When he got home, he immediately placed the $25,000 in a safe in the basement, where it would stay until he funneled it to an offshore account. He began reading through the material he received. Since it was already March fourth, two days after the envelope had been sent, Dom knew he had to get moving in order to eliminate the target within the next two weeks. He purchased a Canadian sniper rifle at a gun show in Syracuse the following day and spent the weekend honing his skills in a rifle range fifty miles away. He also collected and arranged his other equipment over the weekend: fishing pole, tackle, a Zodiac seven foot inflatable boat, outboard motor, compass, gutting knife, and a life vest, just in case.

As always, Dom knew his success depended on planning and rehearsal, so he drove to Winthrop on the ninth to make a dry run. On his way to Massachuetts he used the NY and Mass. throughways so his car would be spotted going through the tollbooths and his trip would be recorded. When he got to Winthrop, he slept in his car which was parked in a church parking lot and awoke early the next morning to start fishing off Deer Island in the Boston harbor. While fishing, he scouted nearby Lord's Island and found to his surprise that he could get to within 800 yards of the island. From that distance he could see a lighthouse, other buildings and a dock without the need of binoculars. His eyesight was still as good as when he was in Vietnam,

Dom noted that the dock was encircled with a chain link fence and only accessible from two points: the water and the stairs leading to the lighthouse. He also noticed that during the low tide in the afternoon a circular rock twenty feet in diameter rose five feet out of the water. The rock was flat and stood about 750 yards from his target, making it a perfect spot to set up his rifle and take his shot.

He hopped onto the rock with his fishing gear and tied his boat to a small crevice

He waited, pretending to fish, until he saw a boat approach the dock at exactly four-thirty. Dom watched as a small man jumped out, stretched his arms up and climbed the stairs. Dom quickly threw his fishing gear back in the Zodiac and sped back to the car. He drove home feeling confident about his plan and pleased that his last hit would surely be a flawless one.

The following Tuesday using back roads he drove to Nashua, New Hampshire where using a flase ID rented a van. He drove to Winthrop and parked along the shoreline. He again slept over night and then sailed out to the rock off Lord's Island in the morning. He waited all day for the boat he had seen earlier to leave the island, but there was no action at all. He remembered that it was St. Patrick's Day and decided to wait one more day before calling off the hit. The next day he could see from where he stood on the shore that the boat from the island was gone. He headed back to the rock in his Zodiac, tied it up, and waited under a tarpaulin colored similar to the rock's.

It was nearly dark when the launch returned from Boston. Paulie stepped off the boat, but it was too dark for Dom to take a shot. When Paulie walked toward the stairs leading from the dock he was spotlighted by a single floodlight attached to a metal pole. Dom knew he had only a second or two. It was going to be a single shot aimed at the chest. When Paulie started to climb the stairs an agent from the boat called to him. He turned and suddenly looked down at his shirt as he flew back against the guardrail. He slid down tearing at his shirt as he began to convulse. His silk shirt turned from white to red in a matter of seconds.

Dom immediately slipped off the rock. On the way back to shore he broke down the rifle into three pieces and wrapped lead weights around them with duct tape. He threw the pieces over the side and watched them disappear into the depths of the ocean.

Thirteen

Deidre Cleary had arranged a family trip to Maine to visit her parents for the long weekend, and Jerry wasn't looking forward to it. He committed himself to going, however, because the thought of getting a divorce was far worse. After hearing from Paulie Strata that his indiscretions with Betsy Gallucci had become public knowledge, Jerry feared the information might spread to the wrong ears. Jerry had to execute some serious damage control with his wife. What was more frightening was the idea that Deidre's parents would get word of his extracurricular activities and would delight in demanding that their daughter get out of the marriage, and get as much money out of the marriage, immediately. Deidre's parents, Mama and Papa Craven, as the kids called them, would hire the best divorce lawyers in Boston and suck him drier than a California raisin.

Jerry drove to work on Friday morning instead of taking the train so he could make a quick getaway in the afternoon, pick up Deidre and the kids, and head north. With the Graves' trial looming large, he hated the idea of leaving the office even for a day, let alone the weekend. He desperately needed to get the thing back on track and decided to use the precious time he had before his weekend imprisonment in the Craven compound.

First, however, he needed to do something about his stuffed

up nose. It was either the air conditioning or the change in weather, but something had been plugging up his nasal passages for weeks. He rummaged around in his desk looking for a nasal inhaler the nose and throat doctor had prescribed to him. Finally he found the applicator and snorted the mist into both nostrils, feeling immediate relief.

Breathing a bit easier, Jerry decided to check up on his associates to make sure everyone was pulling their weight. He strolled down the hallway and poked his head into each office, happy to find that most of them were talking with clients as opposed to staring at the ceiling or hunching over the phone with their backs to the door. When he arrived at Jason Damon's office he knocked on the door while opening it partway, interrupting the young lawyer who was with a client.

He smiled at the client sitting opposite to Jason and said, "I'm sorry to interrupt your meeting, but could I spare a few minutes with Mr. Damon?" The client nodded, seeing that he didn't really have a say in the matter anyway. Jerry raised his eyebrows to Jason and pointed with his thumb in the direction of the hallway.

Once out of earshot of the client Jerry asked, "What's his story?"

"It's no big deal. He got out of bed after a shot of morphine, fell and hit his head. He's been having headaches ever since," Jason almost sounded embarrassed to be discussing such an insignificant case with his boss.

"What was he in the hospital for?" Jerry asked.

"He had a hernia repair and says he got disoriented. Claims the nurses ignored him, weren't watching him."

"Damages?"

"Well, he's been unable to work. He was working at a gas station running the cash register and swiping cards. I found a neurologist who will say that this is a typical case of post concussion headache. Could go on for years." His voice dropped as he finished speaking and he looked at the wall behind Jerry, "It's probably bullshit, but I told him there's probably enough there to get him something."

"Sounds like one you should settle, not waste a lot of time on. What hospital?"

Jerry wanted to end this conversation quickly and move on to what was really on his mind.

"St. Mary's"

"Jason!" he nearly shouted. He felt his fists clench as he continued talking through his teeth, "How many times do I have to tell you people we aren't suing St. Mary's? I'm on the Board of Directors there and on their foundation board too. Tell the client this firm has a conflict with representing him. Send him over to Bradley and Cummings. They like simple, no-brainer cases. The complex ones they send to us anyway." Calming down a bit, he added, "You'll get a nice one back."

Jason wanted to argue with Jerry, but he knew it would be a foolish move. "Okay," he muttered.

"When you're through meet me in my office. We need to talk about the Graves' trial. It's coming up in a few weeks and we are nowhere near ready." Jerry didn't wait for a response as he quickly turned back to his office. He felt like he had already wasted too much time.

"Eddie Collins is on the line," his secretary said as he brushed past her and into his office.

Jerry sat down at his desk, gave a deep sigh, and punched the blinking light on his phone.

"What is it Eddie?" he asked.

"Thanks for the check. It helps." Eddie could tell from Jerry's tone that he was in a foul mood. He wouldn't waste any time getting to the point. "But," he said, "that's not why I'm calling. Did you see the papers this morning?"

"No, and I don't have time for the twenty questions. Just tell me what's up for chrissakes."

"Chill, pal," Eddie said. He was getting tired of being treated like a lap dog. "Your potential witness, one Paulie Strata, was murdered yesterday afternoon."

Jerry realized he had been holding his breath for a couple of beats. He had no use for the two-bit criminal, but still, Paulie Strata was somebody's husband and father, and someone he just met less than twenty-four hours ago. "What else?" he managed to ask, "Tell me what you know." He had already regained his composure and was ready to deal with the stunning news. After all this is was what Jerry did best.

"I read about it this morning before leaving for the office. And since I've been here the phone hasn't stopped ringing. It seems Chief Rastellini got blasted by the US Attorney who now blames him for Strata's death. Since Strata's location was such a highly guarded secret, no one can understand how anyone found out. So Rastellini drags in the cops at the harbor, one of them rolls on me, told Rastellini I'd been by asking what island they were bringing Paulie Strata in from."

"Well, Eddie, that's just brilliant. Why didn't you just go down there with a loud speaker and ask if anyone knows where Paulie Strata is?"

"Hey, take it easy counselor. I keep the identity of my client's confidential. No one knows you hired me to find Paulie. The only person I told about the island was Lenny DeGrazie, who, and I would bet the wife and kids on this one, told the Santoris. You got nothing to worry about from that angle."

"What do you mean from that angle?"

Eddie lowered his voice and said, "Well, the Chief told me that Krosnowski said that you had come to visit Paulie. After you left, Paulie told Krosnowski that he wanted a new court reporter because you were *seeing* the one they had, if you know what I mean."

"That's bullshit. It's just a rumor." Jerry felt beads of sweat forming on his forehead. An image of Deidre's father flashed in his mind. He was holding a noose.

"Hey, I got no problem with you milking the neighbor's cow. I'm just warning you that it could get in the papers."

Jerry was about to deny the allegation again but realized that the more he protested the more he sounded guilty. It was best to keep Eddie on his side before he got rid of him, "I appreciate that Eddie. I did have drinks with her in a bar once. I guess that was a dumb move on my part, knowing how rumors start and all. Anyway, anything else?"

"Yeah, sure, I understand," Eddie said, sounding like he understood all too well.

"I take it you won't be calling Strata as a witness," Eddie chuckled.

"Very funny," Jerry said. He sensed Eddie was getting a little too cocky. Jerry would have to remind him of his debts. "You know, I did learn from Paulie yesterday that you were set up by a couple of your colleagues when you took that fall I bailed you out of. Paulie didn't know which ones screwed you, but it was Lefty Santori who arranged to get Paulie off your back."

"Hey, you know I'm grateful. I'll never forget what you did for me," Eddie knew Jerry's game better than Jerry. "Anyway, I hope they find out who did it. I gotta go. Let you know if I find out anything else."

Jerry rubbed his eyes and sniffled again. He squeezed some more spray into his nose. *What next?* A dead witness, his indiscretions with Betsy Galluci about to be exposed, and a big trial staring him in the face. As if on cue his secretary buzzed him.

"A Mr. Krosnowski on the line. You want to take it or should I have him call later?"

"Put him through," Jerry said, heaving a big sigh.

"Good morning, Jerry. I suppose you heard the news? Just how did you find out we were deposing Paulie Strata?"

This was going to be a short conversation. "It was in the papers. Remember? In fact, you announced it yourself."

Ignoring him, Krosnowski continued, "According to Chief Rastellini a certain private investigator by the name of Eddie Collins was asking questions about Harbor Islands. That was nearly two weeks *before* the papers ran the story."

"What can I say? I'm certainly not going to tell you how I run my practice nor do I reveal what private investigators I use. What they do in their investigations is beyond my control."

"Really? You mean they don't act under your orders, or tacit orders, as the case may be?" George asked with dripping sarcasm.

Jerry had heard enough. "Anything else?"

"That court reporter you been seeing. I find out she talked to you about something she learned during secret testimony and she'll never work at that job again. I won't even mention the jail time she could serve."

"What would that prove? How big a prosecutor you are? How do you know she's the one that leaked the location?"

"Paulie spilled the beans yesterday. Says her old man and Lefty Santori are tight but not connected. Said you been seen at motels with her...he even named a few of them. Isn't that right, *Mr. Smith?*"

Jerry never had anything so important in his life spiral out of control this fast and in quite this way. He should have listened to Betsy. He shouldn't have gotten involved with Strata and his ilk.

"Listen, George, I'm busy over here. I actually have to work for the money I make. You have your job to do and I have mine. And I'm not doing yours for you." He hung up without waiting for a reply. Any further conversations with that man would have to be under oath, if it ever came to that.

Without missing a beat, his interoffice buzzer went off again. Before his secretary could say anything, Jerry told her to send in Jason. Moments later Jason entered looking very serious and still a little peeved that his case was taken from him. He eyed Jerry carefully to determine his mood as he took a seat in front of his desk.

To Jason's surprise, Jerry couldn't have been nicer. "Jason, I'm sorry about the St. Mary's thing, but it's important for this firm not to be seen as a bunch of greedy ambulance chasers. St. Mary's is a good hospital and most of the doctors over there are on retainer status with this firm. We don't sue them and, in re-turn, that's where we go when we get sick. Enough said. Now, the expert deposition for defense is docketed for depo next week. Are you up to speed on the Graves' case?"

"Yessir," Jason said straightening himself in the chair.

"Good, because I want you to fly to New York for Dr. Davis's deposition. I talked to Stokes and he won't be there. He's send-ing an associate, Lisa Harding, to get the experience. Of course, she's a lot cheaper too and it'll keep the insurance guys off his back. Anyway, I want you to prepare the questions you are going to ask Dr. Davis. We'll go over them early on Monday. The depo's next Wednesday. Just to be safe you should fly down on Tuesday," Jerry said all this in one breath. He expected his associates to be quick and on their toes.

"I'm honored you would put that kind of trust in me. I will do my best," Jason smiled.

"I'm sure you will. But there is more to it than that. Having you do the deposition means he won't have faced me before the trial, so he won't know what to expect. I'm hoping it will throw him off base a little because I've heard he is quite sure of himself. He mocks attorneys when they mispronounce medical terms. As a matter of fact, he went to law school for two years so he knows a little bit about this process. Be sharp."

"Thanks for the heads up. I will see you on Monday." Jason left Jerry's office much happier than when he arrived.

Jerry leaned back, pleased with himself. He had put Krosnowski back in his cage and settled potentially divisive issues with Jason. He wanted to keep Jason on and maybe actually make him a partner someday. "Cleary and Damon, Attorneys-at-law" had a nice ring to it. *About time I shared the spotlight.* He was feeling so good that he toyed with the idea of leaving the office now and getting a jump on the trip to Maine. Driving to Portland would take several hours in the best conditions, but on a Friday evening the traffic would be murder. He buzzed his secretary and found that he had only two appointments in the afternoon. He told her he was going home and to have someone else in the office take his appointments. Jerry stood and stretched. He put on his coat and shot his cuff links. Every thing was going to work out. As he strode to the door the buzzer made one final plea. "Shit," he muttered. He saw the blinking light on the phone bank. "Mr. Cleary, Betsy Gallucci is on line one. She sounds upset."

"Thank you. I'll take it." Before he picked up he took a deep breath and slowly let it out.

"This isn't going to be good," he mumbled.

"Hello, Betsy," he said, without emotion.

"Is anyone in the office with you?" she sobbed quietly.

"No, of course not. What's wrong?"

"You know damn well what's wrong. Your dirty little nose sticking itself in places it doesn't belong got Paulie Strata killed. Not that it's any great loss, but now Krosnowski is hopping mad. Says I spilled the beans to you. Says I told you, you told Collins and Collins informed the Santoris."

"Take a deep breath, Betsy. Krosnowski is a prosecutor and they find things out by intimidating people. He's got nothing. He knows nothing. You have to pull yourself together."

"Pull myself together! He's banned me and my employees from the Federal Building and canceled our contract with the court. That was *half* our business," her sobbing became louder, more out of control.

Jerry waited for her to calm down. "You always told me what a pain it was working down there anyway. Low-life criminals and tweedy lawyers. I've got enough business here to keep you guys busy. I only use other people because you're working down there."

The sobbing subsided into hiccups. "Krosnowski said I should get a lawyer because there's going to be an investigation."

"Okay, okay, look, start from the beginning and tell me everything that happened," Jerry was curious to hear her take on it.

"After you went up to Krosnowski's office I finished my coffee with one of my employees. She's new to the building, so I showed her to the office she was supposed to report to and I helped her set up. Then I went to king shit's office around ten o'clock. I was setting up in the witness room across from the elevator...that's when I watched you leave. You looked angry, didn't even look in my direction. I wondered why you ignored me." The sobbing increased.

"I had just finished with the recently departed witness. That would be enough to make anyone angry. He knew all about us, but I played dumb."

"That shouldn't have been hard for you," Betsy said bitterly. She was able to stop sobbing long enough to sling insults.

"Ouch. I guess I deserved that." Jerry pushed back in his chair and propped his feet on the desk. It was easier to deal with mad

Betsy. "Go on."

"Well, we didn't get started on time. Around 10:30 Krosnowski comes storming out and nearly dragged me into his office. They had moved Strata to another room so he couldn't hear. Then he laid into me saying I was having an affair with you and my dad was good friends with Lefty Santori, blah, blah, blah. He ordered me off the floor, told me to change places with the girl I had brought upstairs. I was off the case permanently."

"So far so good. He was right in doing that. You should have recused yourself because of your family ties. You didn't even mention it to me." Jerry liked it better when he had the upper hand.

"You were too busy trying to bed me to think of asking about my family. You never would've paid any attention to what I said anyway. Besides, my dad and I rarely talk about business. He's been cutting Tony's hair since high school, has never once mentioned a word about him. It's called loyalty, something you wouldn't know anything about. This is crap. Whose side are you on anyway?" She was just getting started.

"Yours, of course. But we have to be smart here. How did Paulie find out about us?"

"I don't know. He might have heard about it from my dad when he and Tony were still working together. I mentioned going out to dinner with you to dad once. He probably told Tony, who then put two and two together, told Paulie, maybe, when you were defending Collins. I don't know."

"Is that it? So you are saying that Krosnowski heard third hand that you and I once had dinner. That's like reading one sentence and then telling everyone you read the book." Jerry was feeling more confident. Krosnowski's conclusions were based on hearsay of the worst kind. If it ever came to anything it would be hard to cross-examine a dead witness. "Where are you now? I'm just about to leave the office for the day, maybe we could meet for lunch or something?" Jerry was still hopeful.

Betsy ignored the invitation, "There's another way he could've heard about us. I learned from Krosnowski today, after he told me my contract was terminated, that Paulie was allowed to call his brothers and his wife while he was being held on the island. He kept up on everything. Krosnowki says he has witnesses who saw us at a motel together." Besty started to sob again, softly this time.

"How could that be? I was always careful. This all sounds like a fishing expedition." Jerry reminded himself to look over the prenuptial agreement Deidre's father had shoved down his throat. Alimony for one ex-wife was bad enough.

"Jerry, sometimes I think you are very naive. Paulie and his brothers have soft drink machines in every fleabag hotel or mo-tel in the city. That's how they got so much money. His brothers aren't in the Mafia business but they know what they're doing when it comes to making a buck. They own apartment buildings, bakeries, you name it. Haven't you heard of Strata's Bakery?"

"No. But what does that have to do with us?" Jerry plopped his feet back down on the floor. He was preparing to end this conversation and get on the road.

"One of his guys collecting from a machine saw us come out of a motel room together. He recognized me right away."

Jerry tensed. This sounded more serious. "How the hell does he know it was me?"

"Because your ugly mug is on the back of every bus and bench in the city, as well as TV. He checked the register to be sure and found the room registered to a Mr. Smith."

So that's how Krosnowski knew his alias was Smith. Stupid. "Well, even though we talked about Paulie you never mentioned one word about his deposition. I think you're clear, and that's just what I'll tell anyone who asks. The only thing you told me was that they had him stashed on a Harbor Island."

"Apparently that was enough for your investigator who spilled the beans to the Santoris."

"Hell, it could have been anybody who overheard that in his office."

"You dummy, Jerry. There were two agents in the room with me. They were whispering and when they saw that I might have overheard them the one guy, real nice, smiled and asked if I'd been listening. I told him no." The thought of having betrayed a

Seeds Of Doubt

confidence was too much and Betsy began to sob again.

Jerry saw all the ways this might blossom into real trouble for him. If it ever came to anything, Betsy would be forced to turn on him. He would take the fall for everything, especially with his tinkering in this case. "Damn Eddie Collins. He's too thorough," he said to himself.

Returning to his conversation with Betsy he said, "I think we better hang up and hope that Krosnowski doesn't pursue this. I'll talk to you next week."

"Jerry, I told you not to get involved with these people. Once they start it's like a fly trying to get off flypaper...everywhere you step there's more trouble. Watch yourself. This isn't the end of it for you. Krosnowski said that Paulie told him that if you didn't drop this suit against Dr. Graves, you'd pay for it...and just because he's dead doesn't get you off the hook. He has two brothers and I'll tell you right now they are not happy. Avenging Paulie's death is uppermost on their minds right now. It's a Sicilian thing."

"You can cut the dramatics. They'll never find out, and even if they do they aren't about to go bumping off a lawyer," he said with a little less than his usual bravado, not quite believing it himself.

137

Fourteen

Two issues sit front and center in almost all litigation for malpractice. One, the plaintiff lawyer always wants to know if the treatment-plan, whether it's surgery or medication or a combination of the two, was indicated—an issue that may not get resolved until the trial is completed, depending on the judgment of the "expert witnesses." And two, did the doctor properly explain the risks vs. benefits of a treatment to the patient and then carry out that treatment exactly as planned? Invariably, the doctor's interpretation of what the patient was told does not necessarily match with the patient's interpretation of what he or she heard. Despite whatever distortions arise across these lines of communication, one thing remains certain: the oral contract between a doctor and a patient is as binding in court as a paper contract that has been witnessed and signed.

Informing a patient of his risks is a delicate art, and any doctor will tell you that he or she must balance the need for being honest and realistic against unnecessarily scaring the patient. But patients have a certain responsibility in keeping themselves informed.

When patients enter the hospital for major surgery it is implied that they know why they are there and what the potential risks and complications of the procedure are. Patients sign an operative consent form usually in the presence of a nurse or clerk. By this time the patient should know a surgeon's record, and they should have a reasonably good idea about both the doctor's and the hospital's percentages or probability of a bad outcome.

Doctor Tom Trimble had been dealing with the matter of informed consent for twenty years. Unfortunately for him, he had experienced the gut wrenching and time consuming rigors of malpractice litigation first hand. Early in his career as a heart surgeon he had a patient with severe aortic stenosis who needed an aortic valve replacement. Since finishing his training, he had done fifty aortic valve replacements that had ended in four deaths, making his mortality rate 8%. Statistically speaking, that number meant that one in ten patients would die with him performing the surgery. Not a great record, but also not a record that told the whole truth. Because Trimble was fresh out of residency, he was looked on as someone who knew how to care for the sicket patients and some who was familiar with the latest technology. This is the usual story for the young surgeon fresh out of training. Not unexpectedly and with good reason, the new man is often referred the tougher cases. In order to compensate for the skewed results of his mortality rate, he quoted to the patient with severe aortic stenosis a mortality rate that represented the latest number of all the surgeons in the hospital, which was 2%. After the patient died from the complications of a sternal wound infection, Trimble was promptly sued. The family remembered that Dr. Trimble quoted them a very low possibility of failure, and the clever plaintiff attorney subpoenaed his records in order to show how Trimble had played with the numbers to make himself look good. Ultimately, Trimble won the case in court, but it was a process so grinding and depleting that he swore never to go through it again.

The whole experience motivated him to devise a risk-adjusted score that broke down patients into subgroups. Those patients who had more risk factors involved were quoted a higher risk of complication or death at surgery. Such risk factors included things like age, sex, previous open-heart surgery, smoking, lung disease, diabetes or other physical or mental disorders. Once word got out about Trimble's new system of risk adjustments, the scoring system became the norm for all doctors. Now Trimble was studying the issue of informed consent to see if patients really comprehended and understood the risks and complications he so carefully explained to them before surgery.

For Tom Trimble, a man like Jerry Cleary represented everything he despised and feared about medical malpractice. But while Cleary depended upon having hospitals and doctors make mistakes, Trimble was dedicated to eradicating them. On the same Friday afternoon Cleary was carting his family to Maine, Tom and Nancy Kimball, his research nurse, were sitting in the audiovisual office at University Hospital waiting to meet Bill Platt, the director of the audiovisual department. In an effort to answer the question of whether the informed consent process was effective, Tom had initiated an in-hospital study of preoperative patients. He conceived of a way to videotape his discussions with patients and the hospital agreed to install three unobtrusive cameras and recording devices in a room designated for his purpose. Each patient was aware their conversation was being videotaped and they signed a special consent form allowing this to happen irrespective of who else was in the room. The purpose was to compare what was said and understood preoperatively by the patient with what they recollected postoperatively. The patients were then interviewed three weeks after surgery, six weeks after and, finally, six months post-operative.

"I wonder what's keeping Bill?" Tom asked.

"Oh, I forgot to mention. He paged me to say he was videotaping a case in the OR and would be a couple minutes late," Nancy said. She was an attractive, middle-aged woman who had a very diplomatic manner with the doctors and patients. She had formerly worked in the cardiac surgical intensive care unit and had known Dr. Trimble since his days as a resident

"I hope he isn't too late," Tom said, "We have a lot to go over and the American Thoracic Surgery conference is in two weeks. By the way, are the slides for the presentation back yet?"

"I have them in my briefcase." She smiled. "Don't worry everything is all set. The data are on the slides. I reviewed them today and they look great." She gave him a motherly look while she patted him on the hand.

"I still can't believe the results. Especially when you consider the fact that the patients knew they were being videotaped. Only half could accurately remember what was said before surgery."

"I know. It's incredible. But what's more surprising is the people who sat with them! They had bad memories as well. You'd think they would remember better since they were not under as much stress as the patient," she said.

"I agree. But maybe the person who's going to be waiting in the lobby doesn't want to hear about all those numbers and possible doom and gloom scenarios. Maybe they're under just as much stress."

"Could be. As for the patients, there is memory loss after major surgery, but by six months memory has returned in most cases." Just then the door burst open and Bill rushed in.

"Sorry I'm late. That Dr. Stannovic is the slowest orthopod in the world. Did you ever have to videotape a bunion operation?"

"Fortunately, no," Tom said.

Bill shot a smile back that said "lucky you". Bill had started work at University ten years ago and had worked himself up from an assistant EKG technician to head of the audiovisual department. He was the kind of employee who dot the landscape of all hospitals. The kind who blend into the woodwork but whose competence and willingness to go the extra mile kept the hospital running.   Bill spent his years at University Hospital applying to every new job as long as it meant an advance in pay and prestige. If he were not familiar with the work in the advertised position he would sharpen his skills with night courses and library time. Now, without any prior experience, he had worked his way to becoming one of the best photographers and videographers the hospital had ever employed.

"Dr. Trimble, I have selected six videos of you and your patients," Bill said.

"I gave him the names of three people who had remembered the preoperative interview and three who didn't," Nancy added.

"Right, I spent all day yesterday blacking out their faces. It runs about three minutes per case. How long is your presentation?" Bill asked.

"Well, it's not eighteen minutes, that's for sure. Let see the videos. I'll pick out one each between those who could remember and those who didn't." Bill placed the tapes in a playback machine and they watched the interviews.

After the screening was over Tom said, "The only common thread here is that the ones who seemed to remember facts about the preoperative discussions were the ones that asked the most questions. The ones who didn't remember also didn't seem too interested and were a little impatient." Tom looked around to see if there were any nodding heads. "Well, what do you guys think?" he prodded after there was no spontaneous response.

Bill said, "If I were a patient and I had come this far...sick, primary care doctor, cardiologist, the whole bit...I think I would know what I was in for. I wouldn't want to hear about what bad things might happen, especially the night before surgery. Maybe people just don't listen. You know, tune it out. I mean, it's like somebody standing by the entrance to an airplane explaining to me all the risks and complications of flying just before I'm about to board."

"Good point. Nancy, what do you think?" Tom asked.

"I've cared for hundreds of patients and their families after open-heart surgery," Nancy replied. "No one has ever thought that surgery was without risks or the possibility of dying. It's just that in interviewing these patients you get the sense that your discussion prior to surgery is a disclaimer. They want to know the facts, but then again they don't. Using Bill's analogy, everyone knows that if a plane crashes you'll most likely die, but you don't think about that risk anymore once you've landed. Once you're safe you simply move on. I think these people were so happy to have the surgery behind them that they didn't care about remembering what was said."

"Hmm." Tom was thinking that his study really wasn't going to show much or change anything. The patients have to be informed of risks, and some will remember that discussion while others won't. Formalizing the consent process with written contracts, voice recordings, or videotaped chart documentation might be good legal practice, but it wasn't necessarily good for the patient's well being.

"Well thank you both. I'll review these tapes at home tomorrow. Bill lets get together on Monday and edit things down."

Tom stood up and prepared to leave when Bill asked, "What do you want me to do with these other tapes?"

"What other tapes?" Tom asked.

"I forgot to tell you," Nancy said, "there were three people admitted to the study room who weren't your patients. You either weren't in town or the hospital was short of beds. They used the video monitored room."

"Did the patients or doctors know that they were being recorded?" Tom asked frowning. He hadn't heard this before.

"I checked the records and all three patients had signed a general consent form giving permission for videotaping any aspect of their care. It's a similar form to the one your patients signed but only covers the patients," Bill said hesitantly. He wondered if he had screwed up.

"I thought only cardiac patients were to be taped?" Tom asked. He wasn't sure what to do with the tapes or whether they might create a problem.

"When we first got underway with the study, all admissions to that room were recorded. So this happened early in the study, but then never happened again," Bill said.

Tom turned to Nancy for advice. "What should we do?"

"Well, who are the doctors on the videotapes?"

"Let's see." Bill picked up the cassettes and looked at the names written on the sides to be sure he got it right. "There's Doctors Graves, Nicolette, and Jordan." He looked at Dr. Trimble and said, "I called Dr. Graves' office about it several weeks ago. He never got back to me."

Tim Graves was Tom's close associate, and Tom knew he wouldn't care about the videotapes. "Oh hell, toss them. That was over two years ago anyway," he said, somewhat frustrated.

"Okay," Bill said.

"Don't you think that would be like throwing away a part of the patient's chart," Nancy asked. Having been the watchdog at the hospital for so many years she knew the rules and knew what got people into bureaucratic or legal binds. She realized that she had saved doctors and the hospital from countless lawsuits by her vigilance over details. "Why don't we contact the doctors about the tapes? Or, better yet, give them to me and I'll deliver them to their offices tomorrow."

"Sounds like a plan," Tom said, grateful that Nancy had come up with a solution.

Fifteen

It had been four days since the murder of Paulie Strata, but to Jerry it seemed like a year. His weekend in Maine with Diedre's parents had dragged on. While the setting was nice, Jerry couldn't understand why Deidre's father, for all the money he made, didn't live in a better house. He hated sharing a bathroom with his three daughters and the old New England spring bed he slept on sagged and creaked every time he moved, leaving him sleepless and sore. He wouldn't have slept much anyway, since the haunting threat of Paulie Strata weighed heavily on his mind. Even though Paulie was burning in hell, his threat still bothered Jerry. Those two Sicilian brothers were out there somewhere and who knew what they might pull. As if it weren't bad enough that Jerry had to worry about getting his throat slit by a couple of wop, bullies, he had to listen to Deidre's father rant on and on about how lawyers were ruining the world. "I spent more on legal fees last year to fight environmentalists than I did on my employees," he'd say, adding, "It's a damn shame you lawyers make all that money and don't contribute anything to the economy." Jerry couldn't even count the number of times he'd heard that speech.

After spending most of his weekend longing to be somewhere else, he was finally back in his office on Monday morning preparing to meet Jason and go over his deposition questions. Jerry's approach to depositions was always to get the defense experts to ramble on. Since they were doctors, they loved to show off all the knowledge they had. Ask them a question, Jerry would tell the younger lawyers in his group, and you get an encyclopedic answer. The doctors were always hoping that they would have a brilliant answer- knock a homerun- that would make the lawsuit seem silly. Instead, all they did was give the attorney more avenues to pursue and, eventually, more opportunity to nail somebody. The interoffice buzzer rang and Jerry told his secretary to send in the young attorney.

"Good morning, Jerry. Nice weekend?" Jason seemed confident and prepared. He had spent his Saturday and Sunday writing down questions for the deposition, just as Jerry had asked him to do, and he felt sure he would impress his boss.

"It was okay. Are you ready? This guy Davis has been used by Stokes before. He's pretty good in court. Your job is to poke holes in his testimony anytime you see an opportunity. Get my message?" Jerry asked, ignoring Jason's good mood.

"Yessir." Jason was on his best behavior. "I plan to take him through the consent process, try to get him to say that Dr. Graves was remiss in not telling the family about risks or other treatment options. Standard of care issues like 'Isn't it true that doctors tell patients about alternative forms of treatment?' That sort of thing."

"Those 'isn't it true questions' are okay, but a smart witness can dodge 'em. Just stick to the facts of the case. He will tell you what he really thinks of Graves' cavalier approach to informed consent if you ask him how *he* does it. That will provide the contrast we need. Doctors as experts tend to give an idealized version of how to do things so ask him what he does, not what Dr. Graves did."

"I understand. Then after that I am going to press him on the surgery. His results. What he would have done. Whether or not he would have done anything differently," Jason said. He was beginning to lose confidence. How was he going to ask a neurosurgeon questions he himself didn't know the answers to?

Jerry sensed his insecurity. A doctor wouldn't know what questions to ask a lawyer about the law, and a lawyer would feel unsure asking a doctor about his specialty. "Look, Jason, you'll never know enough about medicine to ask the right medical questions. So you ask questions that are simple, pertinent and something the doctor knows. Like 'what is a cerebral aneurysm, how do they happen, are they always fatal, do they all have to be clipped' then let him tell you."

"I understand. I should ask, 'Do they all have to be clipped?' and when he says no then I ask if Mr. Bradford's needed to be clipped?"

"That's the idea. And remember we're not in court. Histrionics in a depo only antagonizes the witness. You get more with syrup than with acid." Jerry was proud of his analogy. "I do the heavy hitting in court. He won't know what to think after a soft-ball deposition."

"I've been through enough of these to know what not to ask," Jason said while trying to pump himself up. He knew Jerry wouldn't take kindly to any screw-ups on his part.

"When are you leaving?" Jerry asked.

"Tomorrow afternoon. I fly to Laguardia and the depo is at ten on Wednesday morning. I'm staying at a Holiday Inn right next to Eastside Hospital. His secretary told me his office connects to the hospital, so there shouldn't be any delays."

"Good. Call me if you have any questions. I'm in court tomorrow most of the day dealing with an appeal, but will keep in touch with the office. Good luck."

Jason arrived at Dr. Davis's office before ten, eager to start the deposition. The young woman eyed him from behind the open frosted, glass windows and told him to take a seat in the waiting room. Dr. Davis was with a patient, but would be available shortly she told him, closing the window without so much as a smile. A few moments later Lisa Harding arrived and tapped lightly on the glass. The receptionist received her more warmly and ushered her back to Dr. Davis' office. Jason knew it was going to be more than a few minutes wait for him. Lisa Harding was most likely back there filling the doctor in on the latest and warning him about potential land mines. Jason didn't care how much she was prepping her expert witness. He knew how to handle it. He would simply ask Dr. Davis what they had just been talking about. Doctor experts always think their meetings with defense attorneys are privileged. He couldn't wait.

Jason wasn't the only person in the waiting area. Every seat was filled and some people were standing. He could see the names of four doctors on the wall and they were all listed as neurosurgeons. The door opened and closed like the entrance to Grand Central Station with patients and families moving from the front to the examining rooms in back; patients with dressings on their heads, arms, and neck, kids screaming on the floor and older patients with canes. *Boy, are they busy here.* He'd have to speed up his deposition and not inconvenience the doctors or patients. Lawyers had enough PR problems without adding to the perception that all they cared about was money.

The door opened and in walked Betsy Gallucci. What the hell? Was he in the wrong city? She also knocked on the frosted window and was told to have a seat. She noticed Jason after she sat down, placing her recording equipment next to her.

"Am I dreaming or is that you Betsy?" Jason was still single and oozed charm.

"It's me. Jerry wants continuity and accuracy," she said modestly. "He called yesterday and is paying the air and hotel. Came down last night. Glad to get out of town."

Before Jason could ask about her plans after the depo, the waiting room door opened. They were ushered back to the doctor's office. Dr. Davis' office was simply decorated with the usual degrees, pictures and plaques that doctors use to adorn their walls. Dr. Davis introduced himself to Betsy and Jason since Lisa had stepped out to the ladies' room. Betsy set up her recorder and Jason sat down and opened his briefcase, taking out a yellow legal pad. Soon the attorneys for the hospital and anesthesiologist arrived. When Lisa returned she was surprised to see Betsy but seemed pleased. After pleasantries, the lull before war, Betsy swore in Dr. Davis.

"Good morning Dr. Davis. For the record I am Jason Damon with Cleary and Associates in Boston. I expect you have had your deposition taken before?"

"Yes."

"How many times?"

Dr. Davis looked to be in his late forties or early fifties. He was the type of individual that no matter how bad his day he seemed pressed and ready to go. He stood almost six feet tall, lean with graying hair. He had piercing blue eyes and a jutting chin. He could be an actor on TV. "I can't recall exactly but around twenty-five times"

"How many times as an expert?"

"About twenty."

"And the others?" Jason noticed Lisa begin to fidget in her chair.

"I've been sued three time if that's what you are asking," Dr. Davis said nonchalantly.

"Doctor have you ever had any judgments against you as a result of a medical malpractice lawsuit?"

"No."

"Has your license ever been suspended or revoked?" Jason looked serious.

Dr. Davis was getting visibly annoyed by the line of questioning that had nothing to do with his expertise. "Perhaps we can get through this line of questioning by me simply telling you. I have never had a judgment against me for any reason. I have had a New York medical license for twenty-five years. It has been renewed successfully every four years. I have never been disciplined, reviewed, investigated. I only drink socially and I have testified for the plaintiff approximately five times and the defense fifteen. Cases are referred to me I review them and make a decision based on the merits of the case. I reject many more than I accept. Any income generated from this activity is donated to the medical school research foundation. It amounts to about $15,000 per year. I charge $150 per hour for chart review and deposition time and $1,500 flat fee for appearing in court."

"I would like to agree that we can get on with it. The doctor is busy and we've been here a half hour and so far you have asked no questions relevant to the litigation at hand," Lisa said. She was doing her job. The others attorneys joined with Lisa.

"I beg the esteemed counsel's pardon but I will ask the questions. I am only laying foundation here. I will try and speed it up to accommodate the doctor's schedule," Jason said with a stern look on his face. After all he was a hockey player from South Boston and he was not one to back down over some lawyer's rant. There was a gleam in his eye that indicated he didn't like women telling him what to do.

"Doctor, what is a cerebral aneurysm?" Jason asked as politely as he could.

"It's a bubble on a blood vessel in the brain."

"How often do they occur?"

"About one in five hundred to a thousand people have them?"

"Are they dangerous?"

"Yes. They can rupture and cause brain damage and sometimes death." Betsy was happy with Dr. Davis' short answers without a lot of medical terminology.

"How do you treat these aneurysms?"

"Depending on their size and location they can either be watched, clipped with surgery or thrombosed, excuse me, clotted, with a catheter." *Keep it simple stupid.*

"Who makes the decision to choose what is done?" Jason had calmed down and was going through the questions he had laid out for himself.

"I do. Or I should say the neurosurgeon does. The use of catheters, although helpful, has not been as applicable as first thought. Ninety percent of aneurysms need surgery. That is the anerysms that are doable, 90 percent of the time surgery is indicated and about 10% can be done with the catheter. There are a certain number for one reason or another are not interventional or surgical candidates."

"Do you give your patients the opportunity to choose which therapy they might select?"

"I don't know what you mean." Dr. Davis was on guard now. If he says he leaves it up to the patient then the lack of informed consent alleged by the plaintiff might get some legs. "I tell patients what the choices are and give an opinion as to which one I would select. They then decide. Is that what you mean?"

Jason chose to ignore this answer. "Would it be below the standard of care to not inform patients of alternative treatments to surgery?"

Lisa was nearly out of her chair when she said, "I object. Lacks foundation. Too broad a question. Are we talking about this patient or all patients?" The attorneys for the hospital and anesthesiologist joined in with Lisa.

Jason felt good. He was asking the right questions. Unconcerned with Lisa's histrionics he said, "Doctor?"

"I'll answer the question this way. The neurosurgeon's obligation is to inform the patient of the risks, complications, and benefits of surgery. Information regarding the treatment other than surgery should come from referring doctors or neurologists. It is not below the standard of care for a neurosurgeon to not inform the patient about treatments that are either experimental or beyond the expertise of the surgeon."

Lisa liked that answer. Jason didn't. He pursued it from different angles trying to get Dr. Davis to criticize Dr. Graves' handling of the case but couldn't. He did get Dr. Davis to admit that documentation of who was present during the informed consent was essential because after all sometimes it was the relatives who are left behind that begin the litigation process. He produced his office's rather lengthy informed consent document, which every patient signs, along with whomever else is present.

Jason was unhappy with the deposition and needed something more. He had been frustrated by Dr. Davis' answer and considered him an informed witness largely because of his legal background. Toward the end of the deposition out of desperation he said, "Dr. Davis how many cerebral aneurysms have you done?" Jason pointed his finger at Dr. Davis. Lisa wondered why he pointed there was no other Dr.Davis in the room. Lisa assumed he was getting frustrated.

Dr. Davis sought to answer this question as accurately at possible. Finally he said, "Well I have been in practice for more than twenty years and I do about twenty or so aneurysms a year. Well over four hundred."

It seemed like an astounding number to Jason. If he could catch the doctor exaggerating his claims it might just discredit him as a witness. "How many patients survived the surgery?"

"I only operate at this hospital and they keep running tabs on our results. I would say all but one or two patients per year or about a 5-10% mortality."

"Doctor I am going to request copies of all the operative reports and discharge summaries. Patient's names will be redacted of course. I will need them in let's say two weeks. Trial begins in three weeks." Jason looked over at Lisa expecting her to come flying out of her chair with legal gibberish but she remained calm and silent. In fact she had a little bit of a smirk on her face.

Sixteen

Betsy Gallucci was such a successful court reporter because her documents were accurate, words weren't misspelled, and she had a rapid turnaround time. It was easy to get behind in her work because of the sheer number of depositions done on a daily basis. Her goal was to have the typed deposition back in forty-eight hours. After leaving New York and dodging the ever-eager Jason Damon she arrived home from Logan Airport around 6:30. She spent the rest of the evening completing Dr. Davis's deposition so it could be in Jerry's office by the next afternoon. As far as depositions went it wasn't too bad and ended up being ninety pages.

Jerry had been in court with pleadings on Thursday and missed seeing the deposition until he arrived at work on Friday. Jerry never liked to go to court on Fridays since they were usually half-day sessions and a waste of his time. Judges liked to get out early and excused juries for the weekend. As he sat down at his desk he noted the Davis deposition in his in-box. *Holy cow she's quick*. He reminisced for a minute, thinking about his good times with Betsy, then picked up the document. He thumbed through it. Where it might take a doctor or any non-lawyer hours to read a ninety-page deposition, not so with most lawyers. They read rapidly and seem to be able to find the meat in depositions quickly and in an uncanny manner. "Oh no," Jerry moaned minutes into the deposition, loud enough for his secretary to hear him through the closed door.

In a nanosecond Jerry was buzzing her to tell her to get Jason in his office immediately.

When Jason arrived she only pointed to Jerry's office without saying a word. The frown on her face spoke volumes. Jason had no idea what was amiss. When he entered the office he could feel the anger. Jerry's face was red. The only thing missing was smoke coming out of his ears.

Jerry sat staring at Jason for at least thirty seconds attempting to gain control. Finally he said through clenched teeth, "What in the world possessed you to request Dr. Davis' work experience?"

"I don't know," Jason stammered. Rather than remain obsequious, his background kicked in. Nobody, including his self-absorbed, arrogant boss was going to intimidate him.

"Yes I do. The doctor was full of himself and very condescending. I got nothing from him so I decided to call his bluff. He way over-stated his experience and I called him on it. When we get the true numbers he will have to explain," Jason finished by sitting straighter in his chair.

Jerry looked at him, softening somewhat. After all this was Jason's first big deposition where a great deal of money was on the line. Perhaps he'd overestimated this young man's capabilities. If so, he had only himself to blame.

"When I was just getting started and had left the DA's office I took on a case against a very well known heart surgeon in this city today. I asked him for his work experience, which I believed to be different than what he quoted." Jerry paused to be sure he had Jason's attention. The young lawyer was listening attentively. "Well it forced him to detail the results in front of the jury and he proved his point. That was bad enough. The defense lawyer requested the same information from my expert and it was a disaster. The hack had only done three aortic valve replacements in the previous ten years. He had given me a different story, of course. 'Oh I've done plenty of those'" Jerry mimed.

"The doctor claimed he had done over four hundred brain

aneurysms. Let him prove it if he is such a big time expert," Jason said with more conviction.

"This is not a science fair. An expert is someone who knows more than the jury. If he has done one, legally, in our system he is considered an expert. It's up to me to either poke holes in that or support it as the case may be. Now that you have asked for his work experience he can ask for my expert's."

"Well I am at a disadvantage here. I don't know who your expert is and we didn't discuss this possibility on Monday," Jason said tossing the ball back into Jerry's court.

"Listen to me carefully. You're not going to find an expert of Dr. Davis' stature testifying against someone like Graves. That could prove to come back at him if the defendant wants payback. Doctors are not stupid. My expert cannot compare to those two on a medical basis but as experts they are on equal footing as far as the court is concerned. All you've done is allow the defense to take shots at my expert's credentials."

Jason sat back and began to realize what Jerry was saying. He had painted himself into a corner letting his emotions get the best of him. Dr. Davis was smooth and it had pissed him off. Not smart. "I'm sorry Jerry. What do we do?"

"We," Jerry said pointing to Jason, "will need to go over those records with a fine tooth comb and hope the doctor was way off on his numbers. That's all for now." Jerry couldn't resist turning the knife. "I was hoping to send you to Los Angeles next week for our expert's deposition but I guess I'll have to do it myself."

Jason looked crestfallen as he excused himself and left the office.

The following Monday a package arrived from Dr. Davis' New York office addressed to Jason Damon. When Jason opened the box he was presented with a stack of redacted operative reports and discharge summaries, as well as a note. The note was from one of Dr. Davis's office personnel and stated that she could only go back sixteen years the rest of the reports were on microfilm or in storage and did he really need them? Jason looked over the stack and counted five hundred operative reports and four hundred fifty discharge summaries. It was worse than he had thought.

Along with the letter there was an invoice for $1,500 charging for overtime and copying fees. Jason spent the next twenty-four hours reading the discharge summaries and scanning the operative reports. By eight o'clock Tuesday evening he had the bad news. He called Jerry's home and spoke to Deidre who told him that Jerry was on the way to Logan Airport to catch the American Airlines red eye to Los Angeles.

Jason waited until an hour before the flight was scheduled to leave and called the American Airlines Ambassador lounge. The lounge attendant found Jerry within moments since the area was not crowded.

"Hello," he said not knowing who was calling.

"Hello Jerry, it's Jason Damon. I'm glad I caught you. Bad news. I received the operative reports and discharge summaries from Davis' office. Worse than I thought. He did slightly over five hundred brain aneurysms."

"Shit. What's that twenty into five hundred? About twenty-five a year. One every other week! I'll be damned!"

"Well not exactly. They only sent his last sixteen year experience so it would be sixteen into five hundred or thirty-one a year," Jason squeezed his eyelids tight expecting a blast.

It didn't come.

"He's doing too many. A lot of unnecessary surgery. I can make the case for that. Make him look bad," Jerry said in desperation.

"I read most of the discharge summaries and they appeared to be legitimate cases. I'm sorry Jerry."

"Well it was a thought. I just won't dwell on it at trial. I'll find something to discredit him. Maybe he beats his wife," he chuckled softly. "Say, guess who's here in the lounge with me? Edwin Stokes. He's doing the deposition himself, says he's looking forward to hearing about Shamski's surgical experience."

This jab wasn't wasted on Jason. "I apologize again. What do you want me to do with this $1500 bill from Davis' office?"

"Simple. You pay for it out of your own expenses and don't delay on that. I don't want them using it at trial. Oops. They're calling for me to board. See you Thursday," Jerry said. It was time to put this behind him and move on.

Before his plane landed in L.A., Jerry fetched a toothbrush and toothpaste from his briefcase and brushed his teeth in the lavatory. He tidied up his tie and brushed the wrinkles out of his coat. He smelled his armpits and everthing seemed ok. He by-passed baggage claim and headed for a limo waiting to take him to Marion Street in Beverly Hills. He offered Edwin Stokes a ride but the defense attorney refused saying that he had ordered a cab from the sky phone and had a quick appointment before the deposition. Jerry planned to meet with Dr. Shamski at 9:30. The other lawyers would meet at ten. He had thought about bringing Betsy Gallucci along but that would be indiscreet. Good thing, since Edwin Stokes would have suspected something right away.

Dr. Shamski's office was in a plain two story building on Marion Street south of Santa Monica Boulevard. It was two blocks north of the Santa Monica freeway in a neighborhood filled with lower rent apartments. The people who lived here were the work force for Beverly Hills. With briefcase in hand Jerry got out of his limousine. He gazed at the neighborhood. *Strange place for a Doctor's office*. The building had a parking lot next to it where there was an attendant collecting parking fees. He slipped the driver twenty bucks and told him to pick him up at noon for a flight back at two o'clock. He sniffed and pulled his nasal spray out of his pocket and took a snort in each nostril. *Stuffy airplanes*. It was nine o'clock and on the first floor of Dr. Shamski's build-ing there was a small coffee shop and luncheonette. He stopped in and ordered a donut and coffee. There was a used LA Times on a small table. Jerry sat down and pulled out the sports page. It was nearly the start of baseball season and there were lots of stories about rookie hopefuls and traded old timers. There was a brief story on the Red Sox featuring a pitching staff that included the left-handed phenomenon Joey Santori. There was a quote where he hoped the team would do better this year with the addi-tion of some big hitters. There could be a bigger story about this young man Jerry mused to himself. He glanced at his watch and put down the paper.

Outside he saw there was a stairway located at the center of the building facing the street. Jerry climbed to the second floor and at the top to his left was an office. The sign on the door said Dr. Jules Shamski MD FACS, Neurological Surgery, Neurology, and Workman's Compensation Specialist. *Is there a workman's compensation specialty?* He shrugged his shoulders and opened the door. Inside there was a small waiting room with chrome chairs lining the walls. Directly opposite the door was a brown plastic counter top that framed a closed frosted glass window. On the counter was a chrome bell reminiscent of the kind he had seen in numerous motels. The rug on the floor was dark orange shag that needed a cleaning. The color of the rug matched that of the vinyl material covering the chairs.

Jerry walked over and rang the bell. It was exactly 9:30. Plaintiff attorneys were always on time unlike their defense counterparts. After a short period the glass partition slid open and sitting in a chair was a middle-aged woman who was swatting the air in front of her face. Jerry smelled cigarette smoke. He gazed at the no smoking sign on the wall behind her desk.

Her nametag spelled out "*Terry Long*" in bold letters. Wisps of smoke escaped from her lips as she asked, "Can I help you?"

"Yes. Ms. Long is it?"

"Close enough. And you are?"

"Jerry Cleary. I'm here for Dr. Shamski's deposition," Jerry smiled. Terry Long was about forty-five years old with streaky blond hair. She was heavily made up with bright red lipstick. Her eyebrows were plucked to a thin line and her face was tan and seemed wrinkle free. Jerry wondered who had done her face-lift. Her voice was hoarse, consistent with her penchant for smoking. She wasn't attractive but she wasn't unattractive. On a lonely night he might not turn her down.

"Oh. Right," She flashed him a suggestive smile "Are you in town long Mr. Cleary?"

"I've got a flight out at two."

"Too bad," she said pouting her lips. She pushed a button under her desk and Jerry opened the door next to the window. "I'll take you back to the conference room." She wore black nylon stockings and pink pumps. "Would you like something to drink? Coffee?" she asked as she opened the door to a small conference room.

As Jerry walked into the room she did not move aside, forcing him to brush past her. He could feel her breasts on his right arm. They felt like billiard balls. *Bad silicone job. She should see a lawyer.* Surprisingly, he didn't detect the strong odor of perfume, which generally would have completed the package. "No thanks," he said. "Is the doctor in?" Jerry wasn't sure about this operation after he gazed around the conference room. There were bookshelves lined, not with medical textbooks or journals, but legal boxes and stacks of depositions. The table could seat six people and at the back of the room there was a window that overlooked the building's parking lot. They were covered with cheap, white, polyester curtains.

"Yes. He'll be right with you," Terry said as she removed from the table an ashtray filled with cigarette butts and a coffee cup stained with lipstick. Jerry watched as she tidied up.

She smiled at Jerry and left. Moments later Dr. Shamski entered. He wore an expensive silk suit with a bright red tie. Dr. Shamski was sixty years old and had a dark, leathery Palm Springs tan and a slightly wrinkled face. When he smiled he seemed quite affable and unassuming. His hair was gray and carefully groomed. His glasses had clear thin frames. He approached Jerry with an outstretched hand and said, "Finally we meet. Have a seat. How was your flight?"

Jerry noted that Dr. Shamski was at least four inches shorter than he and had the trim build of a swimmer or tennis player. "Well I'm glad I can put a face to the voice. The flight was uneventful. I hope this will go quickly because I have a flight home at two. Mr. Stokes himself has traveled out here for this. He's very prompt and thorough. He will not waste your time."

"Well then can I get you anything to drink? Coffee?" Jerry shook his head no.

As he sat down he placed his briefcase on the table and snapped it open. He removed a yellow legal pad on which he had scribbled a number of questions. "A few things I'd like to go over before the others arrive. There has been considerable concern by me that Dr. Graves acted in a cavalier fashion, not informing my client and the deceased about the risks of surgery. Also the possible use of catheters to clot the aneurysm." Jerry looked at Dr. Shamski as he sat down. *The guy looks like a surgeon right out of central casting. He seems confident and self-assured but not arrogant. Perfect.*

"To start with there is no question in my mind that what you say is true. I graduated from Harvard medical school and we used to have an old saying when I was there. 'You can get a lot of information out of Boston but not much gets in'. There is no question that two years ago this would not have been a surgical problem here in Los Angeles. I work primarily at Los Angeles Westside Hospital where we do about 20 cerebral aneurysm procedures a year. At our hospital this one would have been treated with a catheter."

"So what would the treatment have been in, let's say, St. Louis? Catheter or surgery?"

"Well probably surgery since we are the pioneers in this type of treatment. The rest of the country still hasn't caught up with us."

Jerry was not sure that this attitude would go over well with a Boston jury. Sounds too much like bragging. Better tone it down. "That's interesting doctor. But could we just say that in your opinion this should have been treated in a non-surgical manner?"

Dr. Shamski caught what Jerry was trying to imply. Don't overdo it. "Yes, of course. Surgery is an option but I would have recommended using a catheter. At least I would have informed my patient of the various possibilities. Not to do that is of course below the standard of care."

Jerry began to worry that this expert was saying just what he wanted to hear. "The other issue besides lack of informed consent is the techniques used. When we talked several months ago you said that the surgery was performed incompetently. That Dr. Graves had not freed up the aneurysm enough and when he placed the clip it tore the vessel. Do you still feel that way?"

"In my experience an aneurysm like this needs to be carefully teased up at the neck. Look at the operative report. An hour after the skin incision he was trying to place a clip. When he tore the vessel, he decompensated. I have read Dr. Graves' deposition. Most surgeons would have taken hours just to identify the neck of the aneurysm to be sure it was free."

Just then the door opened and Terry stuck her face in and said, "The court reporter and other attorneys are here." She smiled at Jerry.

"It'll just be a moment," Jerry said. Dr. Shamski seemed to know what he was talking about, but he wondered how he would stand up against Mr. Stokes' cross-examination. "By the way, speaking of your experience have you read Dr. Davis' deposition?"

"Oh yes. He's quite an authority on cerebral aneurysms but 400 cases? Give me a break."

"Speaking of experience my associate requested his, Dr. Davis's records, also to verify his numbers. Turns out he's done even more than he estimated. Unfortunately now Mr. Stokes can ask you for yours." Jerry carefully eyed his expert to see how he was going to react to this. He knew that experts tended to brag to their lawyers about their experience but under oath became more realistic.

"That could be a problem. My records were destroyed in a fire several years ago and office records are no longer available. In the past several years I've cut back in my practice and have not done nearly as many."

"Give me a guesstimate on how many you do or have done per year?"

"Oh around five or six. Most of them are done now by the catheter technique."

The door opened again and Terry stuck her head in and said, "How much longer? I've got a bunch of cranky lawyers out there." This time she wasn't smiling.

"Bring them in," Jerry said. He would have to let Dr. Shamski handle himself with Edwin.

Moments later the small conference room was filled with lawyers representing all the parties involved in the suit. After introductions Jerry stood up and cracked the window. Dr. Shamski was sworn in and when the usual procedural questions were answered Mr. Stokes got down to business.

"I see by your curriculum vitae you graduated from Harvard and did your neurosurgical training in New York. How long have you been in practice in Los Angeles?"

"About ten years."

"Before that?"

"Well various places. I was an attending at Cook County in Chicago for several years. Did the academic thing. Then I was drafted into the army for two years. Spent a year in Vietnam. After that I was with a group of neurosurgeons in Phoenix for about a year. Then I moved to Oregon and worked with another group of neurosurgeons and finally decided to try California."

"Have you ever had your medical license suspended or revoked in any of those states?"

"Well no. I did have a problem in Phoenix and was requested by my group there to resign. It was a financial dispute. Nothing to do with medical care." Dr. Shamski was holding up well under fire but Jerry knew there was more to come.

"I see by the research my office did on you that you testify in court a lot. Plaintiff or defense, mostly?"

"Well mostly plaintiff work."

"And how much of your time is devoted to medical legal matters?"

"Do you mean what percentage of my time is taken up with medical-legal matters?"

"Yes."

"I would say approximately thirty percent of my time." As he finished Mr. Stokes punctuated his answer by looking at all the legal documents lining the bookshelves. The only medical book was an outdated Physicians Desk Reference or PDR.

"By the way doctor, have you ever been sued?"

"I object," Jerry said. "The question lacks relevance and foundation but you may answer it."

Dr. Shamski looked at Jerry to let him know that he knew how to answer the question. Truthfully. "I have been sued before."

"How many times?"

"Three. Once by my ex-wife. Twice for alleged malpractice. One was over a retained foreign body. It was a nursing error and I was dropped from the suit and another over a wound infection. Same outcome."

"No other suits?"

"No."

"Any judgments against you?"

"No."

Edwin decided to move on and said, "I see by the sign on your door you do Workman's Compensation cases. How much of your time is devoted to that?"

"I would say about thirty percent as well." Dr. Shamski answered Edwin's questions forthrightly and seemed proud of his practice.

"Can I assume the rest of your time is spent on clinical medicine?"

"No. I also do chart reviews for Medicare and review claims for neurosurgical care for an HMO. That takes about ten percent of my time. The remainder is for clinical medicine."

"Now last week we deposed Dr. Davis in New York. By the way he sends his regards through my associate Lisa Harding. Seems you two know each other."

Dr. Shamski was a skilled witness and he wasn't going to offer any information. It wasn't a question and he remained silent.

Noting the lack of response Edwin's demeanor suddenly became more businesslike and he asked, "How many cerebral aneurysm procedures do you do a year, Doctor."

"Well if you mean surgery, three or four a year. With the catheter maybe ten or so per year." That was already less than what he told Jerry.

"Do you have records for these cases?"

"I have records which go back for two years. Records before that were destroyed in a fire."

"Do you have records at the hospital that can be accessed?"

"The short answer is no. The long answer is that since doctors are now vying for contracts from insurance companies, they no longer can have access to results. That includes their own cases. It seems that some doctors were reporting their competitions' results inaccurately while giving their own results a white wash. The hospital didn't want their record rooms involved in fraud. I can look at my own records on an individual basis but cannot copy them or remove them from the record room."

"I see. I guess your office records will have to do. Could you provide for me your entire two years experience either way you treated aneurysms. The names on the documents should be redacted."

"Of course. It will take some time, I will have my secretary send them to you."

"Thank you. Now you have read Dr. Graves', Dr. Davis', and Mrs. Bradford's depositions. What in your opinion were the problems with Dr. Graves' care of Mr. Bradford?

"I object. That question is overbroad, lacks foundation, and assumes that Dr. Shamski has criticisms of Dr. Graves." The other lawyers for the hospital and anesthesiologist agreed. Jerry was trying to warn his expert to be careful and not go over the top.

Dr. Shamski was clearly up to the task. He had been here before many times. "First let me say that Dr. Graves has a very fine reputation. I hear from my colleagues in Boston what a fine job he is doing. But everyone makes errors. In this case Dr. Graves fell below the standard of care in his informed consent, and techniques of surgery." Jules went on in very measured and clinical tones and explained what he meant by that, following carefully the questions asked by Edwin.

Jerry relaxed. *This guy is good.* He spelled it out that without informing Julie Bradford and her deceased husband about the dangers and alternatives to surgery, Graves fell below the standard of care. Dr. Shamski had painted a good picture and did not waver in his testimony.

"Doctor we are almost done now. It's nearly lunchtime. Let me get this straight. Other than your criticism of Dr. Graves' surgical technique, if Dr. Graves had informed the patient and his wife in the manner you suggest then he would not have fallen below the standard of care."

"Yes."

"That's all I have," Edwin said and asked the other attorneys if they had questions. After they asked the usual questions to be sure Jules wasn't going to criticize the care their clients had provided, the deposition was ended. Jerry asked Edwin if he wanted a ride to the airport and he accepted. Jerry waved good-bye to Terry as he left, almost sorry that he wasn't staying in town longer. She, too, seemed disappointed.

As they settled in the limousine's back seat Edwin raised his eyebrows and cocked his head in the direction of the office they had just left said, "Same ol' Jerry. Do you ever give it a rest?"

"What on earth are you talking about?" Jerry feigned ignorance. "Well what did you think of Dr. Shamski?" Jerry asked, quickly changing the subject.

"Very smooth. He will do well in court. I'll be interested in seeing his work experience. Should be a contrast with Dr Davis' or Graves' for that matter."

"Dueling experts. The jury will disregard them as usual and pay attention to what our respective clients say. Look, I know Dr. Graves has a great reputation. Why don't we settle this thing without a trial?" Jerry decided to test the waters and see how far the defense was willing to go.

Edwin sat looking out the window as the limousine headed down the 405 freeway to Los Angeles International Airport. It was a lovely day in Southern California making him wonder why in the world anyone lived in Boston. He could see private homes mixed in with industrial businesses and endless shopping malls. Maybe that's why.

"Jerry I grew up with you. I saw you get into many fights. In fact you always tried to pick a fight with me. If it weren't for your older brother I wouldn't be here today. You never gave up. So, let me say that you offering to try and settle a case would be like Hitler willing to go the extra mile with the Russians."

"Love your analogy. Makes me feel good. You always tried to

make me feel stupid by spouting history stuff. You deserved to have your black ass kicked," Jerry laughed. "Seriously. Give it some thought."

"I'll talk to my client and the insurance company. Any settlement still goes on his record and he feels strongly that he did nothing wrong. I realize he is naive about the legal process and you can't wait to rip him a new one in court, but don't underestimate him."

"If I were you. I would settle this case. There is no way a jury is going to vote against this grieving widow. She's young and attractive. Think about it. The hospital is about ready to settle."

This was news to Edwin and not good news. Edwin continued to watch the Southern California wall to wall building landscape then he said, "Let me ask you a question. If you had a brain aneurysm that needed fixing and there were only two choices, would you go to Dr. Graves or Dr. Shamski?"

Jerry had no answer.

Seventeen

Tim Graves pushed his tray along the cafeteria line. The broccoli had had the life steamed out of it. The mashed potatoes were lumpy and the chicken pieces, with leathery brown skin, languished in a pool of fat. He decided to pass. He stopped by the salad bar. As least the greens and vegetable toppings were fresh. Tim grabbed a half pint of milk and headed into the doctor's dining room. He didn't particularly like the hospital's policy of doctors eating apart from the rest of the hospital staff. Invariably a colleague would sit down next to him and begin griping about one thing or the other. The idea of isolating doctors from the remaining cafeteria crowd, especially the nurses, was an effort to control gossip and the possible violation of doctor/patient confidentiality. More than once a slip of the tongue led to a lawsuit. More importantly, Tim lamented to himself, doctors were cut out of the really good gossip. It was the nurses who seemed to know everything. Tim spotted a table that was empty and be made a beeline for it. He knew some of the doctors in the room but the majority were new faces. Before he could dive into his salad he heard, "Mind if I sit with you?"

Tim looked up and saw John McConnell, his old nemesis, already settling into the chair opposite his. "Be my guest," Tim replied half-heartedly.

Taking a clue from Tim's dour expression, McConnell said, "Let me guess. It's the lawsuit isn't it? I just left the risk management meeting. I overheard the administrator say the suit with the hospital settled this morning."

"Great. My attorney called me late last night and warned me it might happen. How much?" Tim asked chewing on a sliver of carrot.

"You don't want to know. One million. They thinks it's a good deal what with all the fuss over this case."

Tim eyed McConnell carefully. When McConnell was medical staff present it was he who made the fuss. Unnecessarily so, Tim felt. It was McConnell's maneuvering that led to Tim's suspension. That punishment didn't accomplish anything except to create a lot of anger and resentment. He didn't say anything but McConnell got the message.

"Hey I know what you're thinking. I was wrong. It was stupid and unnecessary, and even after all I did to you, you went to bat for me over the kidney screw up. I am forever grateful."

When Tim had "returned from the dead" he chaired a medical staff committee looking into a case done by the chief resident while McConnell was supervising. In that case they had removed the wrong kidney and the patient died while on dialysis several weeks later. Tim had discovered that the x-rays were mislabeled and McConnell got off with a warning. The patient at autopsy was found to have cancer throughout her body and the hospital settled the case with the family.

"What's done is done. I just want to get through this and get on with my life."

"I know what you're going through. I've been there myself, twice. We won both times but the process nearly did me in. Someone who hasn't been sued doesn't know what it takes out of you."

"Tell me about it! It's on my mind all the time. I talk about it with Meg every night or worse, I don't talk at all."

"Have you been deposed yet?" McConnell asked looking around the room to be sure no one was within earshot.

"Yes. That was a trip. The lawyers say don't take it personally. What BS. It's very personal." Tim dug his fork into his salad but came up empty. Even his salad had lost its appeal.

"Did the subject of your suspension come up during the depo?" Jerry asked.

"Yes, and it shouldn't have. What do you know about it?"

"I know Cleary, been an expert witness for him. When you were 'dead', I told him privately about your suspension. Said I would testify in court about it if his case came to trial."

"Well thanks a lot," Tim said with a touch of anger.

"Back off. You were 'dead' and I wanted to keep Cleary on my side. Preventive maintenance if you will. The guy's a bull-dog. It was a business decision. Relax, I called him several weeks ago, told him I wouldn't testify. He could subpoena me of course, but I doubt he'd do that."

"Thanks. I suppose," Tim said in a more conciliatory tone.

McConnell looked around the room. It was nearly one o'clock and most of the doctors had left. Leaning into Tim he said, "We can't talk about the facts of this case but why hasn't your attorney subpoenaed my medical records. I mean Bradford's records?"

"What are you talking about?" Tim asked, surprised. "We have all his records."

"Think now. Who sent you this case in the first place?" McConnell asked in a whisper.

"A neurologist. Stan Giddings."

"And who sent the patient to Giddings."

"An internist. We have his records. It was a doctor in Wellesley named Peterson or Patterson. I'm not sure. Why the twenty questions?"

"Jim Patterson. I know because I sent the patient to him. Mr. Bradford was my patient. He didn't want anyone to know he was seeing me. Strictly confidential."

"Okay. So am I supposed to ask why he was seeing you or what?" Tim asked, uncertain of the legalities in this situation.

"You could but I won't tell you. All I am doing is giving you information that you didn't solicit from me."

"Well okay. What am I supposed to do with this information?"

"You've heard what I have to say. You don't want to answer questions under oath about our conversation. That's all. I gotta go. No hard feelings?"

"Hey it's over," Tim gave a tight smile. He would never really trust McConnell.

Tim dumped his tray and headed to his office. He had an afternoon of appointments and paper work. The lawsuit was hanging heavy and seemed to dominate his day no matter where he went or whom he encountered. He had talked to more lawyers in the past several weeks than he had in his entire life. As he strolled down the hallway to get the elevator to his office he heard someone behind him shout his name. He turned around and saw Nancy Kimball the cardiovascular nurse running toward him.

When she caught up to him she was out of breath and between gasps said, "I've been meaning to give you this for over a week." She stopped while she caught her breath and fished around in a large book bag looking for the videotape of Tim's patient. "I saw you coming out of the doctor's lounge, wanted to give this to you personally. I don't trust the hospital mail," she laughed, finally catching her breath.

"What is it?" Tim asked.

"It's a videotape of one of your patients. Remember several years ago my boss was doing a study on informed consent in heart surgery patients. They videotaped in one of the private rooms, 204. A patient of yours was put in there when the neurosurgery floor was full."

Tim thanked her for going to so much trouble as he accepted the tape, his mind still focused on his encounter with McConnell.

"Hey this isn't the Tim Graves I know. Why the long face? Although I think I know," she said with a concerned look on her face. She also remembered Tim when he was a resident and nothing seemed to bother him.

Tim pulled her to the side away from the traffic in the hallway so they couldn't be overheard. "What have you heard?"

"Well let's just say that nurses do talk. I heard from one of the nurses involved in your malpractice suit that the hospital settled. The hospital feels it was a good deal because they don't see how you can win a suit like this."

"Great. Just what I wanted to hear," Tim said leaning his back against the wall and staring at the ceiling as he shoved the VCR tape into his pocket.

"If it means anything the nurses are pulling for you. They think the hospital pulled the rug out from under you. But I suppose it was a business decision."

"Thanks," Tim said, "I have to get to the office. Give my best to your boss," he said as he turned and pushed the button for the elevator.

Upstairs he entered his office for some appointments before clinic in the afternoon. He waved to Lisa Harding who was sitting waiting for a one o'clock meeting.

"Come on in," he said to her. "Are there any messages I need to return right away?" Tim asked his secretary Judith Winters.

"No," she said.

"Hold the calls," he said as he waved Lisa into this office.

Tim took the videotape out of his pocket and tossed it into his lower desk drawer already filled with videotapes of prior operations or commercial videotapes of medical products. "Well how are you today?" he said to Lisa as he sat down.

"I'm doing well. I hope you are not interrupting something for me. I asked Judy if she could work me in today. Things are heating up with the litigation against you."

Every time Tim heard the word litigation his heart sank. He wondered if he would ever get used to being the target of a malpractice suit. He rubbed his hands over his face and sat back and said, "How so?"

"Well Mr. Stokes deposed Dr. Shamski in Los Angeles yesterday. He said he was quite critical of your care. Mainly the informed consent issue and the way in which the surgery was done. Claimed that the operation should not have been done. He would have recommended using a catheter."

"I suppose if you looked at this from a medical point of view, he has his opinion and I have mine. By the way who is Dr. Shamski? Am I supposed to know him?"

"Well he has a modest neurosurgical practice in West Los Angeles. Does mostly medical-legal work and workman's compensation. Says most of his patients have their aneurysms treated with the catheter."

"I've said it before and I will say it again. That aneurysm was too large for catheter clotting. Did he even bother to look at the angiograms?"

"I don't think he did, I'll ask Mr. Stokes. But I'm pretty sure he didn't want to get into that with him, save it for trial." Shifting gears she said, "As you probably already know by now the hospital settled with the plaintiff. It's been in the works for a while. It does raise questions at trial and it doesn't look good to the jury."

"Whose side are they on anyway?" Tim asked still unclear about the litigation process. He couldn't be any more discouraged.

"Well they're on their own side. If they could they would have you pay the whole schmeer. It's about business."

"Let's see. I bring in hundreds of patients, get charged overhead on my grants, and in return the hospital slips the knife in my back."

"I'm sorry," she said and truly meant it. "That's all I wanted to tell you. I told Judith that we are looking at the first week in April for trial. I expect it will go on for three weeks. You should plan to be there every day."

"That's impossible. What will I do with my patients?" Tim protested.

"We can't force you to be there, but it's the right thing to do. In a trial such as this appearances are critical. We need you there, looking confident and capable. The jury will be watching you."

Could it get any worse? What had he got himself into? Everywhere he turned there was a wall closing in on him.

Lisa stood to leave and Tim stood as well. There was something else he meant to tell her. Of course, his conversation with McConnell.

"I've wondered if you have obtained the medical records of Mr. Bradford from the offices of Dr. John McConnell?" Tim asked.

Lisa furrowed her brow. "John McConnell the urologist?" she asked.

"You know who he is?"

"Yes. We've represented him in the past. He did well. I didn't think he would, he fooled us all. Why would he have records of Mr. Bradford?"

"He asked me today if we had them. Out of the blue. Right after he told me he had informed Mr. Cleary of my suspension after the Bradford case."

"When did he do that?" she asked obviously annoyed.

"This was back when it was thought I was dead and Cleary was going after everyone in sight. McConnell thought since I was dead it wouldn't hurt to give the information of my suspension to Cleary. Apparently he and Cleary worked together on several cases."

"Still that information is privileged and protected from discovery except if someone voluntarily comes forward."

"McConnell knows that, he has refused to testify in court against me," Tim said coming out from behind the desk.

Lisa wasn't about to leave just yet as she processed what she had just learned. Finally she said, "He, plaintiff counsel, didn't bring it up at your deposition. Maybe he plans to spring it at trial." She turned and slowly walked to the door. "He'll probably subpoena McConnell and get him to testify against you."

Tim looked even more deflated by that news. In a barely audible voice Tim asked, "By the way, Ms Harding, what about the issue of my disappearance. Is that off the table now that Paulie Strata is dead?"

Lisa stopped and turned to look at Tim. "Well Mr. Cleary won't have the opportunity to call him as a witness. He could bring up the facts about your relationship with the mob. Ask probing questions about why someone would want to murder you."

"Who do you suppose killed Paulie? You know he was a patient of mine. I got to understand him a little. He had his own set of rules about life." Tim had mixed feelings about Paulie's death. He and only a handful of people know why the young mobster tried to kill him.

"I guess you haven't been reading the papers. They arrested a guy in New York. A cop in Winthrop wrote down his New York license plate number a week before the killing. Got him on tapes in the Interstate tollbooths. His uncle is a big time mafia guy in New Jersey."

"So it's all over then. They got the killer?"

"Well not exactly. Seems that they can't place him in Winthrop the day of the killing. No license plate number or Interstate photos. They searched his house and farm in New York and got nothing. Several nights ago on the late news the US Attorney for that district issued an apology. Said that the guy they caught was not their man and that the investigation was going in another direction," Lisa turned and waved goodbye.

"We'll probably never know who did it. Like Jimmy Hoffa."

"Read this morning's *Bulletin*? Some reporter dug deeper, found out the US Attorney was in this guy's platoon in Vietnam. Sounds like the good old boys network slammed the door on this one. See ya and buck up. Your best defense is to get your head into the trial. Don't just be an observer, get proactive." With that she waved goodbye.

Eighteen

Later, at home with Meg, Tim reflected on what Lisa Harding had said when she left his office. Since his "return from the dead" the lawsuit had been hanging over his head like an executioner's blade. He had been short with people lately and was losing interest in practicing medicine. Basically he was going through stage one of a lawsuit. Depression. It was clear to Tim that the patient's wife was lying about her interaction with him and the informed consent process. What could he do about it? Her statements made Tim look callous, uncaring, and sloppy. Just the opposite of what he stood for. That was it. He was worried about his image and how it was being dragged through the mud. Rather than fret about it he decided to take Lisa's advice and stop being such a wimp. How could he fight back? He was sitting on the living room couch watching the late news with Meg. The news commentator was blabbing away about the Paulie Strata killing when he had enough and clicked him off.

"Thanks," Meg said, "Every time I hear that name it sends shivers down my spine. He was such a cold-blooded animal. I don't know how you were able to operate on him, save his life after what he tried to do." Meg slid over and snuggled up to Tim. They had been living together for almost a year and were planning to marry after the lawsuit was over. Fortunately it was moving along quickly. Trial was set in two weeks after a mandatory settlement conference imposed by the judge. That was scheduled for the next week.

"I know I've been a pain in the ass. Not talking about it. The lawsuit I mean. Operating on Strata was an easy decision. This lawsuit has got me going in the wrong direction. I've been feeling sorry for myself. I just can't stand to hear the accusations made by that asshole attorney Cleary." Tim pounded his fist into the couch to emphasize his frustration.

"I know. I've been walking on eggs, afraid to set you off. It's good to talk about it. Your feelings?"

"Well it's hard to put into words. I know I'm human, not perfect. I know that there are risks for both the doctor and patient, but I'm a damned good surgeon and I know I made the right decision for the patient, regardless of the outcome. It just seems unfair that this case where the risks were high and chances for success small would be the one that ends up in court. I have made errors in judgment before that I should have been called on but wasn't."

"So this is the time you have to face the music. Like it or not, you have to be more active in your defense. You keep waiting for the lawyers to do something. How often do you call them?"

"Never. I don't want to hear bad news. Every day when I come to the office I expect to see one of those damn lawyer letters with thick paper, menacing words that I am being sued or more accusations by Cleary. I hate to even look at my mail anymore."

"Well now there's a start. You must call them periodically, the attorneys, find out what's going on. Do some research on your own. Particularly read the deposition of the expert witness to be sure your lawyer asked him the right questions. See what the expert's responses were." Meg was getting more animated as the plan formed in her mind. When she was getting started as a reporter *The Globe* assigned her to the courthouse and she covered trials for three years. Considered herself to be something of an expert in reading the directions a trial would take.

"That expert is an no-name neurosurgeon in Los Angeles. You know that gives me an idea," Tim brightened, "I'll call Jim tomorrow and see if he can find out anything about this expert." Jim was Tim's younger brother who was a defense attorney in a large Los Angeles firm. "I've been so embarrassed about this lawsuit that I haven't even talked to my in-house attorney who worshipped his older brother when we were growing up. Didn't want to disappoint him. He thinks I'm perfect."

"Now you seem to be getting it. No one thinks you're perfect except maybe your mother. But why wait for tomorrow. They're three hours behind us. Call now," Meg nearly ordered.

Tim reached over and grabbed the address wheel sitting on the table next to the couch and thumbed through it until he found Jim's number. He picked up the phone and dialed. It was eight o'clock in Altadena where Jim lived. "Hi, little brother," Tim said when Jim answered. After the mandatory pleasantries, the next half hour was spent telling Jim about the lawsuit, who was representing him, and about the expert neurosurgeon in Los Angeles. He went over what he could remember from skimming through Dr. Shamski's deposition.

When it was Tim's turn to listen Meg heard a string of "ok's," "no kiddings," and "I'll be damned." Meg stood up and mouthed that she was going to bed. Finally, at nearly midnight, Tim hung up the phone. By this time Meg had showered and was in bed. He walked into the bedroom stripping off his shirt and said, "I'm glad I did that. He was so supportive. Said I would win but it would be a big fight. He seemed to enjoy it. Wasn't bothered that I was being sued. Said doctors get sued on an average of three to five times every five to seven years. Says I've been lucky," Tim beamed. He felt better, much better than when he had talked to his own attorneys. Of course they had to face the reality of possibly losing while his brother was free to be a cheerleader.

"So what did he say about Shamski? That's why you called," Meg said patting the bed, inviting him to sit down and tell her everything

"He knows him. Has faced him in court before. He's very smooth but has limited clinical experience. Spends most of his time with worker's comp cases and testifying. Against doctors mostly. I told him about his records being lost in a fire and Jim was going to look into that. He remembers something about it. Suspicious fire." Tim leaned back against the pillows and sighed. It seemed like the more he talked about it the better he felt. He had kept everything bottled up inside for so long it was like popping the lid on a can of soda after shaking it.

"Anything else?"

"Yeah. He said the most important thing was for me to read my deposition. Be sure I don't change anything at trial. Thoroughly read the medical records and the expert's depositions. Sometimes attorneys don't always ask the right questions. Says I should be leading my defense not following it. Says the best doctors to defend are those who know the case cold, every aspect of it."

"Well. Where are the medical records? You haven't been reading anything here at home."

"They, Harding and Stokes, didn't want me reading the medical record before my deposition but that's about to change. I have the various depositions but I've only glanced at them."

"Well tomorrow's Friday. You get everything you can and we'll spend the weekend working on it. You know it just occurred to me that Cleary hired an investigator to snoop around. Why can't we do the same? I mean me. That's what I am, an investigative reporter." Meg had been a reporter with *The Globe* but shortly after her return from the "dead" was let go. Budget cuts they said. She was now working for *The Bulletin* and liked it. It was more upbeat, less liberal and more willing to look at both sides of a controversy. Besides she had grown tired of the elitist attitude at *The Globe.*

"Where will you start?" Tim asked.

"You say that the plaintiff is lying. Well we'll have to see what kind of a life she's led. I know some of her background won't be useful but some may. I'll start tomorrow. Give me her full name and address, maiden name, and telephone number if you can get it "

"Tell you what. Tomorrow I'll bring home all the depositions and you can read hers. All I know is that her name is Julie T. Bradford and her dead husband is John H. Bradford. I remember that from glancing through her deposition." Tim wasn't sure whether he could allow someone else not directly involved in the trial to read the deposition but at this point he could care less.

The next morning Meg was up early for her but it was long after Tim had left for his morning rounds and surgery. She took the MTA from Chestnut Hill and by seven thirty walked into the offices of *The Bulletin*. She climbed three flights of stairs to the third floor and entered her cubicle. *The Bulletin* had only been in business seven years but they were going modern and scanning their copy into a large IBM computer. It was a godsend for an investigative reporter, since not only were articles from her own newspaper in the computer but there were others including *The Globe*. The latter's editions dated back fifteen years. She started by typing in the name of Julie T. Bradford and John H. Bradford then waited patiently for a response. After several minutes, fifteen articles with those names appeared on her screen. One was clearly not the Julie T. Bradford she was interested in since it was an obituary of an eighty-year-old woman in Weymouth.

The first article from an old edition of *The Globe* was the announcement of the marriage of Julie T. Lacey to John H. Bradford of Wellesley. Later in the article it stated that this is the first marriage for Lacey but the second for Professor Bradford of MIT. It stated that his divorce had been final only a week before the announcement. A Seth Goddard is going to be best man in a private ceremony. It went on to say that Mr. Goddard is a graduate student of Professor Bradford who is chairman of the astrophysics department at MIT. Mr. Bradford also was the founder of a software company in Dedham named Outer Space Solutions.

Another article chronicled the death of Mr. Bradford two years ago after surgery for a brain aneurysm. Then there was a notice of the filing of a lawsuit against a Dr. Timothy Graves and University hospital. The third article was more recent and from the *Wall Street Journal* announcing an IPO of Outer Space Solutions Inc. Early results had been remarkable as the stock took off with

181

announcement of the company being awarded military and NASA contracts. The article went on to say that Seth Goddard the CEO and Ransr Gupta CFO were the only stockholders of record prior to the offering. The founder of the company had died and before the stock offering his wife had sold her one million shares for pennies on the dollar. She would have netted thirty million dollars if the shares were sold at the time the article was written. That bit of information peeked Meg's interest. That was a lot of money to lose. Is that why the widow was so anxious to sue Tim?

She continued to open all the Bradford stories and read them intently but didn't find anything of interest. She then typed in Julie T. Lacey. The same wedding announcement appeared. The only other article was published in a Detroit newspaper. It was brief but to the point. It stated: "Scandal rocks the University of Michigan for the second time in two weeks. Twenty year old undergraduate student, Julie T. Lacey, was expelled for cheating. She had obtained the final exam answers for a course in computer science from a married student instructor with whom she was allegedly having an illicit affair. The instructor whose name is unknown was fired. The university has been under fire recently because of several sexual harassment lawsuit involving faculty and students" Wow! What a mess. Interesting information but probably couldn't be used in court. Nevertheless she copied all the articles and would save them for Tim to give to his lawyers.

Meg thought for a moment then spun her Rolodex, which listed the names of all her contacts over the years, and came across a name of an old high school friend who worked at MIT. Billie Hogan was one of her best friends in school and they had kept in touch over the years. Mostly when Meg was doing a story on some political issue or scandal at MIT. Billie worked in the personnel office and had become an assistant director after years spent in various jobs at the prestigious institution. Later in the morning she made contact and they agreed to meet for lunch.

Meanwhile, Tim was on his own crusade. He had left early, kissing his sleeping fiancée on the forehead. He called Judith from the operating room just after eight o'clock to have her arrange a telephone conference as soon as he finished his surgery. At eleven-thirty he breezed into his office and Judith noted a distinct spring to his step that had been missing for too long.

"Good morning," he said with a grin.

"What's with the new attitude?" There had been a pall over the office as the lawsuit progressed toward trial. Judy was hoping for some good news.

"So you noticed. I've been a beast lately, but this is the new me, or rather I've decided to be more like the old me. The lawyers may think this is a game, but it's a game I'm going to win. Now, let's get Lisa Harding on the phone...please."

Judith reached for the phone. "That's more like it! I'll get her right away. When I talked to her earlier she said she would be available for your call."

"Thanks." Tim went through to his office and sat at his desk. He sifted through his inbox and was pleased that there were no thick, odious letters. Soon Judy buzzed him and he picked up the phone.

"Dr. Graves here."

On her end Lisa could detect a change in Tim's voice. Something positive."Good morning, Dr. Graves. You wanted to ask me something?"

"Yes. The McConnell records on Mr. Bradford. Where do we stand?"

"I'm sorry, what was that again?"

Trying to sound patient but firm, Tim said, "Don't you remember our conversation? Bradford was a patient of Dr. McConnell's. We need to get those records."

"Yes. Yes. I'm sorry. I'll be honest it did slip my mind. I don't think it'll be anything pertinent but I'll get a subpoena today and we'll copy the records on Monday. Anything else?" she asked brightly, hoping that was it.

"I don't agree. They could be very important. For McConnell to stick his neck out to help me, those records must be important. It would be better to have them sooner than later. I would like this all handled today."

"I will do my best. Anything else," Lisa answered stiffly. No more miss congeniality.

"Yes. Would you please send over to my office your copies of the medical records and depositions? Today. I have my own, Dr. Shamski's, and Dr. Davis' but I need all the others. I plan to spend the weekend reading all this material."

"It will be done." Lisa hung up and cursed herself for lighting a fire under their client. She had a feeling she was going to pay for that.

Nineteen

By the time Meg had taken the MTA and arrived at Kendall Square it was past noon. She hustled over to the Legal Seafood restaurant. It was mobbed but while Billie waited she had found a table and ordered two lunch specials.

They chatted like long lost friends. High school relationships seem to trump all others for their permanence and depth. Meg wondered why that was. It wasn't the best time in her life. It was more of a 'sink or swim'. I guess you remember fondly the ones who swam with you. Billie was Meg's age but not nearly as attractive. She had one failed marriage and was working on a second. She never felt secure enough with either man to leave her job. She had no children and her work was her life.

When they came to a break in their conversation Billie asked, "What's this meeting all about? I know you didn't come all the way over here in the middle of the day to reminisce." She laughed self-consciously.

"That's not true. I've been... well you know, caught up with personal things. I'm glad to see my old Southie friends whenever. But there is something you possibly could help me with." Meg went on to explain about Tim, the lawsuit, Julie Lacey aka Julie Bradford, the cheating scandal at Michigan and the sold shares in Outer Space Solutions. Soon their lunches arrived and

185

they dug into the seafood platter of shrimp, cod, lobster, and crab over a mound of angel hair pasta.

"You mean you want what I know or what I can find out? Because even though we go back a long way, it's been hard to get where I am, it means a lot to me. Especially since my husband is between jobs - again. So I can tell you what I know. That okay?" Billie forked a shrimp from her plate and plopped it into her mouth.

"Of course. This is probably nothing that will be used in court. I'm just trying to get background. You know. Know thine enemy."

"Well let's see. Professor Bradford was a real nice man. The kind that could never say 'no'. He was always polite to the people in the personnel office. He came in one day when I was screening applicants for fellowship positions, showed me a letter from a student who was living in Boston. Asked me to interview her first, see if she was okay. He always did that whenever he was looking for someone. Make sure they could pass my smell test as it were."

"That's smart. So did she? Pass, I mean."

"I interviewed her. She was very attractive and well spoken. Came from a messed up family in Chicago but was smart. Said she had been at the University of Michigan in computer science, had to quit to earn money. Came to Boston with one of the software firms, didn't like her work there. Answered an ad for a position here. She passed my review with flying colors. But there was something about her I couldn't pin down. A little too quick with the answers."

"Too smooth, in other words," Meg smiled knowingly.

"Yes. But there was more to it than that. Anyway Professor Bradford hired her. And wouldn't you know it before long there were rumors. I mean Bradford was seeing her on the side if you get what I mean. Somehow the missus found out and one thing led to another, bingo Bradford's divorced and Julie and he get married. About this time I got curious and checked with the University of Michigan, found out about the cheating scandal there but didn't tell Bradford."

"Well why didn't you check on her before that? I mean when

she was applying?"

"I was going to go through the regular process when Bradford called me after her interview with him, told me to hire her and I did." Billie picked up the napkin in her lap and dabbed some pasta sauce off her chin.

"Is that it?"

She put her napkin down on the table and said, "No. Six months after they were married Seth Goddard who was a graduate student with Bradford was rumored to be 'cozy' with Julie Bradford. Bradford never knew I guess because they remained 'happily' married." Ater throwing her air quotes Julie picked up her fork and went on, "Had children. He and Goddard of course left and started their company. Too bad John, Mr. Bradford, won't get to enjoy the company's success."

"Wow. That's more info than I expected."

"Universities are like small towns. The gossip gets around." Billie looked around the room and noticed the lunch crowd was nearly gone. She looked at her watch but didn't say anything.

"I wonder if they are still an item? Mr. Bradford being dead, the company doing well. Maybe Seth has moved on to greener pastures." Meg ate the last of her pasta.

"Can't say for sure. But one of the girls I work with saw them together in a restaurant in Natick three or four months ago. It didn't look like a business meeting if you get what I mean."

"The plot thickens. I guess she would want to keep that a secret until after the trial. Well it's great background but I don't think it can be used against her. Billie, I appreciate you taking the time, being so open. No one will ever know we talked. Lunch is on me."

"Thanks. Let's get together sometime when it's not about business. Now I should get back it's nearly one-thirty." She stood and smoothed her skirt.

"You got a date. As soon as this trial is over I want to have you and your husband over." Meg put enough money on the table to cover the bill and a generous tip and walked out of the restaurant with Billie. She came up short just as she stepped outside. She was sure she recognized Eddie Collins sitting in the corner eating by himself. Was it a coincidence or had he followed her?

The next day Tim and Meg sat down in the living room and spread the lawsuit documents on the floor. With mugs of coffee and a plate of buttered toast between them they began to tackle what appeared to be a mountain of paper. Tim began with a thorough review of the medical records and when he finished he glanced at the clock to see that three hours had gone by. Tired of being cooped up he and Meg pedaled their bicycles to Coolidge Corner where they found a delicatessen near the location of the famed Jack and Marion's that went out of business in 1971. During his training it was a real treat for Tim to eat at that venerable delicatessen. They ordered hot pastrami and Swiss cheese sandwiches on rye bread served with gobs of potato salad and pickles. Since there was so much left to do they went back home with their food.

After lunch Tim opened the envelope that had arrived from Lisa Harding's office by courier late the previous afternoon. There were about ten pages of hand written notes from Dr. McConnell's office. Nowhere among the papers could he find copies of outgoing letters to referring physicians. When Tim finished reading the record he was shocked.

"Listen to this," he said sitting up on the couch. "This is McConnell's office history and physical: 'This is a forty-four year old former professor at MIT who complains of burning on urination. Present for two weeks since returning from a trip to Japan. Has a discharge. Claims to have had sexual intercourse in Tokyo. Has had intercourse with his wife infrequently the past three years. Sites incompatibility and impotency. I thought they were hot and heavy," Tim stared at Meg with open palms that said 'what gives?'.

"I just finished reading Julie's deposition. Although Harding hit her hard on the sex thing she stuck to her guns. Claimed they were doing it four times a week." Meg winked at Tim.

"Well this record certainly disputes that. It goes on to say that a urethral smear was positive for gnids. Some gram negative organisms were also seen consistent with NSU," Tim said, laughing, knowing how much she hated medical acronyms and abbreviations.

"In English please?"

"Gnids is a shortened version of gram negative intracellular diplococci. Get it G.N.I.D," Tim spelled it out for Meg who still looked puzzled. "It means positive for gonorrhea which is a common type of venereal disease seen in Japan and elsewhere where prostitution is legal or allowed to flourish unregulated."

"So he had a fling. What does that prove?" Meg was skeptical.

"There's more. He gets treated for the infection and then returns for further evaluation. Says he had difficulty having an erection and holding it. Thinks his wife is seeing his associate. Not sure. Takes hypertensive medicines. McConnell does a complete evaluation including x-rays and cystoscopy. Finds nothing and treats him with nitroglycerin cream. Doesn't work. Then here is his last visit where he complains of headaches when he uses nitroglycerin. McConnell refers him to an internist but Bradford makes the appointment. Doesn't want anyone to know he was seeing McConnell."

"Well that's understandable. So we have a witness who is lying about her sex life with her husband. Rumors abound that she is having an affair with Seth Goddard and is still seeing him according to Billie Hogan," Meg said.

"All very interesting but it only goes to her credibility which as far as I am concerned doesn't exist. Here you have a young woman who lied about her background and gets a job at MIT. Then has an affair with her boss, breaks up his marriage and immediately marries him. Then she starts fooling around with her husband's associate. Tells colossal stories about this sex life that doesn't exist. Her behavior at Michigan should have been discovered by Lisa Harding. What about her current status with Goddard? Are they still seeing each other?" Tim stood up and stretched. It was slowly dawning on him that the truth would not always set you free.

"Well we're amateurs but look how much we learned while your lawyers haven't a clue."

They spent the remainder of Saturday and most of Sunday reviewing the material presented by Lisa Harding. Tim was convinced that other than the actual events in the operating room, most of the criticism leveled against him by Julie Bradford and the expert testimony of Dr. Shamski could be refuted. It was boiling down to how he could explain to the jury why he was unable to complete the surgery. And why John Bradford bled to death. The remainder of the lawsuit was aimed at discrediting him. He would insist upon a meeting with his attorneys in his office before Wednesday's mandatory settlement conference.

Twenty

Late Monday afternoon after he had spent eight hours in the operating room removing an olfactory tumor and seeing patients in the clinic, Tim met with Lisa and Edwin in his office. He'd was damned if he was going to drive downtown late in the day to talk to those two, especially since they were being compensated for their time by the insurance company. Tim, that is the new Tim, was not intimidated by the presence of the two lawyers in his office, as he would have been just several weeks earlier. He was beginning to get a feel for what actually was going on and was more comfortable now that he was taking an active role in his defense. Before, he felt like he had to sit and listen to the accusations and innuendos as if they were gospel. This had the desired effect of planting seeds of doubt in his mind when it came to his own abilities. As far as he was concerned the plaintiff didn't have a thing on him and he was going on the attack. He knew if he presented his new data at once to the lawyers they would have time to digest what he had said and come back with lawyerese to tell him that while this information is interesting it would have little bearing on the case. Then they would turn right around and use it to hammer Cleary. He decided to play it their way and ask the questions.

"I'm sorry to get you down here on such short notice but the settlement conference is Wednesday. Is that correct Edwin?" Tim was not going to be any more deferential to his defense team than they were to him. So first names were in play.

"As far as I know. What is it you wanted to tell us? We were using this afternoon to prepare our case for the arbitration." There was just a trace of anger in his voice.

Calmly, Tim said, "If you are too busy to meet with me perhaps I've got the wrong people defending me. I only requested you because of your reputation. I think my reputation as a neurosurgeon probably matches yours as a defense attorney. But if you were my patient I would never imply that I was too busy to see you."

Lisa sensed potential fireworks and broke in, "I think you have misunderstood what Mr. Stokes was saying, Tim. He only meant to say that he wanted to put his full effort into Wednesday's meeting and time is short."

"Thank you, Lisa, but I can fight my own battles. Dr. Graves is correct and I am sorry to have seemed perturbed about today's meeting. I detect that the esteemed neurosurgeon has become more involved and for that I am gratified. This is not the same Tim Graves I saw at the deposition several weeks ago." Edwin smiled pleasantly.

"Well I have become more involved thanks to some prodding by Lisa. I also was able to talk over everything with my fiancée and with my brother who is a defense attorney. That has helped me understand what's going on. Since time is short, I would like to begin with the issue of consortium. What is consortium and what constitutes loss of consortium?"

Lisa looked at Edwin and he shrugged as if to say 'it's all yours'. "Consortium is a legal term that means the joining together of two or three entities for a common goal. For example, two companies that are rivals might join together to form a bigger company. In terms here it means joining of two people who comfort and love each other. That includes intimacy such as sexual intercourse."

"And of course loss of this would be if the two were separated by death or divorce. Now what if one partner is having an affair during, in this case, her consortium." Tim wanted to pin down his lawyers as much as he could. He knew they twisted words to meet whatever argument they were making.

Edwin couldn't stand it any longer and jumped in. "Loss can also be if they are still together but for some reason or another, a medical procedure or medication produces impotency. Then the person can claim loss of consortium even though they are still partners."

"What if one partner secretly seeks outside sexual gratification and contracts a sexually transmitted disease? Can the other still claim loss of consortium?"

"Well that gets a little harder. It wouldn't look good in front of a jury that's for sure. The party with the social disease might claim it was a once in a lifetime thing, etc. But again juries aren't going to buy that," Edwin stated.

"What if the party claiming loss of consortium actually was having an affair outside the partnership and lied about her own sexual history under oath?"

Edwin was getting tired of the hypotheticals and said, "Enough with the twenty questions Tim. Let us know what you have."

"It's actually what we have. The records of Mr. Bradford you obtained from John McConnell's office." Tim looked at Lisa who was slowly turning pink.

"Mr. Stokes, I apologize. Dr. Graves had informed me late last week about this matter with John McConnell. It seems Mr. Bradford had been a patient of his. I subpoenaed the records late Friday and had a copy messengered to Tim. I must confess I have not looked at them."

Edwin wasn't about to dress down his young associate in front of a client. That would come later. "Well, Dr. Graves, let's hear it."

"Pardon me while I recover here. I'm just a bit stunned that you were unaware of the subpoena. I guess important things can be overlooked in a busy lawyer's office." Tim wanted both Edwin Stokes and Lisa Harding to hear his message, loud and clear.

He went on, "The short answer is that John Bradford contracted gonorrhea in Japan on a visit. As well as non-specific urethritis. He also had been virtually impotent for three years before he died and sought help from Dr. McConnell with no success. He also suspected that his wife was stepping out on him with one of his associates Seth Goddard. Meg, my fiancée did some snooping and found out a lot about our grieving widow."

Edwin was silent as he processed what he was hearing. Finally he said, "Let's hear what Meg found out."

Tim went on to tell him about Meg's lunch with Billie Logan and Julie's lying on her application for work as well as the rumors with Seth Goddard. The trouble at the University of Michigan. Also the recent sighting of Seth and Julie at a restaurant in Natick. Meg spotting Eddie Collins in the restaurant where she was meeting with Billie Logan. Edwin listened intently and when Tim finished he shook his head.

"Some of those things like the lying on the application about her status at the University of Michigan would require us subpoenaing her employee file at MIT. The article in the Detroit newspaper would be helpful to have. Certainly the rumors about her sexual proclivities would be difficult to verify. The records of John McConnell are damaging to her sworn testimony." Edwin looked over at Lisa to see if she wanted to add anything. Lisa simply nodded in agreement.

"Here's the way I see it," Tim said. "Mr. Cleary hires a professional investigator and knows more about my personal life than I do. He probably broke into Luther Kennedy's office and his mother's home." Tim had heard from Luther about the break-ins presumably by Eddie Collins. Luther had received a report about the unlocked door in his office and swore that he had locked it before he left. When he checked his files he could clearly see they had been rifled. A visit to his attic sealed his suspicions. "They nearly tear my life apart, but we can't fight back?"

"That's a good question and maybe we should. But there is a risk in every endeavor. It wouldn't look good for the defense to be ganging up on a grieving widow now would it?"

"When is a grieving widow not a grieving widow? What is the judicial system, a crap shoot? Why not lay the facts on the table and let the jury decide. If Julie Bradford lied about one thing then she'll continue to lie. She was sitting in her husband's hospital room when I went over everything. Now she claims not to have been there. She's lying."

"I wish it were that simple. That's not how it works. We, Lisa and I, have a lot of work to do with this new information. Mr. Cleary is not going to like it when I tell him."

Lisa spoke up and said, "I'm sorry I didn't pay more attention to Dr. McConnell's records. They certainly speak for themselves and will be a great help. Is there anything else?"

"I am not happy with the questions presented to Dr. Shamski at his deposition. It would have been important to establish that he actually reviewed the angiograms before he commented on the type of management he recommended."

"Since I did his deposition I'll address that," Edwin said. "He stated that he would have thrombosed the aneurysm with a catheter based on what he read in the radiology report. I plan to pursue that angle in court. Get him to admit that he had never seen the angiograms before he rendered an opinion."

"I see. Is this what you call strategy or did you just come up with this answer?" Tim looked doubtful at Edwin's explanation.

Edwin kept his cool at this rebuke and said, "I tried to call you several time to go over what questions I should ask. I left messages here at your office and my calls weren't returned. Before trial we will go over everything thoroughly."

"That's a fair criticism. I did dodge those calls expecting bad news. No one likes to return calls to a lawyer. But that's the old Tim Graves. I want to know everything that goes on. Here is my home phone number." Tim wrote down his number on two business cards and gave one to Lisa and one to Edwin.

"Well that should wrap it up," Lisa said. "I'll call your secretary late tomorrow and confirm that the settlement conference is on for Wednesday." Lisa stood, picked up her briefcase and smiled at Tim. "Well it seems as if Mrs. Bradford may have bitten off more than she can chew when she tangled with you. Trial begins in two weeks so this will be over before too long. Welcome to the team."

Jerry Cleary had spent a sleepless night and was irritable when he arrived at his office on Tuesday. His nose had been stuffy all night and several times he felt the jab of his wife's elbow while trying to breathe through his mouth. He had received a phone call the day before from Eddie Collins giving him a 'freebie'. He told Jerry that he had spotted Meg Logan the reporter and soon to be wife of Tim Graves having lunch at Legal Seafood in Cambridge. It was purely by chance he was there, he told Jerry. He was tailing a lawyer whose wife had hired him to follow her husband. Her suspicions proved true as he witnessed him having lunch with a beautiful young thing half his age.

He had followed Meg's companion back to the main administration building at MIT. It seems her name was Billie Logan and she worked in the personnel department. Even had her name on the door. This was too much of a coincidence. Meg could very well be snooping around and chasing down his client's past. Hell, he didn't even know much about his client's past. She wasn't the one on trial but still he worried. She seems so smooth and self assured yet so vulnerable. In the good old days clients came in with a run of the mill "slip and fall" case, he got them some money, problem solved. Now he is hiring investigators and so is the defense or so it would seem.

He sniffled again and fumbled with his nasal inhaler before giving two puffs in each nostril. The medicine just wasn't working as well it did when he first started using it. That meant a trip back to that old quack ENT doctor again. But that would have to wait until after the trial. He was too busy getting ready for the court-mandated arbitration tomorrow. He had called Julie Bradford yesterday afternoon after Collins called. He wanted to go over her testimony and be sure he wasn't going to be blindsided by something Meg Logan discovered on her own. He read through her deposition and with the exception of her exaggerated claims about her sex life everything seemed in order. Jerry still liked his chances. The hospital had settled last week and this put him in a stronger position to deal with the defense or if it came to it, would help him at trial.

Just as he finished the review of Julie's deposition his secretary announced that Mrs. Bradford had arrived. Jerry opened his office door to greet his client just as she was settling into a chair. Jerry smiled at her and motioned for her to come in. She stood and smiled sweetly at Jerry's secretary and said, "That was quick." Julie was wearing make-up today with deep red lipstick and dramatic eye shadow. She was dressed in a two-piece green pants suit with yellow pinstripes. Perched on top of her hair was a chic beret.

"Have a seat. Can I get you anything? Coffee, water, whatever," Jerry smiled.

"Thanks for asking," Julie said as she sat down in a chair across the desk from where Jerry sat. He wanted to keep the tenor of the meeting more businesslike since he might have to ask some tough questions. "But no thanks. What's this about?"

"Well tomorrow we'll be meeting for a mandatory settlement conference. It happens in almost every civil case. The judge wants to see if we can get through this without a trial. Just like we did with the hospital. Some issues have come up since we last met," Jerry said cautiously. He didn't want to imply that he doubted her story.

"What kind of issues?" Julie looked puzzled. Alert.

"Well we know that the defense has been over to MIT probably looking into your work history there. Is there anything I should know?" Jerry eyed her closely waiting to judge her response.

As if on cue tears appeared at the corner of her eyes. "Of course not. How humiliating to be investigated like this. I'm not on trial."

Good performance, but Jerry but didn't believe her. "Are you sure there isn't something you want to tell me. Say about Seth Goddard. You were there when he was weren't you?"

Julie straightened up and said, "Seth was a graduate student when John and I were married. In fact he was part of the wedding ceremony. There was nothing going on between us. Oh we met for coffee when John was on one of his trips out of town. I suppose that could have been misconstrued by the campus rumor mill. We had nothing to hide."

"Anything about your job application I should know about?" Jerry wasn't convinced about her story.

"No."

"Please Mrs. Bradford. I need to know everything if you expect me to represent you to the best of my ability."

Julie stared at her attorney trying to decide if he had found something about her past. She decided to be forthright and said, "Well, okay, there was an incident at the University of Michigan when I was a starry eyed sophomore. I was seeing an instructor who was married. One thing led to another and he helped me in just the slightest way on an exam. The department chairman found out and before I knew it I was expelled. The instructor was fired." She finished by looking down at her hands folded in her lap.

"And did you put this little episode on your application to MIT?"

She looked up and coldly said, "Of course not. I would never find work if I did that. That's in the past. Twelve years ago. Why does that have to do with anything?"

"Well it could be used against you. Goes to your credibility. Meg Logan, our doctor's fiancée, was an investigative reporter for *The Globe* and now *The Bulletin*. If there is anything to find out she will do it."

"Well as far as deep dark secrets go that's it. Do I have to be at this settlement conference?" Julie asked, tearing up just a bit.

"Technically no. But the judge wants this formal with a court reporter and referee. Ordinarily these proceeding are done at the courthouse a week or two before trial in front of an alternate judge. But things are so busy over there that we are using a private arbitration service in the Hancock. There are a bunch of old, retired lawyers or judges who hear these cases. It would not look good to have you missing this. Dr. Graves will be there."

"Oh, brother. This is getting to be complicated. But I need this to go right. Things are tight," Julie sighed.

"Is your fiance getting antsy? The settlement with the hospital should help you get through the rough patches, but you won't see any of that until the trial is over. That's part of the agreement and as I told you before we have to prevail in court to get that settlement. There's no appeal for the hosptial."

Julie quit work when she got married and the thought of going back to work did not appeal to her. She needed this lawsuit to go her way, and soon.

The next morning, promptly at nine o'clock, Jerry entered the offices of Bay State Arbitrators Inc. He was greeted by a secretary who sat behind a desk in the plush lobby. The massive offices encompassed more than half of the fortieth floor. The attractive secretary was framed by a floor to ceiling window with a spectacular view of Boston laid out as if in a living portrait. Jerry was told that his arbitrator this morning would be Judge Nathan Wilcox retired superior court judge. Since this was a private service the secretary led him to his assigned conference room and offered to get him coffee. Jerry accepted and when he entered the conference room found Betsy Gallucci setting up her recording devices. Jerry smiled at her but was not in a playful mood.

Betsy smiled back as Jerry sat down and opened his briefcase. He was it for the plaintiff today. No Jason Damon. No battery of supporting lawyers for him. The facts were straightforward. Dr. Graves through his negligence had done in his client's husband and she was destitute. Well sort of destitute he told himself.

"It's awfully nice of you to keep the business coming my way. I wouldn't blame you for using someone else." Betsy looked around to be sure no one by the door was listening.

"Betsy you are the best in the business. It's a business decision. Nothing more."

She pouted and said, "Jerry is having a downer is he? Well thanks anyway. Are you set for this?"

"You bet. It's not a matter of if, it's a matter of how much," Jerry chortled confidently.

Betsy nodded her head not in agreement but in acknowledgment of why Jerry would think that. "Remember. I told you. I don't believe your client is being totally candid. She puts on a good show but there's something about her."

Jerry stared at Betsy with a blank face. He didn't want to tip his hand but he was beginning to agree with her. "How's your family?" changing the subject.

"Good. My dad was shocked but not surprised that Paulie Strata bought the farm. Said he's never seen Tony Santori so happy when he cut his hair last week. You know they're thinking of dropping the case against him and his brother?"

"No I didn't know that. I've been busy. Haven't read a newspaper in days. That Krosnowski hasn't called me since he blamed the murder on my snooping around."

"Well, shouldn't he?"

"Can we not talk about this now. I have a splitting headache."

As Betsy was about to reply Lisa Harding breezed into the room. She smiled brightly at Betsy and Jerry. With a feeling of dread, Jerry wondered why she seemed so cheerful. "Mr. Stokes is right behind me. Dr. Graves is waiting in the lobby. So where's your client?"

"She'll be here. Don't worry." Jerry's tentacles were up. Just then Edwin Stokes strolled in with Dr. Graves following. Betsy Gallucci watched the show out of the corner of her eye. Dr. Graves was dressed in a very nice, dark pin striped suit and appeared quite handsome, she thought. He didn't have that dour look she remembered from his deposition. The anesthesiologist's lawyer arrived and there were greetings all around. There were no hospital attorneys and Betsy knew right away what that meant.

"What great weather we're having for the end of March," Jerry said. "My client will be here momentarily." He was beginning to feel like he should have brought Jason Damon along just to even up the sides.

The secretary from the lobby popped her head in and told the assembled group that Mrs. Bradford had arrived and would be in as soon as she stops at the ladies room. After everyone turned down offers of refreshments the secretary said that Judge Wilcox would be ready to begin promptly at ten.

Minutes later Julie Bradford entered and the room was suddenly quiet. Jerry pointed to the chair next to his. After she was seated quiet conversation began again. She did not look at Dr. Graves but he eyed her openly. She was wearing simple clothes again, a black skirt and white blouse with a black knit cardigan. She wore light makeup and black pumps with no stockings. The appearance of someone still in mourning. Tim just shook his head slightly at seeing her again after two years.

Suddenly the door opened with a swoosh and Nathan Wilcox entered with a stack of papers under his left arm. The retired judge was seventy-five years old but still had a bounce to his step. He wore a dark suit with a red tie. Nathan Wilcox was almost six feet tall but slightly bent over to a degree consistent with his age. He had a handsome, wrinkled face with a thin gray mustache above his upper lip. "Good morning everyone," he boomed, "I trust we are all ready for today's proceedings." With that he sat down at the head of the table and motioned to Betsy to begin.

He said to her, "Today is the 31st of March 1988. We are meeting here at the request of superior court Justice Robert Cull in the matter of Bradford versus Graves et al. Would you please swear in everyone Miss Gallucci."

Betsy had worked at their office before and Judge Wilcox remembered her well.

Betsy swore in each of the participants and when she finished Judge Wilcox said, "I have received written summaries from each of the parties involved and reviewed them in their entirety. The purpose of this meeting is to see if we can't settle the complaint against Dr. Graves. The hospital has settled with plaintiff but compensation has been held until the trial is over. Mr. Cleary would you begin."

"Thank you your honor. As you know to bring a malpractice action against a physician or institution in the state of Massachusetts there is now a tribunal process introduced in 1986. This was actually one of the first cases to go through that process and plaintiff received a favorable ruling. You have all the documents related to that your honor. In that meeting we satisfied the five criteria of the statutes before a lawsuit can go forward. One there was a patient/doctor relationship. Two, the standard of care owed by Dr. Graves to Mr. Bradford. Three, the defendant acted negligently. Four, plaintiff's husband suffered injury. Five, the defendant doctor caused plaintiff's husband's injury. In this case death."

Tim sat there with a bemused look on his face. Just two or three weeks ago a verbal attack on him would have brought anger and frustration. But now it was only something that he had to endure. It seemed that lawyers had their own language and there was nothing he could do about it. By using the most hyperbolic words initially in their complaint such as outrageous, gross negligence, uncaring, incompetent, egregious, indifferent, there were few acceptable words left in their arsenal if they wanted to kick things up a notch. By this time Tim had become desensitized to their language and short of swearing there was nothing Mr. Cleary could say that hadn't already been said. Perhaps he is holding something back for trial. Like scumbag, miscreant, or even asshole. Tim was amusing himself while Jerry droned on with the same legal rhetoric he'd heard before.

When Jerry was through, Judge Wilcox asked Edwin to respond. Edwin liked Wilcox because he had not only been a good attorney when he was practicing, he was very practical and used common sense as a judge. By some mistake he was appointed to the bench not because of political connection but because he was competent. In fact, he had been appointed by a Democrat Governor who was well aware of his anti-abortion leanings. Nathan Wilcox was a practicing Catholic with six children but he worked hard to keep his personal feelings separate from his judicial duties.

"Good day Judge Wilcox, it's nice to see you again." Edwin was from the old school where there was civility in the courtroom. Since there was a court reporter and the witnesses were sworn he chose to use courtroom decorum. Judge Wilcox nodded but did not audibly respond. Edwin continued, "The action brought against Dr. Graves, who is one of the leading neurosurgeons in the world, is an outrage. There is nothing in his behavior or action that warrants any compensation for damages. However, his insurance company has authorized me to consider any settlement offer that might be proposed by plaintiff, so I am bound to do that." The lawyer for the anesthesiologist joined with this statement.

Nathan Wilcox allowed Edwin's words to sink in. Tim was wondering why Edwin didn't just call Julie Bradford a liar and show them McConnell's records. "Well Mr. Stokes it seems as if the tribunal thought there was negligence based on expert testimony by Dr. Robert Hastings of St. Mary's hospital. He is a well-known neurosurgeon in the community and was very adamant about it. In fact the tribunal vote was three to zero. You aren't going to give some wiggle room here?"

"We'll listen to what Mr. Cleary proposes but we are set for trial."

"Mr. Cleary do you care to respond."

"The defendant's lawyer must be kidding. Dr. Graves, without proper consent or care fell below the standard of care by not informing his patient of the risks of this procedure. He also performed the surgery carelessly leading to Mr. Bradford's demise. As a result we have Mrs. Bradford with her two children left to fend for themselves. She has lost her husband of ten plus years and his companionship, which was very important for her. The loss of consortium extends deeply in that they had a loving relationship of longstanding. I will not go into detail but suffice to say they enjoyed a healthy marital relationship." Jerry stopped to let his words sink in. He went on to add some more details and then finished his spiel.

Judge Wilcox nodded to Edwin who weighed in that informed consent had been given and that plaintiff was present. He acknowledged that the meeting was not documented in the progress or nursing notes. Judge Wilcox took notes during the discussion.

Finally after an hour of back and forth the Judge called for a fifteen minutes break.

Edwin and Tim retired to the men's room. While standing at the urinal Tim couldn't hold out any longer and said, "What the hell's going on? Why all the dancing around? Just tell the Judge the plaintiff is lying."

"Settle down. Now you're in my bailiwick, I'll call the shots. Let Jerry put that rope out as far as he can then we'll snap it. I'm just about ready but be patient." Edwin smiled at Tim. "You know if we lawyers listened to you doctor's about strategy we'd lose every time."

"Does that include finding documents that destroy her credibility? Finding out she was kicked out of school for cheating. If Meg and I hadn't uncovered those things we would not be in a very good position here."

"You did well. No question. But I'm talking strategy. The time will come when it will be apparent to even you that the hammer must drop." Edwin could dish it out as well as Tim.

Back in the conference room everyone resumed their seats. Judge Wilcox reminded all present they were still under oath. "Now Mr. Cleary, I think we have heard your side and the defendant's rebuttal. What are you asking in the way of damages? "

"Because of financial considerations, my client was forced to prematurely to sell her husband's privately held stock to his surviving partners. That stock was sold for pennies on the dollar. Although the sale netted her 100,000 dollars, today it's worth thirty million. She had to pay excess medical bills despite her deceased husband having excellent health insurance. At the present she has little left to live on. Along with that she has lost a loving companion and has been depressed since his death. Because Dr. Graves was so cavalier about my client's husband and his problems we are seeking punitive damages. Putting that all together we are asking for eight million dollars."

Judge Wilcox nodded in a non-committal way and turned to Edwin.

"Your response, Mr. Stokes?"

Edwin began to shuffle papers and finally found what he was looking for. "We find the demand totally unacceptable. In fact we are prepared to challenge at this time that Mrs. Bradford is an injured party. I have obtained the medical record of Mr. Bradford's visits to Dr. John McConnell and I would like at this time to enter them into evidence."

Jerry wasn't about to let that happen. "This is an outrageous attempt by the defense to discredit my client. I move that these documents be reviewed by me before they are allowed," he nearly shouted. His headache was getting worse and this bit of news was not good therapy.

"Perhaps all parties should be excused from the room and principal counsel will discuss this with me off the record. That includes you Miss Gallucci," Judge Wilcox smiled.

After the room cleared and only Jerry, Edwin and Judge Wilcox were left looking at each other. Judge Wilcox asked, "Edwin what's this all about? Isn't this a bit dramatic?"

"I apologize your honor but I only received these documents on Monday. I was hoping they wouldn't have to be used. Since plaintiff has demanded such a large settlement I am forced to do it."

Jerry was fuming. "Cut the courtroom stuff Edwin. Let's hear it."

"Very well. Mr. Bradford was a patient of Dr. John McConnell for approximately three years before his aneurysm surgery. He was treated for impotence or at least lack of sexual desire for his wife. He had contracted a venereal disease on a trip to Japan and was treated for that. In the doctor's notes there is a statement that Mrs. Bradford was having an affair with his partner Seth Goddard. Also I have a news clipping here regarding the expulsion of Mrs. Bradford from the University of Michigan for cheating and having an affair with a married instructor. Do you want me to go on?"

Jerry could have wrung the neck of his client. But she had told him about the expulsion and she might not have known about the visits to Dr. McConnell. The affair issue is hearsay.

"Well I was aware of her expulsions twelve years ago and it is not pertinent to the case. She was unaware of her husband's problem, which was of his own creation. Also she denies vehemently that she had anything but a platonic relationship with Seth Goddard Mr. Bradford's partner," Jerry said.

Judge Wilcox was having a hard time getting his mind around Jerry's argument. Certainly the expulsion was not relevant but it did speak to her credibility. Her loss of consortium argument had taken a big hit. "If I were ruling from the bench I would find these records damaging to your case Jerry. Certainly she can be queried about her past if it has to do with her character."

Edwin continued, "I took the step of subpoenaing her personnel record from MIT yesterday. They were very cooperative. Under the question 'have you ever been dismissed as a student, employee, etc for punitive reasons' she answered no."

"I was also aware of that. How was she going to find work if she disclosed this regretful indiscretion? One can hardly blame her for not being candid."

"I believe the very nature of these pre-employment questions is to determine if a potential employee is honest about any past indiscretions. To have made mistakes is understandable, to lie about it is unacceptable," Edwin stated.

Before Jerry could sputter his reply the judge intervened. "Enough. We have to continue these proceedings. I will step out of the room and you two decide what you want to do," Judge Wilcox said.

The judge left and Jerry and Edwin sat staring at each other. It was obvious to Edwin that he, for the moment, had the upper hand. He had to get as much as he could. "I might suggest a compromise," he said. "You drop the punitive damage claim, do not refer to my client's unsolicited brushes with the mob, and any reference to your fishing expedition about his being a sperm donor. In return I will not present these medical records or her past history at MIT."

Jerry looked at Edwin and sighed. How had he let his client lead him down this path?

"Ok. I'll draw up the necessary changes in the complaint and issue a sworn statement that what you mentioned won't be brought up at trial. Do you have a copy of McConnell's record?"

"I have one copy and my client has another. That's it. I'll make a motion to exclude these records at trial or any reference to the past employment status. I assume there won't be a settlement today?"

"Hardly seems likely, now does it? I've got a headache, my nose is stuffed up, and I have a client who has misrepresented herself. What's worse I might have to actually try this case based on the medical issues. Bummer," Jerry laughed. He was recovering rapidly as he began to plan his approach in court. "See you in court next week."

When Tim heard about the deal Edwin made with Jerry Cleary he wasn't quite sure whether they were to his advantage or not. It seemed to him incontrovertible evidence of a plaintiff lying under oath was solid stuff. Edwin had insisted it was about sex and pride. She would state that she lied because she was embarrassed to admit her marital problems in public. But it was she who had started this lawsuit so she should be prepared to live with the consequences. Edwin insisted that the jury would overlook it. In return, he argued, you have the punitive charges dropped as well as no reference to any past activities that might cast you in a bad light. Again Tim felt there was only so far he could go and then he had to trust his attorney's judgement. There was no time for second opinions and in some corner of his brain he was beginning to feel that Edwin knew what he was doing. The strategy to not expose the plaintiff's misrepresentation and lurid details of her husband's venereal disease was probably good legally, but Tim felt it was also a high-class move by Edwin to keep the fray out of the gutter. All in all, Tim thought, there comes a time when he had to let go and let the system work.

Twenty-one

It was Monday morning and Tim was waiting outside court-room 18 of the superior court. Inside Judge Robert Cull was hearing pretrial motions and establishing ground rules. Jerry and Edwin, with their associates Jason Damon and Lisa Harding, had been in the courtroom over an hour. They were going back and forth while the judge listened or shuffled papers. Tim had gotten an earful on Friday about Judge Cull. Unlike Nathan Wilcox, Cull was strictly a political appointee. He had been a so-so plaintiff's attorney for twenty years. During that time he had become a big deal in the Trial Lawyer's Association, fighting for his right to make as much money off the system as possible. Of course to accomplish that he paid into the coffers of Democrat candidates who knew the score and either fought against tort reform or facilitated legislation that allowed the broadening of the tort process. One of Cull's favorite candidates had become governor and as a reward for his support the politically active lawyer had been named to the bench.

Edwin went on to say that Cull's parents had emigrated from Ireland and were as poor as "white folks can get". Judge Cull had clawed his way out of the Projects by working during the day and going to school at night. When he finally graduated from law school it was a banner day in the Cull household. Judge Cull wasn't the sharpest tool in the shed and it took several attempts before he passed the bar. He was a diehard Democrat in the tradition of Mayor Curley who was credited with refining class warfare in the political process, at least as far as Boston politics were concerned. Judge Cull could not shed his background, heritage, or personal feelings on the bench. He constantly came down on the side of the plaintiff, especially if they were poor or fighting the establishment. For Judge Cull, doctors were the establishment.

Tim had drifted off waiting for the trial to begin. He had gotten up at four thirty to see his patients, make rounds and catch up on his dictation. Then he made a mad dash down town to be at the courthouse by nine thirty only to sit and wait. He felt someone shaking his shoulder as he dozed and was startled to see Edwin's black face staring at him.

"Don't sleep out here. It will look bad to the jurors. They will think you're bored. Understand?"

Tim stood and said, "Yes. But they wouldn't be wrong. Why am I here so early? I'm just sitting out here hearing people complain about their legal troubles while you're in there," Tim said, stifling a yawn.

"If the judge calls on you for any reason, you need to be here. Anyway we have other problems. This judge and Cleary are like long lost brothers. He didn't rule on any of the motions to suppress McConnell's records or drop the punitive damage claim. Even when we stipulated that we agreed to these motions the judge wanted to spend more time reviewing them. Worse he didn't accept Jerry's revised complaint. We're still working under the old one."

"Great. So what do we do now?"

"They'll call in some jurors in a little while so we can start selecting. You need to be here for that so they can put a face to the name. Remember don't look bored, angry, happy, just neutral. You may laugh if there is something really funny so that the jurors see that you're human."

Lisa Harding came up behind Edwin and she had her business face on. "Remember if the judge asks if you have any questions during the jury selection just say no sir. Unless, there is a burning question that you don't think we can answer," Lisa said.

"I understand but I have this feeling things are spinning out of control, suddenly moving too fast."

Edwin smiled at Tim and said, "I think Mr. Cleary wants to get on with this trial. He feels that your 'untimely death' had delayed things enough. What with the malpractice mess in the State the judges are pushing to get these cases either settled or done in a timely manner. Having said that, this has been accelerated for some reason and Cull is not slowing it down either."

The three of them stood while approximately forty jurors filed into the courtroom to fill the witness seats as well as the jury seats. Jerry Cleary and Jason Damon were standing off to the side looking anxiously down the corridor for their client. Suddenly as the end of the hallway she appeared and walked slowly toward her attorneys. It was pathetic, as if she were attending the funeral of her late husband. No make up. Her hair was casually brushed back. She was dressed in black, right down to her shoes and didn't wear any jewelry except for the large diamond ring on her left hand. The corner of her mouth was turned down and she forced a tight smile when she saw Jerry. He put his arm around her shoulder but quickly released her. They talked for a while and then the deputy requested that the parties be seated.

When Tim stepped through the courtroom door he had that 'struck in the gut' feeling. Here he was for all the world to see. The surgeon gets to be sliced and diced instead of the other way around. The potential jurors who were talking in low tones suddenly stopped when the lawyers and clients entered. After a moment of hushed silence and staring, the low buzz began again. The door to the judges chambers opened and the deputy said, "All rise. The superior court of the Commonwealth of Massachusetts is now in session. Judge Cull presiding."

Tim looked at the Judge with immediate dislike. He was short with gray hair and what could only be described as a sadistic smirk. He obviously enjoyed his position of power and prestige. Judge Cull wore glasses with narrow lenses so he could read with them and then gaze out at the courtroom over the top of the lenses. He had an intimidating presence about him despite his short stature.

"Good day ladies and gentlemen. I wish to thank you for being here and hope that you feel happy to be here?" There was tittering around the room. "Madam clerk would you please read the complaint?"

A fat, fiftyish woman with a double chin struggled to stand up. When she was upright she reached for the glasses hanging between her pendulous breasts. Her blue dress had flakes of dandruff scattered on both shoulders. This chronic scalp condition left her open to much ridicule, but always behind her back. She had been Judge Cull's courtroom clerk for as long as anyone could remember and she enjoyed his protection.

"The matter of Bradford versus Graves et al. is before the court. Number b-789456-cd. All parties are present."

After she sat down Judge Cull paused a beat before saying, "This is a malpractice case involving a Dr. Graves who is seated over at the defense table. Would you please stand Doctor?"

Tim stood halfway and was getting ready to quickly sit back down when the judge said, "All the way up, and remain standing." Tim complied with the most neutral look on his face he could muster. He was not going to like Judge Cull at all.

"Now Mrs. Bradford is the plaintiff in this case. Please stand," he said with a polite smile. "Representing the defense is Edwin Stokes and," he paused to look down at a piece of paper, "Lisa Harding." He gazed around the courtroom over the top of his glasses to be sure all were being attentive. "Counsel for plaintiff is the distinguished Jerry Cleary and his associate Jason Damon." The latter names he remembered without looking at his notes.

Tim made a move to sit down when Judge Cull ordered in a slightly irritated voice, "Remain standing Dr. Graves. I will tell you when to be seated. Now Mrs. Bradford claims that the death of her husband was directly related to the negligence of Dr. Graves. It will be the charge of some of you to listen to the evidence and testimony given and render a verdict. Our judicial system requires that at least eight out of twelve jurors agree with the verdict to decide a civil case. Counsel and their clients may now be seated."

"Today," the judge went on, "there are forty of you in this room and twelve with four alternates will be selected to hear this case. Do any of the potential jurors present know either counsel or Mrs. Bradford or Doctor Graves? If so would you please raise your hand?"

Two hands immediately shot up. One was an elderly lady in her seventies and the other a young man in his late twenties with a ponytail.

"Would you please step forward and come to the side here so I can hear what you have to say."

They approached the judge on his right side and he cautioned them to speak softly. The elderly lady said, "Dr. Graves was my husband's doctor years ago when he had a brain tumor. It's terrible what the doctor has to go through." The judge nodded gravely and told her she was excused.

The young man said, "I know the lady. She was my prof's wife when I was at MIT. I'll just leave it at that." Judge Cull didn't know what to make of his statement but excused him as well.

"Now if there is no one else with personal knowledge is there anyone here who has been involved in a malpractice case either as a defendant or plaintiff?" There were no other hands raised. "Is anyone here related to, married to or an offspring of a physician? Three hands shot up. One said that her dad was a doctor and she still lived with him. She was excused. The second said his cousin was an orthopedic surgeon who worked at University hospital. He was also shown the door. The third had been married to a physician but they are now divorced. She was told she could stay.

There were now thirty-six potential jurors and they were given a list of questions written by both the plaintiff and defendant. When the questionnaires had been returned to the judge he said, "We can now begin voir dire. That's a fancy word for interrogation. Each lawyer can disqualify six jurors without cause and after that unless there is some compelling reason not to we will pick the jurors."

The first juror was a postal worker who appeared to be about forty years old and seriously overweight. After he was sworn in Mr. Stokes asked, "Have you ever had a bad encounter with a doctor?"

"No. But I don't waste my time going to see them."

"Why do you call it a waste of time?"

"They're in it for the money. They charge for everything they can find to charge and keep sending bills."

"Judge I would like to excuse this juror," Edwin said while seated.

"Very well," Cull said.

The next juror was an attractive, married schoolteacher. She had had no bad experiences with doctors and would listen to the testimony before making a decision. In addition, Jerry liked her looks and thought he could charm her so she was selected. By the lunch break they had named six jurors and excused an additional six others. Judge Cull requested a meeting with the attorneys.

In his chambers he removed his robe and settled into his seat. The others either stood or sat in hard back chairs. "I want to settle these motions and exclusions. Just so I don't say something prejudicial let's go over them in more detail now that I have heard your arguments." Lisa was famished, having missed breakfast. The judge should have ruled on these things at the morning session and she struggled to appear patient.

"Let me understand. The plaintiff lied on an application to MIT about cheating at the University of Michigan. Therefore you want to drop punitive damage claims and any reference to the doctor's past activities and alleged disappearance. Is that correct?" he asked the room at large.

"Essentially, yes," Edwin said. "But she also misrepresented herself during her deposition regarding the matter of loss of consortium. There is strong evidence that she was having an affair with her husband's associate for some long period of time. I believe it is still ongoing."

"How did you establish that?" the Judge asked.

"Well, we have obtained medical records of the plaintiff's

husband. In those it is clear that Mrs. Bradford and her husband were having serious problems," Lisa said. "Also corroborating hearsay evidence of her involvement with Seth Goddard."

"Where are those records? They're not included in the documents you gave me today."

"We, plaintiff and defense, agreed that they were potentially harmful to the deceased husband's reputation and would not have an advantage to either side," Edwin said.

"Well that's unacceptable. Please produce those documents," Judge Cull said in a high-pitched whiney voice. Edwin reached into his briefcase and handed the Judge his copy. After spending ten minutes reviewing Dr. McConnell's records of Mr. Bradford's visits the judge sat back and stared at Jerry and Edwin. His mind was churning, facts fighting prejudices, fighting integrity, fighting hate all going on at once behind the pince-nez glasses.

Finally the judge sighed and said, "The record and statements about the Michigan-MIT issue are excluded. There will be no reference made regarding the plaintiff's past or present affair with a Mr. Seth Goddard. Since the records are excluded and the husband's speculations about his wife' philandering are hearsay, the loss of consortium claim stands. In return the punitive damage claim is disallowed. I have been managing this case since it was filed. The disappearance of the doctor for a year certainly has become public knowledge. I can't see where that is not a part of this lawsuit. Therefore any reference to that episode is allowed."

Edwin was nearly out of his chair. He attempted his most outraged expression and said, "Plaintiff counsel and I have already stipulated to not allow that information to infect this trial. I object to this judicial interference in the management of our case."

"So noted. Are there any other issues?" the Judge asked glaring at Edwin.

"Well now that you mention it, Judge Cull, what about the reference to the doctor's past sperm donation during his training?" Jerry asked. "That relates to his activity with the mafia,"

"Yes. Quite so. That avenue may also be explored."

Lisa suddenly lost her appetite as she saw their defense going out the window. *Dr. Graves will be devastated.* The Judge terminated the meeting and they made their way to the cafeteria for soggy sandwiches and tasteless coffee. Lisa and Edwin avoided Tim but they knew it was only a matter of time before they would have to tell him.

In the afternoon session the remaining jurors were picked. There was a postal worker, schoolteacher, retired personnel manager, an engineer, working mom, retired nurse, and others who represented a cross section of the community. Neither side felt like they had a jury favorable to their case. In the hallway on the way out Edwin and Lisa stopped and pulled Tim over to the side and told him about the judge's rulings. He was overwhelmed with anger and disappointment. This case was like a roller coaster ride. One day he was up and the next day he was down. It seemed hopeless.

Meg and Joe Macintosh, a photographer for *The Bulletin,* sat in Meg's red Pinto watching a house on Liberty Road in Horsham a small community of upscale homes outside of Dedham. It was the day the trial began and she had heard from Tim during the noon recess about how agonizingly slowly things progressed. Lots of long winded arguing and posturing. It was a show and right in the middle was Julie Bradford playing the role of the bereaved widow. Hearing this Meg decided to take matters into her own hands and do a story about the grieving widow. How bad off was she? Meg told Tim her plan and that she wouldn't be home until late. She let her editor know that later in the afternoon she would be out chasing down a story. She would need a photographer and he had told her to take Joe. It was four o'clock when she finished the first installment for the next day of an expose about the malpractice crisis in the state. She found Joe, who had just come on duty, playing checkers with one of his associates. She coerced him into going with her on a 'secret assignment'. He didn't know what to expect but shrugged his shoulders and grabbed his camera. During the drive to Horsham Meg kept silencing Joe's questions with "just wait and see."

Now that they were parked down the street from Julie's home Joe tried again. "So can you tell me now what this is all about? Whose house is this? That's a hot Cabrera in the driveway."

"I'm sorry I was a bitch driving out here. I have a lot on my mind. It's a long story but essentially we have a lady suing a doctor. The lady has claimed that her husband's death deprived her of companionship. This is the address the lady gave during her deposition. I want to see if she is as lonely as she claims. Is your film time stamped?"

"Of course. Time and date. Learned that a long time ago. I check it everyday." Joe raised his camera and peered into the eyepiece. "Yep. April 4, 1988, 6:30 PM. So why are we here? Right now I mean."

"I'm not sure. A friend of mine said she is hot and heavy with a guy she had been seeing before her husband died. Way out here in the sticks, away from the Hub who's to know."

"You mean she was seeing the guy before her husband died?" Joe asked. "What's the big deal about that?"

"A couple of million dollars and my fiancé's sanity. He, my fiancé, is the doctor being sued. He says she is lying about everything. Says she wasn't told about the risks of surgery, you name it."

"Well duh. Isn't she supposed to say those things? She is suing after all," Joe said giving the whole situation a younger generation's perspective. Joe was twenty-four and after a two year stint in the military where he learned photography, did not give much thought to any weightier issues other than his next paycheck and a date with his girlfriend. "Judging from the two story house, and huge lot she can't be suffering much. Whose Porsche is that anyway?"

"Enough with the twenty questions. I'm thinking. I don't know who owns that sports car. Let's drive by, get a picture of it. It's getting dark." Meg started the car and slowly drove past the driveway that led to a three-car garage attached to the two story Tudor house. There were no other cars in front of the house or further up the driveway.

"Don't worry about the light. I can take pictures in a dark-room," Joe said as the camera clicked softly while the car drove past. Meg read the Porsche's license plate number out loud so they could both remember it while she pulled ahead and stopped. She wrote down the number on a piece of paper and tucked it in her purse.

"Lot of good that's gonna do you. You'll never get that through the motor vehicle toadies."

"I've got my connections." She looked back and she could see the front door open. Meg observed Julie talking to a teenage girl. Just then a young man in his early thirties stepped outside. He wore a dark sports coat with a white open collared shirt and a gold chain around his neck. "We have to get a picture of them getting into the car. Is it dark enough for you to hide?"

"Consider it done." Joe opened the car door and running low entered the trees bordering the property. He arrived before the home's front door was closed. As soon as the pair approached the car he began shooting pictures.

Moments later Meg's car door opened and Joe slipped back inside. "I don't think they have a clue. I overheard them say they were going to the Block and Tackle in Dedham."

"Good work. They'll have to pass us so scrunch down." Moments later with a grinding gears the Porsche passed them. Meg started her car and pulled into the street.

"What's next Dick Tracy? You buying dinner? I hear it's a great seafood restaurant."

Meg kept her eye on the Porsche's rapidly disappearing tail-lights. "I'm glad you heard where they're going. This clunker can't keep up."

"Ain't that the truth," Joe said while he replaced the film in his camera.

"We're not exactly dressed for the occasion so let's slip into the bar. I've been there before. There's a nice bar off the dining room and you can see into it easily."

"What you don't like the way I'm dressed?" Joe feigned hurt feelings.

"Pony tail, sweats and sneakers aren't going to do it. We'll be lucky to get into the bar." Several minutes later Meg pulled into the restaurant parking lot and spotted the Porsche. She parked a discrete distance from the sports car. Joe placed his camera in a paper grocery store sack he found in the back seat and together they strolled into the restaurant. The bar was to the left as they entered. Sitting at the bar one could peer over a half wall topped with a row of lathed wood pillars rising to the ceiling. The place wasn't that busy on a Monday night and they headed for two stools that gave the best view. Meg ordered a coke and Joe ordered a beer.

"Joe looked over his right shoulder and Meg asked, "Well do you see them?"

"They're in the corner like a couple of teenagers in heat. If they got any closer you'd think there was only one of 'em there."

"Go on. Tell me more."

"Well the guy is whispering in her ear and she's laughing like crazy. Looks like she has found that companionship she lost. Their hands aren't on the table. I wonder what's going on under there?"

"You're a degenerate. Can you get a picture?"

"They're way over in the corner booth but the restrooms are back behind them. I'll just take my paper sack and visit the head." Joe left and Meg held her breath until returned minutes later.

"I gotta admit she's a knock out. Nice rack on her."

"Shut up you pig! Did you get a picture?" Meg asked eagerly.

"Of course. No problemo. It was a lot harder than this in the military I'll tell ya. What's next?" Joe asked. He was getting hungry.

"We can eat at the bar here." Meg signaled the waiter for a menu. Dinner was uneventful and they finished their meal just as the lovebirds were standing up preparing to leave. Meg left cash on the bar and she and Joe followed the couple out. The Porsche was all fired up when they reached the Pinto and Meg could see them kissing while vapors came from the car's twin tail pipes. Joe caught a clear picture of the lovebirds in action. Meg and Joe climbed in her car and backed out as soon as the Porsche left the parking lot.

It was a lot easier following them after dinner. Julie's companion must have had several glasses of wine since he was over-cautious as he drove home. After they arrived back at Julie's house the car pulled into the garage. Meg did a U-turn and parked out of sight. Moments later the front door opened and the teenager she had seen earlier waved goodbye to someone in the house. The young lady walked up the street and into a driveway several houses away. Joe slumped down in his seat. "What's next?" he asked. "I've got to get my eight, I'm off duty at midnight it's just about that now."

"We need to take a picture of the boyfriend, whoever he is, leaving the house in the morning."

"How are you planning to do that? Wait in the car all night. No kinda way. Uh uh. Not me."

"Shut up. You're so negative. We obviously can't drive back to Boston and come back in the morning. There's a Howard Johnson's about a mile from here. We'll stay there."

"What's Sammy Surgeon going to say? Spending the night with the likes of me," Joe said with a large grin.

"He would say that he was disappointed in my taste in men. Don't worry he knows I'm here. Let's go. Separate rooms."

"Aw gee you're no fun."

Promptly at six in the morning a groggy Joe and an eager Meg were back at their surveillance site. Joe took some pictures of the house, which was still shrouded in mist. "The least you could do was get coffee. We passed a *Dunkin Donut*. What was the big rush?" Joe asked as he set his camera on his lap.

"I promise as soon as our mystery guest leaves we'll grab breakfast. It's not going to be

easy getting back into town with the traffic going that way. So just relax and we'll get a full breakfast before we head back. On me."

"Look, there's the dude now. In a bathrobe picking up the paper. I'll snap a bunch of pictures."

"Did you check your time stamp?" Meg asked.

"You know you don't listen. Here look in the view finder and read me what it says."

Meg took the camera and looked into the viewfinder. "It says April 5, 1972 and its 10 AM."

"Bull shit. Give me that thing." Joe took the camera and looked in the view-finder. "April 5, 1988 6:30 AM. Very funny." Meg laughed and they fell silent as the mist began to lift and the sun shone through. About an hour later the mystery guest drove away in his Porsche while Joe was vigorously snapping photos. "Well I guess that's it," he said when the car sped down the street away from them."

"Breakfast's on me. Let's go," Meg said.

After a large breakfast in Dedham at the *Bacon Rasher* the two headed back to Boston. Meg dropped Joe off at his apartment in Cambridge and headed home for a shower and clean clothes.

Later, after she was refreshed, she called the Boston Police Department. Following a series of transfers she was able to speak to Chief of Police Danny Rastellini. Since her name was easily recognizable to the Chief he did not hesitate to take the call. "Meg, how are you? Long time no talk. How are things going at *The Bulletin?*"

"Great Chief. Love it. I'm doing fine. I know you know that Tim is in the middle of a trial. I overheard him talking to you about it last week. I have a favor."

"Shoot. By the way thanks for the great coverage you guys gave us on the neighborhood watch program. It really helps."

"You're welcome. Listen, Tim has been accused of all kinds of things by the lady suing him. She claims she is lonely without her husband. Last night we, a *Bulletin* photographer and I, staked out her house. It seems she has a live in -boyfriend who probably has been a lover from way back. Any hope you can find out who it is?"

"Well I need a little more than that," Danny laughed.

"Oh. Dumb me. Here is his license plate number." She gave him the number and waited while the Chief wrote it down.

"Just to be legit. Did you observe this individual breaking the law?"

"He was doing at least 85 miles per hour on the back road in Horsham and was driving slowly after splitting a bottle of wine with our lady in question."

"So you are making a citizen's complaint?"

"Sounds good."

"I'll get back to you in about fifteen minutes. Ciao."

He hung up before Meg could say thank you. Twenty minutes later he called back with the name of Seth Goddard. The Chief also found out that he had five outstanding unpaid traffic tickets. One was for speeding. He was going to call the Dedham police and have his car impounded. Meg laughed and thanked him for his hard work.

While Meg was talking to the Chief, Judge Cull was bringing the court proceeding to order. Tim looked over at Julie Bradford and her despondency was palpable. The jurors were seated and every once in a while Tim snuck a peek in their direction to see if he could measure their reactions. After Mr. Cleary and Mr. Stokes argued some point of law Judge Cull announced that opening arguments would begin. As is customary the person bringing the complaint opens first. Jerry was dressed in a pinstriped dark suit with a bright patterned tie. His hair was slicked back and he was ready to go. He stood and sniffed once or twice then slowly walked over and stood in front of the jury box.

"Today begins a very important trial and you will decide the outcome. We live in a form of democracy where the majority has the edge. Notice I didn't say the majority rules. Everyone gets a voice in our society with its representative government. Ours is not a true democracy but a republic with three branches of government underpinned with checks and balances. But a jury is the purest form of democracy. You vote and the majority rules. All it takes is for eight of you to find in favor of my unfortunate client Julie Bradford."

He looked around at the jurors. There were six women and six men. He had tried to get single mothers and had succeeded in two cases. The sixth female juror was a fifty year-old librarian who had never married. This was Edwin's choice. The other unmarried juror was a Cambodian lady who cleaned hotel rooms for a living.

He walked over near the defense table and continued, "Now over here is the defendant. Dr. Timothy Graves. He is a well-known neurosurgeon. Has a busy practice but we will show that he was too busy. Too busy to sit down with my client and explain to her the risks and potential complications of surgery. Too busy to tell her that there were other ways to treat brain aneurysms with less risk. Too busy to properly perform the surgery on her husband." Jerry was nearly preaching as he addressed the jurors.

He went on in a commanding voice to say, "We will show that he rushed through the surgery and when he got into trouble he fell apart, letting a doctor in training finish off the surgery and Mr. Bradford." Jerry went to describe how callous and impersonal medicine had become. How doctors were interested only in the bottom line. Medicine was a big business now. Jerry purposefully stayed away from the issue of Tim's disappearance. He didn't want to give the jurors too much too soon.

He walked over to his side of the room and looked down at Julie Bradford and explained to the jurors how her life had been torn apart. She was nearly broke and had to sell her husband's stock for pennies on the dollar. Was nearly bankrupt and without companionship. He explained loss of consortium and what it meant. Finally after an hour he turned to the jurors. "You must send a message. It's time doctors took an interest in their patient's families. The ones left behind. They are left to pick up the pieces, go on with their lives. They, as well as the patient, must be informed of the risks. Thank you." Jerry went over and slowly sat down while he solemnly looked at his client.

Edwin looked over at Jerry to be sure he was really through with his ranting. Jerry was seated, nose behind a cupped hand, discretely using an inhaler to clear his nasal passages. *Whew*, Edwin thought, *thank God that's over. What drivel.* Jerry didn't know the difference between a democracy and a dictatorship when they were growing up. Edwin stood and shook his head and said, "In reality most doctors are compassionate, caring, and measured in their care of patients. Dr. Graves not only sat down and talked with the patient and his wife," he looked over at her for emphasis, " he told them everything. What the risks are. Why surgery over other methods? What to expect afterward. Plaintiff, Mrs. Bradford, you will find has misrepresented the informed consent discussion." He wanted to plant that seed right away. Leave no doubt who is lying here.

Edwin walked over to the jurors and stood in front of them. He was glad to see two black faces, one female and one male. The female had raised three kids after her husband, a white construction worker, was killed in an auto accident. The male was a postal worker who seemed interested in being a juror and not particularly swayed one way or the other. "Dr. Graves is a neurosurgeon with a worldwide reputation and has patients come to him from all over the world. He **is** busy but each patient is special to him. We will not drag in former patients of his to bore you with testimonials to this but you will see for yourselves when he testifies." Edwin decided to go with his golf analogy. "Doctors are human. They are not gods, as we so often tend to think. They eat, breathe, laugh and cry just as we do. This case is about a bad outcome. If any of you have played golf or watched it on television you'll understand what I am talking about." Several jurors nodded their heads affirmatively. Jerry had noted that two of the jurors had put down golf as their recreation.

"A professional golfer makes nineteen wonderful shots only to have the twentieth go awry. A bad outcome. Was it the golf swing, the wind, mud on the ball? Whatever it was the outcome was bad. The professional golfer makes the adjustment and suddenly he's out of trouble and back on track. When **we** play golf we have nineteen bad shots and the twentieth shot sails perfectly straight and lands at our target. We say to ourselves "why can't I do that every time?" Well that's the difference between a professional and an amateur. The professional makes **adjustments** and moves on. Dr. Graves is a professional. A professional neurosurgeon. He had a bad outcome with Mr. Bradford. You will see that it had nothing to do with his technique or skill. It's something that happens in a business where millimeters count and risks are great."

Edwin looked out over the jury. He was glad to see they were listening. He wasn't going to drag it out. "We put doctors on a pedestal because they are the barrier between life and death. A life free of illness. There have been many great strides in medical knowledge and miraculous treatments. Doctors are their own worst enemies. They have done so well with so many problems that we have grown to expect great outcomes every time. If there is an errant shot something must have gone wrong. It's the doctor's fault we reason." The jurors were still rapt watching the defender of the doctor hold forth. Edwin had a cultured stately manner. Who was this man? A black man. He did not fit the stereotype. How did he get here? Defending a respected neurosurgeon. The jury wanted to know so they listened and observed.

"Now Mr. Cleary is a very well known lawyer. Why you see his face on television, on bus benches, all over town. Now he is a busy man! You have to ask yourself is **he** prepared for this. Where does **he** find the time being as busy as he is? How can someone be so busy and yet be able to devote enough time to one client? Well let me tell you he's ready. He has hired the best experts money can buy."

Jerry was out of his chair before Edwin could finish, "Objection. Is Mr. Stokes going to present my case?"

"Sustained," Judge Cull said, "Mr. Stokes confine your remarks to your defense."

Edwin smiled at Jerry and said, "Yes your honor. I will show through expert testimony that the defendant, my client, acted wholly within the standard of care regarding Mr. Bradford. He will give us the story himself," he said gazing at the jurors. "Thank you."

After Edwin was seated Judge Cull pointed to Jerry to begin. Jerry stood and said, "We will begin at the beginning. I call Julie Bradford to the stand."

Julie stood and carefully pushed her chair back in place. She walked slowly to the stand with head high but did not look at the jurors. When she was seated she adjusted the microphone in front of her and vowed to tell the truth. She took a quick look at the jurors and all eyes were on her.

Jerry cleared his throat after she was settled. He asked her name, address, what her husband's name was, how old she was, where she met her husband. About twenty minutes of background or foundation. The preliminaries dispensed with, Jerry asked, "Can you tell us about the events leading up to the surgery?"

uietly she said, "John, my deceased husband, came home one evening with the news that he had a problem. He explained it as best he could but he said the doctor was rushed and didn't go into a lot of detail. Said he spent about five minutes with him. Anyway, Dr. Graves," she looked over at Tim, "had told him that he needed surgery right away. It was a routine aneurysm." She was careful to pronounce the last word correctly and then briefly gazed at the jurors. She was satisfied that they all were paying attention.

Jerry looked over at Tim then turned and looked at the jury. He also was satisfied that they so far were paying attention. Returning his gaze to Julie he asked, "Did you ever talk to Dr. Graves about your husband's surgery?"

Julie looked at Tim and with just a faint bitterness in her soft voice said, "No."

"Louder please and will you elaborate."

"I never talked to Dr. Graves before surgery. The first time I met him was in the waiting room after my husband had died." Julie took a handkerchief from the pocket of the sweater she was wearing and dabbing prettily at the corner of her eyes. Tim saw that she would certainly get the sympathy vote.

Jerry went on to cover more ground about the informed consent process. How she and her husband were never informed of possible alternative treatments. When he was through he asked, "How has it been since your husband's death?"

Julie sighed and looked away. "I miss him so. His laugh, his playfulness, our intimacy. It's been hard on the children as well. No father at home has been a big change in their lives." For the first time Julie took a prolonged look at the jurors. She spied one female wiping her eyes with a Kleenex. "I more or less have been at home and unable to get my life back to together."

"Are you dating?"

"Not really. I have no interest in that. John's loss was so sudden that I haven't fully recovered from it."

Jerry went on to explore her financial situation and how she had to sell company stock for pennies compared to their current value. He finished up and Judge Cull dismissed proceedings for lunch. It was a great start for Jerry. He felt he was in the driver's seat but he knew Edwin wasn't going to roll over. He cautioned his client at lunch that she had a bumpy road ahead of her. Julie seemed unconcerned.

Tim, Lisa, and Edwin walked out of the court building and found a sub shop. While Tim was picking at his lunch he asked, "Well should we settle now or should we go on?"

Edwin was wolfing down a sub sandwich and laughed when he heard Tim's negative comments. Suddenly Meg burst into the shop and made a beeline to their table. She pulled up a chair. Tim smiled at her and said, "You should have seen the performance by Julie Bradford. It was a tear jerker."

"Well you should have seen her performance last night. She had on a different costume."

With that Meg pulled some photographs out of a manila envelope and began showing them to Tim. Edwin and Lisa put down their subs as Tim passed the pictures around.

Meg went on, "You can see she's decked out for dinner with someone who I now know is the mysterious Seth Goddard. Here's a shot of them entering her home and a shot of him in a bathrobe the next morning picking up the paper."

Angry, Tim said, "She just testified that she rarely goes out and has not been dating anyone. What bullshit. Edwin what do we do with these?" Tim asked, pointing to the pictures.

"The chances of Judge Cull allowing the jurors to see these pictures are as likely as me giving the keynote address at a Ku Klux Klan convention. I will try, see if I can, but don't hold your breath. Either way this is good since I can question her about where she went last night. Ask who Seth Goddard is. This will be very helpful."

Lisa had been quietly looking at the pictures and when there was a break in the conversation asked, "How do you know this is Seth Goddard?"

"You see the blow up of the license plate? License tagged for 1988. Through unnamed sources I have verified that this is Seth Goddard's Porsche." Lisa nodded and didn't pursue the issue.

After lunch Meg kissed Tim on the cheek and said she would be home when he finished in the courtroom. He said he would be late because he had to make rounds at the hospital. When they were back in court Jerry, Edwin and Judge Cull met in chambers to review the pictures. Jerry was livid that someone was spying on his client, ignoring the fact that she was a pathological liar. Judge Cull said the pictures although time and date stamped needed independent verification of when they were taken. Edwin pointed out that the license plates are dated 1988 but that didn't satisfy Judge Cull. Also he stated that they were an intrusion into the plaintiff's privacy. Edwin pointed out that she is the one that made her privacy an issue by claiming loss of consortium. Judge Cull did allow that Edwin could question her about the events in the pictures but could not make reference to them.

Back in court it was Edwin's turn to cross-examine Julie. He waited while Jerry and Julie, who had stepped out into the hall after their session with Judge Cull, returned to the courtroom. While she was taking the stand Edwin planned his questioning. He asked himself should he be careful and go slowly or charge ahead. Before he could decide he asked, "Who is Seth Goddard?"

Julie, immediately on guard, sat forward in the witness chair and said, "Seth is a dear friend and my husband's former partner. He has been so good to me during this ordeal." She looked over at Tim as she finished.

"Mrs. Bradford when was the last time you saw Mr. Goddard?"

Julie glanced at Jerry and his face was blank. She became wary and decided this was the time to tell the truth. The pictures weren't in evidence but she could be questioned about the circumstances they portrayed. She wondered what else does this nosy black lawyer have up his sleeve.

"He called last night to see how I was doing and took me out to an early dinner. He knew the trial has started and he offered a diversion for a few hours."

She's good Edwin thought. *Very good.* "What time did he go home?"

"I..... he didn't go home right away so I don't know. He'd had a little too much wine to drink. I told him he could sleep on the couch and leave whenever he wanted. He was gone when I woke up this morning." Julie quickly glanced over at the jurors and found they weren't quite so rapt with this testimony.

Edwin thought it was time to move on. Without the pictures in evidence Julie can fabricate any story that suits her. He should have just asked these questions without tipping off Cleary by trying to get the pictures into evidence. He obviously told his client about the pictures and she had time to prepare her answers. This was one clever woman and not to be underestimated. He went over her testimony about the informed consent and finally asked, "On the evening of admission, what room was your husband admitted to prior to surgery?"

"Well originally when I came to see him the night before surgery I went to the neurosurgical floor but he wasn't there."

"Did you asked the nurses on the floor where your husband was?"

"No. They were all sitting around talking at the nurse's station and didn't acknowledge me. I called on the phone to the admission's office to find out. They told me. Said I went to the wrong floor, he was on the cardiac surgery floor. Room 204, I believe."

"When you went to the cardiac floor do you remember what time you arrived?"

"I remember seeing the eight o'clock news on the TV in John's room. So sometime after eight."

"Did you talk to anyone?"

"You asked me these questions in my deposition. The answers then are the same as they are now. The nurse told me that Dr. Graves had been by briefly and was too busy to come back. A student doctor went over the risks of surgery with me."

"Did you ever see Dr. Graves before surgery." She staying right on message Edwin thought to himself.

"Like I said before, I didn't meet Dr. Graves until after surgery," Julie answered with a petulant tone to her voice.

Edwin asked more questions to try to pin her down but she stuck to her original story and it was getting late. He looked over at the jury and they were tired. Some were doodling on pads of paper others were rubbing their eyes. He decided to wrap it up and Judge Cull dismissed the jurors.

On the way out Jerry buttonholed Edwin and put on his angry face. "My client got a call from Seth Goddard during lunch. Seems his car was impounded. You wouldn't know anything about that now would you?"

"Of course not. You know me better than that. Curious you would be bringing that up as an issue when you sent a private investigator after my client." Edwin was miffed at Jerry's insinuation that he had done something unethical.

"Still don't want to talk settlement? You fired your best shot at my client and it bounced off like a Beebe hitting a tank."

"Your client has misrepresented the facts since day one. In short she is a liar and you know it. It's my job to expose her and this is only round one," Edwin said pulling away and heading for the elevator.

"I'm putting on Shamski tomorrow so watch out," Jerry laughed at Edwin's departing back.

Tim was discouraged as he left the courthouse. He knew the plaintiff was lying but Edwin had not done much to destroy her credibility. He could feel the sympathy on the part of the jurors and she had wiggled out of the Seth Goddard thing neatly. After rounds at the hospital he arrived home at nine o'clock more exhausted than if he had spent all day in the operating room. Meg had dinner ready for him. She had made a valiant effort the night before to gather incriminating evidence but to no avail. After Tim ate he sat down to his mail. There was a letter from his brother Jim. Tim tore it open and there was a letter plus an article from the *Los Angeles Post*. He read the letter then the article. Meg watched him, bursting with curiosity.

"Well?" she asked as he finished.

"My brother checked up on Shamski. He has had his privileges temporarily suspended at two hospitals for suspected fraud. Billing MediCal for services he never performed. It seems that when they were closing in on him a couple of years ago there was a fire in his office. All of his records were destroyed."

"What does the newspaper article say?" Meg asked.

Tim handed her the article. "Here read for yourself. This is from last week. Says Shamski was cleared of any wrong doing because of the destroyed records. He claims there were errors on some billing forms but it was all a misunderstanding," Tim finished with a discouraged shake of his head. "It seems like this whole case is stacked against me. How do you deal with a liar like Julie Bradford and a disreputable physician like Shamski?"

"Now don't get discouraged. Dr. Davis will make Shamski look like the phony that he is. The jury has to see it. You have to look confident in the courtroom not like you look now."

"I know. I thought with the pictures, McConnell's records this case would be dismissed but the truth doesn't seem to matter."

"Now, now. Let's not wallow. You can do this." Meg was being a cheerleader but inside she began to have doubts. Whichever direction they took they were blocked by the judge or some rule of law. "Get a *Bulletin* in the morning. They finally after several delays are running my investigation into the malpractice crisis."

"You've been awful quiet about that article. Is there something you don't want me to know?"

"No. You know I wouldn't keep anything from you. It's just that I don't want people to think you influenced the article. Keep it on the up and up."

Tim gave here a loving kiss and said, "Come on. Let's go to bed. I have to get up early again for rounds then go to my favorite place, the courtroom." All Tim felt was dread. He honestly didn't think he could ever go through this again. He tucked Jim's letter and the article into his pocket to remind himself to take it with him the next morning. There was something in Julie Bradford's testimony today that rang a bell in his brain but he couldn't put a finger on it. *Oh well, it will come to me.*

The next morning he kissed Meg goodbye as she lay sleeping. He tiptoed out of the bedroom and headed off to the hospital for rounds. When he finished it was eight o'clock and he took the

MTA to the Common so he could get an early morning walk. Jim's letter and the newspaper article were in his suit pocket. It probably wouldn't do any good but he was going to show it to Edwin. He stopped at a coffee shop off the Commons and purchased a *Bulletin* and a cup of the house blend. As he sat reading at a table outside the cafe he came across the article by Meg. Whereas Massachusetts at one time had one of the lowest claims records against doctors that had all changed. Now the state was one of the worst. So much so that the legislature stepped in and passed some tort reform and fee restrictions over the objections of the trial lawyers. Tribunals had been instituted. Tim tried to recall the name of the neurosurgeon at St. Mary's that said he had practiced below the standard of care and allowed this suit go forward. Oh yeah Dr. Hastings. Now there is someone who should know what the standard of care is all about. The article finished with announcing the next installment will concern the judiciary and their role in the malpractice crisis.

As he folded the newspaper Tim remembered that when he first joined University staff Dr. Hastings was a junior resident on the neurosurgical service. He was a very weak resident and was not offered a senior residency to complete his training and had to go elsewhere. It had been Tim's recommendation along with the then chief of neurosurgery to not allow him to complete the program. Tim had caught him lying about patient information when the young doctor had been too lazy to look over the patient's records before rounds. A sure sign of someone you didn't want taking care of you or a member of your family. He also on two occasions couldn't be found in the middle of the night when a brain injured patient was in the emergency room. As the years passed Tim recalled having run into Hastings at meetings both in Boston and out of town. On all of those occasions Hastings was cool toward him. As far as Tim knew all he did were back fusions, some uncomplicated craniotomies and was a frequent witness in court.

Tim glanced at his watch. It was time to meet with Edwin. He stood up, stretched, and looked out at the common. Spring was in the air and it was a beautiful day. The trees were beginning to show their leaves and flowers were blooming. Days like this made him wish he had settled on a baseball career. Moments later he met Edwin and Lisa in a conference room off the court-room.

"We're ready to go," Edwin said. "What do you have for us today. Yesterday it was pictures. Even though they were excluded they were a definite plus for our side."

"Last night I got a letter and an article from my brother. It seems that Dr. Shamski has dodged a bullet. He was being investigated for fraudulent billing and what do you know his office records mysteriously were destroyed in a fire. It seems the fluid in his copy machine exploded when he turned it on. A defective switch." Tim handed the letter and article to Edwin who in turn handed them to Lisa when he had finished.

"Very interesting. This is why he was unable to document his experience with brain aneurysms. Very convenient," Lisa said when she finished reading the documents.

"I love the part where he sues the copy machine manufacturer and wins a rather large award. What's the word? Chutzpah. He has it," Edwin said. "I can use this today. Pin him down. As far as we know he has done only a handful of cases since this incident."

"What difference does it make how many he's done? He's going to say this should have been done with a catheter anyway. By the way the guy that does these catheter obliterations remembers going over this case with me. How come he hasn't been deposed?" Tim was curious.

"I did talk to him," Lisa answered, "But when I talked to him he couldn't remember enough detail and was evasive. I just felt he didn't want to get involved, could possibly hurt rather than help you."

"Great," Tim said. "Like rats on a sinking ship."

"Buck up. There's a long way to go," Edwin said.

They walked into the courtroom walking past the jurors gathering outside. When Tim and his counsel were settled into their chairs, Jerry and Jason strolled in looking confident and laughing together. They waved to the defense and threw their briefcases down on the table. Soon Julie shuffled in looking depressed and then the bailiff summoned the jurors. As they filed past the plaintiff and defense tables all stood in deference to them. Odd, Tim thought, as he stood watching the charade. Why should he be standing out of respect for them, as if they cared one way or the other?

"All rise," the bailiff announced in a booming voice as Judge Cull waved everyone to their seats. Once he was settled he asked Mr. Cleary if he was ready with his first witness. He replied in the affirmative and he called Dr. Shamski to the stand. Tim was surprised. He remembered seeing this man sitting out in the waiting area and thought at the time that he looked like an actor. He was tan and fit and looked to be in his early sixties. This guy looked the part of an expert and appeared very comfortable on the stand while he was being sworn.

"Dr. Shamski please state your full name for the record," Jerry said.

"Bernard Donald Shamski."

Jerry went through the usual questions about where he lived and what was his medical background. He emphasized to the jurors that Dr. Shamski was a graduate of Harvard Medical School. When he was through with the standard questions, Jerry asked, "Have you ever been investigated for fraud."

"I don't know what you mean by fraud. But several years ago I had a new secretary in my office and she messed up the billing. It was all a mistake and any incorrect billing was resolved ..... I paid back what was collected in error." Dr. Shamski gave a fatherly look at the jurors as if so say it was no big deal.

"Wasn't there a fire in your office? Destroyed your records."

"Yes. That was caused by a faulty switch on the copy machine and it ignited flammable fluid. It was purely coincidental that this happened while the investigation was getting underway."

How convenient Tim thought. He stole a quick glance at Edwin who sat staring straight ahead. Jerry went on. He had beaten Edwin to the punch again.

"Tell the court what you reviewed in order to render an opinion today." Shamski listed all the depositions, hospital records and reference materials he used to come to his conclusions. "Dr. Shamski where did Dr. Graves fall below the standard of care in his treatment of Mr. Bradford?"

"He did not properly consent the patient or family. He rushed through a surgery that was not necessary and the patient died."

Jerry looked over at the jury to be sure there were taking it all in. Several time during his direct examination of Dr. Shamski Jerry had to stop and use his nasal inhaler to clear a stuffy nose. Jerry continued, on making Tim look less than competent and finally finished up with a question. "Dr. Shamski did Dr. Graves fall below the standard of care in the treatment of Mr. John Bradford?" Jerry starred at his client as he asked the question.

"Absolutely," Shamski's responded.

"Thank you. No further questions for the witness at this time."

Judge Cull banged his gavel and announced a twenty-minute break and the next session would start at eleven and go for an hour until lunch.

Tim, Lisa, and Edwin walked away from the courtroom. Tim said, "He didn't spend that much time with his witness. Got him to say the same old things. No surprises. Now I know that means something to you two. What is it?"

"Well he doesn't have the strongest expert in the world there. Just enough to cast doubt on your judgment and care. He didn't want to go too far with this guy. He has baggage with that MediCal fraud charge," Edwin said.

"Did you notice that he did not review the angiograms? Are you going to ask him about that?" Tim asked.

"You wait and watch. It's time to get back in there." Edwin seemed confident.

After everyone was settled the judge reminded Shamski that he was still under oath. "Dr. Shamski how many time have you been sued for malpractice?"

"Well you asked me that during my deposition. I'll answer it now as I did then. Twice."

"Doctor would you look at this document for me." Edwin walked over to Shamski and handed him four sheets of paper. Shamski quickly glanced over the document and looked up.

"Would you read to the court what it says on the first page?"

"It's a complaint filed in Maricopa County Arizona. Page vs. Shamski et al. I can explain this," he said with a slight hitch to his voice.

"Please do."

Jerry decided that the quicker he got the doctor out of here the better and kept his objections to himself

"Well," he went on, "Page was a ten year old girl who had a head injury. I saw her late in her illness and there was not much I could do. She died after a long illness."

"What was the outcome of the litigation?"

"It was settled by the hospital and my insurance company."

"How much?"

"One hundred thousand dollars."

"Now when you say your insurance company you really mean it was a settlement against you." It wasn't a question.

"Well. Yes. I suppose so." Shamski shrugged as if no big deal.

"Doctor would you please open your deposition and go to page twenty line 15 through 30 and read what it says."

After fumbling nervously to find the right page he began to read his testimony about how he had been only sued twice and never had a judgment against him."

After he finished Edwin said, "Now which is it two suits and no judgments or three suits with one settlement?"

Jerry had had enough. The once cool and urbane Shamski was coming apart at the seams. "I object to counsel's questions. They are argumentative and he is badgering the witness."

Cull looked satisfied and said, "Sustained."

"Dr. Shamski, which is it, twice or three times?"

"Three times but I thought you only wanted my experience in California."

"Are you telling me that there are more than three since you practiced in a number of states before you came to California?"

Dr. Shamski shifted in his chair and folded his arms onto his chest in a defensive posture. Edwin was definitely getting to him. "No. Those are the only lawsuits I've had."

"Doctor would you describe for me the aneurysm that Mr.

Bradford had."

He unfolded his arms and felt a little more comfortable since the questioning shifted away from him. "Well it was about three and a half centimeters which is large for a brain aneurysm. It was sacular with a neck of about one centimeter. It was located in the left middle cerebral artery."

"On what date did your review the angiograms, Doctor?"

Dr. Shamski glanced nervously at Cleary but there was no help there. He knew what was coming. "Well I never actually saw them. I asked for them but they were never presented to me."

"Why didn't you insist on seeing them before you came to your conclusions about Mr. Bradford's treatment?"

"I was busy and I never got around to seeing them but the radiology report are quite descriptive." His tone was almost condescending as if to say I know what I'm doing.

"So as we sit here today you have never looked at the cerebral angiograms."

"Ah.....no."

Edwin pulled several x-rays out of a folder he had brought to court and walked over to a view box. He placed the films on the view box and snapped on the light. After gazing at the films he asked, "Would you like to look at them now?" There was a slight trace of sarcasm in Edwin's voice. Jerry immediately jumped up and said, "I object to counsel's badgering of this witness. These x-rays were not available for Dr. Shamski to review."

Judge Cull sat and looked at Jerry for a moment. His client did come to the conclusion without seeing the x-rays Jerry would have to live with it. "Overruled," he said and added, "Let's get on with it it's getting near lunch time."

Dr. Shamski got up from his chair slowly walked to the view box. He had been embarrassed enough.

"Now that you have seen the x-rays first hand have you changed your opinion?"

"No. It's just as described in the report." He returned to his chair.

"Dr. Shamski your testimony was that this aneurysm should

have been treated by clotting it. Do you do the clotting procedure or does someone else do it?"

Shamski was immediately on guard. This lawyer was tricky and he had something up his sleeve. "Dr. Singh in our radiology department actually does the procedure," he answered cautiously.

"Now despite the size of this aneurysm and it's wide neck you still contend that this should have been treated in the radiology department?"

"Yes."

"Doctor I have here an article written by Dr. Singh in the 1987 Journal of Indian Medicine. Would you be so kind as to read to the court the portion underlined in red?"

Shamski read silently and frowned. "Doctor?" Edwin prompted.

"In our experience at Los Angeles Westside Community Hospital, we have found that aneurysms over two centimeters with a wide base are not amenable at this time for thrombosing and continue to be a surgical problem.' Let me explain what he means here because things have changed. We now do larger aneurysms."

"But doctor this was published in 1987 and the study includes the time period in which Mr. Bradford had his surgery. You are not still supporting thrombosing when your own radiologist does not recommend it, are you?"

"Well," and he folded his arms again, "what's written isn't always what's done. I would have talked the radiologist into doing it."

Tim couldn't believe what he was hearing. Was there no end to this? Dr. Shamski was making a mockery of his profession. No wonder doctor's call some expert witnesses advocates and whores. This guy would say anything. Edwin was doing an excellent job of destroying his testimony.

"One last thing doctor then I'm through with you. How many of these aneurysms do you see in a year?"

Dr. Shamski looked at the jury members. They were all waiting for his answer. "Well about three or four a year." He stuck to his deposition testimony.

"We asked for your operative reports on these cases and only received two for the prior two years after the fire in your office. Where are the remaining reports?"

"Well my office personnel couldn't find the reports since we don't catalog things by diagnosis in my office. That's all that we could find."

"Doctor the difference between three and four is twenty-five percent. Was it three or four per year?"

"Most likely three."

"So for the six cases you did in two years you could only find two?"

"Yes."

"Thank you Dr. Shamski. I have no further questions for this witness." Judge Cull asked

Jerry if he any more questions for his witness. He shook his head no then said "no" out loud for the court reporter. Dr. Shamski stood and stepped down from the witness chair. He hurriedly walked past the jury, Julie, and Jerry, while looking straight ahead. It had not gone well for him and he wanted to get back to the land of sunshine and roses.

The judge excused the jurors for lunch. Tim, Edwin, and Lisa remained seated at the defense table until everyone left the courtroom. Tim broke the silence, "Now I know why you're considered the best. Where did you come up with all that information and detail?"

"You sound surprised. I have two experts at my disposal. You and Dr. Davis, who has been extremely helpful. He got me onto Dr. Singh. Thank you for your kind remarks but there's a fine line between destroying one's credibility and humiliation. The jurors might react unfavorably to the latter. Anyway let's get lunch. Jerry has more 'experts' this afternoon," Edwin finished, wiggling his eyebrows.

The afternoon court session went about as expected. Jerry presented experts in nursing care outlining the standards of informed consent and documentation thereof. Operating room nurses detailed the procedures for sudden blood loss during surgery. All of it appeared to make Tim look bad but Edwin managed to defuse most of the testimony by getting the nurse experts to admit that there was nothing done by the defendant that was below the standard of care. Thursday he had an anesthesiologist expert who was going to comment on informed consent and the conduct of Tim as well as the anesthesiologist, Dr. Cryer, during the critical episode of bleeding.

Everything seemed out of synch to Jerry. His expert, Dr. Shamski, was a disaster. The nurse experts were critical but they did not come down hard enough on the surgical team. His own anesthesiologist expert wasn't that tough on Dr. Cryer. Jerry was thinking about a settlement offer to the anesthesiologist or dropping him outright from the trial. No way was he going to win this case on his client's credibility and he needed to destroy the testimony on cross examination of Dr. Graves' and Dr. Davis's. He didn't have much on Davis to use and here it was Friday morning. He was going to wrap his case up on Monday with a psychiatrist explaining the prolonged grieving process that his client had experienced.

It was Friday afternoon, the morning having been spent wrapping up motions and details about the trial. The judge gave the jurors Friday afternoon off. Jerry buzzed his secretary and requested that she find Eddie Collins. He had two issues to discuss with the investigator. Moments later the phone buzzed and Jerry picked up.

"Hello Eddie. Jerry here. You got anything for me," Jerry asked abruptly.

"Hi Jerry. I don't feel the love. Is there something wrong?" Eddie didn't like bending over and spreading his cheeks..

"Sorry. This trial is giving me a headache and I literally mean a headache. My expert looked like a toy doctor today compared to Dr. Graves. Funny how the same medical school can turn out such diametrically opposite doctors in the same specialty. Anyway that's for another time. Did you find out anything I can use on Dr. Davis?"

"Well, yeah and no. I had an investigator go to his hometown in upstate New York. I'm supposed to hear from him later. I'll let you know anything new. What I know so far is that he's been divorced twice. One kind 'a messy with mistresses and hidden assets. Not the kind of mistresses you're thinking of. I'll know more later. His medical record is clean. A couple of malpractice suits that didn't go anywhere."

"Is he married now?" Jerry said discouraged, bored. Divorces weren't going to do it for him.

"No. And there are rumors the guy is a fag. Excuse me gay. That's what I mean about the mistresses. They were guys."

"Ugly. But that's better Eddie, you don't want to be taken for a bigot. With attitudes changing the way they are I'm not going near that issue." Changing subjects Jerry said, "I've decided to use the info you gave me on Graves' escapades as a sperm donor. I'll need that documentation you said you have but don't tell me how you got it."

"Aw shit Jerry. Do you haft 'a have it?"

"Yes I 'haft' a have it," he mimed in a whiney voice. "It cost me five thousand bucks and I need it." Jerry was getting a little irritated with Eddie's reluctance.

There was silence on the other end and Eddie thought about the consequences of what he had done. Once he presented the paper to Jerry and it was used he was in trouble with the Kennedy's. But that was life. "Ok. I have it stashed. I'll bring it to the courthouse on Monday. I'll find you there."

"See that you do." Jerry hung up and pinched his nose. He did have a headache and for sure he would see that nose doctor at Saint Mary's at the end of the trial.

Twenty-two

Peter Strata was in the back of his bakery in East Boston waiting for the ovens to reach the right temperature. The early morning was his favorite time of the day, the sweet smell of yeast fermenting, no customers to worry about and the coffee was perfect. He had brewed it himself. Each morning at five o'clock he started work baking the bread and other bakery items to be sold or delivered that day. He would be joined soon by his younger brother Raphael, who liked to work out front and deal with the customers while Peter made the deliveries. Peter had a copy of the *Post* and was reading a story on the second page when he slammed the newspaper down. *What kind of bullshit is this*? The article was a follow-up on a series investigating the killing of his brother. A reporter had dug deeper and found out that the US Attorney in New York and Dominic Milano were in the same platoon in Vietnam and once on patrol credited Dom with saving the whole unit. "There is no way this outstanding citizen had anything to do with the murder of Pualie Strata" the attorney was quoted as saying.

Just then Raphael walked through the back door and poured himself a cup of coffee. He was taller than his two brothers and the youngest. Being taller than Paulie or Peter didn't make you a candidate for playing center on the Celtics team but at least at five feet nine inches he was taken seriously. He was husky like his other brothers but slow to anger and liked people. Peter was in the middle. Paulie, his older brother had practically raised the two after their mother died when they were teenagers. Their dad had been killed in a robbery shortly after Raphael was born.

"I can tell you're not happy about something. What's in the paper?" Raphael held the coffee pot out and Peter accepted a refill.

"Seems this guy in New York was a war hero to the attorney who's supposed to be investigating him. It's come to a dead end."

"What difference does it make? Paulie's gone. We'll never see him again. The only thing we can do is keep the business going and help Rita." Rita was Paulie's wife.

"I know but it bugs me that guy gets a pass."

"Listen, Paulie was in a bad business. He planned to rat out the Santoris. He paid for that. What can we do? Go after the Santoris? A couple' a of mafia wannabes taking on the head guy? We wouldn't get to first base. The Santoris have left us alone. We still have the same contacts. They are letting us continue our business. We go at them and it's all over in more ways than one."

"I hear ya. Paulie called me the afternoon they offed him. He said this lawyer Cleary had been by. Knew all about where they were stashing him. Betsy Gallucci was the court reporter working with the lawyers. She could have spilled the beans. Remember you saw them together at a motel."

"Can't forget it. It surprised me that she would be doing a mick lawyer like that."

"To each his own," Peter said as he started to shape the dough for the bread.

"So where does this all lead? Sicilian revenge? Kill everyone. What?" Raphael said.

"Well we have to do something," Peter said as he slid the dough off his long peel into the warm ovens. He closed the oven door and looked at Raphael. "Paulie said this cop who tried to nail him could be the one behind it. It was Cleary who got him off that phony charge the Santoris cooked up against him. He's got his own investigating business now. Off Commonwealth."

"What are you saying? We should go pay him a visit? Is that what your saying?"

"Yeah. Why not? It can't hurt. The two of us can handle him."

"When?"

Peter opened the oven slightly to get a peek at his bread. "How about tomorrow? Today's Thursday. We'll pick him up after work," Peter said as he closed the oven door and began shaping more dough.

"Ok. But let's not get carried away. Ok?"

Peter looked at him and said, "We should carry it as far as we need to. *Voglio Vendetta.*"

Friday evening Tim came home totally wiped out. It was a bad wipe out like the waves he sometimes couldn't handle when he was a surfing in Southern California. A hard day in the operating could get him down but nothing like this. At least Edwin had neutralized Shamski's testimony or so it appeared from Tim's perspective. What about the jury? Nothing he could do about that. When he opened the door to his condo Meg was sitting on the couch watching the evening news. She offered him a quick kiss then she hurried to the kitchen. She returned with a glass of red wine for Tim along with cheese and crackers.

"What's the celebration?" Tim asked as he took a sip and sat down next to her.

"I heard from one of the beat reporters who is covering your trial. Mr. Stokes really shut down Cleary's witness against you."

"Yeah. It was something to watch. Don't know how much good it'll do. Do you mean a reporter was actually sitting in the courtroom today?" Tim asked. He didn't remember seeing any reporters.

"Oh yeah. They come in and out. They're not dressed in little reporter uniforms, so you may not be able to spot them," she laughed.

"You wouldn't publish the ongoing events would you? I mean report it as it's going on?"

"Usually not. Not enough interest. We wait till' it's over and then if there's a big judgment. Whammo right up there with all the gory details."

"Great. Lose and everyone hears about it. Win and no one knows. What a system. You should report things as they happen."

"We'd get kicked out of the courtroom and everyone would be gagged."

"Why did I know you would say that? What's for dinner?" Tim asked with a smile, ready to change the subject.

"Fajita's with skirt steak. Your favorite. Before that let me ask you something."

"Shoot."

"How well do you know Jack Trimble?"

"The heart surgeon at University? Well, we go back a long way. He's a good guy. Why?"

"Well there was an article in *The Globe* from one of their medical reporters about a study he presented in New York last week. He actually videotaped patient informed consents. Found out that most people don't remember what's said. Or disregard it."

"That's true but you have to do a sort of disclaimer like you read on a pack of cigarettes. So what?"

"Wouldn't it be nice if you had a taped interview of your meeting with the Bradford's?"

"I suppose. Of course, this judge would find some way to exclude it and Cleary would find some way to discredit it. In court things are never as they appear. The legal world is so caught up in their language and arguments, their process, that reality as we see is not reality to them. Cleary would argue that his client did not know about the videotape going on or that she was so traumatized by the ordeal that she had forgotten about it."

They went into the kitchen. On the stove Meg had a wok filled with beef bits, sautéed red and green bell pepper slices, onions, and julienne zucchini. Another pan contained black beans and rice. Meg wrapped several tortillas in foil and placed them in the oven to let them soften. She brought salsa, sour cream, cheddar cheese, and lettuce from the refrigerator while thinking about what Tim had said. It couldn't be that bad. She wondered if he was just feeling sorry for himself.

"Still," she said, "I have to believe that taping an interview would at least wipe out some claims. Have you ever seen an informed consent on video? Like maybe yourself just to see how well you do it, is it effective?"

"You know, now that you bring it up. No. But you have made me think. When Trimble did his study two years ago someone admitted one of my patients to the room where they did those patient videos you're talking about. By accident I was videotaped during an interview."

"Well, how did you do? Were you a star or just boring?" she asked playfully as she finished heating the wok. Tim removed the warmed tortillas from the oven and overlapped two tortillas. He proceeded to lay all the ingredients before him on the tortilla and folded it into a burrito. He took a bite and chewed slowly. Savoring and thinking at the same time.

"I'm trying to remember. Nancy Kimball gave it to me and I stuck it in my desk drawer that is filled with videos I haven't seen. How to do this, how to do that." Tim finished with another giant bite of his burrito.

"Well don't you think you ought to look at it? Maybe they videotaped you and the Bradfords."

"Yeah, in a perfect world. I'll look at it someday but I have too many things going on right now. Still there is something bothering me about it, but I can't put my finger on it. Anyway, great burrito. Almost as good as a Hollenbeck burrito."

"What may I ask is a Hollenbeck burrito? What's the difference between a burrito and fajita?" Meg's investigative reporter's mind was as work.

"I thought reporters could only ask one question at a time. That's three. First off it's pronounced fa he ta. The j is pronounced like an h. A fajita is made usually with beef strips from skirt steak. Skirt steak as you know is the diaphragm muscle of the steer. A fajita is served from a hot pan and you scoop the stuff on a tortilla. You just fold the tortilla once and have at it. A burrito is closed up completely like I've done, has beef, beans, rice, sour cream or whatever you want. When I took a month rotation at LA County Hospital as a fourth year the residents and students would go for lunch at a restaurant near the hospital called El Tepeyac. They served the biggest and best burritos. They had a huge one called a Hollenbeck burrito."

"Ok I give up. Why the Hollenbeck?"

"Well near the restaurant was the Hollenbeck LAPD station." Seeing Meg's perplexed look he went on, "They made these burritos for the cops sorta like doughnuts. Pretty soon everyone wanted the Hollenbeck burrito or so the story goes"

"I think I'm sorry I asked" Meg laughed.

Changing the subject Tim said, "I saw your first article on the malpractice crisis. It was right on. What's next?"

"Monday it's about judges. I went and looked up their records. You know how judges are shielded from scrutiny by the press and public. They're appointed for the most part.

Well judges judge each other and they have their own watch committees. It seems that one of the biggies they look for is the number of appeals from their courtroom and outcomes of those appeals."

"Is that the only process for review?" Tim had finished his first burrito and was making his second when he asked.

"Pretty much. Oh they look at conduct and professionalism, things like that, but the one that gets their attention is the appeal factor. The founders of the country placed the judicial at arm's length away from the executive and legislatives branches of government. Keeps things on an even keel. For the most part it works unless you get a bad judge then getting rid of him is not easy."

"What about Cull. How does he stack up?"

"He's at the top of the list. That is top of the worst list. He had more appeals with turnovers than any other of the superior court justices. He's been admonished but nothing happens to him."

"Great. And I get him."

"Well look at this way. If you lose you can appeal some of his decisions. But they have to be based on legal questions not the amount of the judgment. For example excluding our pictures is a basis for appeal. The excuse that they invade privacy or lack corroboration is BS."

"What about this article coming out during the trial. Won't it anger him? He must know about our relationship." Tim was getting wobbly again.

"Yeah. It might. But it's nothing that's not public record and he should be able to handle it. Judges are supposed to be immune to these kinds of attacks."

"Let's hope. What's for dessert?"

"Now or later?"

Twenty-three

Peter and Raphael sat in a black closed paneled van. They were parked on the second level of a parking structure across the street from Eddie Collin's office waiting for the detective to leave for home. They guessed that the car two spaces away belonged to Eddie because it had old police parking stickers on the windshield and bumpers. It was a Chevy and just looked like a car a former police detective would drive. It was nearly six o'clock and shadows were beginning to fall. The structure was nearly empty because it was Friday and most of the patrons were long gone for the weekend.

"This is going to be tricky. This guy's an ex-cop, tough. He won't take any bullshit off us. You ready Raph?"

"As ready as I'm going to get. I'm glad Paulie did this shit. I'm not cut out for it."

Raphael was always the kid brother. Protected by his older brothers but now Paulie was gone. He was anxious about becoming involved in something as serious as kidnapping and probably murder. He had the urge to right the wrong done to his beloved older brother but he also knew the consequences if he was caught

"Shut up you woos, here he comes"

They watched as Eddie walked up to his car and looked around like any good cop would do. The brothers slipped quietly out of

251

their van and circled around behind while Eddie placed his key in the lock. Suddenly he felt his arms being pinned behind him. Peter had him in an arm lock and Raphael wrapped his wrists in back of him with duct tape. They had rehearsed this maneuver. He finished wrapping Eddie's ankles and Peter whispered into Eddie's ear, "Take it easy. No one gets hurt here. All we want is information."

Eddie didn't believe that for a minute. He began to squirm but the two brothers were much too strong for his efforts. They taped his mouth and carried him squirming to the van and tossed him in the back. Peter looked around and seeing no one got into the van with his brother and drove off. They were already guilty of kidnapping an ex-BPD officer. There was only one way this could go.

Peter drove outside the city observing all speed limits and traffic signs. Soon they were heading north on interstate 93 and night had fallen. Outside Newburyport he turned off the highway and onto a back road. After several miles he pulled up to an abandoned quarry. Raphael looked puzzled. He had been silent during the trip but now he was confused.

"I thought we were going to take him to a motel and have a talk. What gives?" Raphael asked.

"Change of plans. If things get rough I'm not moving him from a motel. Paulie used to take us here when we were kids. Swimming and stuff. Remember?"

"Yeah. So what? I don't like what I'm hearing."

"Shut up and give me a hand." The two climbed out of the van and Peter popped open the back doors. Eddie was on the floor where they had left him. In the shadows he could see two figures then he was unceremoniously pulled by his ankles until he bounced to the ground. Peter ripped off the tape covering his mouth.

"Now we're going to have that conversation," he said.

Eddie blinked up. His nose bled from banging against the bumper when the brothers pulled him out. His lips and face were swollen. Despite this he was is not ready to talk. He simply glared at the two.

"You micks are always yakking. Cat got your tongue," Peter taunted. Raphael didn't say anything. He had never seen his brother like this.

"Don't be such a chickenshit. Undo me like a man and we'll talk."

Peter kicked him in the ribs and Eddie groaned. "What do you know about Paulie's gettin' killed? Did you finger him?"

Eddie didn't respond and only glared up at his captors through the gloom. Two swift kicks caught him in the right flank. He screamed. Raphael looked around but they were way out where no one could hear them.

"Jesus you sonafabitch. What do you want to know?" he asked through clenched teeth.

"Paulie called me the day he died and said this asshole lawyer Cleary knew all about him and where he was? How did he find out where Paulie was? Simple. You answer and we go home."

Eddie knew he was in a hard place. If he told the truth he was going to die. If he didn't he would die anyway. At this point he thought of his wife and children. What a waste this was. He had led a mostly good life. Why was it going to end like this? "C'mon Pete. You and your brother have never been busted before. That was Paulie's wish. To keep you guys out of it. Why do this? They'll find you and you'll spend the rest of your life in Walpole."

"Maybe so. But I'd be happy knowin' I got back for Paulie."

"I didn't kill Paulie. It was all mob," Eddie panted as the pain in his side returned.

"Oh we know that, but who let them know where he was?" That's the thing." He got ready to kick Eddie again when Raphael grabbed his arm. Peter glared at his brother but stopped. "Ok," he muttered.

"Eddie, I don't want this to end badly. Tell what you know and I swear to God we'll let you go. That's a promise."

There was something in the younger brother's voice that gave Eddie hope. He'd give them something and hope they were satisfied.

"Since you know that Cleary was my boss there's nothing to hide, I guess. He was seeing Betsy Gallucci who does the court reporting. She overheard where Paulie was and told Cleary."

"How do you fit into this? We already know about Gallucci and Cleary. Raph saw them at a motel together a coupla years ago."

Eddie didn't want to implicate himself so he remained silent. This got him another kick except it was to the ribs on his left. Now both sides hurt to breathe. He gasped for air and took short shallow breaths.

"Ok. No more of that stuff......shit it hurts," he panted. "Cleary hired me to find out where exactly the feds had stashed Paulie. I talked to a cop at the harbor and he let me know. In order to find out other information from Lenny I traded what I knew for what he knew. He's still bitter about Paulie offing his old man.....he told the Santoris."

Peter and Raphael walked away out of Eddie's earshot. Peter was pumped up to finish off Eddie and put him in the quarry.

Raphael was beside himself. He didn't want any part of this and said, "Doing an ex-cop who had nothing to do with the actual killing of our brother is dumb. Paulie didn't want us involved in this. He always protected us. It would be like killing him all over again if we do murder."

"I gotta live with myself and you gotta live with yourself. Somebody has to pay. That's just the way it is. We leave this guy around and go after Cleary then he'll know who did it."

"Wait. You want to kill a big shot lawyer? You crazy? They'd really come after us."

"They'd never find out it was us. I gotta plan. Maybe we could use Eddie to help us get Cleary."

As the brothers talked over a plan to lure Cleary to meet with Eddie, the hapless ex-cop was doing some thinking on his own. Although both sides hurt as if he had been stuck with hot pokers he was able to roll over several times and clear the back of the van. If he could roll away into the nearby underbrush he could hide in the dark, at least that was his prayer. The tape on his legs was loosening and he could slightly bend his knees. He rolled so he was perpendicular to the van. He kept logrolling and easily cleared the front of the van. The activity helped loosen the tape on his arms, which gave him more mobility. Although the pain was excruciating, he kept going. Soon he would be able to sit and then stand and hop. Approximately twenty feet beyond the van he came to some bushes and was able to wriggle around them as he moved farther away. He could still faintly hear the two talking when he felt a small ledge that he was able to jack knife himself onto. His legs were nearly free of the tape. He decided to drop over the ledge to the other side and make for the trees he could just see in the darkened skyline.

Raphael and Peter were still arguing when they heard a blood-curdling scream. "What the hell?" Peter began running back to the van. There was no Eddie Collins. "Shit he must've rolled away. Dumb shit. He made it to the quarry and fell over."

"We gotta see over. Maybe he's hung up on a ledge, needs help." Raphael searched in the back of the van for a flashlight. The two made their way carefully toward the quarry, about thirty feet in front of the van. Peter carefully peered over the side and shined the light downward. He scanned back and forth. The only thing that caught his eye was the rippling of water. "Man it must be hundred and fifty feet down to the water. He musta bounced off the sides on the way down and hit the water."

"What are we going to do?" Raphael moaned. "It's just like we killed him. We should never have left him alone."

"Shut up. No one knows we're here. It'll be weeks before anyone finds the body, if they ever do. That water's cold. He's going to stay down for a long time. Let's go."

The two brothers piled into the van and carefully backed away. On the road home Peter said, "It may not have been what we wanted but I'm beginning to feel good about it already. That guy did himself in. We were going to let him go."

"Nice. That's bullshit and you know it. We killed him as good as if we put a bullet in his head."

"We never need to talk about this again. We still have Cleary to deal with."

"We? You've got to be kidding!"

Twenty-four

Monday morning arrived and Jerry was preparing for trial. Today he would wrap it up and tomorrow or Wednesday Edwin would start his rebuttal case. He needed the information from Eddie Collins on Davis. He hoped the weekend had been fruitful for the detective. He was due in court at nine thirty and it was already nine o'clock. Jerry could hear the office coming alive outside his closed door. He had come in early to get some work done away from his kids who were noisiest in the morning. He had two experts today. A psychiatrist will tell the jurors that the shock of her husband's death had permanently damaged Julie Bradford's psyche. He thought it was worth a shot. The other was a pathologist who had reviewed the autopsy results along with photographs showing the rather unsightly ligature on the middle cerebral artery. Jerry planned to make a big deal about that.

Jerry stopped and gazed out onto the Common watching the city come alive. He loved

Boston at this time of day. The phone buzzed and he picked up. He learned Joan Collins was on the line and punched the blinking light.

"Hello Joan," he said without giving her a chance to identify herself.

"Hello Mr. Cleary. So good of you to take my call," she said but the anxiety in her voice was palpable. Joan Collins had worried many times in the past when her husband was on the BPD. But this time things felt different.

"Something wrong? You sound terrible."

"I don't know. Eddie didn't come home Friday. He said he had talked to you earlier, was thinking he might have to go to New York. He said he was on his way home but he never did get here. I'm very worried Mr. Cleary. I know he's a tough cop, can handle himself but this is not like Eddie. I've checked with his friends and associates. No one's seen him."

"I don't know what to say. When I talked to him Friday he was satisfied with an investigator he hired in New York, didn't say anything about going there. Eddie's reliable. He wouldn't go anywhere without you knowing. Have you called Rastellini?" Jerry also began to get a bad feeling about this. He automatically reached for his inhaler to ease his stuffy nose.

"I did. He's going to send Patrick Kennedy around to check his office. Maybe he collapsed there. I don't know. I thought maybe you had called him and he went to New York. He told me that the doctor in New York you were interested in had some trouble in med school. The investigator he hired there had just called him."

Jerry was getting interested now. "What sort of trouble? Did Eddie say?"

"Only that this doctor had been arrested for drunk driving when he was a med student. Had his license suspended for six months. Please Mr. Cleary I'm worried. Can you call Rastellini and make inquiries for me? I feel lost," she nearly cried.

Jerry waited until Joan settled down. "Did Eddie tell you the name of the investigator?"

"It was a guy by the name of Derwin Jones. A black guy Eddie knew. Used to be NYPD. Eddie has worked with him on cases in the past."

I'll need Mr. Jones' help if Eddie has pulled a disappearing act. "Interesting. I'm due in court shortly. But at the break I will call Rastellini. Give me your number." Joan rattled off her telephone number and Jerry hung up.

Eddie could have gone to New York, Jerry thought, but not without telling someone. He supposed he could check with the airlines but he'd let Patrick Kennedy handle that. He told his secretary to call Derwin Jones in New York and explain the circumstances. Rehire him over the phone if necessary and tell him to keep digging into Dr. Davis' past. He hung up when he finished and stood, stretching. He was bothered by Joan's call. It wouldn't take a genius to figure out that Eddie had been involved in hunting down Paulie Strata. Somebody was out there seeking revenge. Jerry knew with Sicilians involved that was bound to happen. Or maybe, he thought it was just a car jacking that went bad. Eddie could be difficult when threatened. He didn't really buy that. Eddie drove a piece of crap. *No. Something else is going on here.*

While Jerry was talking to Joan Collins and dealing with her problem, Meg was across town nursing a cup of coffee. She had gotten up late and phoned the paper to say she was chasing down a story. She received a compliment from the reporter answering the phone about her second installment dealing with the malpractice crisis. The reporter said he wanted Judge Cull trying his malpractice case, then laughed and hung up. *Very funny.* Today she would hunt down that videotape since she knew Tim was a lost cause dealing with the details of this lawsuit. He was too personally involved to see the forest for the trees. He was backsliding into the doldrums that had consumed him for so many months. He was used to fighting his battles in the operating room, not the courtroom.

Meg dressed and caught the MTA to University Hospital and headed straight toTim's office. It was ten o'clock. Judith told her to go right in when she heard what Meg was after. She hoped something would happen to pick her boss up. Meg entered Tim's office and went to his desk. Finding the desk drawers locked she went in search of Judith. With key in hand she returned to the desk and unlocked it. She opened the lower drawer to find it filled with videotapes. After a moment she selected the one that had a strip of tape scribbled with " Dr. Graves and patient #30." It was dated Feb. 16, 1986. How could Tim not notice this? She was aware of the date Mr. Bradford had entered the hospital as a result of her review of the records with Tim. She looked around the room for a video playback. Tim had an inexpensive TV sitting on top of a built in VCR. She found the remote on top and shoved the tape into the slot and turned it on. Soon images appeared on the screen of University Hospital's multiple disclaimers. The patient's name was not on the screen but the number 30 was displayed. Without any further identification the tape showed Tim entering the room and introducing himself to Julie Bradford who acknowledged that they had met briefly in Tim's office. Soon Tim was explaining the surgery and why less invasive methods would not work because of the size of the aneurysm. He also explained that surgery was a risky procedure due to the nature of the aneurysm. Julie asked appropriate questions and nodded affirmatively when he asked her at the end of the session if she understood. *That lying, manipulative…………*

She ejected the tape and hurried from Tim's inner office. She wanted to get to her office to make a copy of the tape before she handed it over to Tim, then she thought that a transcript of the interview would be better yet. As she passed Judith an idea to save time struck her. *Since there wasn't enough time to do everything she wanted why not have Judith type the interview?* She easily persuaded Tim's secretary to watch the tape and type a transcript. After she helped Judith move her typewriter into Tim's office Judith told her to find Bill Platt and he would make a copy for her. By eleven thirty she had the copy of the tape and the typed transcript with two copies. She hurried down to the hospital entrance where a cab Judith had called was waiting. She told the driver to head directly to the courthouse. She'd call her boss later and explain why she wasn't at work.

Jerry's direct questioning of his own expert went as planned, flawlessly, with the psychiatrist presenting everything Jerry wanted the jurors to hear. The psychiatrist was in her late thirties and attractive in a studious way. She wore horn-rimmed glasses, light makeup, and a tasteful business suit. Her hair was long and she kept brushing it back during her testimony. Edwin could see the male jurors were paying close attention. The testimony was outrageous as far as Edwin was concerned. She postulated that Julie had suffered permanent damage with the sudden and unexpected death of her husband. She was still grieving and would likely do so for some time. Later, during cross examination, Edwin got the psychiatrist to admit that Julie had seen her three times and all visits occurred after the lawsuit had been filed.

Judge Cull looked imperiously out over the courtroom when Edwin finished his cross examination and announced, "It's eleven thirty. Time to break for lunch. I will hear Mr. Stokes' motion at one o'clock. The jurors should be back here by one thirty." He banged his gavel.

As Edwin was gathering papers and Tim was shaking his head. "What motion are you presenting to the judge?"

"The pathologist who Cleary hired has some photographs of the autopsy which look rather ugly. To be frank a suture around the middle cerebral artery placed by a resident doctor isn't going to go over well with the jurors. I'm going to try and get them excluded on the basis they are prejudicial and unfair. They were taken at the time the patient was dead, blood everywhere and don't represent the scene played out in the operating room."

"I haven't seen those photographs in two years. They are graphic and don't begin to tell the story of what happened," Tim said dragging out the last word for emphasis.

"That story will be yours to tell tomorrow or Wednesday. Let's go get lunch." Just as Edwin turned he saw Meg hovering near the door. "Here comes your fiancée. I wonder what she has for us today. Her report in *The Bulletin* isn't going to endear Cull to our side," he said in a tone that indicated he was not pleased.

"What difference does it make? He's been against us since the beginning." Tim hugged Meg when she reached the defense table. "You look rushed. What's going on?"

Meg tried to control her excitement. "You remember that tape in your office? Well I went and got it today. You and Mr. Stokes should see it right away. There's a VCR at my office and I have a cab waiting. Let's go."

Lisa was not in court with Edwin since she had gone to New York to bring Dr. Davis up to speed with the trial. The three hurried out of the courtroom and into the waiting taxicab. Several minutes later they entered *The Bulletin* building and quickly went to the audiovisual office where there were banks of televisions and VCRs.

"We need these to tape TV news from all over the world. See if we're keeping up with the electronic media." Meg said over her shoulder and she headed for an unused VCR. She slipped in the tape and they stood and watched.

When the tape was finished Edwin complained, "Why are we getting this tape now? I could have introduced it earlier. Judge Cull is not going to be thrilled about letting us use it now that he has had all this free publicity in your paper." Edwin was not happy.

"So what," Meg said. "If he doesn't allow it then he is being blatantly prejudicial. My guess is that no matter when it was discovered he'd find some reason to exclude it if he could."

Edwin thought about it and finally said, "You're probably right. Let me see if I can guess what he would say. Mrs. Bradford has a reasonable expectation of privacy when she enters the hospital. Mr. Bradford on the other hand signed a general consent form that allows videotaping and photographing for medical purposes, but that doesn't include his wife. Therefore the tapes are excluded. How am I doing?"

"Too well. But if he won't exclude the pathologist using photographs how can he not let this in?" Tim moaned.

"You've got to get a grip, Tim," Meg said. "What if the video was shown with her voice dubbed out and her picture fuzzed over? Wouldn't he accept that? At least it will show the jurors Tim did talk about alternative treatments with Mr. Bradford."

"It's possible. I'll try. How many copies of this are there?" Edwin asked.

Meg wasn't about to tell Edwin she had made a copy herself. "That's it. Oh, I do have a transcript of the video with two copies. You can have them." Meg handed Edwin the transcripts.

"Let me have it. Since we are trying to get this in I will drop my motion to suppress the photographs or perhaps it would be better to make a strong appeal. Make Cleary go out on a limb. We better get back Tim. Thanks Meg and I know you have a job to do, but it would be helpful if you could hold off on the rest of your series until this is over. Please."

Meg simply looked at him. "See you at home this evening Tim," she said and kissed him on the cheek.

At one o'clock, while his client and the plaintiff were out of the courtroom, Edwin stood alone and presented his reasons for excluding the photographs of Mr. Bradford's autopsy. He did so with a great deal of enthusiasm and passion, hoping to bait Jerry. He told the judge that letting these photographs in was tantamount to handing his case over to the plaintiff. He cried out that Mr. Cleary was underhanded and trying to prejudice the jury against his client.

When he finished Jerry rose and calmly said, "Mr. Bradford had signed a consent form which allowed him to be videotaped or photographed. This would include all areas and aspects of his care whether it is in the operating room, at the bedside or at autopsy. Mr. Stokes' motion to suppress the photographs are a clear cut admission that his client screwed up and the pictures are telling," Jerry said raising his voice while slamming his fist on the table. "I see no credible objection to these photographs or for that matter any pictures or videos that might expose the egregious way in which plaintiff's husband was treated by Dr. Graves. Mr. Bradford cries out from the grave for truth and justice to be served here your honor."

Judge Cull, aware of his track record on appeals and today's article in *The Bulletin,* decided to sugar coat his answer. "I have given this a great deal of thought. I agree the pictures are graphic but not to the point of being prejudicial. I'm sure the details of the autopsy when described with words will conger up all kinds of distorted images in the minds of the jurors. Perhaps the pictures might even clarify those images, better the devil you know, and all that. Might even soften them and help your client, Mr. Stokes. Motion denied. The pictures are allowed. If there is no further business before the court we will begin the afternoon's session in ten minutes."

"Your honor there is one item that has come to my attention. It seems that unknown to the plaintiff and defense alike the informed consent session of Mr. Bradford and Dr. Graves was videotaped. At the time of Mr. Bradford's admission there was an ongoing study at University Hospital and Mr. Bradford was admitted to the study room due to overcrowding on the neurosurgical floor. The tape quite clearly shows Dr. Graves discussing the pros and cons of surgery along with other techniques to treat the cerebral aneurysm. What's interesting is that plaintiff, who denied she had met with Dr. Graves the night before surgery, was an active participant in the discussion. I have copies of the typed transcripts." Edwin passed out the documents and stood quietly while Jerry and Judge Cull read.

Jerry was fuming inside. What he had read was very damaging to his case and there was no way he was going to let the jury see the videotape. He better make it good since he had just pleaded for all photographic materials to be admitted as evidence.

"This is a ninth inning theatrical ploy to discredit my client's testimony. I'm sure my client, who has been under tremendous stress as the result of her husband's death blocked out this meeting. You heard the psychiatrist testify that Mrs. Bradford is still in shock and denial. This tape was of a private interview and my client did not give permission to have her words recorded. In fact this is a severe invasion of the privacy she expects to have when meeting with a physician. I move that the transcript and video be excluded."

Judge Cull sat looking at Jerry. Just moments earlier he had ruled in favor of the plaintiff's attorney to let in photographs and now he was being asked by the same attorney to exclude a video-tape. He longed for the good old days when he could run rough shod and his word was law. Now he has newspapers after him, his colleagues are scrutinizing every ruling he makes. Jerry was from the neighborhood and he, Judge Cull, didn't like the uppity black lawyer from Harvard. *Too smart for his own good.* "I will review the videotape tonight and render a decision tomorrow." He directed his clerk, who was taking minutes of the meeting, to secure the tape from Mr. Stokes. She waddled over to Edwin then back to the judge handing him the tape.

Cull looked at the tape and asked, "Are there any more copies of this tape?"

He was looking at Edwin and as far as Edwin knew there were none according to Meg Logan. "No. That's the only tape."

He looked at his clerk and said, "Please note that I have the videotape in hand and there are no copies." He looked at the two attorneys and went on with, "Mr. Stokes how many copies of the typed transcript do you have?"

"I have the original here in my possession and two copies. The one counsel has and yours."

"Those documents will also be turned over to the clerk until the time I rule on this issue. Clear."

"Yes your honor," Edwin said, "but time is running out. We expect to begin our case in the morning with Dr. Graves' testimony. Can I expect to have a decision by then?"

"Very likely. How long does the tape run?"

"Twenty minutes."

Judge Cull nodded and left the bench with the tape and transcripts. In the afternoon the pathologist presented his findings and the photographs. It seemed to Edwin that the jury was bored and not paying attention to the testimony. He could not tell whether that was good or bad. He asked the pathologist several questions on cross-examination. After that Jerry had an actuary detail the potential monetary losses and future financial needs of his client because of her husband's death. Edwin objected to most of the conclusions the number cruncher had arrived at in his research. The session ended with a jury that appeared bored and tired. They were told that the defense would begin their rebuttal the next day.

While the courtroom cleared Edwin remained seated with Tim. He had told him to stay a minute. "Are you set for tomorrow?" Mr. Stokes asked Tim.

"I guess so. It would be a lot better to know whether he's going to let the tape in or not so we can coordinate the presentation."

"That's precisely why I wanted to talk to you. It's better that we don't do that. The jury would see right away that we rehearsed our little dog and pony show. It looks fake, contrived. Just be ready to answer the questions. I'm going to focus on the actual events surrounding the surgery including technical questions that plaintiff didn't ask at your deposition. Exactly what happened in the operating room and why."

"You mean I get to answer direct questions about what really happened? Wow I didn't think that would ever happen. Some legal precedence where you don't answer direct questions because they may be prejudicial or some such thing."

"You better put that attitude on the shelf. It makes you look like sour grapes. Just be truthful and clear in your answers."

"Understood," Tim said giving a mock salute.

Twenty-five

Judge Cull returned to his chambers with the videotape and transcripts. He had already read the printed version of the interview. He knew what would be on the tape. Clearly the plaintiff was lying and Dr. Graves had done his job. But he wasn't about to allow the tape into evidence. As a former plaintiff attorney he felt the courts were stacked against the plaintiff and tilted toward the defense. The videotape would crush the plaintiff's testimony and assure a victory for the defense. This is a courtroom where the trying of facts was supposed to supercede all other considerations. However, he could rule that the facts in this case were obtained by violating the rights of privacy of Mrs. Bradford. *Weak, but effective.* Her testimony is such a gross lie that there was no explanation other than fraud. Still he didn't like the black lawyer and was clearly rooting for Jerry Cleary. What was he to do?

Judge Cull lived in the suburbs west of Boston, forsaking his roots in South Boston. At heart he was a Southie but in mind he was now a well off suburban lace-curtain Irish judge. He hated that characterization but he had worked hard to get where he was. Besides, in the suburbs he was less apt to run into old neighborhood connections asking for favors. As he arrived home in his Suburban SUV, he was greeted by his longsuffering wife who had listened year after year to his pontificating about his day's toil in the courtroom. He kissed her and went directly to his study were he opened a bottle of Irish whiskey and poured himself three fingers. His wife followed him into the study and looked puzzled. Usually Judge Cull would spend some time with her before he asked for a drink and dinner.

"What's the story? No sermons about how bad defense attorneys are," she asked frowning at her husband.

"Oh. Plenty. But I have a problem. Watch this tape and let me know what you think."

"Is this about the malpractice trial going on? *The Bulletin* wrote a not so flattering story about you," she said.

He didn't bother to respond, he would let the tape do his talking. They sat and watched the twenty-minute recording. When it was over she said, "Sounds like a doctor telling his patient and wife the pros and cons and risks of surgery."

"It is. Only trouble is it was recorded without the wife knowing about it. I want to exclude it."

"Let me guess. It would help the defense if this is shown," she said while the judge hit the rewind button.

"How did you ever guess? This is the only copy of the interview," he said while staring at the images being bounced around while the tape rewound.

"When do you have to make this momentous decision? Soon I hope, because I'm hungry."

"Tomorrow. The defense begins their case. This tape would really help them but it was done without plaintiff's permission."

"But she's not the patient. Why does she get to benefit from the 'doctor patient privilege'?"

"I'm not sure she does. But if they appeal I'll worry about precedence then. What's for dinner?"

"Baked chicken with all the root vegetables you can imagine. Carrots, turnips, potatoes, onions, the whole bit. Apple pie for dessert." She stood while she watched the final images parade backwards across the screen of the TV. She wondered why her husband wouldn't let the tape in and let the chips fall where they may. She loved him, but she knew that he often let his emotions and personal bias color his judgment. In short he did not have the right temperament to be a judge.

Judge Cull stared at his wife, wondering why she wasn't in the kitchen. Their little session was over. "I'll be through here in a minute," he said taking a sip of his whiskey. Mrs. Cull took her cue and when she was out of earshot he pushed the record button and went into the kitchen. After dinner he ejected the tape and placed it into his briefcase. The typescripts went through the shredder.

That night Tim did not sleep well. He couldn't cram for his session in court. There was too much material. He did read his deposition marking several pages where he thought Jerry would pounce on him. He noted that the actual events of the surgery itself were not covered in the questions Cleary had asked him. There were more questions about his state of mind or how he informed the patient about surgical risks and rewards. The business about his being a sperm donor while a medical student worried him. He wondered if Cleary would pursue that line of questioning. Edwin had told him to stick to the story in the deposition and not to change anything or freelance and expand on things he had said. Answer the questions truthfully.

He finally fell asleep at two o'clock but was awakened by the alarm at five. Meg rolled out of bed the same time he did and went to the kitchen and prepared bacon, eggs, coffee and toast while Tim showered. It was nearly six when he joined her in the kitchen.

"Is this what I get when I testify in court, sort of a last meal?" he asked kissing Meg on the neck.

"Of course but let's not make this a habit," she smiled. "How do you feel? You were up late and didn't have much to say last night."

Tim sat down and Meg placed the food in front of him. He picked at the eggs and took a bite of the toast. As he chewed he thought about her question. How did he feel?

"Well I feel like I'm going to jail. I hate the courthouse. Every time I walk into that sorry place I can feel my heart beating faster and my stomach churning. How can lawyers stand it day in and day out?"

"They're not the ones on the grill. They love it. A chance to strut and do their thing. They would say the same thing about you going to the hospital everyday. You love it but the patients dread it. Anyway, it's show time. No more feeling sorry for yourself. Be positive. Exude confidence. You did nothing wrong."

Tim appreciated what Meg was trying to do. He took a more substantial bite of his eggs. "I didn't tell you but the judge is going to rule on the videotape this morning. I think he is going to exclude it. I just got that feeling yesterday when he read the transcript of the tape."

Meg shook her head. "This judge is not being fair and it's obvious. As a former plaintiff attorney he's going to lean in that direction. But there's got to be something more. Even the most biased judge puts up a front to appear fair. This judge has denied every one of your motions and even allowed stuff back in that the attorneys agreed should be excluded."

"Tell me about it," Tim said as he took a sip of coffee and stood. He was dressed in his best suit, a crisp white shirt and a blue tie. "How do you like my courtroom clothes? We joke at the hospital that whenever a doctor looks nice it means he.... or she is either going to a funeral or court. Most doctors don't want to be seen in either place."

"You look great. If he excludes that tape I'm of a strong notion that we should run excerpts in *The Bulletin.*" Meg was giving Tim a look that he had seen before. It was the hard eyes and set jaw.

"Good luck. The judge has the only tape and he confiscated the transcripts. They won't see the light of day now or probably ever."

Meg didn't want to implicate her fiancé in a conspiracy. No privilege here, so she shut up, smiled, and said, "You're right. I'll see you this evening." They embraced and kissed. Tim gave a lackluster wave good bye.

In the courtroom Tim felt more anxious that he ever had before any surgery. Jerry was over on his side with Jason Damon and Julie Bradford. They appeared very confident while they shuffled papers and talked in hushed tones. Jerry was particularly pleased with Judge Cull's ruling on the videotape and transcript. They were in violation of the plaintiff's privacy, he ruled. Even if it were basis for an appeal, that would take several years and the best he would get would be a retrial. What a system. Suddenly Judge Cull banged his gavel and announced to Edwin that he could begin his defense.

Edwin stood and gave a summary of the trial proceedings pointing out all the inconsistencies thus far. It was a short presentation and ended when he was assured all the jurors were paying attention. He called Tim to the stand. Now for the first time the jurors would hear his side of the story. They had watched Tim throughout the plaintiff's case, trying to gauge his reaction to the testimony as it was given.

Tim stood and nervously adjusted his tie. He strode to the stand, avoiding eye contact with any of the jurors. After he was sworn he took his seat and adjusted the microphone upward. He was a very handsome man, having retained most of his California sun bleached hair and muscular build. Exercise had always been a part of his life and until the trial began he was in excellent physical shape. He smiled at Edwin to let him know he was ready although he could feel his heart thumping erratically in his chest.

"Good morning Dr. Graves. Could you give us a little background? Let the jury know who you are."

"Yes. I was born in Chicago and grew up in Glendale, California. I graduated from USC and from Harvard Medical School. I did my training in neurosurgery at University Hospital and have been on the teaching staff there since that time. I am currently Chief of Neurosurgery."

Edwin asked more questions about Tim's qualifications trying to paint a broader picture of him than the brief thumbnail sketch of his life that Tim had outlined. When he felt the jury had heard enough he asked, "Did you meet with the plaintiff on the evening before Mr. Bradford's surgery?"

"Yes, I did." Tim hazarded a glance at the jury. He wanted them to see his face and know that he was telling the truth.

"Tell us about that meeting with Mr. and Mrs. Bradford."

Tim went on to detail the meeting including how long it lasted, what Julie Bradford was wearing, and what questions she asked. He was very convincing and now that he could answer direct questions about facts he knew to be true, he was loosening up. He knew Jerry was ready to pounce when Edwin was through. He tried to interrupt Tim's composure with objections and demands for Edwin to be more precise with his questions. But it only slowed things down. Telling the truth was so easy and Tim was determined to not allow that loudmouth to get to him. Not yet anyway. After a thorough examination of the consent process, the court adjourned for fifteen minutes. Edwin told Tim he had done well, but reminded him not to fold his arms on his chest because it was a defensive posture and they were on the offense.

After the break it was time to actually talk about the surgery itself. Edwin asked, "How many patients with cerebral aneurysms have you treated."

Tim thought about that answer. He wanted to be accurate. "Well five years ago I reported my own personal series of surgical cases in the Journal of Neurosurgery. At that time I had done three hundred and ninety cases. Since then I've done an additional one hundred or so. Patients with brain aneurysms who I saw but did not go to surgery number in the thousands." He went on to explain his answer to the jury assuring them that not everyone with a cerebral aneurysm is a candidate for surgery. This reinforced his testimony, which clearly revealed his efforts to inform the Bradfords of alternative forms of treatment. Tim felt that he was getting through to the jurors.

Next Edwin asked Tim to detail the events of the surgery he performed on Mr. Bradford.

"The surgery in this case," he started, "was risky because of the size of the aneurysm. A small aneurysm has a narrow neck like the stem of an apple. On the other hand a larger aneurysm may have a stem more like a squash with a broad stem. The wider the stem or neck of the aneurysm the more difficult it is to clip."

"Tell us what happened when you came to the point of clipping the aneurysm," Edwin interrupted. As Tim became more comfortable he risked giving too much information, revealing something Jerry Cleary might use against him.

Tim thought about this answer. It would be so easy to relate his personal history with a cerebral aneurysm as a way to make the jury understand, but it probably wouldn't be wise. "Years ago a famous surgeon from Boston devised a clip specifically for use on aneurysms and blood vessels. These clips were called Cushing clips named after the surgeon, Harvey Cushing. Since that time the clips have been modified and now come in all different sizes. The clips are applied with this device." Tim reached into his inside coat pocket and pulled out an applier. He showed the jury how it worked. He also showed how it could fail when the tip of the applier did not coapt precisely. This occurs, he explained, when there is a slight imbalance of pressure on the arms of the applier while squeezing it shut. The clip tips then would not meet evenly and have a scissoring effect on the vessel.

"I object to this show and tell," Jerry shouted when he could see the jury finally coming to life with Tim's presentation. He turned bright red. "I have not seen this device and cannot question him about it. Is this an exhibit? What is this, a lecture hall or a courtroom," Jerry asked sarcastically as he sat down. He reached over and took two puffs of his inhaler in each nostril.

Judge Cull had been taken aback as well. What were his choices? Sustain the objection and admonish the jury or let it pass. He decided this wasn't going to help the defense that much and he had to at least put on an appearance of fairness. "Overruled. The device is allowed in as evidence but in the future any such aids will be shown to the plaintiff attorney prior to presentation."

Edwin smiled to himself. "Your honor my client has prepared this presentation on his own. I was unaware of the use of surgical instruments but I must say it certainly lends credibility to his testimony."

Jerry was up again. "I object," he said in a more controlled voice. "Defense counsel cannot determine whether the witness is credible."

"Sustained. Get on with it Mr. Stokes," Judge Cull said impatiently.

"Yes your honor. Now Dr. Graves you have described this scissoring effect. How often does it happen?"

"Depends on the size of the clip. It's less likely with a smaller clip. But with a larger clip, which was needed here with a broad neck aneurysm it is more likely. I would say once in a hundred times and it usually does not lead to the events in this case. Mr. Bradford's aneurysm was quite large. It only takes a small amount of uneven pressure to make this happen. Unfortunately when it occurred the bleeding could not be controlled." Tim went on to explain how he tried to control the bleeding and finally decided that it was hopeless. The chief resident ligated the vessel to stop the bleeding but that led to the brain infarction.

"How did you know there was this scissoring effect?"

"You can tell right away when it doesn't feel right. But further proof is the autopsy photos showed by Mr. Cleary. You can plainly see the clip there and the ends of it are not coapted." Edwin passed around the photo to the jury.

"Dr. Graves what about plaintiff's expert, Dr. Shamski, stating that the surgery was done too fast?" Edwin wanted to put this one away. He didn't want the jury to think that this was slipshod surgery.

"The best I can answer is that as a surgeon learns about a procedure over the years he or she becomes more skilled. When Mr. Bradford had his surgery I had done over four hundred repairs. I am unaware of the number of these operations Dr. Shamski has done but clearly if you only do one or two a year you will be slow, tentative. Everyone has his own pace. Golfers, baseball pitchers et cetera. You've seen pitchers take a long time between pitches, golfers a long time with their routines. People reflect their pace. Some walk slowly others quickly. My pace is different than Dr. Shamski's. When I was a pitcher I was quick, I didn't waste time on the mound."

"That's baseball but isn't the operating room different?" Edwin didn't like Tim's analogy. It might lead the jurors to think that Tim looked on surgery as some sort of sporting event.

"Years ago I had a time and motion engineer come to the operating room and watch me for a week. I wanted to know how to speed things up so that there was less operative time and of course less anesthesia time. That would make it safer for the patient. He observed that the biggest time waster was the surgeon. By patting tissue two or three times before dissecting or asking for one suture then changing his or her mind and asking for another. In short, tentative motions, redundant motions, unsure motions were all a basis for time wasted. By working on these areas I was able to shorten my total operative time and improve the efficiency of the surgical staff during an operation. They could predict better and be prepared."

"Thank you. I have no more questions for Dr. Graves at this time."

"In that case we will continue with Mr. Cleary after lunch. Jurors are admonished not to discuss the case with each other or with anyone else." He banged his gavel and left the bench.

Jerry was angrily putting papers back into his briefcase acting as if he had just heard the largest pack of lies ever uttered in the courtroom. He looked Tim's way and simply glared, using his favorite intimidation persona. Tim didn't appear to be intimidated as he talked casually to Edwin while watching Jerry's show out of the corner of his eye.

Jerry whispered something to his client and Jason then hurried out of the courtroom to find a phone. He dialed his office and spoke to his secretary. She had informed him that Eddie Collins' wife had called and left a number. She also gave him the information the private investigator in New York had uncovered concerning Dr. Davis. Jerry wanted to call Joan Collins but remembered he had promised to call Rastellini. He was able to get through to Rastellini but all he learned was that they were investigating Eddie's disappearance and so far had no leads. All they did know was that Eddie had not gone to New York. If he wasn't found in the next forty-eight hours Rastellini was going to open a criminal investigation.

Jerry dialed the number Joan Collins had left and there was an immediate answer. "Mrs. Collins," Jerry said, "any word about Eddie?"

"None. What trouble did you get my husband into?" she asked coolly.

"I didn't get him into any trouble. He was working for me, but he worked for a lot of people. What makes you think I was the cause of his disappearance?"

"He told me he was working for you and had to do some things that bothered him. I suspect it was something illegal," she said without emotion. "Did you find time to call Rastellini like you promised?" with a slight touch of sarcasm.

"As a matter of fact I did. They have nothing new but if he doesn't turn up in the next few days they'll start a criminal investigation. Judging from the tone of his voice I would prepare myself."

"What was so all fired important he had to stick his neck out?" she asked heatedly.

"I don't know. He was doing routine investigation of a doctor and that's all. Whatever he may have done illegally was on his own." Jerry didn't like the direction the conversation was taking. He knew Eddie had found evidence of Tim Graves' biological relationship with Joey Santori. But he didn't know how he found it and didn't want to. He just wanted the evidence. "Eddie didn't leave any letters or documents for me did he?"

"Is that all you care about?" she demanded but cooled down immediately. "Listen, I appreciate what you did for Eddie when he was in trouble. Lord knows you saved his life. It's just that I'm worried sick. If I find anything I'll send it over."

Jerry thanked her and hung up. No luck he thought. He was about to grill Graves and he didn't have the last link in what was going to be a long and hard session for the good doctor.

Jerry returned to the courtroom and found the jury sitting and waiting for him. He had spent so much time on the phone he had missed lunch.

"Call your first witness," Cull intoned with a scowl at the tardy attorney.

Jerry smiled at the judge and jury. He apologized for being late and then asked that Tim Graves take the stand. Tim stood and looked at Jerry. He could see that the attorney was relishing this moment. He briskly walked to the stand and sat down. The judge reminded him he was still under oath. Tim positioned the microphone to his height and looked at the jury, then Jerry.

Jerry stood staring at Tim for several moments in order to get him off guard and create a tension. He finally started by asking, "Dr. Graves do you know Dr. Shamski?"

"I'd never heard of Dr.Shamski prior to this trial."

"How is it that two neurosurgeons both certified by the American Board of Neurological Surgery be so divergent in their testimony?"

The question raised a red flag in Tim's mind. He was trying to get him to say something negative about his expert witness, hired guns, etc. He had no intention of falling for that. "There are about two thousand board certified neurosurgeons in the United States and I daresay they all have their own opinions. It's the consensus of opinions that set our standards. I believe what I testified to is the consensus of the majority of neurosurgeons."

"Really? Are you talking about academic neurosurgeons who practice in an ivory tower or those who are out in the real world?"

He's really trying to bait me. What an asshole. "I believe the standards are for anyone who practices neurosurgery, whether at a university hospital or private hospital. We all live under the same standards."

"Is that so? Your expert Dr. Davis. Is he an academic neurosurgeon or a real world doctor?"

Tim fidgeted in his chair. Of course Dr. Davis was an academic neurosurgeon at one of the best medical schools in New York. He finally answered, "I'm not sure I understand your question, but I believe he is an academic surgeon."

"Thank you. Now is it your contention that Mr. Bradford's aneurysm was not treatable by a catheter?"

Tim looked skeptical. He was waiting for Mr. Stokes to object to the question as being too broad. Lacked foundation etc. He stole a look at his attorney who was writing on a legal pad. *I guess I'm on my own.* "That was my opinion and the opinion of the doctor who does those procedures at the hospital."

"Is that so?" Jerry shuffled some papers, apparently looking for something. Tim knew that was another ploy to make him nervous and alert the jury to some bombshell that was coming. Cleary knew the name already. Finally he recovered a piece of paper and read from it. Would that be Dr. Stanton?"

"Yes."

"It says here in a memo from your attorneys that Dr. Stanton had no specific recollection of Mr .Bradford's case but does recall reviewing similar cases with you," Jerry smirked. "Do you have any evidence that you and he met and discussed Mr. Bradford's problem?"

Edwin was up in a flash. "I object. That memo is a response to Mr. Cleary's attempts to call Dr. Stanton as a percipient witness. Dr. Stanton stated that he had reviewed many cases with Dr. Graves he just doesn't recall this specific case."

"Overruled. The witness can answer."

"I recall meeting with Dr. Stanton several days before Mr. Bradford's surgery and going over the aneurysms with him. He stated he didn't think the aneurysm was amenable to clotting," Tim said choosing the word clotting so the jury would know what he was talking about.

Jerry rolled his eyes. "The witness is not answering the question. Give me a yes or no. Do you have any evidence when and where you met with Dr. Stanton about Mr. Bradford's problem?"

What a jerk. Am I supposed to carry a tape recorder around whenever I talk to a consultant? "No."

"Now doctor you stated that you reviewed the risks and benefits of surgery with the Bradford's the night before surgery. My client disputes that. Did you document your meeting and what was discussed?" Jerry asked, staring intently at Tim and then looking over to the jury.

Your client is a liar Tim wanted to shout but that would be the sure way to defeat. *I have proof of the meeting but your judge won't let me use it.* "No I did not document specifically who was in the room only that I met with the patient."

Jerry was not getting anywhere with Dr. Graves. His answers were short and he wasn't on the defensive. He was making eye contact with the jurors and conducting himself professionally. He'd better shake him out of this.

"Doctor isn't it true that cerebral aneurysms run in families."

Tim thought about this question. He was worried that Cleary was going to go all out and embarrass him in front of the jurors. "In some cases that's true."

"Would a person such as yourself or for that matter any doctor know this information."

"They should but not all do. It's not an area that is common enough for physicians to be aware," Tim hedged. *Where was he going with this?*

"Doctor would you refer to your deposition testimony on page 57 and read line 18 through 25."

Edwin rose and objected to this line of questioning since counsel has not established its relevance. He was overruled.

Tim nervously thumbed the pages of the deposition in front of him. He remembered that the purpose of a deposition was to lock in testimony and he better make sure his testimony matched what he had just said. He finally found the lines and began reading. "Doctor, do cerebral aneurysms run in families? Answer, that's pretty basic medical school stuff, yes they can."

"Do you want to change your prior testimony? I mean you just testified that it wasn't common enough information for all physicians to be aware. Now which is it 'basic medical school stuff' or uncommon information not knowable to all doctors?"

Tim cursed himself. How could he be so stupid? "It's common information as I said in my deposition, but outside of medical school it is not information that is commonly known among physicians."

"Doctor that's quite an answer."

Edwin shot to his feet. "I object. Counsel is being argumentative."

"Sustained. It's getting late Mr. Cleary let's, move along."

Jerry stared at Judge Cull. He was angry and could feel his blood pressure rising but he had to control himself. He needed to send the jury home with a negative impression of the doctor. He looked down at Jason who was writing something on a legal pad then over to his client who was staring straight ahead in her perpetual mourning mode. "Doctor, didn't you have a cerebral aneurysm, successfully treated obviously, while in high school?"

"Yes I did," Tim said glaring at Jerry.

"Doctor while you were in medical school and during training didn't you donate your sperm for the purpose of reproduction?"

"Objection."

"Overruled."

"Yes I did donate but it was for research not reproduction."

"How many times?"

"Three."

"Did you let the doctor who was using your sperm know that you had this history of an aneurysm? After all it was basic knowledge that they can run in families."

Tim was furious and looked to Edwin for help. This was none of anybody's business and certainly not relevant to the case as hand. "I had no family history of this problem so I assumed it was not a familial trait. I later learned that I had been adopted and my biological mother had probably died of a cerebral aneurysm. Furthermore, since my sperm was not to be used for reproduction, the information was not pertinent."

Shit. That line of questioning backfired. Now the jury will think I'm a prying, sleazeball attorney. Jerry could feel his anger building. Dr. Graves had won that round and made Jerry look stupid. He suddenly felt his nose begin to run. He turned away from the jurors and wiped his upper lip and nose with a handkerchief. When he looked at the handkerchief he was shocked to see blood.

What a time for a nosebleed. Edwin looked over at Jerry, as did Jason Damon. He remained turned away as he pondered the next question. He decided to go ahead and use everything he had. "Doctor," he said as he turned back to Tim while placing the handkerchief back in his pocket, "did you ever have contact with any offspring that resulted from your sperm donations."

Edwin was afraid of this. He didn't know what to do since Tim refused to tell him the whole story about his past relationship with Paulie Strata. He stood and calmly said, " I object. Relevance. How much longer is counsel going to pursue this line of questions about my client's personal life?"

Even Judge Cull was puzzled and despite his leanings was upset with Jerry. "Mr. Cleary wrap it up. Objection overruled."

"Isn't it true that you are the biological father..........." Jerry couldn't finish as blood began to flow from both nostrils, pulsating down onto his expensive suit and tie. The jurors gasped and Tim stared, horrified at the scene before him. Jerry staggered forward and fell to his knees then rolled onto the floor.

Tim leapt from the witness box and immediately grabbed his own handkerchief and applied it to the counselor's nose. He squeezed tightly and immediately stopped the flow of blood but this only changed the direction of flow and Jerry began to cough blood.

"Call 911," Tim shouted to the bailiff while he continued to apply pressure to Jerry's nostril.

In between gags Jerry was trying to tell Jason Damon to take over. The trial must go on. Judge Cull dismissed the jurors for the day. Minutes later two paramedics arrived and quickly shoved Tim aside. One placed EKG leads on Jerry while the other took a history and assessed the bleeding. It was decided to start in intravenous line and transport Jerry to the Massachusetts General hospital. When Jerry heard that he shouted out that he wanted to go to St. Mary's Hospital, all the while coughing up more blood.

"Okay, pal," the medic said, "but don't sue me if you die on the way."

"Jason, Jason, come and see me tonight," Jerry shouted as he was being wheeled out of the courtroom.

"I'll do better than that. I'll go with you." He gathered up all the papers and stuffed them inside his briefcase and grabbed Jerry's and raced out of the courtroom, telling Julie Bradford that he would be in touch.

Judge Cull observed the scene in front of him and shook his head. "Court dismissed. See you in the morning, counselor."

Edwin nodded and turned to Tim who had moved next to his lawyer. "What does this mean?" Tim asked.

"You mean the fact that Jerry was carted out of here or the fact he was about to ask you an embarrassing question? Because neither is too good for us. Since you want to keep things to yourself I can't help you the way I should," Edwin said with a disappointed tone..

Tim got his meaning. "I'm sorry but that subject is off limits and it has nothing to do with the facts of this case. I don't have to tell you all my secrets," Tim said, somewhat irked.

"I stand corrected. I was out of line. Tomorrow we have Dr. Davis and this thing should wrap up on Monday. Go home and see your fiancée. Have a nice glass of wine and stop worrying. From what we saw just now, it doesn't appear that Mr. Cleary will be joining us tomorrow. Damon will have to step in." Edwin slapped Tim reassuringly on the back and they left the courtroom.

The next morning Tim arrived at the courthouse early and sat on a wooden bench waiting for Edwin. He read the sports page but kept a sharp eye out for Jerry. He hoped the attorney couldn't make it. *After all even lawyers get sick, don't they?* Moments later Lisa Harding came bouncing down the hall with Dr. Davis in tow. Although Tim knew his expert by reputation he had never met him. Lisa stopped short when she saw Tim and told Dr. Davis to wait for her while she approached her client.

"Good morning," she said. "Dr. Davis flew in last night and is ready to go. Since there are jurors gathered around out here I think it best if I don't introduce you two. Dr. Davis is very happy to be here and glad to help."

"I appreciate that. What's the word on Cleary? Did he die last night?" Tim smirked.

"Careful. Put your fangs away. No, but Mr. Stokes called last night and said that opposing counsel would not be here for the rest of the trial. Mr. Damon will take over."

Tim wondered why lawyers were so formal when they were in the courthouse. Why couldn't she just say that Jerry is sick? "Something serious?"

"Well he was seen by an ear, nose, and throat doctor last night. The doctor had to staunch the bleeding by packing his nose. But when he looked in there he saw something very suspicious like a tumor. The bleeding's stopped for now but Mr. Cleary is having a biopsy this morning."

"Hmm'. That could mean a lot of things, none of them very good. I hope he has a good neurosurgeon over there at St. Mary's. Sounds like he's gonna need one. I guess he'll request Dr. Hastings since he's the one that testified against me at the tribunal."

"Why do you say that? I discussed this with Dr. Davis and he said the same thing."

"It could very well be a brain tumor which has grown down into his nasal passages. You see how easy I can explain things to a layperson. I wish you lawyers would adopt a more user friendly language rather than your twelfth century legal jargon."

Lisa stared at Tim and wondered whatever happened to that polite, naive, compassionate doctor she met a month or so ago. "I'll take that under advisement," she replied in a steely voice. Suddenly Edwin appeared on the scene and Jason Damon with his bereaved client soon followed.

The bailiff opened the courtroom door and notified those in the hallway that court was in session. After everyone was seated Judge Cull entered from the side door motioning everyone to remain seated. He gazed out over the courtroom and waited until there was quiet.

"Mr. Cleary has taken ill," he announced. "He is having surgery this morning and Mr. Damon will be of counsel for the plaintiff. Are you ready to continue Mr. Stokes?"

"Yes your honor?"

"Mr. Damon, do you have any further questions for the defendant?"

"Yes your honor."

"Begin, please."

Jason adjusted his tie while he stared at some papers in front of him. He had spent all the previous night going over his questions. It was his big moment and he didn't want to screw it up. He wasn't going to continue the line of questions of his boss since he didn't know where he was going on that. Instead he wanted to hit on another issue.

He looked up and asked, "Doctor what time did the surgery on Mr. Bradford begin?"

"I don't recall the exact time but I remember it was late in the afternoon."

Jason picked up the piece of paper he had before him and approached Tim with the judge's permission.

"I have here," he said,"a copy of the anesthesia record. What time does it say the surgery began?"

Tim looked the record over. "It says the surgery began at 2000 or eight PM."

"Was that your first surgery of the day?"

"I don't recall." Tim couldn't remember why they had started so late.

"Well I have here also the surgery schedule for that day," Jason said as he walked back to the lectern and picked up an additional piece of paper. He knew the suspense was building. He could feel it. He walked back to Tim while glancing at the jurors and was happy to see they were following him. He handed Tim the operating room schedule for the day of Mr. Bradford's surgery. "Would you read for the jurors your scheduled cases for the day."

Tim read over the schedule and began, "Seven thirty posterior fossa tumor, two o'clock middle cerebral artery aneurysm and to follow Mr. Bradford's surgery."

"Weren't you tired by the time Mr. Bradford's surgery was to begin? Didn't it make you want to work faster to get out of there? Hadn't you made enough money that day?"

Edwin didn't waste any time objecting to the question on grounds that it was argumentative and outrageous. For once he had an objection sustained but the damage had been done.

Jason stood staring at Tim and let the moment sink in with the jurors. "I have no further questions of the doctor but reserve the right to recall him," Jason said disgustedly. Jason walked over and sat down. He reached over and grasped Julie Bradford's arm and gave her a reassuring squeeze. He was pleased with himself but Julie just sat staring straight ahead with a shocked expression on her face. Perfect theater.

Judge Cull banged his gavel. "Mr. Stokes, call your next witness."

"Thank you your honor. I would like to call Dr. Davis to the stand."

The bailiff left the courtroom and went out into the hallway and escorted the witness to the doorway separating the gallery from the lawyers. Dr. Davis was sworn and he took his seat on the witness stand. Today he looked very composed. He had on a light blue sear sucker suit and white shirt with a conservative tie. His gray hair had been recently cut and he looked confident.

"Dr. Davis do you know my client Dr. Graves?"

"I know who is by reputation but have never met him."

"That reputation is good I trust?"

"Dr. Graves is well known in our field and has an impeccable reputation." Dr. Davis said all of this while looking over at the jurors. He wanted to make eye contact early. It would be up to him to explain many aspects of this case and he needed to get their attention. He glanced back at Edwin but did not look at Tim.

"Dr. Davis I'm going to give you free reign here, explain to the jurors what a cerebral aneurysm is, why it is serious and what do you do about it. You may use the blackboard."

Dr. Davis stood and went to the blackboard and began drawing a picture perfect representation of the brain and it's vascular system. Like many surgeons he was able to conceptualize the anatomy and his artistic ability was above average. He showed where the blood vessels entered the skull, where aneurysms occur, why some can't be dealt with by surgery and others could. He finished up with the surgical techniques and the risks of surgery.

When he completed his fifteen-minute lecture without interruption from the plaintiff attorney, Edwin asked, "Is it below the standard of care to not inform a patient of possible alternatives to surgery?" Edwin wanted to preempt that question by Mr. Damon.

"No it is not. Although, I do it as a routine. For the most part, by the time patients see me they have had all that explained to them."

Edwin didn't like "for the most part." "So in your opinion plaintiff's contention that Dr. Graves didn't inform her and her husband as well, of possible alternatives to surgery was not below the standard of care?"

"Most certainly not."

"In this case is it your opinion that the aneurysm seen on Mr. Bradford's angiogram was not amenable to non-surgical methods?"

"Clearly not. It was well over the acceptable limits of the size one might consider to occlude with a catheter," Dr. Davis looked over at the jurors and corrected himself, "I mean it was too large to clot off."

"We heard testimony from Dr. Shamski that he would have done it that way. What do you say to that?"

"I am unaware of Dr. Shamski's work in this area. I am chairman of the American Society of Neurosurgery aneurysm committee and have never heard of Dr. Shamski or for that matter techniques by anyone to clot aneurysms of the size we're talking about here."

"Another criticism voiced by Dr. Shamski was the speed at which the surgery was performed. Also, plaintiff has made an issue of Dr. Graves' having done two long operative procedures prior to Mr. Bradford's surgery. You have not heard Dr. Grave's testimony and plaintiff's irresponsible questioning on that matter. But what is your response to Dr. Shamski?"

Jason stood up and looked at the jury. "I object to the mischaracterization of my questions as irresponsible," he nearly shouted.

In bored tones Judge Cull sustained the objection and told

Mr. Stokes to move on.

"I beg the court's forbearance but the witness has two questions before him. May he answer them?"

"Very well," Cull said as if he had forgotten that Dr. Davis hadn't answered the question posed to him by the defense counsel.

Edwin nodded at Dr. Davis to begin. "As to the speed of the surgery that is totally based on the skill and experience of the surgeon. Some get things done faster than others. I don't think there is a timetable that says if you go this fast you are sloppy or cutting corners. In fact often the opposite is true. The longer a surgery takes could reflect on the uncertainty, skill and lack of experience of the surgeon. As to the second question, we live in an age where surgery has become highly specialized. There are only so many operating rooms, so much time and a limited number of surgeons of Dr. Graves' ability. It is not unusual to do two, three, and even four cases a day. Cardiac surgeons do it often and there have been no studies that indicate that patients operated late in the day are any worse off than those operated on earlier."

"Thank you," Edwin said and turned to Judge Cull, "I have no further questions for this witness."

Tim thought about what Dr. Davis had said. He does routinely inform his patients about alternative treatments but it's not below the standard of care not to do that. In most cases the patients have been informed about alternative therapies before he sees them. Somehow Tim had the feeling that Mr. Damon was going to pounce on that answer.

Jason started by asking Dr. Davis to explain why Mr. Bradford's aneurysm was not amenable to catheter treatment. After a series of hypothetical questions and maneuverings he got Dr. Davis to admit an attempt to clot the aneurysm might work or partially occlude the aneurysm making subsequent surgery safer. Edwin tried to object to the various questions Jason was asking but was categorically overruled. He glared at Judge Cull after one such episode and was warned that he was flirting with contempt.

"Doctor, what do you mean by most cases, nine out of ten?

Eight, seven?" Jason asked as he approached the witness stand. He seemed relaxed and not at all intimidated by Dr. Davis.

"Well probably nine or ninety percent are informed before they see me."

"Since you inform all your patients about alternative treatments none of your patients are unaware?"

"I suppose you could say that," Dr. Davis answered warily. He could see where Mr. Damon was headed.

Jason turned away from the witness and walked toward the lectern and picked up a piece of paper. "What would you say if I had an affidavit signed by the neurologist that referred Mr. Bradford to Dr. Graves stating that he did not inform the patient about non-surgical methods for dealing with the aneurysm?" Jason held up the paper.

"Well that depends. Maybe he thought after seeing the angiogram that there was no way that this could be treated by a catheter. So he didn't say anything."

"Well what if I told you that the neurologist never makes recommendations but leaves that up to the surgeon. Namely Dr. Graves?"

Edwin shot out of his chair objecting to this line of questioning since the neurologist had not been named as a witness by either side nor had he been deposed. Jerry had planned it that way. "I have not seen any such affidavit," he boomed.

Judge Cull banged his gavel and warned Edwin to be civil. He requested a copy of the affidavit and Jason handed it to him. He also passed one over to Edwin. After reading the affidavit, the judge allowed it to be entered into evidence.

Edwin was furious. The affidavit was dated two days ago and had been a clever move by Cleary. How had this slipped past him?

Tim was beginning to feel the heat. Jason was certainly well prepared. Of course all of this is BS he thought. He had her on video listening to the informed consent, which included alternative treatment methods. He kicked himself again for not having written in the chart the full text of his discussion with Julie Bradford.

After the dust settled Dr. Davis responded with, "I would say then that it would be up to the treating neurosurgeon to do this. Namely, Dr. Graves."

Ouch. Tim was staring straight ahead trying to look unconcerned but Dr. Davis was rapidly becoming an expert witness for the plaintiff.

Jason glanced over at the jurors to be sure they were paying attention. He looked at Dr. Davis for several moments. "Dr. Davis have you ever had your license suspended for any reason?"

Dr. Davis sat upright as if offended by the question and answered, "No."

"Really? I have here a New York district court declaration that your diver's license was suspended in 1961 for six months. I'm sorry, I didn't mean your medical license I meant your driver's license in the last question," Jason said with a practiced look of concern on his face.

"Yes. When I was in medical school it was temporarily suspended for driving under the influence," he said, staring at Jason angrily.

Edwin stood and attempted to repair the damage but Dr. Davis came off poorly when he tried to explain the situation. He had been to a going away party for someone at the medical school and he was tired from a long shift in the emergency room. On the way home an officer saw him weaving and pulled him over. It was too late. The jurors had heard it and Dr. Davis' credibility had taken a hit.

Judge Cull banged his gavel and stopped the proceedings when Edwin said he had no further questions. Since it was Thursday and Friday was a half-day the judge announced the trial would resume on Monday.

After the courtroom cleared Tim stared at Edwin. "Why? How?" he asked.

Edwin looked down and when he had crafted an answer he looked up at Tim and said, "It's ultimately my fault but I didn't know about Dr. Davis's drunk driving conviction nor the neurologist's testimony. I'll fall on my sword but Lisa Harding will have some explaining to do."

Tim couldn't believe what he was hearing. Not one, but two major bombshells and his attorney didn't know about either. Dejected he shook his head and shuffled out of the courtroom.

Twenty-six

Jerry Cleary was wheeled into a private area of the recovery room at St. Mary's hospital. The nasal biopsy was done by Dr. Grissom, ear, nose, and throat specialist. Dr. Hastings, the neurosurgeon, scrubbed in to assist and help expose the tumor. It was hard to tell from gross inspection the exact nature of the tumor but a frozen section of the tissue indicated that it was an unusual and uncommon tumor of the olfactory bulb. After Jerry was settled in and awake a special nurse provided by the hospital brought Deidre Cleary in to see her husband. She was frightened but tried to put on a brave front for Jerry. In spite of their shaky marriage, Deidre loved her husband and planned to stick by her man during this ordeal.

"Well?" she asked.

"I'm fine. No pain. I'll be out of here by tomorrow. Trial is still going on and we're near the end." Jerry tried to sit up but his nurse cautioned him to remain flat.

"Are you sure? Dr. Hastings spoke to me and said that you have a good possibility of a more serious problem than they had thought."

Jerry frowned and said, "Why isn't he here telling me this? I shouldn't have to hear it from my wife."

"Relax. He said it was only preliminary and he wanted to

review the material before he spoke to you. You've gotta back off. Chill. Let the doctors figure it out."

Jerry sighed. "Doctors. That's what I worry about. They are always making mistakes."

"You only deal with the small number that come to you by way of their disgruntled patients and extrapolate from there." Deidre didn't want to get into a discussion about Jerry's practice but she would prefer he pursued something else. Too often she had been shunned by physician wives or discreetly encouraged by doctors to find someone else whenever she or her children were sick. Nobody wanted to take care of them because of Jerry's reputation.

Suddenly the recovery room door opened and in walked Dr. Hastings. He looked around and spotted Jerry and Deidre and came over to their private cubicle.

"Well how's my favorite attorney doing?" he beamed. Dr. Hastings was slightly less than six feet tall with a round soft face and a pudgy body habitus. He had sandy blond hair and wore clear framed glasses. He appeared to be in his mid to late forties.

"Cut the shit doc. What's the bottom line?" Jerry nearly snarled. "My wife already knows more than I do?"

"Wow," he said, "you are a piece of work, aren't you? I always talk to families immediately when I get information. I'm sorry if that upsets you." Dr. Hastings had been the expert against Tim Graves during the tribunal process and got to know Jerry pretty well. He was not intimidated.

Once Jerry saw that Dr. Hastings wasn't going to back down he said, "Sorry doc. I'm a little jumpy. We're in the middle of that trial with Graves you helped me on."

Dr. Hastings, twenty years before, had been a neurosurgical resident at University Hospital but wasn't allowed to advance in the program because Dr. Graves opposed his promotion to senior resident. He learned confidentially from another faculty member that Graves felt he was bright enough but did not have the temperament or technical skills to do complicated neurosurgical cases. He finished at a less demanding program in Texas and then returned to his hometown of Boston. Shortly into private practice

Dr. Hastings realized that he was not cut out to take on big cases and had the common sense to do things he could do safely. He performed back surgery for herniated discs, simple brain biopsies, some straight forward craniotomies and diagnostic studies. To supplement his income he reviewed malpractice cases. He did a lot of that.

"I hate to tell you this Jerry but the trial is going to have to go on without you. There's no way you're going to court in the near future."

"Hey I'm **supposed** to be blunt, where's your bedside manner?"

"Sorry. I never like to be the bearer of bad news, but the reality here is you have a rather extensive olfactory bulb tumor. You'll probably need x-ray treatment and then surgery." Dr. Hastings did not back down or apologize. There was no way to sugar coat it.

Deidre felt like she was being left out of the discussion. "How long will all this take?" she asked.

Dr. Hastings looked over at her and said, "Anywhere from six weeks to three months. If the tumor responds to radiation then it will be shorter. He has a tumor that's been there for some time. I'm surprised he wasn't more symptomatic. It's eroding blood vessels and treatment needs to begin tomorrow after we see the permanent sections."

"You mean this is only preliminary?" Jerry asked with an incredulous look on his face.

"Jerry I saw the tumor. It's nasty. The frozen section we did today is preliminary but I'm ninety-nine percent certain it's an olfactory tumor."

Jerry stared at his doctor. His brusque manner had given him some confidence. He was a no nonsense kind of guy. Sure of himself. "Well doc, when do we start, when will you be doing the surgery?" Jerry asked.

Suddenly Dr. Hastings didn't seem so confident. He shook his head back and forth hesitating to say the next thing on his mind. It was a personal disappointment but something he had faced many times in his professional career. On so many occasions he was good up to the point of treatment. Then he began to waffle.

"Well let's slow down. This is a tricky kind of tumor. We don't do these here at St. Mary's. I'll have to refer you out. These are rare types of tumors and only a few centers see them."

"Doctor," Deidre again interjected herself back into the conversation, "could this tumor be the reason Jerry has been sniffing constantly and can't seem to smell anything, including my perfume?"

Dr. Hastings wondered how long this had gone on. He hadn't really talked to the Cleary's before the biopsy, since he was consulted at the last minute by Dr. Grissom.

"Yes. That's a typical story with these tumors." He wasn't going to comment on any delay in diagnosis issues.

"So, who do you recommend?" asked Jerry.

"I'm afraid you not going to like this. Dr. Graves, whom you are currently suing, has had the most experience with this tumor. I mean in the entire country. He's done like twenty of these and is considered the expert by most of my colleagues. If that's a problem for you then there is man at the Mayo clinic but their experience is less."

"You got to be kidding me. What about that doctor I had in Los Angeles? Shamski?"

"Now Jerry, you know I do a lot of malpractice work and have testified against Dr.Shamski. There is no way he is suited academically or medically to take on a challenge like this. I wouldn't let him operate on my dog. He's a good expert witness but that's as far as it goes. No, Graves is your man."

"How in the hell can I go to a doctor I'm suing. Does he come here?"

"I've seen Dr. Graves here once in twenty years and that was to talk about cerebral aneurysms. I have my own beefs with him but it has nothing to do with his abilities as a neurosurgeon. I can call him now or you can handle it your own way. But, you should be transferred to University Hospital tomorrow," Dr. Hastings stated while he backed away from the bed.

Jerry looked at Deidre and slapped his arms on the bed in

exasperation. "Shit. Nothing's going right lately."

"Make up your mind. I have to get home to the kids. It sounds like you ought to be at University Hospital, the sooner the better," his wife said. She stood and came over to the bed and picked up Jerry's hand. "I'm sorry but this is not the time to fret. You told me Jason Damon is a good lawyer, you'll have to let him run the show for awhile."

"Shit, shit, shit. You're right," Jerry said, calming down. Sitting up on his elbows he said, "Doc call Graves and arrange a transfer to University Hospital. What choice do I have?"

"Good, I'll make the arrangements. By the way there is a Mr. Damon in the waiting room. He introduced himself as I came in. He wants to talk to you. I'll send him in. Sorry Jerry but you'll be in good hands. Goodbye Mrs. Cleary," Dr. Hastings said as he turned to go.

"Thank you doctor. I know you've given good advice," she said with a wan smile.

After Dr. Hastings left, Deidre kissed her husband and said goodbye. She didn't want to be there when her husband and Jason discussed business. Moments after she left the door opened and Jason walked up to the bedside and gave a sympathetic smile.

"Are you in any pain Jerry?" he asked softly after they greeted each other with a hand-shake.

Jerry was subdued and quietly answered "no". He explained his conversation with Hastings to Jason then they got down to business.

"I'll be out of action anywhere from six weeks to three months the doc said. Good opportunity for you to step in, run the show. You know how I work. You do the same."

"I know that you're going to see Dr. Graves, all that. What about the trial? I mean will a doctor that you're suing take care of you?" Jason asked with a concerned look on his face. "Will he want to help you?"

"Yeah, he could turn me down. But I know he won't. Ego's too big. He'll look on it as the last laugh. You wait. I'm not worried about it. So how did the day go? Give me all the details." Jerry laid back and waited for Damon's response.

"Well I think it went well. I got Davis to admit that clotting the aneurysm was possible and may even have been beneficial. He got shot down with the neurologist's affidavit. What a stroke of genius that was. The jury was also listening when he admitted the DUI while in med school."

"Wow. Maybe I should just stay out of it. Let you run it. What's on the agenda for tomorrow?"

"Judge Cull has held the trial over until Monday. So tomorrow nothing's happening anyway. I think Stokes has a few more witnesses then we'll probably finish up by Wednesday afternoon for the jury."

"How's the plaintiff doing? Is she still looking like the funeral was yesterday?"

"Yeah. She's allright. But she's a cold fish. How do you find these clients?"

"I advertise," Jerry laughed. "Forget the client. It's about winning and settlements. She's just the reason we're there."

"Ok you're right. But I still would like to see some appreciation of all the work we're doing. It's all about her."

"You'll learn. Don't expect strokes from the clients. Anyway convey to her my apology for getting sick, leaving her to the likes of you," Jerry laughed. Even in the presence of his current situation, Jerry was going to remain optimistic.

"Well at least your sense of humor is intact. By the way you look terrible with that bloody gauze sticking out of your nose. Reminds me of hockey after the game with all the broken noses."

Jerry waved goodbye to Jason and lay back in bed. *University Hospital. Why the hell they can't treat me here is beyond me.*

Twenty-seven

On the one hand, Tim was glad he was spared another day in the courtroom, on the other he wished the whole pain in the ass process was over. Despite this quandary he called Meg and told her to meet him at Vinny Testas on commonwealth for dinner. After stopping at the hospital to take care of paper work and see several postoperative patients, he drove to the restaurant to find Meg already waiting. The restaurant was moderately busy with waiters and busboys moving about keeping the hungry patrons satisfied. Large platters of pasta flew by their table. The portions were huge, and no normal person could eat a full meal. Usually the remainder was packed and taken home. He spotted Meg in a corner booth sipping a glass of Chianti with a full glass sitting on the place mat across from her. Tim leaned over and kissed his soon to be wife, sat down and took a sip of wine. He was pleased with its taste and smacked his lips when the after taste tantalized him. Tonight he was going to relax and tomorrow he would sleep until seven then enjoy a good breakfast. He hadn't had time together with Meg for over a week and he was looking forward to it.

"Tell me all about it," she said as she grasped his hand across the table. "You look happy tonight. Good news? Meg was dressed in a short-sleeved red blouse, which complimented her hair. She

297

too was in a good mood as her series on the malpractice crisis was selling papers.

"Not really. Judge Cull gave everyone the day off tomorrow. Trial resumes on Monday. I should be unhappy the way things went today. Damon, who's substituting for Cleary, did a nice job of converting our witness to their cause."

"What! I thought Davis was on your side."

"He is but Damon asked these impossible questions laced with hypotheticals to get Davis to say things. Such as 'he could have tried to clot the aneurysm and even if it didn't work the surgery would have been safer'. He got Davis to admit that he always discusses alternative treatments with his patients. Then he gets an affidavit from the neurologist, Stan Giddings, who sent Bradford to me saying he never discussed possible alternatives to surgery." Tim took another sip of wine but didn't smack his lips this time.

He went on. "That's not the worst of it. Davis had a drunk driving arrest and had his driver's license suspended for six months. In med school."

Meg was incensed. "This is crazy," she nearly shouted, "the judge has withheld the video that would make all that discussion moot and lets in a drunk driving incident years earlier." Meg caught herself beginning to sound like a lawyer.

"That's the legal system. It's their playing field. We have to work around it. By the way tell me you made a copy of that video tape and transcript. Have it safely tucked away."

"Of course I do but I didn't tell that to Stokes. You never know. The original could be destroyed, damaged, misplaced. Why do you ask?" Meg asked warily she was beginning to smell a rat.

"Well. I asked Stokes if he had gotten them back from the judge expecting we would need that stuff for an appeal. He told me he had asked Cull and he got an evasive answer like 'he'd look for them at home they weren't in chambers'."

"Sounds fishy. Of course Cull would be delighted if those documents were lost or destroyed. There goes your appeal."

The waiter came by and Tim ordered lasagna and Meg went with a large Caesar's salad with chicken. They each took a healthy sip of wine and smiled as they both started to speak.

"You first," Tim said.

"What if we ran an article on this trial showing the actual photos of her sitting
there while you were telling them all about surgery? We could print the text underneath. It would be an eye catcher."

"Super idea. But when would you do it? While the trial is going on?" Tim asked.

"Could. But Cull might declare a mistrial. You'd have to go through all this again, maybe in another city. No. We wait for the jury's verdict then publish it. Whether you win or lose. What judge in his right mind would exclude it at a future trial?"

Tim pondered what Meg said. It seemed liked common sense answers like reporting excluded tapes would be beneficial to his cause but may actually hurt it. He couldn't wait until the trial was over. "You know what puzzles me is how these lawyers find out so much about things. Davis and his trouble with the law. That happened over twenty years ago. The conviction was actually sealed once he did his probation."

"Investigators. Cleary has them. Eddie Collins ex-BPD was his favorite. I ran into him when I was with *The Globe*. He's not a bad sort, or rather he wasn't."

"What are you talking about? Did he die?"

"I just heard about it at the paper today. He was found by some campers in an abandoned quarry yesterday. A floater. BPD suspect foul play since his hands had been taped behind his back. His wife gave a statement saying that he had been working for a client who was a lawyer. His investigation got too close to the mob."

"How do you know it was a mob thing? Other than personal experience that is," Tim smirked.

"Yeah, you said it. The word is that Cleary's investigator was snooping around for information about you, got too close to Paulie Strata our favorite thug, your patient. He may have tipped his location, bammo."

"How do you know all this stuff?"

"Hey I work with reporters. They have friends at the BPD. I

also heard Collins had his enemies there too."

"You know I don't think I'm hungry anymore."

As Tim was wiping his lips with a napkin his beeper sounded. He had forgotten that he had told his service he was taking call.

"I hope this isn't anything serious. I had other plans for tonight," he winked.

He stood up and made his way to a telephone booth in the front of the restaurant. He placed a dime in the slot and dialed his exchange. The operator told him that a Dr. Hastings called from St. Mary's and to have him paged.

Once they were connected Hastings said, "Good evening. I hope I'm not interrupting anything. I haven't seen you in years but have heard about all the great things you're doing at University."

"Thanks Bob," Tim said politely. He wasn't going to get into his legal troubles with his adversary. "What can I do for you?"

"Right. Well we have a Jerry Cleary over here and he needs your expertise. Seems he has caught himself an olfactory tumor. Been going on for some time. I helped the ENT guy do a biopsy today and on frozen it looks like a neuroblastoma."

"You mean a neuroblastoma or an esthesioneuroma?" Tim asked unable to believe his ears. Olfactory tumors in general were uncommon but esthesioneuromas were literally as rare as hen's teeth.

"Can't say for sure. Needs more tests. It sure looks like it's one or the other. I told Mr. Cleary that you are the expert on this type of tumor, he should be transferred to University tomorrow. He's willing if you are."

"Wow. Let me think. This doesn't happen every day. The lawyer suing you needs your expertise. He's alright coming over to University?"

"Yeah. He wanted to stay at St. Mary's, he's on the Board of Trustees and all that but it isn't going to fly. I don't do these tumors and neither does my partner. You're the expert, I told him. So what's it going to be?"

"Give me some more information. What about his CAT scan? Anything eise?" Tim asked.

"He's in great shape if that's what you mean. Normal EKG, labs, chest x-ray. CT shows the tumor above the cribiform. Invades both nasal passages nearly occluding them. Questionable extension into the right frontal lobe. It's been there for some time. He'll need surgery and radiation from what I can gather."

"Crazy tumor. Can spread to the bones. He'll need a bone scan and then if that's okay, then surgery. You better transfer him. He really bled a lot in the courtroom and he could cut loose again. I'll see him tomorrow. Thanks Bob. I'll keep you posted."

"He's in good hands. Good luck."

Tim sat in the phone booth for a minute thinking about the ramifications of what he had heard. It seemed surreal. Out of a play or book. Well he knew he was the man with the most experience with these tumors. He would have to put aside his personal feelings and do the right thing. He returned to the table and told Meg about the strange turn of events.

The following morning, Tim arose promptly at seven, showered and shaved. To his delight Meg was in the kitchen preparing bacon, eggs, and pancakes. His favorite manly meal. He sat down at the breakfast table and opened *The Bulletin.* There were no startling revelations above the fold but below the fold near the bottom was an article relating to Eddie Collins. There was nothing in it he did not know except a quote by his old friend Chief Rastellini stating that Collins was a good cop and if there was foul play his department would investigate.

"Now tell me. Honestly. Did you or did you not call the Chief yesterday for some of that info you told me last night? Reporter my you know what!"

Meg flipped several pancakes and she turned to smile at him. "You're so smart. Of course I did. Is it in the papers?" she asked innocently.

"What do you think?"

"The Chief said it was definitely a mob hit although not very skillful. He's not sure whether Collins was trying to get away in the dark and fell into the quarry. He was not weighted or wrapped. There were tire marks from a van nearby. He suspects it was payback for Strata's hit. Maybe one of his brothers."

Tim shook his head. "Seems like this thing never ends. Collins was snooping around trying to find dirt on me. Luther thinks he knew about my sperm donations and Joey Santori. Says he feels his office was searched shortly after Collins paid him a visit."

"Any of that stuff come up at trial?"

"I think Cleary was getting ready to reveal it when he developed his ... nose bleed. Well Collins is dead and Cleary is about to have an operation that may alter his personality and memory. Maybe it will all end with you, me, the Chief, Maria Santori and Luther knowing the real story." The only people who knew he was the biological father of Joey Santori.

"Let's hope. Exposing that detail at trial wouldn't help you. Doesn't sound like he told his partner Damon or he would have used it."

"Probably. I'll be seeing Cleary today. He'll need surgery soon and maybe I'll do it on Monday." Tim stood and kissed Meg goodbye and headed to the hospital.

Before leaving for work. Meg telephoned her editor at home. She wanted to run by him the possible use of the videotapes before the trial was completed.

Twenty-eight

Tim made rounds in the morning almost searching for things to do. He had not scheduled any surgical procedures because he had expected to be in court. After seeing the few patients he had in the hospital, he reluctantly went to his office where there was always never-ending paper work. An hour later his secretary buzzed him to say the chief resident was on the line. He picked up and listened while the young doctor identified himself and alerted Tim that Jerry Cleary had been transferred to University Hospital from St. Mary's. Tim agreed to meet the resident in the x-ray department and review the CAT scan sent over with the notorious trial lawyer.

Several moments later Tim was standing before the x-ray view box reviewing the brain scan with the radiologist and chief resident Dr. Lloyd Benning. "This looks quite extensive Mel," Tim said to the radiologist Dr. Mel Lufkin.

"We've seen more of these than most but this looks like it invades the right frontal lobe. I've not seen that before," he said shaking his head.

"What do you think Lloyd?" Tim asked the chief resident.

He thought for a while rather than blurt out an answer. "Well, it's definitely an esthesioneuroma. I've gone over the path slides they sent over with our neuropathologist. Hard to tell if it invades the frontal lobe, that can only be determined at surgery. These tumors do not respond to preoperative radiation. The only option is surgery."

"I agree" Tim said. "This is an invasive tumor and he already has had an extensive epistaxis. Impressive bleed in court believe me."

"How do you know?" Dr. Lufkin said.

Tim regretted he had allowed the conversation to drift in the direction of his trial. Well it was too late. "This is the lawyer that is suing me as we speak. I was in court when he cut loose."

"Are you kidding me?" Dr. Lufkin asked incredulously. "Why would a lawyer suing you use you as their doctor? I've often wondered if that ever happens. Now it has. Of course he doesn't have many options since you're the expert when it comes to this tumor." Dr. Lufkin was short and almost totally bald. He was getting worked up over this seemingly impossible coincidence.

"You can only play the hand that's dealt you. It's not going to be fun but that's never been a criteria, what the patient does for a living," Tim said shaking his head. "Put him on for the first case Monday, Lloyd, and get a bone scan today."

"We'll need a couple of units on standby. I'll see if he wants to have designated donors," Lloyd said.

"Good point. Do everything by the book. Document everything in the chart. Date and time your entries, have a nurse in the room when you talk about transfusion. Wait until I see him first before you hit him with this," Tim said.

"See. He's got you running scared already." Lufkin said sourly.

"What room is he in?" Tim asked.

"He's not on the neuro floor the place is full. Your partners are having a field day while you atrophy in court. Room 204."

"Oh no. I don't believe this. Isn't this typical of the hospital? They put him in the same damn room as the patient whose wife is suing me. Damn." Tim wondered briefly if the video cameras were still in place. He shrugged. He had a job to do and he was going to do it the same as always.

Tim left the radiology department and headed for the second floor. He took the stairs rather than the elevator hoping to avoid meeting any family members or get engaged in a conversation with someone about the trial. When he arrived at the nurses' station he grabbed the chart and with a nurse in tow headed for room 204.

As he entered the room he noticed a woman sitting on the end of the bed. She stood immediately when he entered and introduced herself. Deidre was tall but still had to look up to Tim. Tim introduced himself and the nurse to both Deidre and Jerry.

Jerry still had the nasal packing, which by this time was brown as the pigment in the dried blood broke down. Tim and the nurse remained standing while Deidre moved to the only chair in the room. Jerry waved and broke the ice by saying, "You got me doc. Now it's your turn. What's the story?"

"Suddenly Jerry didn't seem so formidable. Here he was like anyone else facing a terrible problem and trying to be strong. Tim had seen this hundreds of times. Any animus he might have had for Mr. Cleary subsided. This was a bad tumor and could have already spread. He had a fifty-fifty chance of surviving it and maybe not as the same person if his frontal lobe was involved.

He found himself saying in a compassionate voice, "How are you doing Mr. Cleary?"

"Doc," Jerry smiled, "from now on it's Jerry. I'm your patient. The nurse doesn't need to be here. I'm sure she's got better things to do. This is between you, me, and my better half."

Tim appreciated his patient's attitude but he asked the nurse to stay. *Once burned* ....

"Well there's good news and there's bad news. The good news is that the tumor is resectable. The bad news is we don't know whether it has invaded your frontal lobe."

Deidre sat and listened to Tim go on about the tumor and how it had eroded the olfactory nerves eliminating the sense of smell. That it could have spread to bone and if it has then the prognosis was not good. They had to wait for a bone scan to find that out. When he finished Deidre asked, "Is this why Jerry hasn't been as careful with his personal hygiene? Doesn't shower regularly."

"I suppose if you couldn't appreciate your own body odor

that's possible."

"Well that's been going on for some time. How come the ear, nose, and throat specialist didn't pick it up sooner?" she asked.

Tim was beginning to wonder if Jerry was going to ask any questions. He just lay there with his hands folded behind his head and listened.

Before Tim could answer she went on, "Another thing is his sleeping around. He hasn't been interested in me for some time. Could his sense of smell have anything to do with that?"

Tim was stunned. He had only been in the room for fifteen minutes and all the dirty laundry was being trotted out. How do you respond to questions like this? He tried by saying, "These tumors grow slowly over time and can be missed. Diagnosed as nasal polyps or deviated septum. He chose not to comment on Jerry's private life."

Jerry was uncomfortable and could see his wife wasn't going to let up on him even when he was lying there with a potentially lethal tumor. He had to jump in and put an end to this, "Thanks Dr. Graves for your honest appraisal. I know you're the best when it comes to these tumors. I'm at your mercy." Jerry said, glaring over at his wife.

Anxious to move on and avoid Deidre's questions Tim told them that the surgery was scheduled for Monday morning, as long as the bone scan is negative. He went on, "There is an issue that must be addressed. This tumor is close to your right frontal lobe. If it invades the lobe I might have to resect some of it. It could change your personality."

"Will it make him impotent?" Deidre asked.

Jerry had enough. He wasn't going to be shown up by his wife any further. "Dr. Graves will you excuse us. We need to talk. Deidre and I."

Tim gladly left Jerry and his wife to hash out their marital problems. He thanked the nurse for standing by and went to check on a time for Jerry's bone scan.

"Tell me what's going on," Jerry asked when the room was empty.

Deidre glared at him and debated her answer. Her husband

was sick with a serious problem. Should she ease off or let him have it? She had loved him and he was the father of her children. He was a good provider and he claimed to love his family. Still she was not one to be walked over. Finally she went on with a steady voice, "I got a call last night. The caller didn't identify himself. I could tell from his accent that he was one of those Italians who seem to have taken over this city."

"What makes you think that?"

"Becausa he talka likea thisa."

Shit Jerry thought, *don't these sick guineas ever give up?* He looked at Deidre and reluctantly encouraged her to go on by waving his hand in a 'bring it on' fashion.

"Who's Betsy Gallucci? Apparently you have been seeing her at every sleazy motel in the city for a couple of years."

Jerry leaned back on his pillow and closed his eyes. *What next?* First his investigator is killed. He has a serious brain tumor and has to grovel by going to a surgeon he is suing. Now his wife is after him. All he needed right now was to have his family break up.

"What can I say? Yes there was some hanky panky going on. I slipped once. It's over and all I can do is ask you to forgive me." He looked pleadingly at her.

"That's bull shit and you know it. You slip once a week," Betsy said as she stood up to go. She barely touched his hand to say goodbye. "We'll talk about this when you're back on your feet. This isn't over."

Jerry sighed. That's the best he could hope for considering the circumstances. "Drive carefully. Kiss the kids for me."

She gave him a thin smile and said, "Okay." Deidre left and hoped for Jerry's sake that the surgery was successful. After that......she hadn't made up her mind.

Monday arrived and Tim was just starting Jerry's surgery, which could very well take all day. Across town Jason Damon and Edwin Stokes were standing before Judge Cull. The jury had not been seated and there was a motion before the judge. Edwin felt that the jury should be appraised that his client wasn't there because he was performing surgery on Jerry Cleary. Jason was certain that that information wasn't about to help his case. Judge Cull for his part was amused by the coincidence. He had never had to rule on an issue like this. Of course it would be detrimental to the plaintiff if the jury were aware that the lawyer suing the doctor in this case was now undergoing surgery by that same doctor.

"Well, the fact that Mr. Cleary is being operated on by the defendant is prejudicial. It has no bearing on what went on with the plaintiff's interaction with the defendant. Any reference about the absence of either Mr. Cleary or Dr. Graves will be strictly off limits. Let's see if we can wrap this thing up so the jury has it by Wednesday."

Edwin wasn't happy with this ruling. "What do we tell the jury? My client being absent looks bad and the jury knows why Mr. Cleary is absent."

"Judge, if I may intervene here," Jason said, "perhaps a small statement by me about Mr. Cleary's absence and a similar one by Mr. Stokes should satisfy the jury. We can just say that Mr. Cleary has taken ill and is in the hospital and that Dr. Graves is doing an unscheduled emergency surgery this morning."

"Since when are emergencies scheduled?" Edwin scoffed. "Let's just say that Dr. Graves has been called to do emergency surgery. It still doesn't tell the story and I object to your ruling. That kind of ruling makes people wonder about the judicial system. Why can't we say what's really going on and let the jury decide if it has any bearing on this trial."

Judge Cull was beginning to fumble with papers, stacking them in front of him while he composed his response. He was so tempted to make an off color remark. "Nice try. I have ruled, Mr. Stokes. A simple statement by each of you will be enough. Now that's final. I'm going to ask the bailiff to seat the jurors."

The rest of the morning was spent by actuarial reports from both sides telling the jury how long Mr. Bradford might have lived had Dr. Graves not botched the surgery. When Jason introduced his expert and used the word botched, Edwin objected but the judge let it pass. Of course the plaintiff's expert thought Mr. Bradford would have lived well into the next century and earned a gazillion dollars. Edwin's expert gave a considerable lower life expectancy with lower earnings. The jurors seemed bored by the exchange between the lawyers and their experts. Some even were yawning or gazing at the ceiling. All wanted the trial to end today but were surprised when Judge Cull dismissed them early and announced that closing arguments would begin tomorrow and the jury would have the case either tomorrow afternoon or Wednesday morning.

Meg scowled. She was fixing dinner when Tim arrived home after the exhausting surgery on Jerry Cleary. The stress of this particular operation was considerable without throwing in the fact that his patient was out to get him in court. There could be no missteps. He was glad to be home sipping a glass of red wine.

"Are you telling me that Cull would not allow Stokes to tell the jury why you were absent?"

"That's precisely what I'm saying," Tim mumbled while he ran his hand through his hair. "Fortunately the surgery went well. I think I got all the tumor and it hadn't invaded his frontal lobe."

"Big deal. That means he'll live to fight another day. What's with Cull? He has thwarted you on every turn."

"Tell me about it," Tim sighed, "Stokes called me at the hospital and let me know that the summations are tomorrow and he wants me there. Also the anesthesiologist insurance company settle for some small amount. Here I am all alone for the jury to pluck."

Meg was fed up. She was ticked at the way the court was jerking Tim around. Now he would be responsible for all damage claims should things fall against him. It was time to fight back. She toyed with the idea of running a story about the trial and the odd twist it had taken. She turned to the stove and lifted a pot of spaghetti and poured it into a strainer in the sink. She turned to Tim and said, "What if I run a story tomorrow about your involvement in the care of Cleary?"

Tim looked at Meg, unable to comprehend what she had just

said. He shook his head. "Well for starters it would be unethical since it wouldn't take a genius to figure out how you got that confidential information. Cull would blow a gasket and may declare a mistrial. There's no way I want to do this again. I'm in it to the end. This is the trial I want to go with, whatever happens."

Meg poured the pasta onto a platter and then took a pan with simmering sauce and meatballs off the stove. She added that to the pasta and set the platter on the kitchen table. There was a tossed salad and crusty, buttered, sliced bread on the table. She sprinkled Parmesan cheese on the spaghetti and sat down. She slowly poured herself a second glass of red wine and said, "Suit yourself. It was just a thought. Time to eat," she smiled.

Judge Cull banged his gavel lightly to alert everyone that summations were to begin. Jason Damon stood and looked at the jury. Should he tell them about Jerry's situation or stick to the case at hand? There had been no announcement on the night before about the surgery and he scanned *The Globe* and *The Bulletin* this morning. *Nothing*, he thought. He half expected to see a story about it in *The Bulletin*, what with the defendant's ties to a reporter. They were playing it straight up. He certainly would try to get it to the jury if the roles were reversed.

"Good morning ladies and gentlemen of the jury. It's been a busy two weeks for the lawyers but now its time to turn over the reins to you." he smiled. He could see that the jurors were ready to get on with it. "We promised at the beginning of this trial to show that Dr. Graves, who is a fine doctor, slipped up in this instance. He didn't do it on purpose nor do we have to prove that. What we must establish is that Dr. Graves fell below the standard of care when he treated Mr. Bradford."

Jason paused and he was relieved to see that he had the jurors' full attention. There would be no yawns this morning. "Dr. Graves fell below the standard of care when he failed to inform the plaintiff and her husband of the risks of surgery and the alternatives to surgery." He went on for the next hour reviewing the surgery, the opinion of his expert witness and the testimony of Dr. Davis. He emphasized that Dr. Davis admitted that clotting the aneurysm with a catheter might have prevented surgery or at the very least make surgery less risky. He finally finished and smiled at Edwin confidently. He felt the jury had taken his words seriously and it would carry the day.

Judge Cull ordered a fifteen-minute break and during the break Tim buttonholed Edwin.

"From what I can tell of this trial, the plaintiff is lying, the expert from Los Angeles is incompetent and the facts of the case have been excluded by a prejudiced judge. Does that about sum it up? Is this what you call the justice system? Hide the truth and see who can win," he asked bitterly.

Edwin looked at Tim. They were standing in the hall outside the courtroom well away from prying eyes. "I know this has been hard for you. The plaintiff is lying and your testimony is believable but not established. No record. The tapes were excluded and that was unfortunate. But Cull gave his reasons. Whether we can use that on appeal is the question."

"Have you ever gotten the tapes back from the judge or the written transcript of my session with the Bradfords?"

"No. But when the trial is over I will push him on that matter."

"You see, this is where I don't get it. A rational person could look at the evidence and not even allow this trial to go ahead, at least not that part of it. But no, legal maneuvers can obscure the truth. Do you see how frustrating that is?"

"Yes. But the reality is we don't have any recourse. The judge is calling the shots. If we lose, we could possibly win on appeal, get the tapes introduced into evidence. Go for a new trial."

Tim was about to protest further when the bailiff approached and said the trial was back in session. The attorneys and clients went to their respective corners and the jurors filed into the courtroom.

"Mr. Stokes," Judge Cull intoned, "you may begin your summation."

Edwin slowly rose to his feet. He too was frustrated by Judge

Cull. He knew Cull was a red neck Irishman who had a thing about blacks. Edwin in particular bugged him because of the time twenty years ago when he had defeated Cull in a malpractice trial. *Payback,* he thought. No sense in burdening his client with this information. It would only fuel Tim's anger.

Edwin smiled at the jurors. "I too want to thank you for listening patiently during these proceeding. Some of you have been taking notes and I commend you for that. Let me say that my client apologizes for not being here yesterday. He was busy performing emergency brain surgery. I also want to send my condolences through opposing counsel to the Cleary family. Mr. Cleary underwent surgery at University Hospital yesterday for a brain tumor and I hope all went well."

Jason Damon was out of his seat before he thought about it. Instead of shouting an objection which would tip off the jury he asked for a sidebar. Cull granted his request with a frosty stare at Edwin. The two attorneys gathered at the side of the podium away from the jurors. Damon had his hockey face on but managed to turn away from the jurors as he spoke. "Mr. Stokes broke your order and I demand he be reprimanded. No more reference about Mr. Cleary's medical problems," Jason whispered through clenched teeth.

Cull was furious. "How do you respond Edwin?" he hissed.

"I merely stated the facts concerning my client's and plaintiff attorney's absence yesterday. The only thing that links the two events is this silly sidebar. If counsel had made no issue of it, it would have sailed past the jurors. I didn't tell them that Dr. Graves operated on Cleary. Mr. Damon has provided that clue."

"No more references to them Edwin, or so help me."

"Or 'so help you what' you pompous fool. You've been biased during this whole trial."

"That's enough," Cull said with a controlled whisper. "Back to your tables."

When Jason was seated and Edwin returned to the lectern, Cull smiled at the jurors and motioned Edwin to continue.

"Thank you your honor. The plaintiff told you she was not present when Dr. Graves met with her husband prior to surgery and informed him of the risks and benefits of surgery. She lied. Unfortunately we do not have a videotape available to us to show you what actually happened. If we did we wouldn't be here today. So all we have is Julie Bradford's word against Dr. Graves. You must ask yourself who stands to benefit the most here. This answer is obvious. This trial isn't about who's right or who's wrong. It's about money. Lots of money. The plaintiff attorney wants as big a settlement as he can get and the plaintiff does too. So ask yourself, who is going to benefit here."

Edwin went on to explain the difference in the experts' findings based on their experience with cerebral aneurysms. He pointed out that Dr. Shamski had only done a small number and was mistaken when recommending non-surgical therapy. He went over his client's explanation as to what really happened when dealing with delicate tissue with surgical instruments that are not fool proof.

"In conclusion let me say that if I were to have the problem that Mr. Bradford had Dr. Graves would be the only neurosurgeon I would trust to do the job right. Thank you."

Edwin sat down and there was silence in the courtroom. Jason was shuffling papers and was wondering if he should have objected to Edwin's characterization of his client. He had called her a liar but he didn't want to protest too much. *Let the jury decide* he finally concluded.

Judge Cull banged his gavel and then went on for another forty-five minutes with instructions to the jury. Finally at noon he sent the jury off to lunch and after that they were to begin their deliberations. He glared at Edwin. As the jurors left the courtroom Edwin asked permission to approach with Damon.

"You came close to real trouble Edwin," Cull whispered as the attorneys approached. "What is it now?"

"Your conduct throughout this trial has been reprehensible. If the jury hasn't picked up by now on your prejudicial rulings then they must be brain dead. I want the videotape and transcripts so I can begin an appeal."

"Listen you two bit shyster. The reason I'm here and you're there is you don't know how to conduct a trial. With all your years of experience you still can't seem to get it together. The tapes and transcripts have been misplaced and I don't know where they are."

He turned to Jason and said, "Mr. Damon do you have anything to say?"

"No your honor. I feel that you have conducted a fair trial, however."

"Thank you. How is Mr. Cleary today?"

"He's awake and taking nourishment. Quite amazing. His wife said he can go home in a few days. The surgery was apparently very successful." He glanced over at Tim who was still in his customary seat at the defense table.

Jason stepped back, but Edwin looked at Judge Cull unable to control his anger. "You're a disgrace to that robe. You should relieve yourself from the bench," he whispered.

The judge turned red and whispered back, "And you are an uppity black man who doesn't know his place."

Edwin didn't need to hear any more. He abruptly turned his back on the judge and walked away. He was satisfied in his own mind that Cull had let out his true feelings. He didn't like blacks in general and Edwin in particular. Not exactly "fair and impartial" when ruling from the bench.

"Well, what was that all about?"

"Not good news. Judge Cull has 'misplaced' the videotape and transcripts. Unless you have another copy there goes our appeal."

"So you think we're going to lose. Already worried about an appeal," Tim said bitterly.

"I'm just being realistic," Edwin sighed. "You've got to stay ahead in my business. No time for wishful thinking."

"Thanks for sharing. I'm going home. Call me when it's done. I'm not coming back here again," Tim said with a dismissive wave of his hand at the courtroom.

Edwin remained silent and watched Tim leave.

Outside the courtroom, Tim called Meg at her office. When she heard what Tim had to say she was outraged, vowing to bring the whole story to the public's attention while the jurors were deliberating.

After lunch the jurors crowded into a windowless chamber off the courtroom. There was a scarred table with fourteen steel gray chairs positioned around it. Pencils and pads of paper were placed in front of each chair. Some of the jurors used them to fan the stale air. One of the jurors tried to fiddle with a thermostat but to no avail. The bailiff went to find someone to try and improve the ventilation. Soon there was air blowing in from the grates on the ceiling.

There were six women and six men that made up the jury and also two alternate female jurors. They were there for insurance purposes in case someone became ill or had to leave because of a family emergency. The alternate jurors were dismissed and told to standby in another room. Consistent with almost all small group dynamics one juror had taken the lead and sat at the end of the table. When everyone was seated he rapped the table with his pencil and announced, "I'm Justin Baker. Some of you have approached me to be the foreman. I'm an engineer by trade and as you know we like to organize things. Are their any objections to me being the foreman for the group? Please identify yourself and occupation when asking a question."

A black female juror raised her hand and said, "I'm Mary MacGinty, boring widowed mom. I thought we weren't suppose to talk to each other?" There were some chuckles. Mary was in her late forties and moderately plump with a kind face. She was not challenging Mr. Baker. She wanted to know.

"Fair question. I was approached during lunch today after trial testimony had been completed. I'm not pushing for the job."

A third juror raised his hand and said, "I'm the one who approached Mr. Baker. Excuse me my name's Ed Jones, post office. Noticed he was careful about takin' notes, Mr. Baker was, and thought perhaps he be the best."

A fourth juror raised her hand and said, "Maggie George, school teacher. I move that Mr. Baker be our foreperson." Maggie emphasized the last word with air quotes around it so that every-one understood she was into politically correctness.

Mr. Baker said, "I apologize. Yes I should have said foreperson not ...man. How many are in favor of the motion?"

Most of the jurors wanted to get on with the deliberations and all hands were raised.

"Thank you. I'm not an expert in the process since this is my first time on a jury. But I have seen enough movies and read enough books to have an idea how we should proceed. First of all some of you have met before we gathered here but let's get the name and occupation thing out of the way."

Mr. Baker had conveniently positioned himself at the end of the table. He looked to his right and pointed at an elderly female.

"Hi. I'm Janet Giordino, grandmother. Retired nurse. MGH."

She looked to her right and the next juror introduced himself and so it went around the table. When everyone, had been intro-duced Mr. Baker said, "The next order of business is the jury instructions given to me by the bailiff. Essentially we meet until we come to a decision. We can have bathroom breaks down the hall but please no discussing with anyone outside what's going on." Everyone nodded.

Justin Baker was employed by an engineering firm outside of Boston. He was not a local, having grown up in Indiana and at-tended Purdue University. He had lived in Boston long enough to get his name on the voter's role but not long enough to under-stand all the ethnic subtleties. Oh sure he knew there were the Irish, Italians, blacks, wasps and more recently hispanics and asians. *One big segregated melting pot* he mused. His Midwest-ern upbringing never emphasized one race over the other. People tended to get along and tended to look at people as, well, people. As he looked around the room all the factions seemed represented here.

"I think to start out we should poll our group and see where we stand on the issues," he said.

A hand shot up and he pointed to Simon Murphy, retired BPD. "I've sat on a jury before. I don't think that's a good idea. Some people haven't made up their minds yet. Better to discuss it first and then vote."

"Thank you Simon and judging from the nodding heads I guess everyone agrees. Why don't we start with you Simon since you have made a good suggestion."

"Well I'm one of those who hasn't made up my mind. What bothers me is that we're asked to judge whether the doc didn't live up to standards. Whose standards, that quack from L.A.? Also, who's telling the truth, the woman or the doc? He sounded sincere when he said he talked to her before surgery. She sounded almost as sincere in saying she wasn't talked to."

A small Cambodian lady who worked cleaning hotel rooms raised her hand. "I looked at lady very hard. She lie. Doctor tell truth. Westerners can't hide faces." That was it. The plaintiff was a liar.

Two hands shot up. The first to speak was an elderly gentleman who was a retired personnel manager of a large business in Boston. "I spent a good part of my life interviewing people. The lady is not a liar and she comes across as a woman who is still in mourning for her husband. I have to respectfully disagree with the last lady."

"Hey it's been two years since her hubby kicked the bucket. Get over it already," said another juror who was a mechanic in Somerville.

Justin decided to step in and take control, " Okay, I think we've heard some strong opinions here. Let's look at the facts. The plaintiff, Julie Bradford, says the doctor did not inform her and her husband of the risks of surgery. Let's deal with that one issue first. Let's hear from some of you who haven't said anything."

He pointed to the retired MGH nurse and nodded at her. "Well, as I've said. I'm a retired nurse. I spent a good part of my life obtaining consents. Some patients are smarter than others. Some listen and some don't. On the hospital record exhibit they showed us Mr. Bradford a former professor at MIT clearly signed a consent for surgery to clip a left middle cerebral artery aneurysm. Now to my way of thinking he was informed. I couldn't tell whether his wife was telling the truth or not."

"Well do you think he also informed them of alternative treatment?" the foreman asked.

"How do we know? It wasn't documented so it's her word against the doctor's. If I were voting on this one issue, I'd come down on the doctor's side. It's so standard now for someone along the way to inform the patient about other methods of treatment. So do I think he did? Yes."

The foreman looked around the room and there did not appear to be any interest in discussing this further. Finally a file clerk in the city's administration building said, "It's just like sex. He said she said. We'll never know but I tend to believe the plaintiff. The doctor sounded too positive on this issue. He is busy and he forgot. Not only that he didn't document the discussion. Even his own expert said he routinely talked to relatives and always talked about other forms of treatment. And always documents it."

With these remarks a lively discussion ensued for nearly an hour. Justin said, "It's getting late. Let's take a vote on this issue then come back in the morning and deal with the doctor's conduct during the surgery. Heads nodded around the table. They had beaten this issue to death and there was little more that could be said. "Okay, by hands how many think the doctor fell below the standard of care regarding his informed consent?"

Eight hands shot up. "How many don't?" The retired nurse, Cambodian lady, and two others voted in favor of the defense. Justin thanked everyone and reminded them all to keep the discussion confidential and do not read the newspaper or watch the news since there might be media coverage of the trial. The jurors were quick to gather up their things and go home.

Twenty-nine

Meg couldn't get over Tim's phone call. She had had enough of this sham of a trial. Television often chronicled high profile murder trials and reported findings in real time. Why couldn't she do the same for a boring malpractice case? Jurors in murder cases are often sequestered so that they were not privy to sensational reporting by the media, but what about in a malpractice trial? Not a whole lot of interest there. Why would someone want to listen while experts are interviewed on television about the subtleties of medical care? A murder trial now that was juicy stuff. She had to find a way to make the story newsworthy and convince her editor to run it now, while the jurors were deliberating. She had twelve hours at the most

Reaching into her desk drawer she pulled out the only copy of the video of Tim's preoperative discussion with the Bradfords, along with the typed transcript. Meg picked up the phone and dialed the extension of Joe Macintosh her favorite photographer.

Moments later Joe entered her cubicle and dropped into the chair across from her desk. "What d'ya want now. Another sleaze ball stake out?" he asked with a friendly smile. He still liked Meg's looks.

"No, but close. I have a video and need photographs from this video showing a doctor discussing surgery with a patient. I want a photo of the three in the room together off the video. Can you do it?" she asked with a broad smile.

"Does a wild bear..... aw forget it. Of course. Let's go to the TV room, I can do it now." The smile worked but she didn't need it. Joe would have done anything for Meg with little prompting. He had always admired her spunk.

While they were viewing the tape Meg pointed out the best shot showing Tim talking to Julie and John Bradford. The video had a time and date in the corner and this was used to key the typed text of the ongoing conversation. When Tim got to the point of talking about alternative methods for treating cerebral aneurysms she stopped the video. "I need a photo of this segment with the time and date stamp."

Joe rubbed his chin. "Okay. I've got it marked. I'm going to use another TV, which has a larger, flatter screen. Give us a picture that looks like a picture and not a fish bowl. You got ze?"

"I got ze. How soon?" Meg asked, to build a fire under Joe who was beginning to look bored over this less than challenging assignment.

"An hour," he yawned. "I've got to get more sleep. On your desk by three o'clock sharp. That is if there are no emergencies."

"Thanks. I'm also including in this article your shots of the boyfriend along with her sworn testimony about how her intimate life had been ruined."

"Remind me not to get on your bad side." Joe took the video out of the machine. "Since this is so important do you want me to make another copy.?" he asked waving the cassette at her.

"You are so considerate. Yes. Now I've got to go get this article ready by five."

Back at her desk Meg began to bang away on her copy. The words flowed easily since she had been over the subject with Tim so many times. She even found herself using medical terminology without hesitation. At the end of the piece she put in that the famous plaintiff attorney Jerry Cleary had undergone brain surgery by the doctor he was suing. The article was quite long and she had included nearly everything that had transpired at trial. While she was working Joe dropped off the videos and photographs - that were just perfect.

She typed a subtext to the photograph, quoting the words of Tim and then placed after them Julie's sworn testimony. When her work was complete it was just a few minutes past five and she congratulated herself. The jury would reconvene in the morning and she wanted this in the morning addition. Her only problem now was getting this by her editor George Longley. It was George, who had come over from the sports page department at *The Globe,* who encouraged Meg to join him at *The Bulletin* when she had returned from the "dead". Meg had a special fondness for him and vice versa and she hoped to cash in on it. She hurried to his office having promised to show him the article by five.

George Longley had been a sports reporter at *The* Globe for twenty-five years before taking the editor's job at *The Bulletin.* He had proven to be a good find for the more conservative paper in the year or so he'd been on the job. George was a friendly person, quick with the one-liners but very cagey. His folksy side had always made access to professional athletes easy and fun. He read over Meg's article, then yanked off his glasses and looked at her.

"You're not serious are you? Interfering in an ongoing trial. Your fiancé is the plaintiff. Inside information. Why, there wouldn't be enough left of me to spit at if I ran this. I'd be covering high school football games in western Mass," he drawled.

"It goes on all the time with murder trials. There are leaks from attorneys. It happens all the time," Meg nearly begged.

George eyed her as a father to a daughter. He had gone to law school, but flunked the bar exam enough times to decide being a lawyer wasn't his lot in life. He still had enough legal knowledge to be dangerous. "Meg we go back a long way. You know me. I'd run anything if I thought it was worth the effort. But think about it. You're too close to this. Me thinks you should back off."

"You mean don't run it at all? Not even in my series about the malpractice crisis?" she pleaded. "It's so unfair." She thought about tears but that wasn't her style.

"Do you ever watch baseball or football games? Of course

you do. How many times have you seen the ump miss a call or a ref miss a fumble call. We, the fans, have replay. We get to see things after they've happened, slowed down. But the fan doesn't have a say in the decision. It isn't about right and wrong. It's winning and losing. It's the game's rules, the fans don't get to vote." George was pleased with his analogy.

"What are you saying? I shouldn't poke my nose into things I'm not part of. I might as well stay at home," she said with a sharp edge to her voice.

"Now take it easy. Slow down. There's more. Look on lawyers as the players, the judge is the ref, the jurors are the scorekeepers. In a trial the scorekeepers rule. It's much better than football. It's their game and their rules. The lawyers let twelve citizens decide who wins and who loses. You have to let it play out. Unlike sports, there are plenty of ways to correct wrong or unfair outcomes."

"More lawyers and more judges. Appeals. Why not inform the public what a travesty this is? Expose Cull for what he is, a pigheaded, bigoted Irishman from the old school. The problem with your juror/scorekeeper analogy is that the scorekeepers don't have all the facts!" Meg was aware that her voice was rising and she calmed down enough to say, "I really want to do this George.

George thought for a while. In spite of himself he had to admit that she had a good point. "Ok. Here's what you can do. Run the article the day after the verdict is in. Leave out the part about Jerry Cleary's surgery unless you and Dr. Graves want an invasion of privacy suit. You have to respect doctor/patient confidentiality."

Meg sighed heavily. She felt she had been rebuffed but knew George was right. "Okay. Today's Wednesday. The jury will probably come back with a verdict today – it's not brain surgery (ha, ha). I'll tentatively run it for tomorrow and will cut out the Cleary surgery part."

She hadn't gotten everything she wanted but maybe the article will stir things up. It certainly will make Julie Bradford look like a lying gold digger. *I wonder what her boyfriend is going to say when he sees his picture in the paper?*

Wednesday morning at nine the jurors in the matter of Bradford vs.

Graves et al. gathered in the conference room. There was a quiet expectation that they would quickly wind things up, but there was no sense of relief or joy. Whatever the decision there were no winners in this case. Justin Baker appeared ready for action. He was dressed in a dark suit with a gold and black striped tie. The other jurors had also dressed up and had abandoned their sneakers and tee shirts. Most were TV presentable. They had the feeling that today was their day to be in the limelight.

When everyone was seated, Justin looked around the table. All the jurors were present. "Yesterday we voted on the issue of standard of care regarding the informed consent. Today we will discuss the actual circumstances of the surgery and determine if Dr. Graves met the standard of care in his treatment of Mr. Bradford. Now let's assume that Mr. Bradford had lived and had an excellent outcome. Would we be here today?"

"That's kinda silly question," said the postal worker. "Course not."

"So what I'm saying is that the fact we are here is because things didn't turn out the way the Bradfords wanted. If things had we wouldn't be here. Do we all agree on that?"

Everyone nodded affirmatively.

"Another way of approaching this is to accept that all the experts and defendant doctor agree that Mr. Bradford needed something done. The issue was how it was to be done. Correct?" All the jurors nodded their heads.

"Okay, so what we are dealing with here is a bad or unexpected outcome. If a plan goes the way the doctor wanted and it benefits the patient, then there is no issue regarding the standard of care. Both the experts agreed that the aneurysm needed treatment. One wanted to clot the aneurysm with a catheter the other said surgery was advisable. Were they both right? Is there more than one way to skin a cat?" Justin was happy with the way he was leading the discussion.

"Well. From my experience at the MGH, there is more than one way to deal with most medical problems," said the retired registered nurse. "Two doctors may disagree on treatment and both be right. It seems to me that the neurosurgeon from Los Angeles was saying things he wanted his lawyer to hear. His surgical experience was very modest compared to Dr. Graves and Dr. Davis."

"That's true. But Dr. Davis did say that clotting the aneurysm even if it didn't completely fix it would make the surgery safer. So he may have had less experience than the other doctors, but the Hollywood doctor had a point." said the mechanic.

The Cambodian lady raised her hand and before she could be recognized blurted out, "Hollywood doctor look like movie star. Not real doctor. I no believe him."

"I'll agree with that," another juror blurted out, but the big time doctor from New York was arrested for drunk driving. Can you trust a doctor like that?"

"That's ridiculous," said the matronly housewife Mary MacGinty, "I'll bet everyone in this room at one time or 'nother operate a car while under the influence at least legally. That was years ago when he was in med school. Doesn't mean anything."

The discussion was becoming heated and Justin jumped in and said, "Well let's put aside for a moment the expert witness testimony. At best it seems like a wash. What about the actual surgery itself? Was it done according to standard of care?"

"The Hollywood doctor said not but he had only done three of these surgeries in the last two years, by his own admission they were small aneurysms. As a mechanic I know that you have to rely on your tools. I think Dr. Graves gave a reasonable explanation of what happened. I mean he's done over four hundred of these aneurysms."

The discussion went back and forth and two emerging opinions dominated. Granted Dr. Graves' informed consent fell below the standard of care but the surgery was indicated and the surgery was a technical misadventure. Some had made up their minds and weren't going to change, others wavered either way. Soon the ties came off and the shirt collars were unbuttoned as time dragged on. After lunch a vote was taken and it came out six to six. They worked until dinner and broke. Justin informed an unhappy Judge Cull that they were hopelessly deadlocked. I wouldn't do any good to try further. The judge would not accept that and ordered them to continue after dinner.

Thursday morning came and Tim was beside himself with anticipation. He hadn't heard a word from Edwin on Wednesday. He felt like calling his lawyer at home but instead, dressed quietly while Meg slept. She had come home late and did not discuss her article that was to appear today. Tim skipped breakfast and headed off to work. As far as he was concerned no news was good news.

Edwin awoke Thursday morning after a sleepless night. He didn't like the looks of things. A prolonged jury deliberation could not be good for his client. While he tried to control himself he let his imagination take over. His imagination wasn't generating positive thoughts. He also dressed but skipped his office and went directly to the courthouse.

It was nine o'clock when Edwin arrived outside the courthouse. He purchased a *Bulletin* and a cup of coffee. He went into the courthouse and sat in the lobby drinking his coffee and reading the paper. He had an uneasy feeling about the jury deliberations. Theoretically, in one sense it was good for his client that they were still in session. But in another way he was concerned they were just haggling over how much money to award the plaintiff.

Tim was at the hospital having lunch where he discovered that everyone in the hosptial knew about Meg's article except him. Just as he finished he was paged. It was Lisa calling from her office telling him that the jury had come to a decision and were to be seated in an hour. Mr. Stokes felt it would be appropriate that Tim be present when the verdict is read.

Tim left the hospital and drove to the courthouse. He had trouble finding a parking spot and it was nearly one thirty when he arrived outside the courtroom. Jason Damon was standing with

Julie Bradford. They were chatting amiably and both looked confident. Tim approached Edwin and said, "Well, do we appeal or what?"

"Take it easy. It could be good for us. We'll soon know. Sorry to make you come across town but it's important that you be here."

Jason Damon caught Tim's eye and gave him a cocky "thumbs up".

"Shit, how tackless." Tim muttered so only Edwin could hear. Just then the bailiff opened the courtroom door and announced that the jury was on its way in. The parties to the lawsuit slowly walked to their respective tables. Jason pulled out a pad of legal paper and began jotting on it. Tim thought the plaintiff attorney was probably calculating his take. When the jury was seated, Judge Cull approached the bench and everyone made an unenthusiastic gesture to stand but the judge waved them down.

"That ol sonnafabitch can kiss my ass before I'll stand," Edwin whispered to Tim. Judge Cull may have heard part of Edwin's remark since he glanced menacingly at the defense table but said nothing.

Judge Cull looked at the jury and frowned. "Do you have a verdict?"

Justin Baker stood and cleared his throat. Tim couldn't tell yet what was about to happen since reading the faces of the jurors was useless. They all appeared subdued. That couldn't be good news.

"We have spent the better part of the last two days and into late last night in heated discussion your honor. It has been civil for the most part but each person has his or her own opinion. Unfortunately we are divided right down the middle."

Judge Cull was clearly unhappy. He had done everything he could possibly do to assure a plaintiff verdict. Exasperated he said, "I want to poll each juror to see if there is some way to get you people off center." Judge cull proceeded to question the entire jury and in the end saw that there was no one wavering and further deliberation would be fruitless and a waste of the taxpayers' money. In the end he reluctantly announced that it was a hung jury and no verdict was forthcoming. He instructed a shocked plaintiff attorney and his bewildered client that they could re-file the case if they wished.

When he finished Edwin stood and said, "Judge Cull I would like to interview the jurors myself." Cull eyed him suspiciously. Why would he want to bother, he had a victory of sorts. At least he didn't have to appeal the case. However, since it was standard practice to interview jurors after verdicts, Judge Cull granted his request and also that of Jason Damon to do the same.

Edwin sat and nodded to Jason to go first. Jason strode confidently to the jury box and asked the jurors who voted for his side what compelled them to do so. The six who had voted for Julie agreed that the informed consent issue was uppermost in their minds. They felt the experts were flawed in one respect or another and disregarded their testimony. Too positive in Dr. Shamski's case and too evasive in Dr. Davis' case. The latter seemed to side with the plaintiff more than the defense. That gave him credibility but also weakened the defense's case. This happens often enough to defense attorneys when they rely on their experts to make their case.

Jason was less interested in the six who voted against him. If Jerry decided to re-file the case this would be valuable information and Edwin chalked it up to inexperience although Jason had acquitted himself as a formidable replacement to Mr. Cleary.

When Jason sat down Edwin was convinced that the jurors were willing to forgive Dr. Graves for trying to treat a tough surgical problem. There was a bad outcome but it wasn't the overriding issue. His explanation of the technical pitfalls when using surgical clips seemed to resonate with them. He decided to stay away from questions about the surgery itself and talk only about the informed consent. He reached for his briefcase and slowly unsnapped the two locks, the sound resonating in the quiet of the courtroom. Judge Cull was annoyed with Edwin's theatrics and urged him to move along.

"Thank you your honor I plan to do so," was his response. Edwin pulled out a copy of *The Bulletin,* which had just hit the streets that morning. Meg had called him the night before and urged him to read her article. After Edwin had read the paper he had folded it and put it into his briefcase.

"First of all I want to thank the jurors for giving up their time and performing their civic duty in such a professional manner. Naturally I'm disappointed that some of you didn't see it our way and it is to those I wish to ask this question." He stood directly in front of the jury box. "It is clear that six of you voted in favor of the plaintiff based on the informed consent issue. If I told you that the plaintiff had misrepresented herself and she was in fact present during the conversation with her deceased husband and Dr. Graves would that change your vote? If I told you further that in that conversation Dr. Graves clearly outlined alternatives to surgery and what their chances were, how would you vote?"

Justin Baker answered for the group. I was part of the six in favor of the plaintiff. If you could prove what you've just said it would have changed my vote and I suspect that of the other five who voted with me." There was nodding of the heads of the other five jurors.

"In other words presented with those facts the jurors would have held for Dr. Graves."

It was not a question.

Justin scanned the faces of his fellow jurors and nodded in agreement.

Edwin let that sink in while he slowly took the folded newspaper out from under his left arm and opened it to show a picture below the fold on the front page. The picture had the date and time stamped on it and clearly showed Dr. Graves, Julie and her husband in a hospital room. "This picture is from a video shot during the informed consent of Mr. and Mrs. Bradford on the night before his surgery."

"Pardon me, Mr. Stokes," Justin intoned, "how can that be? Why haven't we seen this video?"

Suddenly the Cambodian lady shouted out, "She lie. She no good. I knew that."

Judge Cull had heard enough and banged his gavel and stopped the proceedings. He thanked the jurors, dismissed them, and ordered Mr. Damon and Edwin into his chambers. Tim looked over at Julie Bradford to let her know of his disgust for her. She kept her eyes down looking at a spot on the table.

Edwin and Jason settled into chairs in front of Judge Cull. "What was that stunt all about? How did *The Bulletin* get a hold of those pictures? No respectable person reads that rag anyway. You told me when you gave me that video that **it** was the only copy." He punctuated "it" with stabbing his index finger into his blotter.

"That reminds me your honor where is that copy I gave you? Have you found it yet?" Edwin smirked.

"This is unbelievable. Excluded evidence in a civil trial appears in a piece of shit newspaper. How are we supposed to re-file when that prejudicial material is out there?" Jason sputtered. He was clearly distraught and also dreading the prospect of facing his boss with this news.

"Actually," Edwin said, "it was the reporter who provided me with the original copy and told me there were no others. I guess she must have been mistaken. Again Judge Cull, where is the original video and its transcript?"

Judge Cull glared at Edwin but relaxed and said, "It's a real shame. I took it home and was watching it on my playback. My wife accidentally recorded over it. What can I say? You have my apologies. The original transcript and copies have been misplaced but I'll keep looking for them."

"In other words for the next trial should Mr. Cleary decide to re-file I can expect that we will not have the original tape?" Edwin asked with frank sarcasm.

"You, Mr. Stokes, can also kiss my ass. Gentlemen we are through here."

Thirty

Jerry Cleary sat in his office putting the finishing touches on a pleading he was preparing in yet another malpractice case. He chuckled to himself. The doctors just couldn't do enough for him. How could he have been so lucky as to find a profession that never seemed to run out of customers? There are bad doctors and there are good doctors. It didn't matter to him. That wasn't the issue. Could he make a case? That was the issue, and there was no one better at it. Curiously, since his surgery he was less inclined to use cutthroat tactics and he was settling more cases than he had in the past. Was he getting older, mellowing, or did that Dr. Graves cut out some part of his brain that was the trial part? Either way he was happy he was alive and vowed he would never sue Dr. Graves again. If it ever came to that he would refer it out.

He was brought out of his reverie when the intercom announced that Julie Bradford had arrived for her ten o'clock appointment. Jerry was clearly not looking forward to this meeting but like the trouper he was said, "Show her in."

Jerry's secretary opened his door and ushered in Julie who refused the offer of a beverage. Jerry smiled at her as he came around his desk. She didn't look as alluring as she did a year ago and was in fact, quite unattractive to him. But the new Jerry wasn't' straying far from home. Deidre had issued her ultimatum and Jerry now found it easy to be the husband and father she expected him to be.

Julie was dressed in a fashionable navy blue pants suit with matching shoes. Her hair was longer and loosely curled. She shook Jerry's hand and sat down. After stiffly exchanging pleasantries, Julie got down to business, "Well when are you going to re-file this lawsuit?" she asked.

Jerry leaned back in his chair, swiveling from side to side while he eyed her. The new Jerry wasn't looking at an attractive thirty two year old woman, she was merely a client. Julie's charm was not even an issue.

"I've given a great deal of thought to your case. First, since Dr. Graves is my physician I would have to withdraw. I turned your files over to Jason Damon who as you know has left my .....ah practice for greener pastures. He gave your files to one of my junior associates. He, let me be frank here, is unenthusiastic about re-filing your case."

Julie looked horrified and asked, "Why not? It was good a year ago it should be good now."

"How is it going to look to a jury that you were less than forthcoming about your meeting before surgery with Dr. Graves. All the falsehoods you presented in the first trial can be used in the second. It would be a disaster."

"Well get the judge to exclude it. Cull did. Can he be my judge again?"

"I'm afraid not. Judge Cull has been severely sanctioned by his peers for his conduct in your trial and bless his soul his conduct in general. He currently presides over traffic court in Brockton."

"That's unfair. What am I to do? Seth has left me. I have no income. The house is mortgaged to the hilt. My girls are wearing the same clothes as last year." There was a break in the usually stoic facade offered by Julie as tears began to from at the corners of her eyes.

"I'm afraid I can't help you there. You might consider selling your house and getting a job. I don't think your salvation is in the courtroom," Jerry said dismissively.

Julie stood and glared at her former attorney. "You bungled my trial by getting sick just as you were about to nail Dr. Graves.

What were you going to ask him before you passed out? Why couldn't Mr. Damon have done the same?" Anger flashed in Julie's eyes.

Jerry had been through this before. She could threaten to sue him, but since she'd lied to him from the very beginning, she wouldn't get very far. "I think our business is over, Mrs. Bradford. Good luck to you." Jerry stood.

"Julies turned and headed for the door. "I hope your malpractice insurance it up to date. I'll see you in court!" she tossed over shoulder as she opened the door.

Jerry wondered why he ever got involved with that shrew, a cheater, liar, home wrecker, and gold digger. The new Jerry would have to be more selective in his clients, money wasn't everything (something he would never say aloud). He returned to work on his pleading.

After putting in a long day, Jerry turned out the light and left his office. As he walked to the elevator some of the young associates were still on the phone or interviewing clients. Injured working people, disgruntled patients, people on crutches from slip and falls, it was great. He could go home at seven o'clock and the others were still working.

He stepped out onto Boylston Street and turned left toward the parking garage. The traffic should be light and he was anxious to get home to his wife and daughters. He'd come a long way in the past year, actually bought into the whole "family values" thing. What a concept.

He stepped off the curb between two cars to cross the street.

Suddenly a shot rang out. Jerry ducked and went to his knee when the windshield of the car parked to his left shattered. Nearby to his right there were sounds of a scuffle. Another shot, muffled. Moments later he heard distant sirens.

Jerry couldn't tell where the shots had come from and he was afraid to move. There were no other sounds. The street was deserted. He would stay right where he was until the police arrived.

"Why did you do that, Raphael, why?" Peter cradled the bloody body of his brother in his arms and sobbed.

Printed in the United States
50278LVS00003BA/85-93

9 781886 571211